middlewest

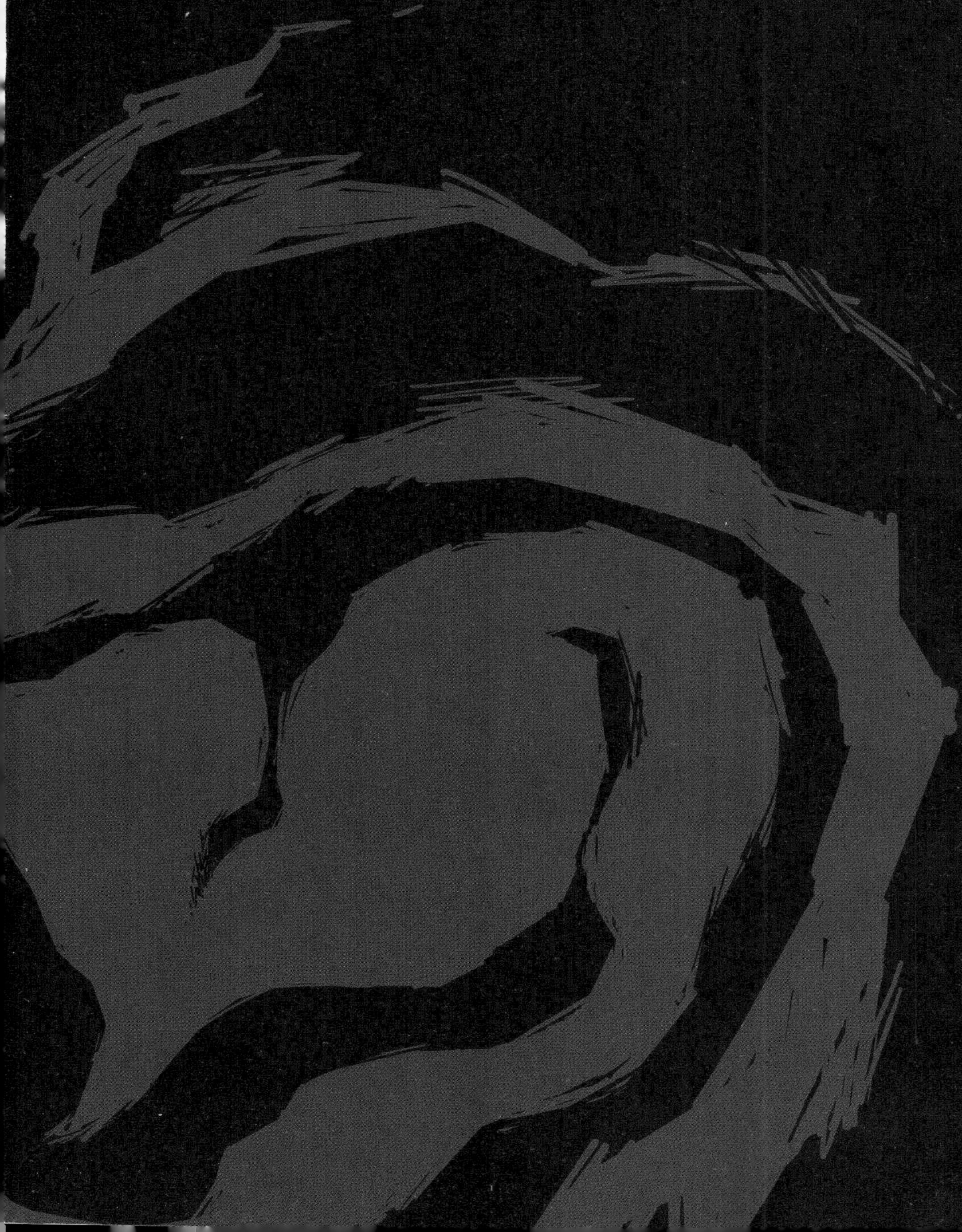

IMAGE COMICS, INC. ROBERT KIRKMAN: Chief Operating Officer • ERIK LARSEN: Chief Financial Officer • TODD MCFARLANE: President • MARC SILVESTRI: Chief Executive Officer • JIM VALENTINO: Vice President • ERIC STEPHENSON: Publisher/Chief Creative Officer • JEFF BOISON: Director of Publishing Planning & Book Trade Sales • CHRIS ROSS: Director of Digital Sales • JEFF STANG: Director of Direct Market Sales • KAT SALAZAR: Director of PR & Marketing • DREW GILL: Cover Editor • HEATHER DOORNINK: Production Director • NICOLE LAPALME: Controller **IMAGECOMICS.COM**

middlewest

STORY
SKOTTIE YOUNG

ART
JORGE CORONA

COLORS
JEAN-FRANCOIS BEAULIEU

LETTERING
NATE PIEKOS OF BLAMBOT

COVER ART
JORGE CORONA &
JEAN-FRANCOIS BEAULIEU

EDITOR
KENT WAGENSCHUTZ

DESIGN
CAREY HALL

CHAPTER
SEVEN

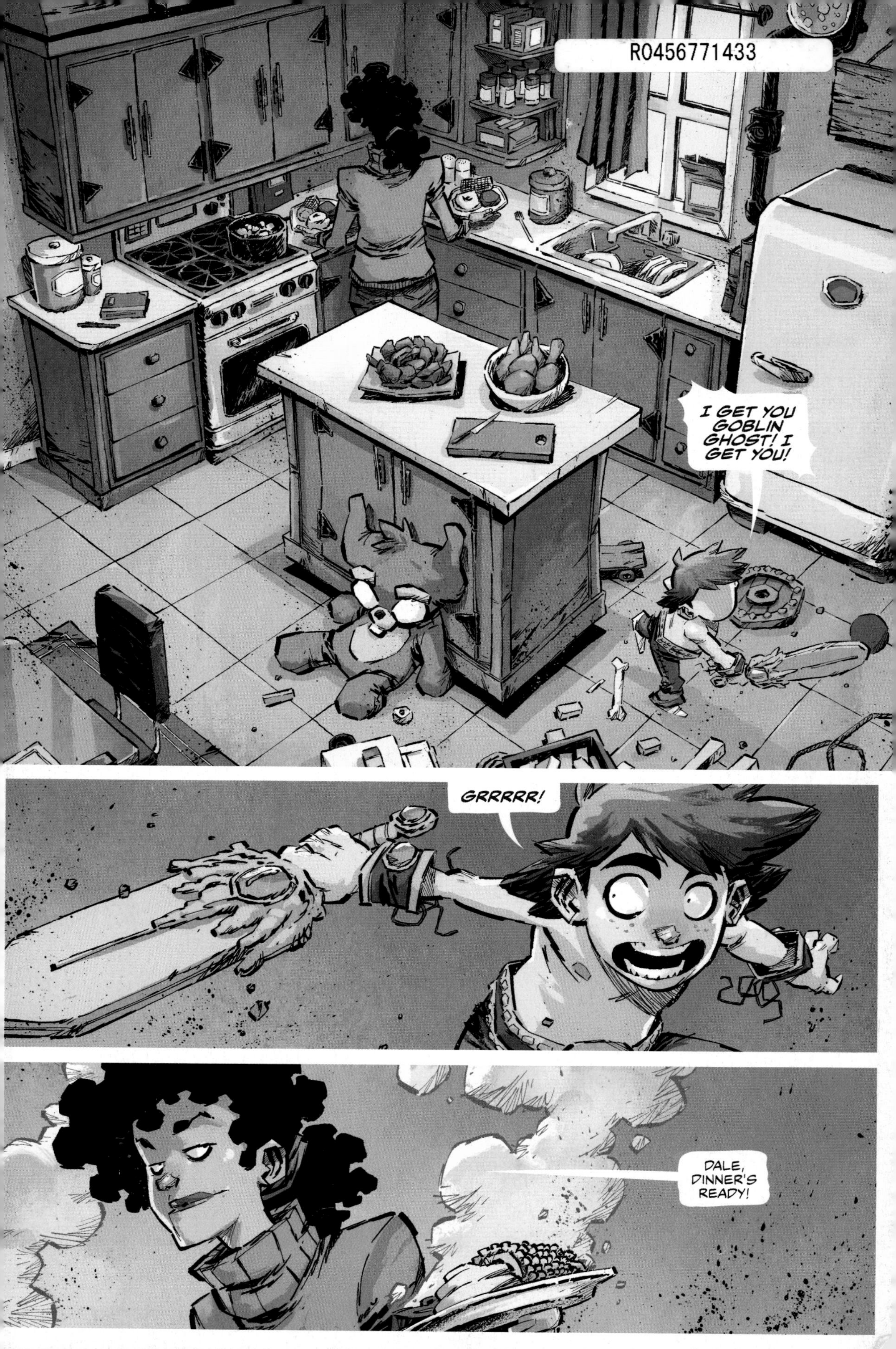
I GET YOU GOBLIN GHOST! I GET YOU!
GRRRRR!
DALE, DINNER'S READY!

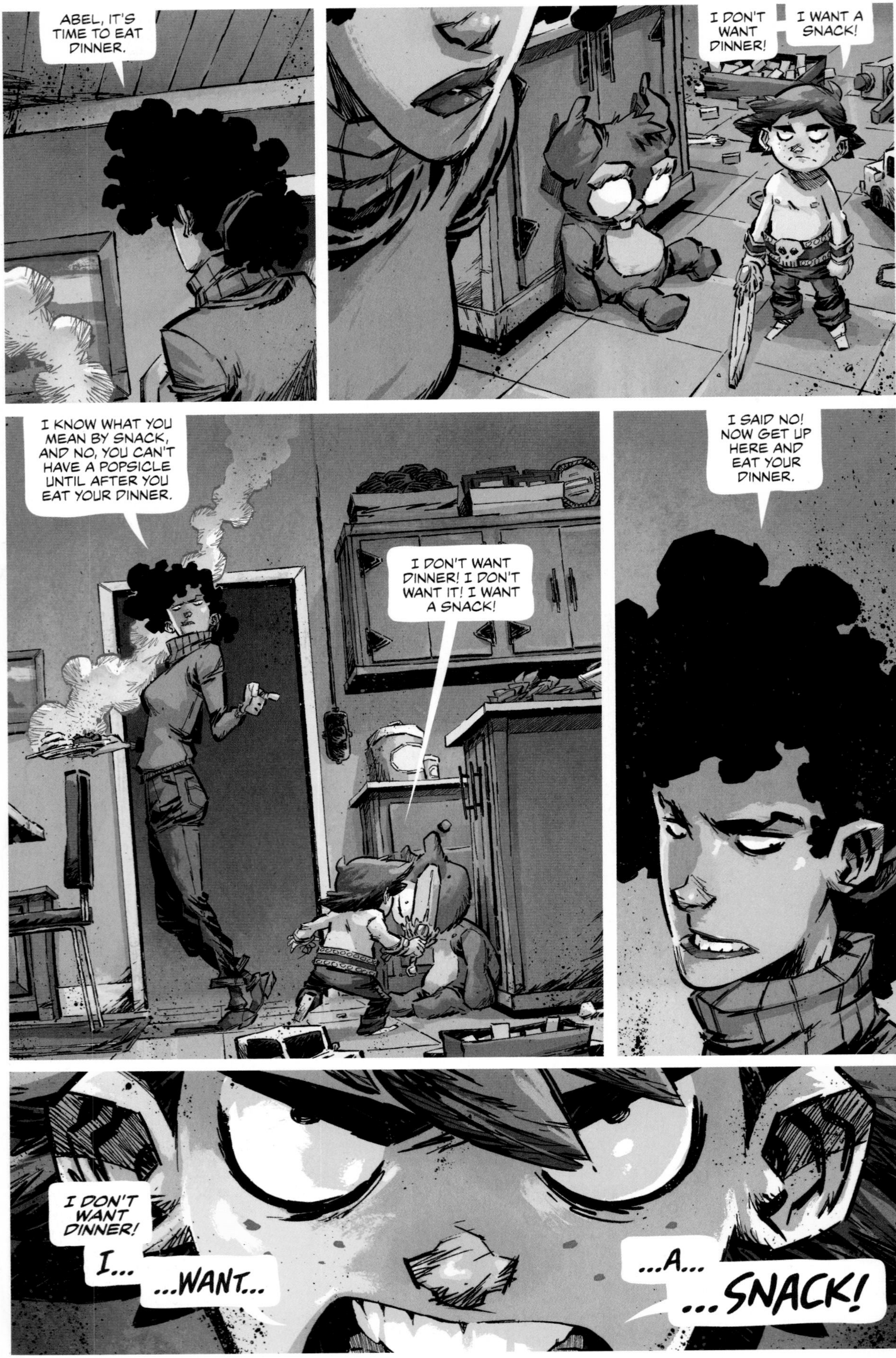
ABEL, IT'S TIME TO EAT DINNER.
I DON'T WANT DINNER!
I WANT A SNACK!
I KNOW WHAT YOU MEAN BY SNACK, AND NO, YOU CAN'T HAVE A POPSICLE UNTIL AFTER YOU EAT YOUR DINNER.
I DON'T WANT DINNER! I DON'T WANT IT! I WANT A SNACK!
I SAID NO! NOW GET UP HERE AND EAT YOUR DINNER.
I DON'T WANT DINNER!
I...
...WANT...
...A...
...SNACK!

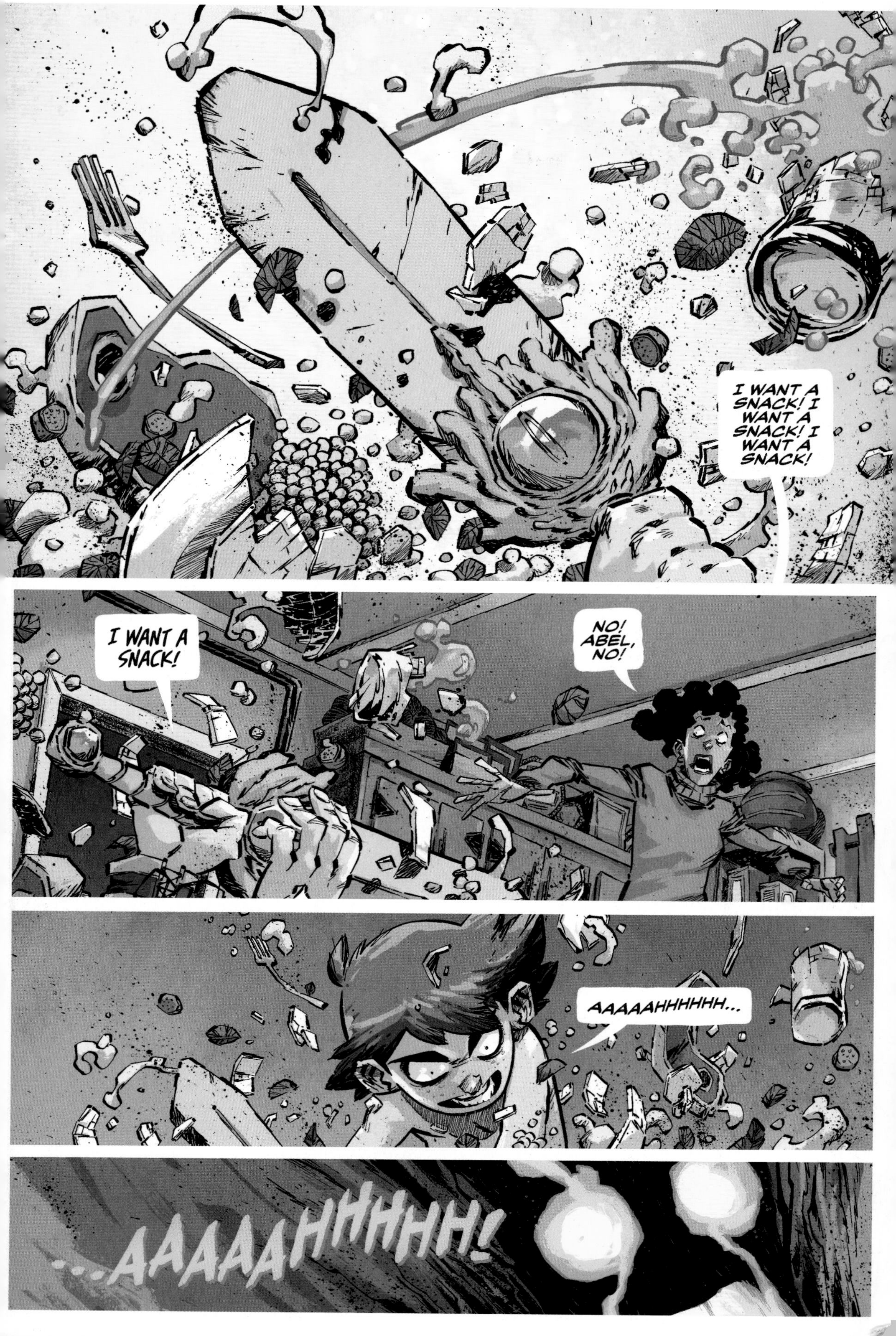
I WANT A SNACK! I WANT A SNACK! I WANT A SNACK!
I WANT A SNACK!
NO! ABEL, NO!
AAAAAHHHHHH...
...AAAAAHHHHHH!

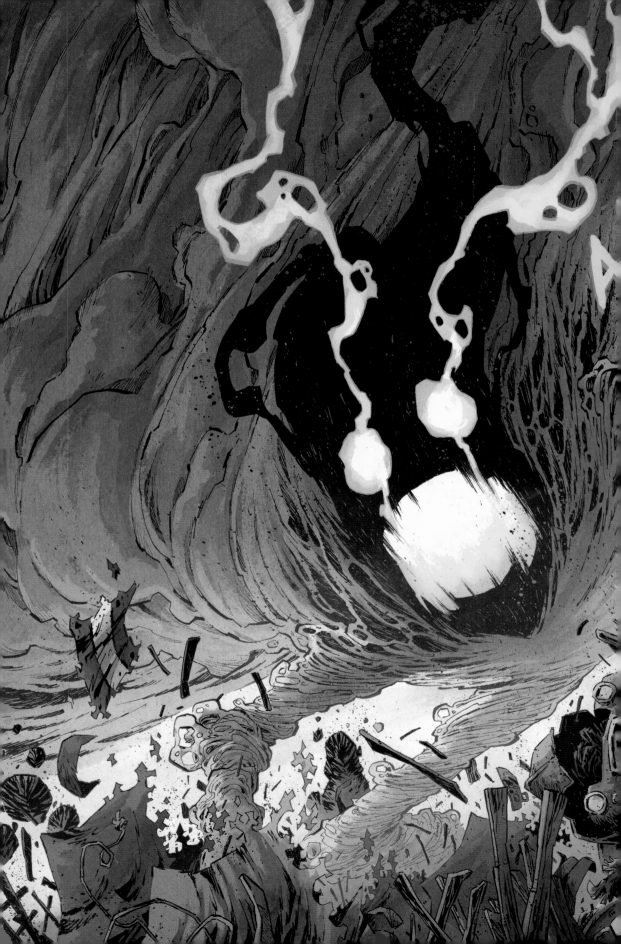

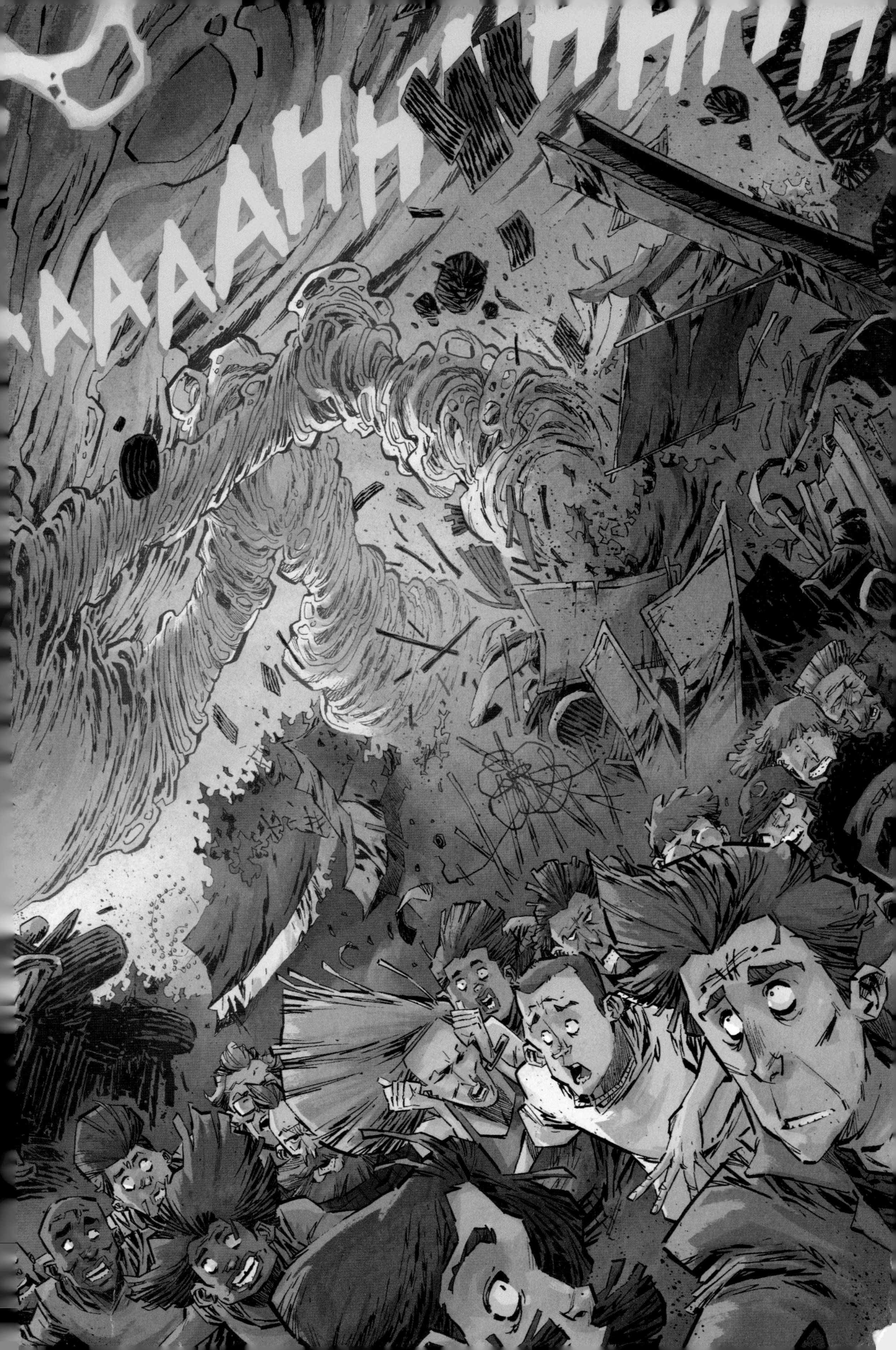
AAAAAHHHHHHHHH

OH...

...FUCK.

BOBBY! GET OUT OF HERE!

MAGGIE, NO! YOU'LL GET YOURSELF KI--

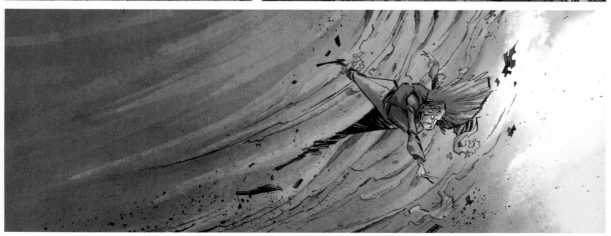

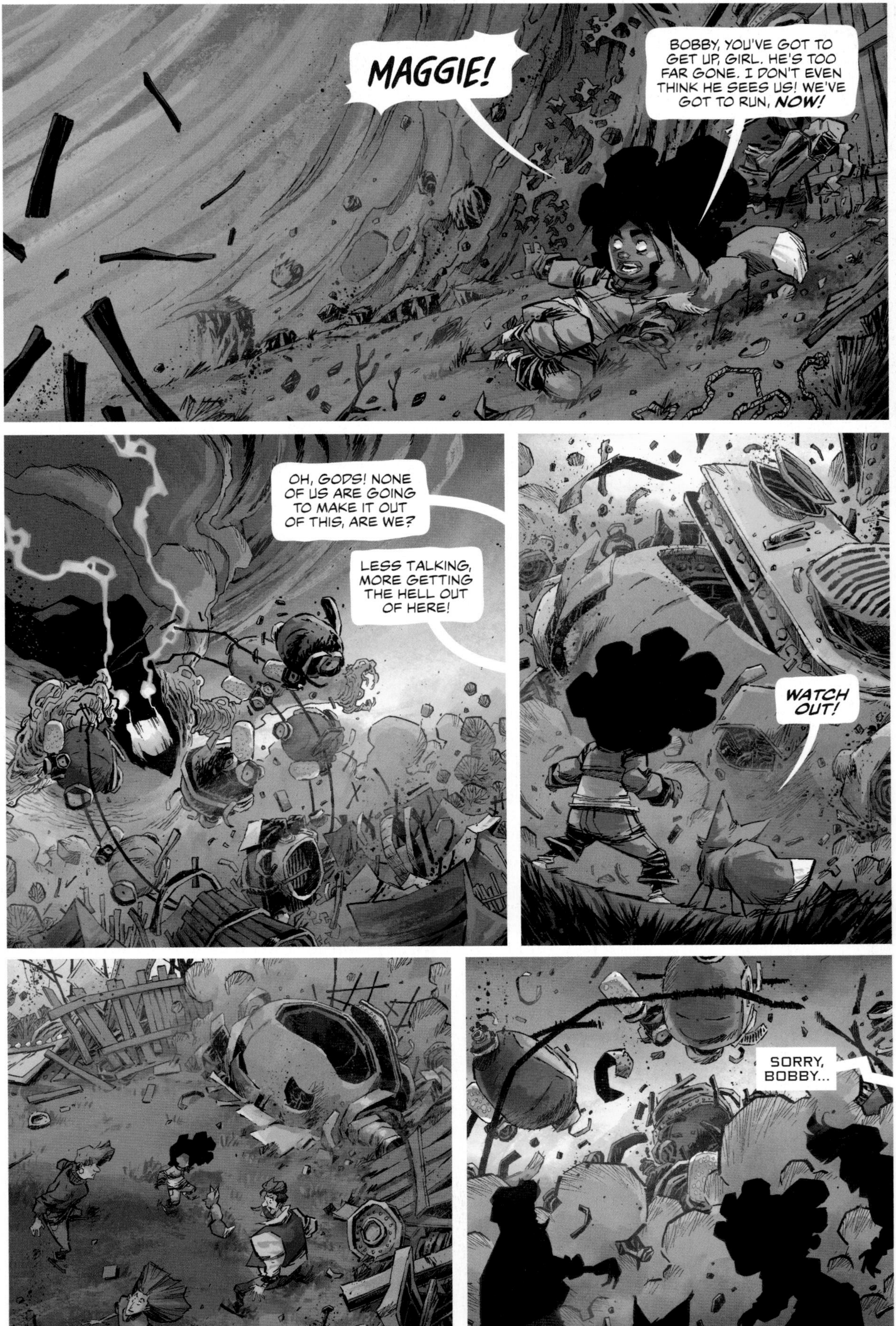
MAGGIE!
BOBBY, YOU'VE GOT TO GET UP, GIRL. HE'S TOO FAR GONE. I DON'T EVEN THINK HE SEES US! WE'VE GOT TO RUN, NOW!
OH, GODS! NONE OF US ARE GOING TO MAKE IT OUT OF THIS, ARE WE?
LESS TALKING, MORE GETTING THE HELL OUT OF HERE!
WATCH OUT!
SORRY, BOBBY...

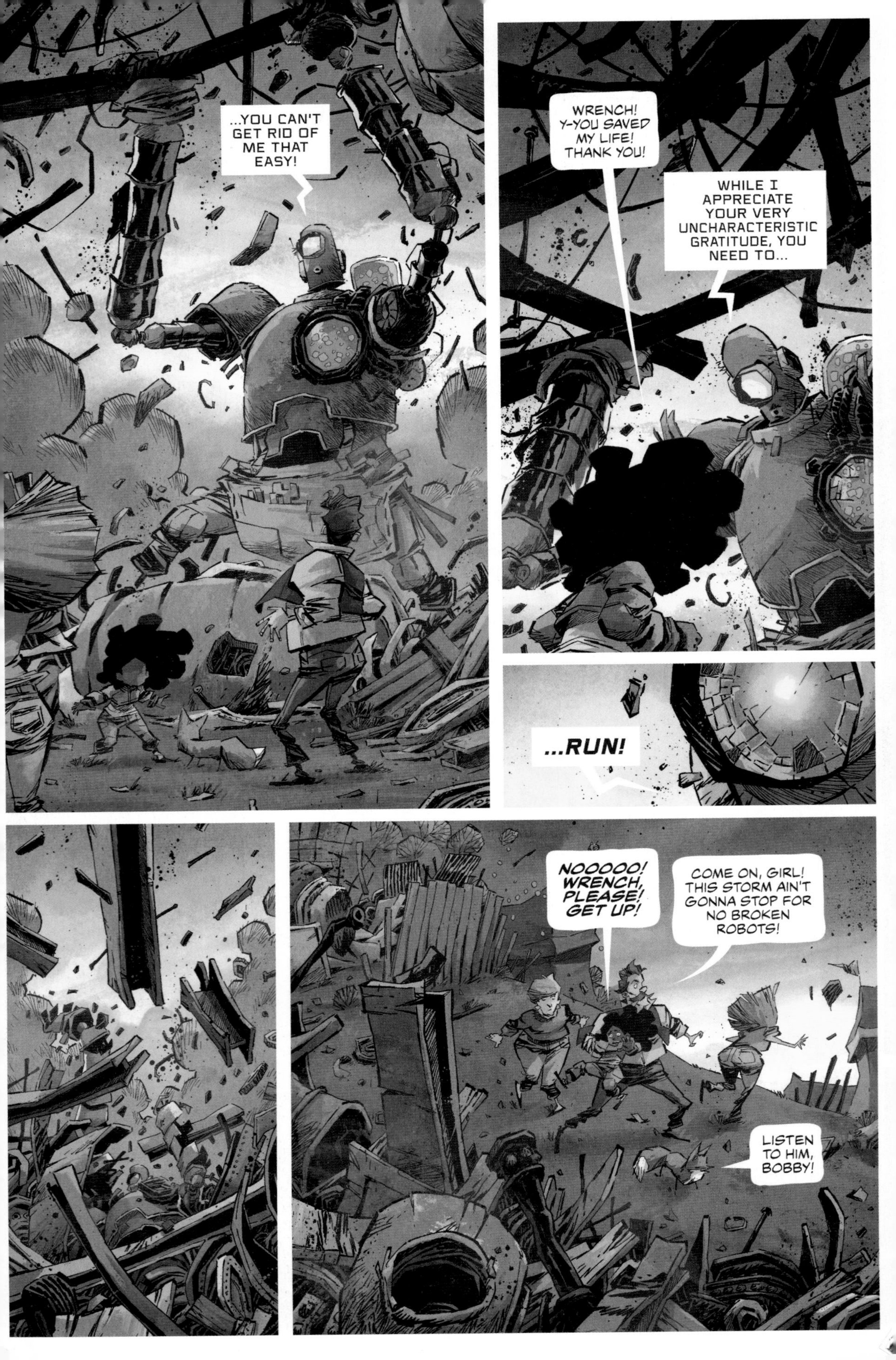

...YOU CAN'T GET RID OF ME THAT EASY!
WRENCH! Y-YOU SAVED MY LIFE! THANK YOU!
WHILE I APPRECIATE YOUR VERY UNCHARACTERISTIC GRATITUDE, YOU NEED TO...
...RUN!
NOOOOO! WRENCH, PLEASE! GET UP!
COME ON, GIRL! THIS STORM AIN'T GONNA STOP FOR NO BROKEN ROBOTS!
LISTEN TO HIM, BOBBY!

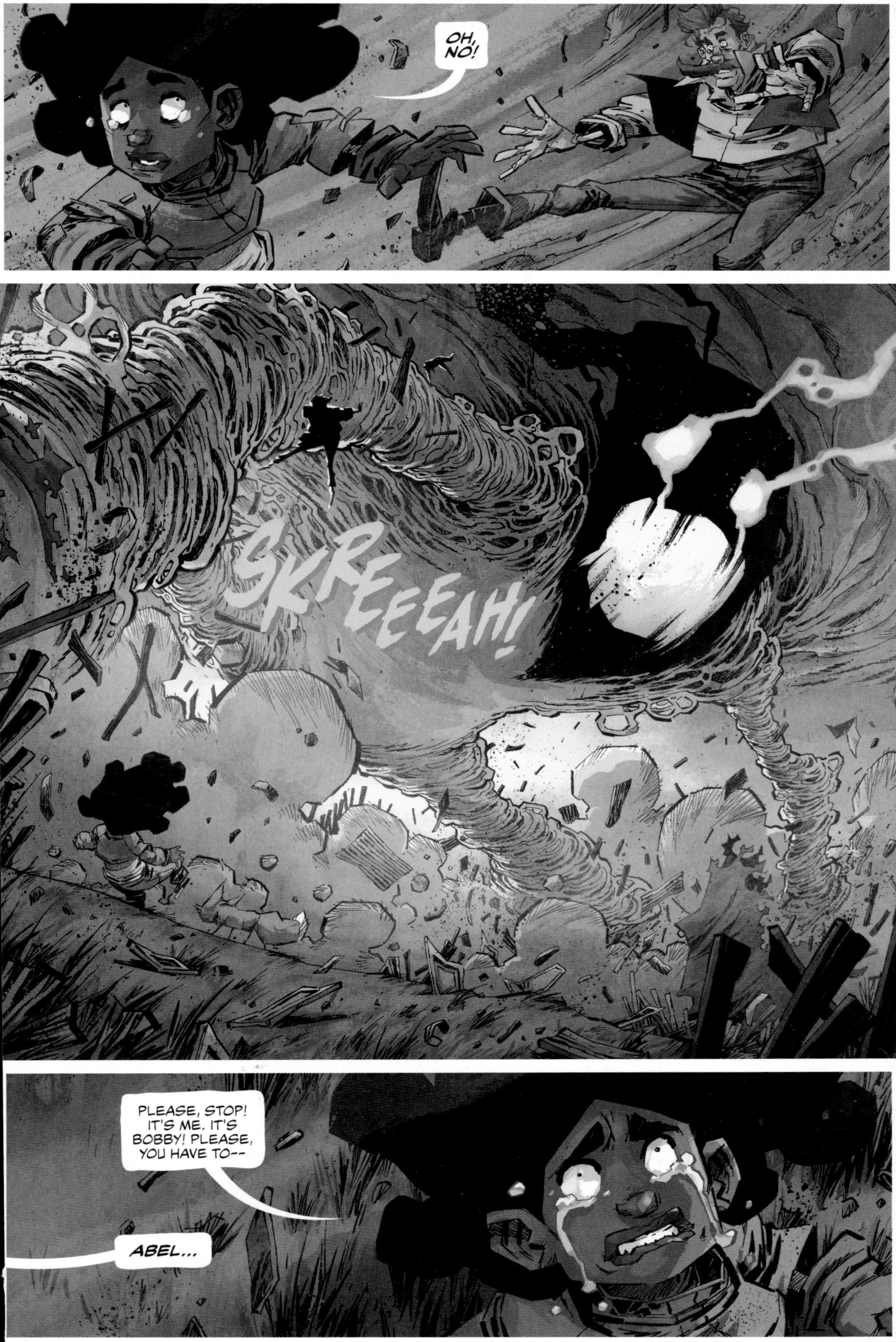
OH, NO!
SKREEEAH!
PLEASE, STOP! IT'S ME. IT'S BOBBY! PLEASE, YOU HAVE TO--
ABEL...

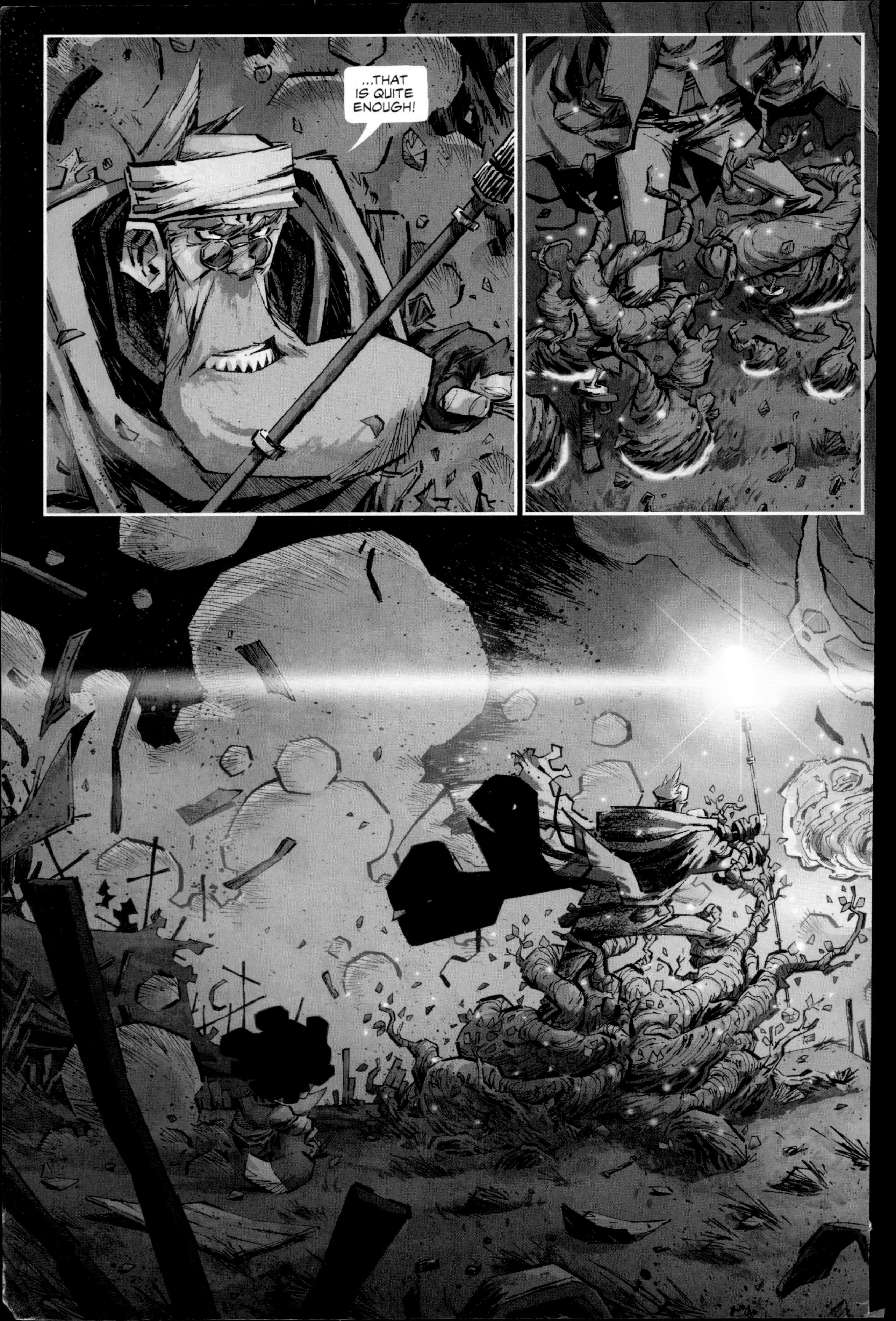
...THAT IS QUITE ENOUGH!

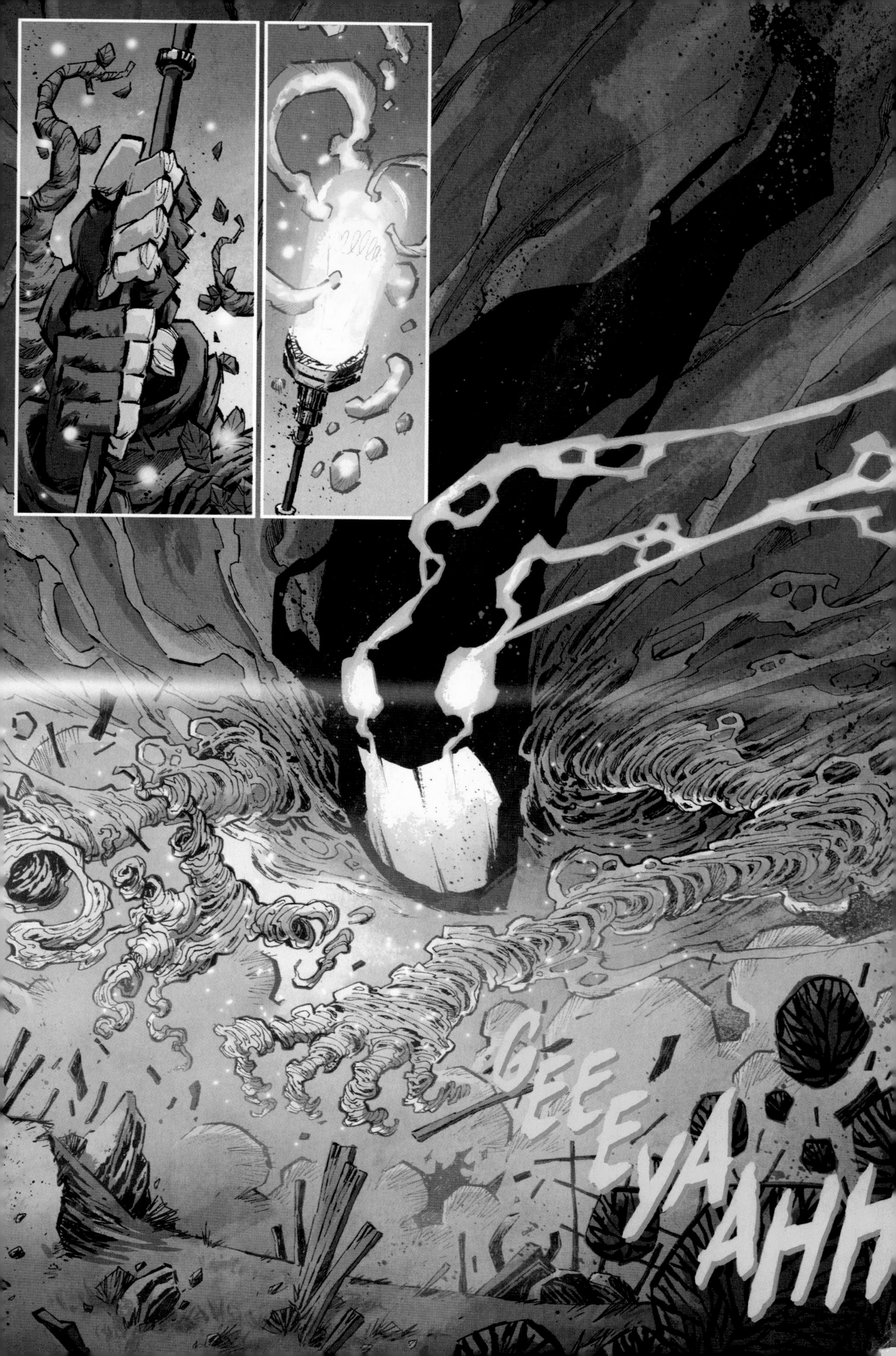
GEEEYAAHH

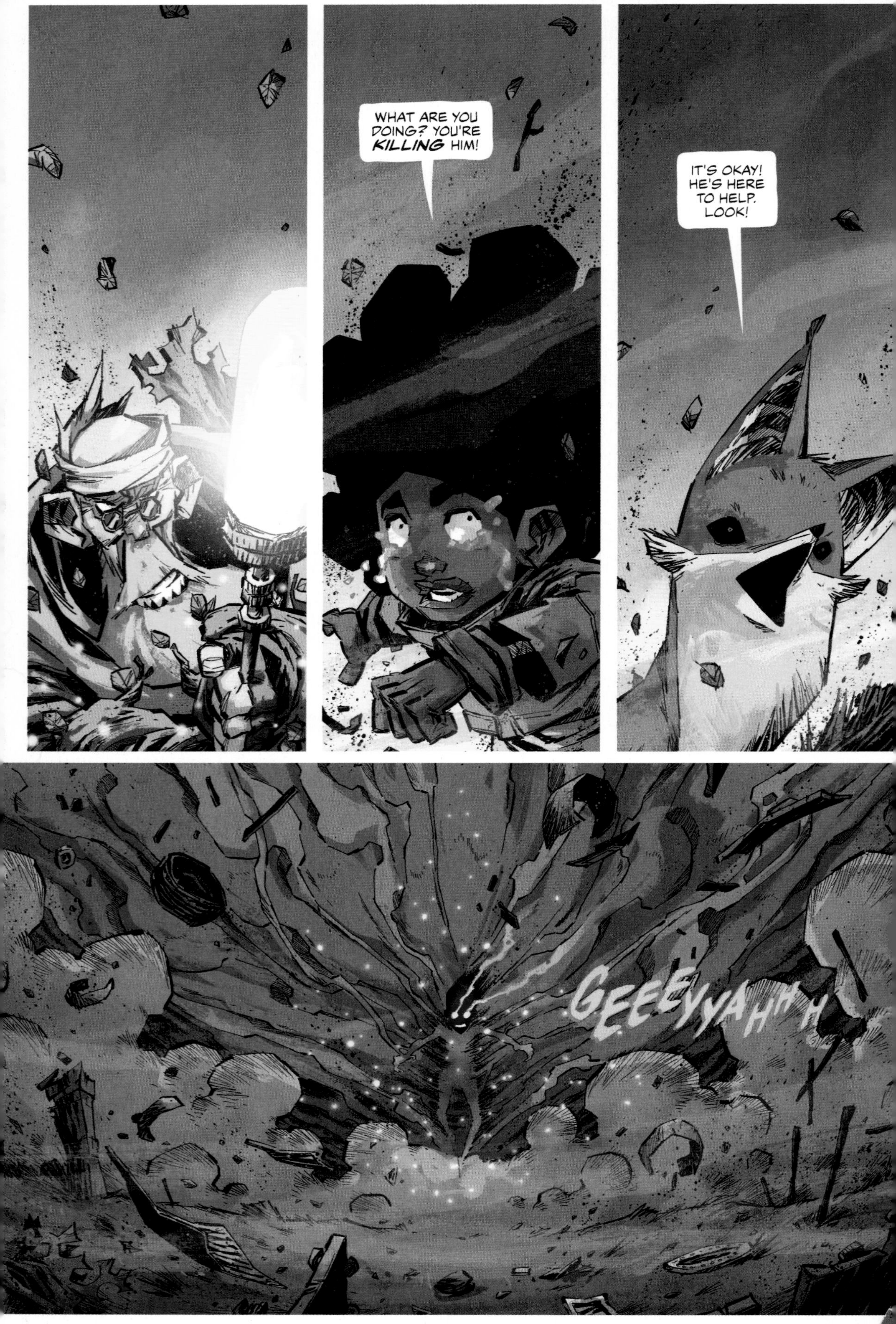
WHAT ARE YOU DOING? YOU'RE KILLING HIM!
IT'S OKAY! HE'S HERE TO HELP. LOOK!
GEEEYYAHHH

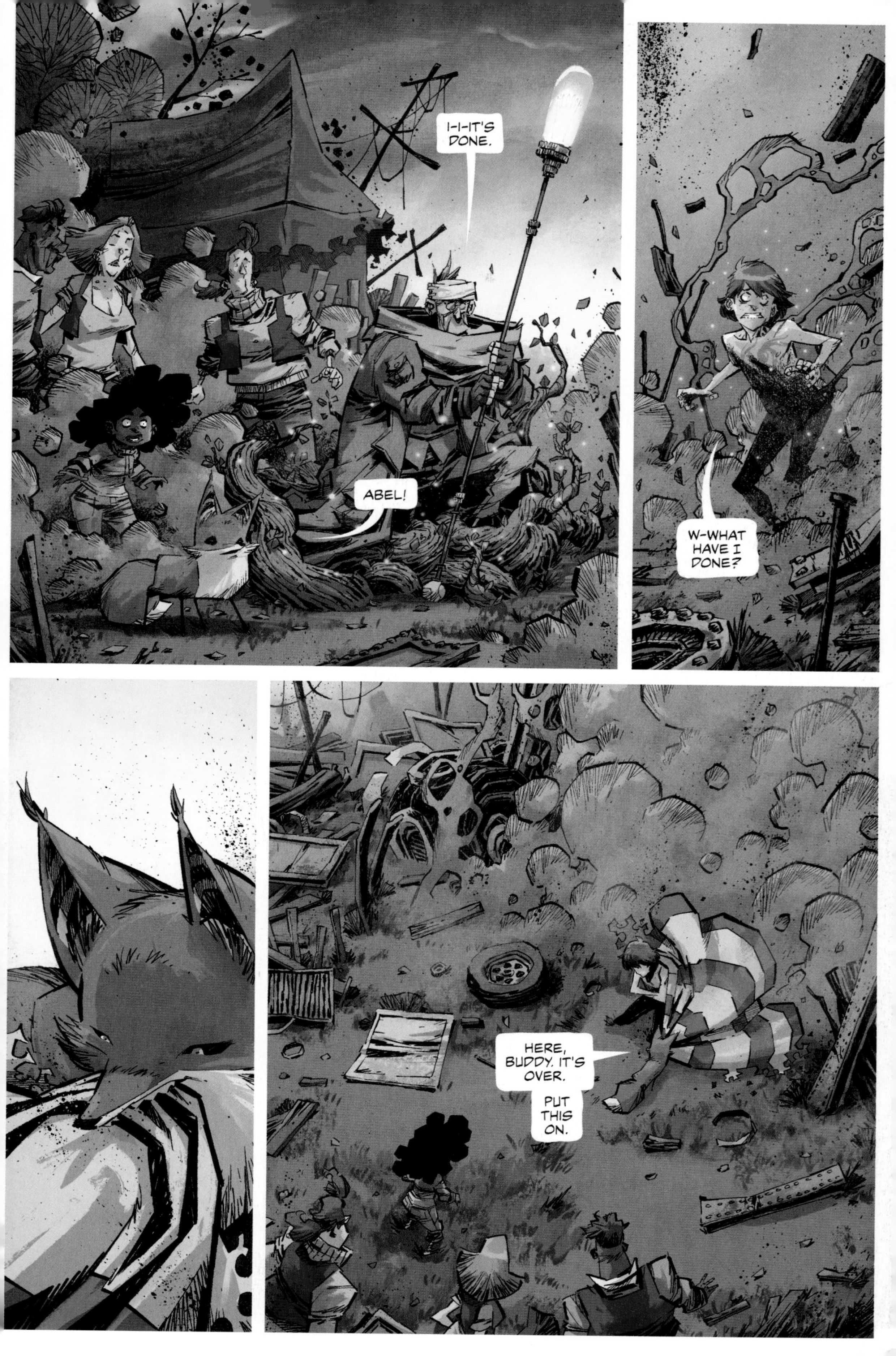
I-I-IT'S DONE.
ABEL!
W-WHAT HAVE I DONE?
HERE, BUDDY. IT'S OVER.
PUT THIS ON.

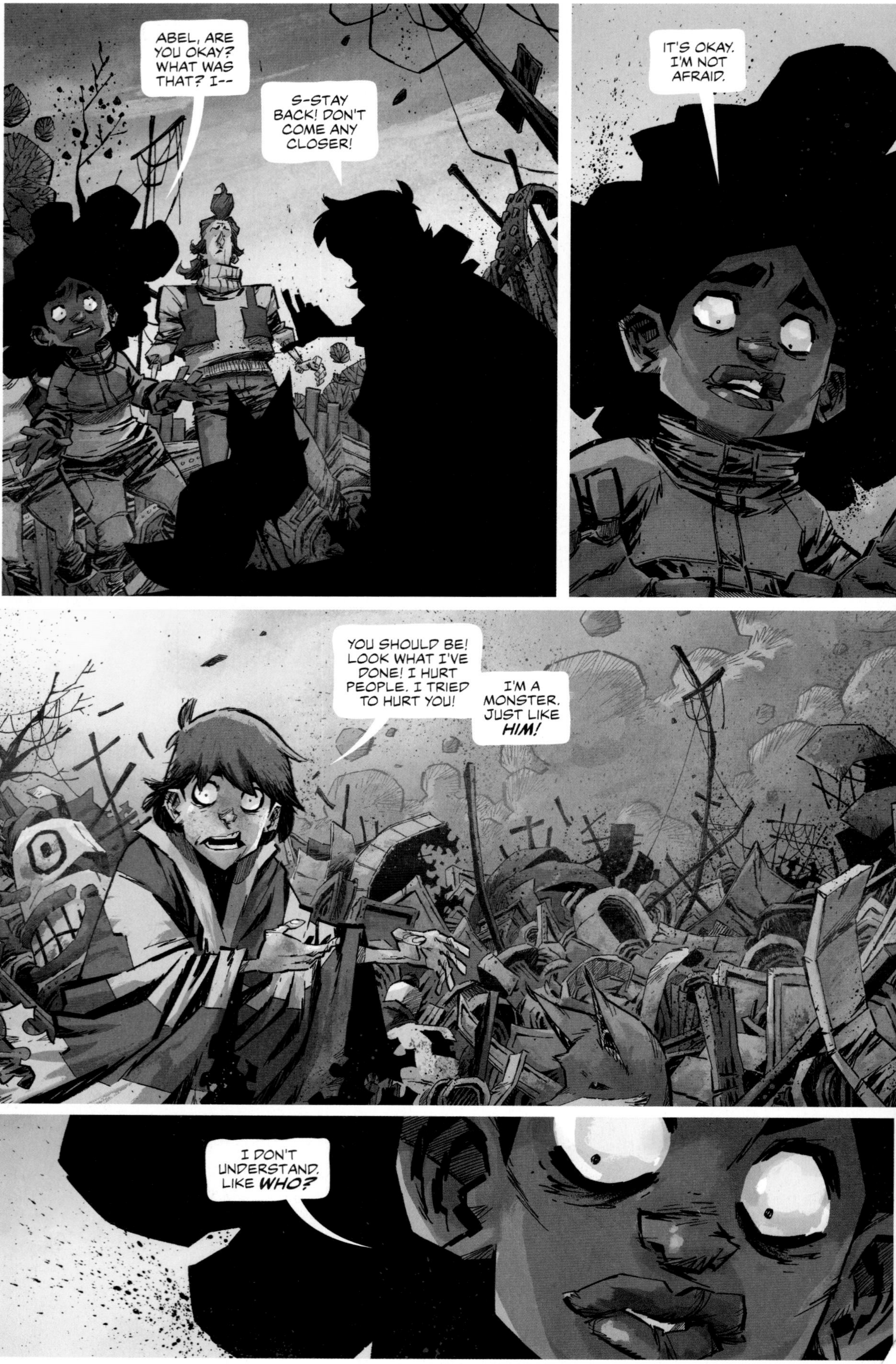
ABEL, ARE YOU OKAY? WHAT WAS THAT? I--
S-STAY BACK! DON'T COME ANY CLOSER!
IT'S OKAY. I'M NOT AFRAID.
YOU SHOULD BE! LOOK WHAT I'VE DONE! I HURT PEOPLE. I TRIED TO HURT YOU!
I'M A MONSTER. JUST LIKE *HIM!*
I DON'T UNDERSTAND. LIKE *WHO?*

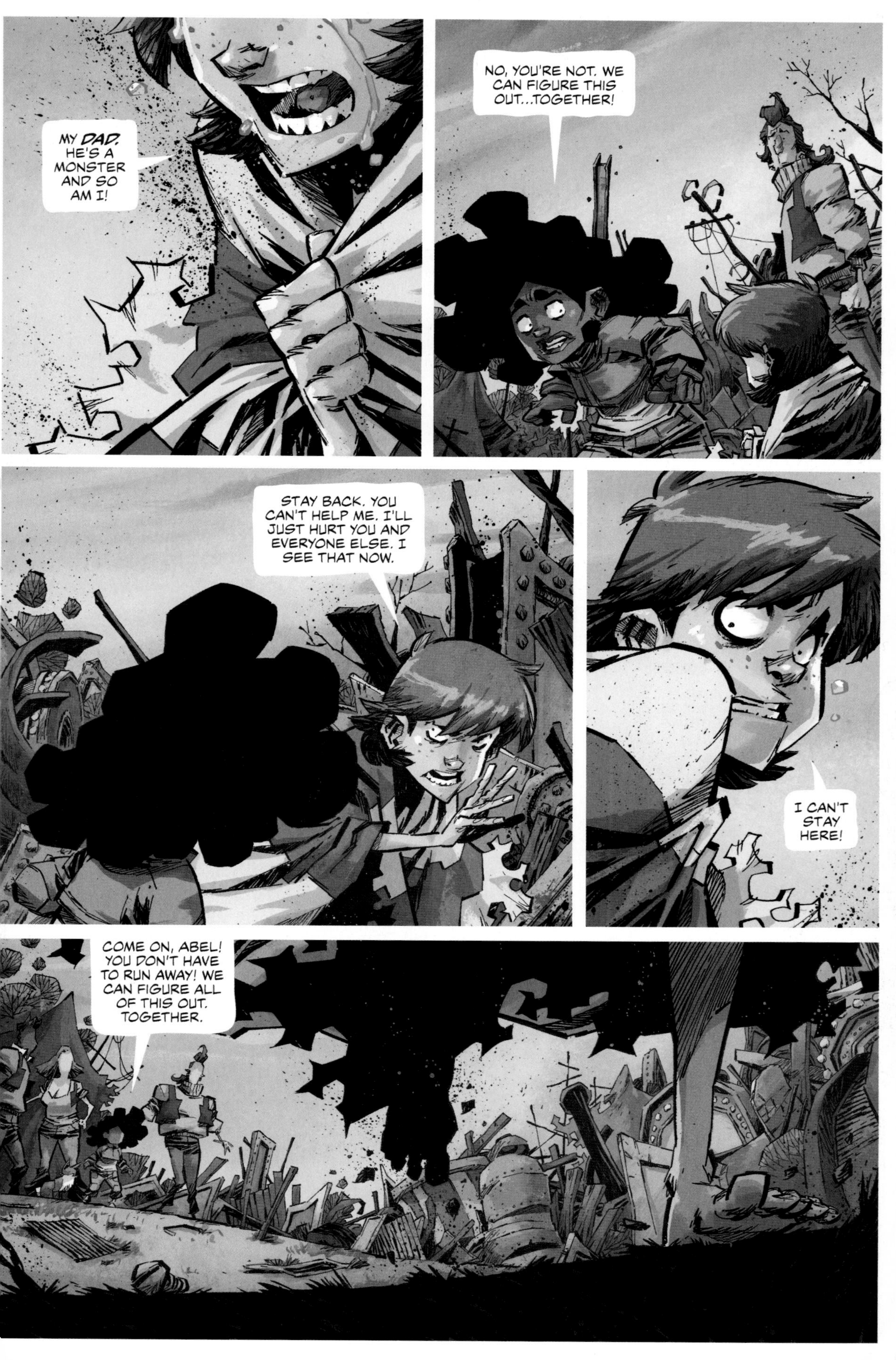
MY **DAD.** HE'S A MONSTER AND SO AM I!
NO, YOU'RE NOT. WE CAN FIGURE THIS OUT...TOGETHER!
STAY BACK. YOU CAN'T HELP ME. I'LL JUST HURT YOU AND EVERYONE ELSE. I SEE THAT NOW.
I CAN'T STAY HERE!
COME ON, ABEL! YOU DON'T HAVE TO RUN AWAY! WE CAN FIGURE ALL OF THIS OUT. TOGETHER.

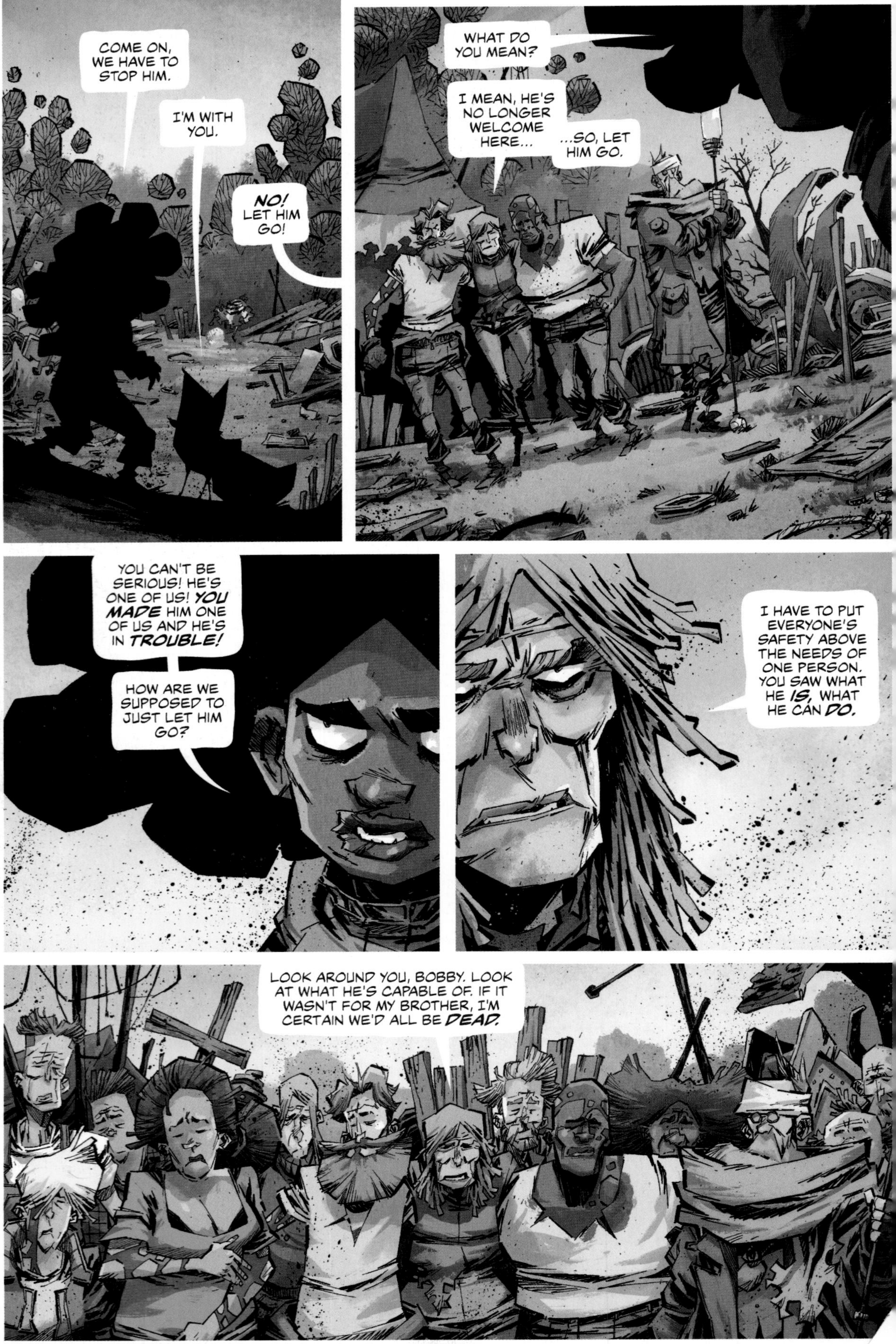
COME ON, WE HAVE TO STOP HIM.
I'M WITH YOU.
NO! LET HIM GO!
WHAT DO YOU MEAN?
I MEAN, HE'S NO LONGER WELCOME HERE...
...SO, LET HIM GO.
YOU CAN'T BE SERIOUS! HE'S ONE OF US! YOU MADE HIM ONE OF US AND HE'S IN TROUBLE!
HOW ARE WE SUPPOSED TO JUST LET HIM GO?
I HAVE TO PUT EVERYONE'S SAFETY ABOVE THE NEEDS OF ONE PERSON. YOU SAW WHAT HE IS, WHAT HE CAN DO.
LOOK AROUND YOU, BOBBY. LOOK AT WHAT HE'S CAPABLE OF. IF IT WASN'T FOR MY BROTHER, I'M CERTAIN WE'D ALL BE DEAD.

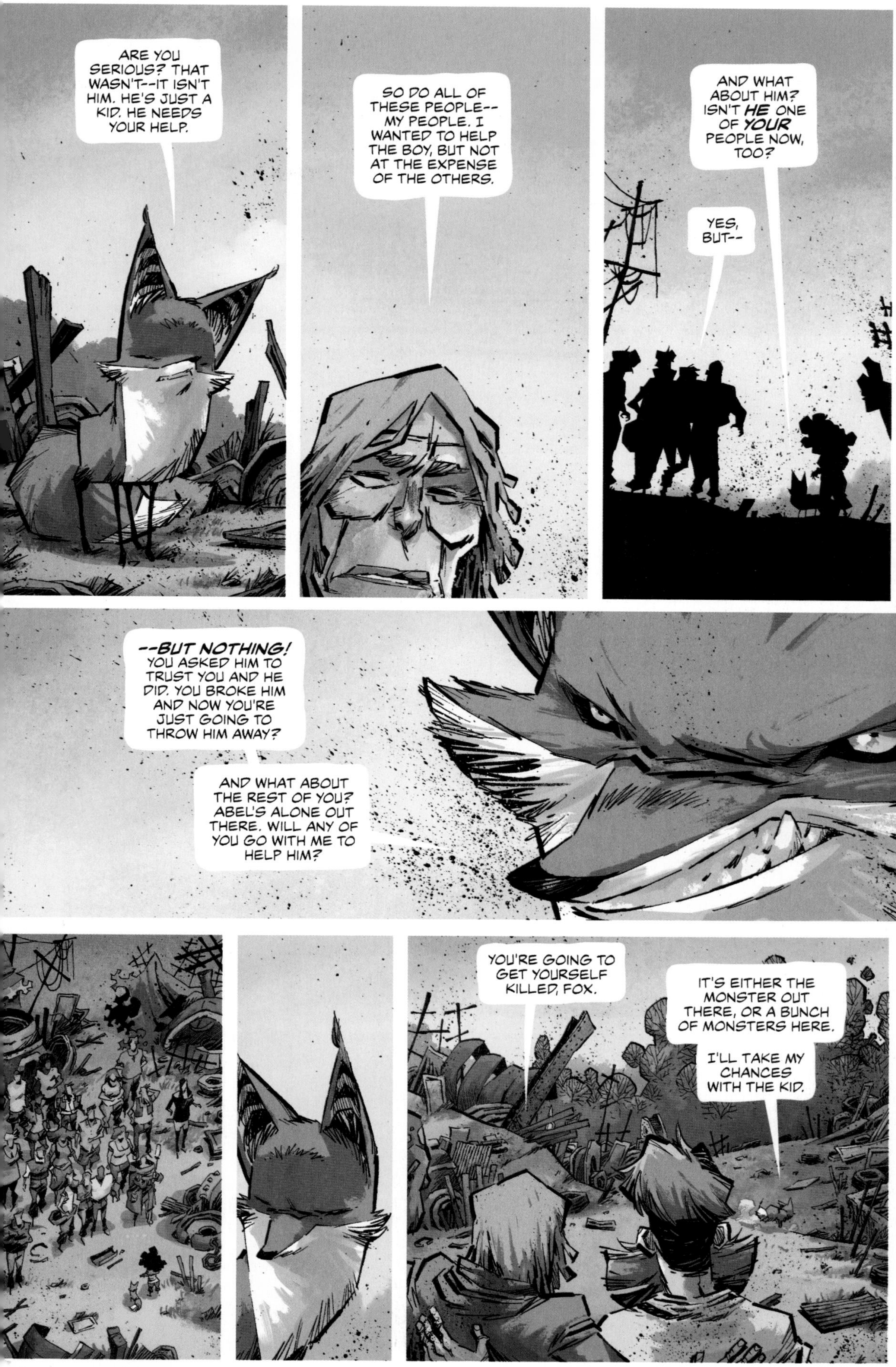
ARE YOU SERIOUS? THAT WASN'T--IT ISN'T HIM. HE'S JUST A KID. HE NEEDS YOUR HELP.
SO DO ALL OF THESE PEOPLE-- MY PEOPLE. I WANTED TO HELP THE BOY, BUT NOT AT THE EXPENSE OF THE OTHERS.
AND WHAT ABOUT HIM? ISN'T **HE** ONE OF ***YOUR*** PEOPLE NOW, TOO?
YES, BUT--
--BUT NOTHING! YOU ASKED HIM TO TRUST YOU AND HE DID. YOU BROKE HIM AND NOW YOU'RE JUST GOING TO THROW HIM AWAY?
AND WHAT ABOUT THE REST OF YOU? ABEL'S ALONE OUT THERE. WILL ANY OF YOU GO WITH ME TO HELP HIM?
YOU'RE GOING TO GET YOURSELF KILLED, FOX.
IT'S EITHER THE MONSTER OUT THERE, OR A BUNCH OF MONSTERS HERE.
I'LL TAKE MY CHANCES WITH THE KID.

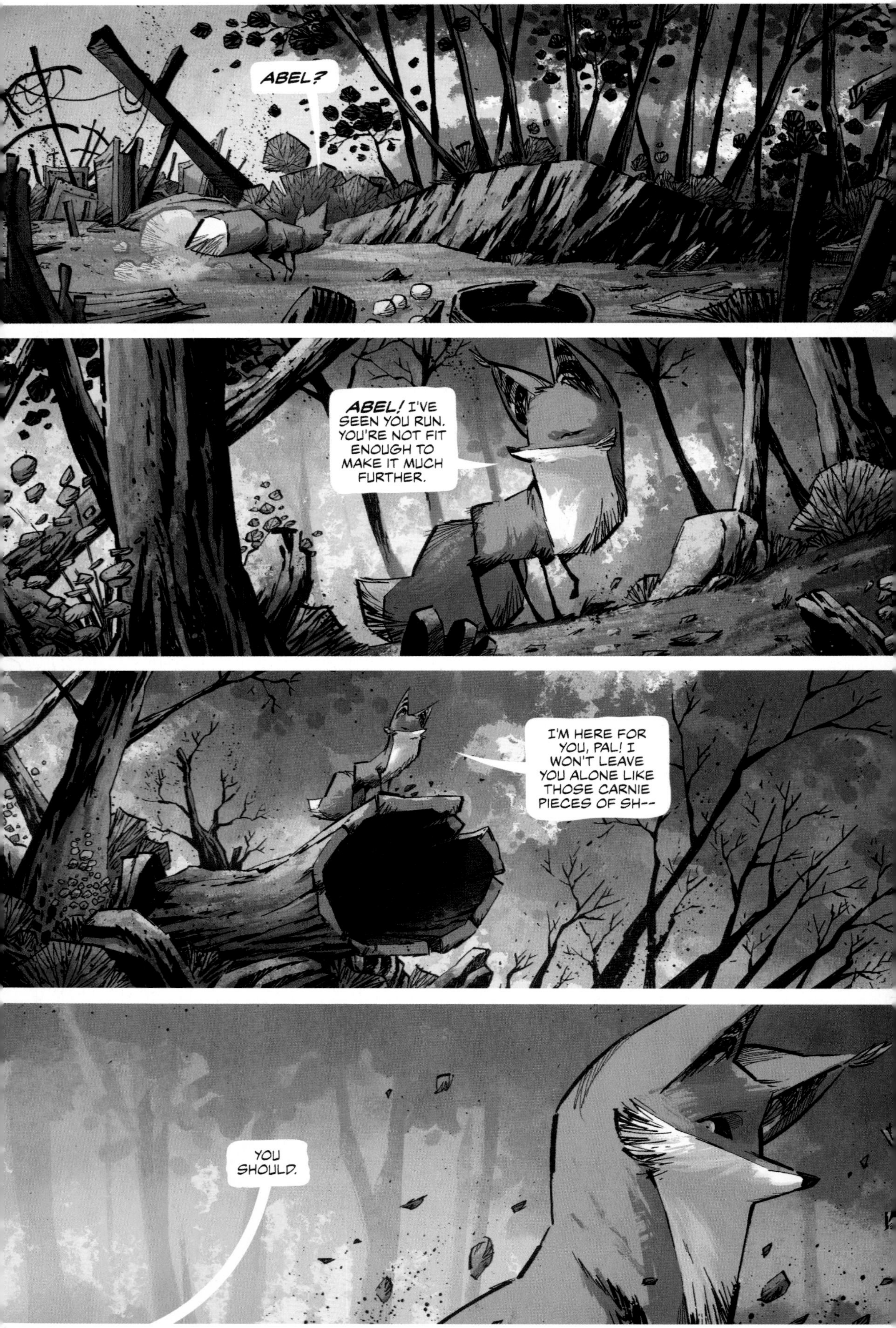
ABEL?
ABEL! I'VE SEEN YOU RUN. YOU'RE NOT FIT ENOUGH TO MAKE IT MUCH FURTHER.
I'M HERE FOR YOU, PAL! I WON'T LEAVE YOU ALONE LIKE THOSE CARNIE PIECES OF SH--
YOU SHOULD.

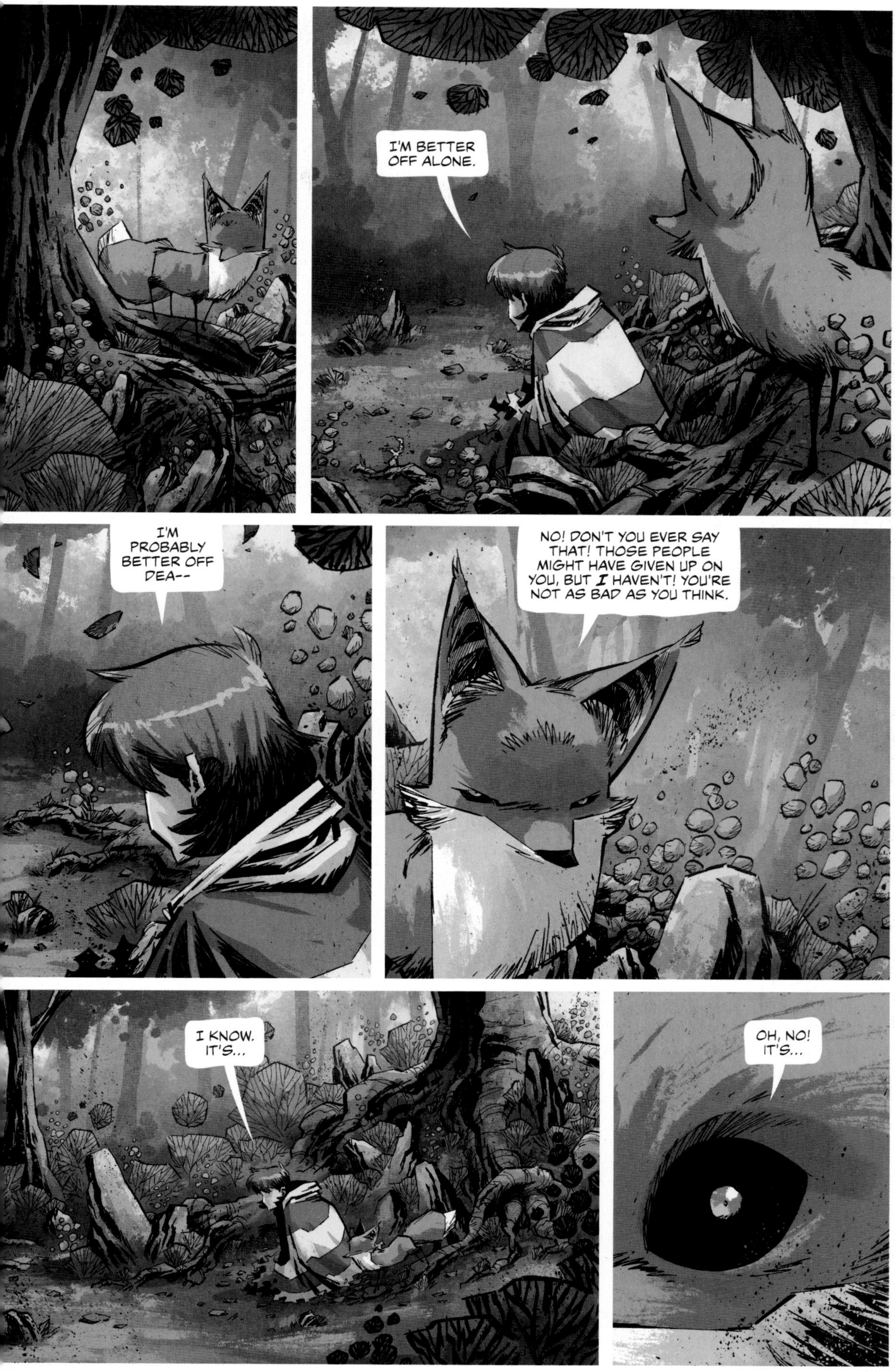
I'M BETTER OFF ALONE.
I'M PROBABLY BETTER OFF DEA--
NO! DON'T YOU EVER SAY THAT! THOSE PEOPLE MIGHT HAVE GIVEN UP ON YOU, BUT I HAVEN'T! YOU'RE NOT AS BAD AS YOU THINK.
I KNOW. IT'S...
OH, NO! IT'S...

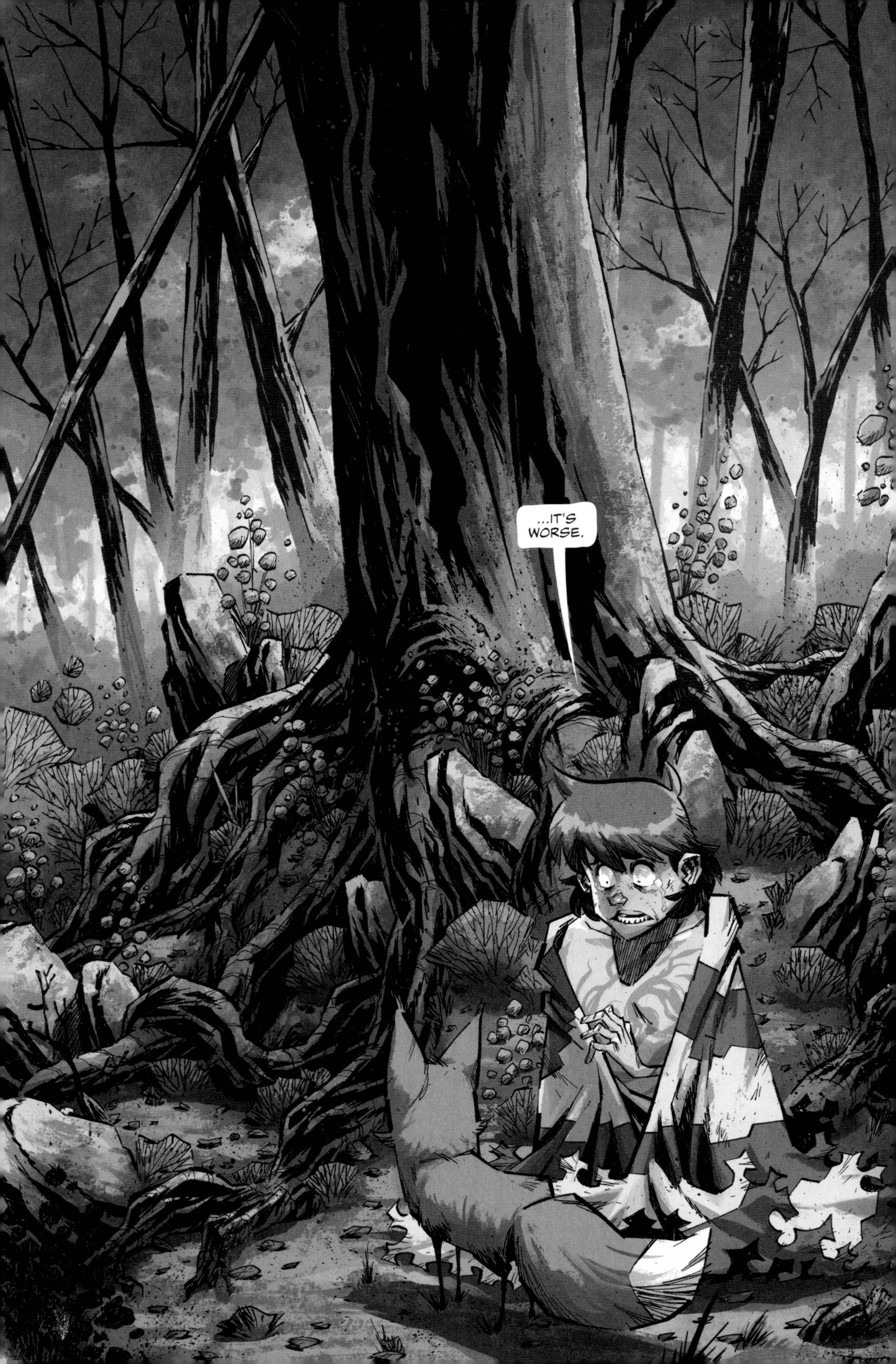
...IT'S WORSE.

CHAPTER
EIGHT

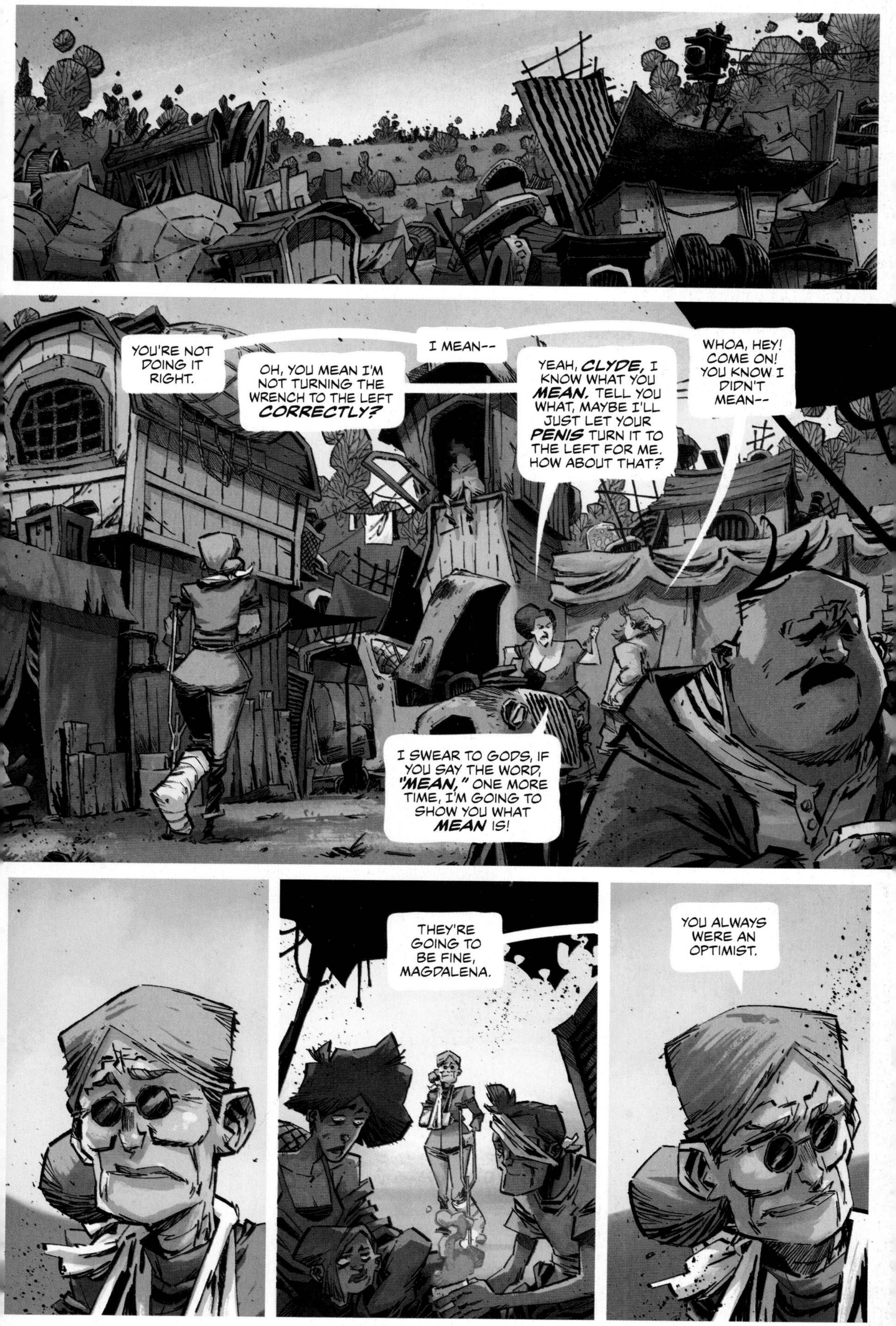
YOU'RE NOT DOING IT RIGHT.
OH, YOU MEAN I'M NOT TURNING THE WRENCH TO THE LEFT CORRECTLY?
I MEAN--
YEAH, CLYDE, I KNOW WHAT YOU MEAN. TELL YOU WHAT, MAYBE I'LL JUST LET YOUR PENIS TURN IT TO THE LEFT FOR ME. HOW ABOUT THAT?
WHOA, HEY! COME ON! YOU KNOW I DIDN'T MEAN--
I SWEAR TO GODS, IF YOU SAY THE WORD, "MEAN," ONE MORE TIME, I'M GOING TO SHOW YOU WHAT MEAN IS!
THEY'RE GOING TO BE FINE, MAGDALENA.
YOU ALWAYS WERE AN OPTIMIST.

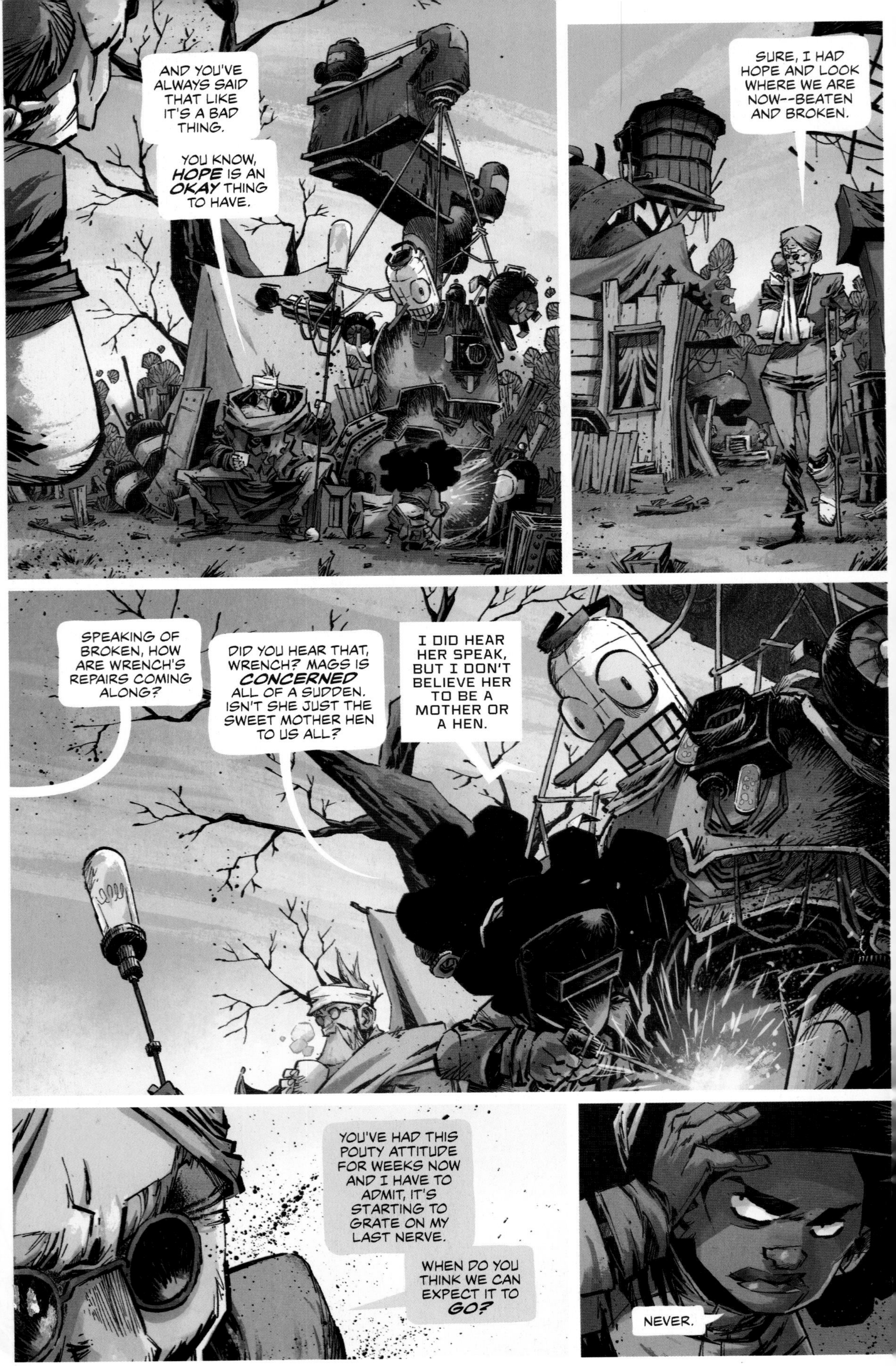
AND YOU'VE ALWAYS SAID THAT LIKE IT'S A BAD THING.
YOU KNOW, HOPE IS AN OKAY THING TO HAVE.
SURE, I HAD HOPE AND LOOK WHERE WE ARE NOW--BEATEN AND BROKEN.
SPEAKING OF BROKEN, HOW ARE WRENCH'S REPAIRS COMING ALONG?
DID YOU HEAR THAT, WRENCH? MAGS IS CONCERNED ALL OF A SUDDEN. ISN'T SHE JUST THE SWEET MOTHER HEN TO US ALL?
I DID HEAR HER SPEAK, BUT I DON'T BELIEVE HER TO BE A MOTHER OR A HEN.
YOU'VE HAD THIS POUTY ATTITUDE FOR WEEKS NOW AND I HAVE TO ADMIT, IT'S STARTING TO GRATE ON MY LAST NERVE.
WHEN DO YOU THINK WE CAN EXPECT IT TO GO?
NEVER.

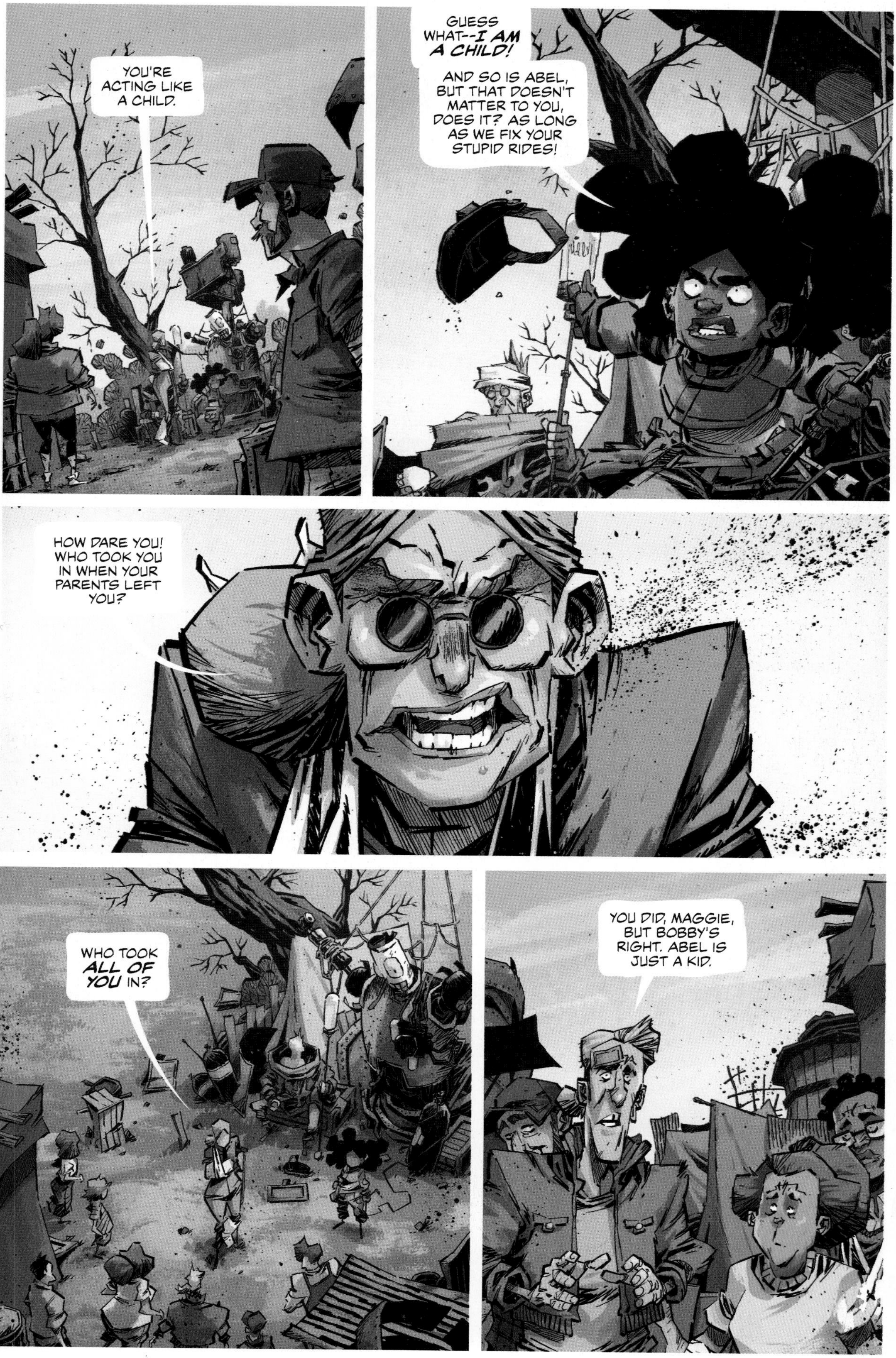
YOU'RE ACTING LIKE A CHILD.
GUESS WHAT--*I AM A CHILD!*
AND SO IS ABEL, BUT THAT DOESN'T MATTER TO YOU, DOES IT? AS LONG AS WE FIX YOUR STUPID RIDES!
HOW DARE YOU! WHO TOOK YOU IN WHEN YOUR PARENTS LEFT YOU?
WHO TOOK *ALL OF YOU* IN?
YOU DID, MAGGIE, BUT BOBBY'S RIGHT. ABEL IS JUST A KID.

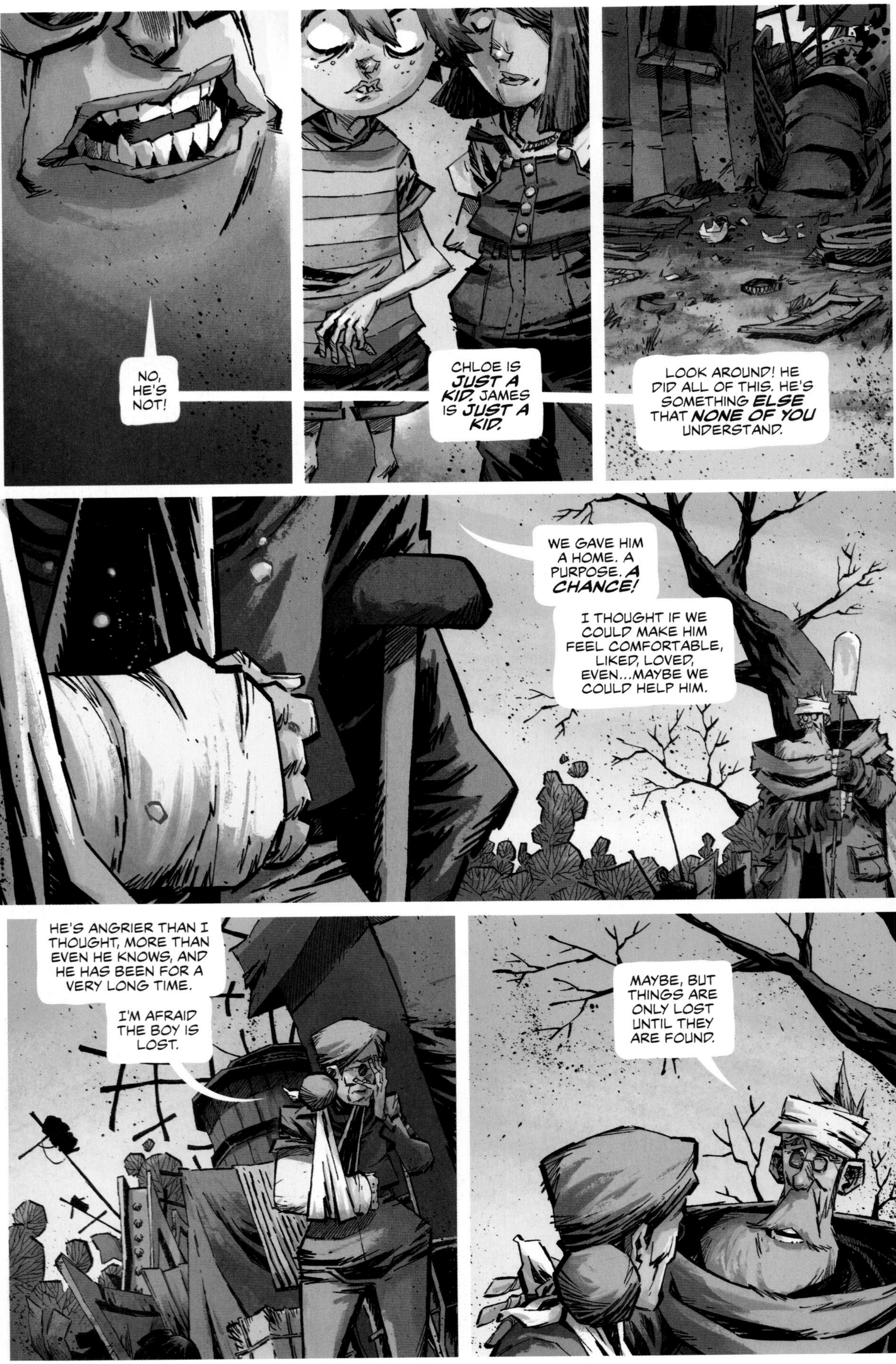
NO, HE'S NOT!
CHLOE IS JUST A KID. JAMES IS JUST A KID.
LOOK AROUND! HE DID ALL OF THIS. HE'S SOMETHING ELSE THAT NONE OF YOU UNDERSTAND.
WE GAVE HIM A HOME. A PURPOSE. A CHANCE!
I THOUGHT IF WE COULD MAKE HIM FEEL COMFORTABLE, LIKED, LOVED, EVEN...MAYBE WE COULD HELP HIM.
HE'S ANGRIER THAN I THOUGHT, MORE THAN EVEN HE KNOWS, AND HE HAS BEEN FOR A VERY LONG TIME.
I'M AFRAID THE BOY IS LOST.
MAYBE, BUT THINGS ARE ONLY LOST UNTIL THEY ARE FOUND.

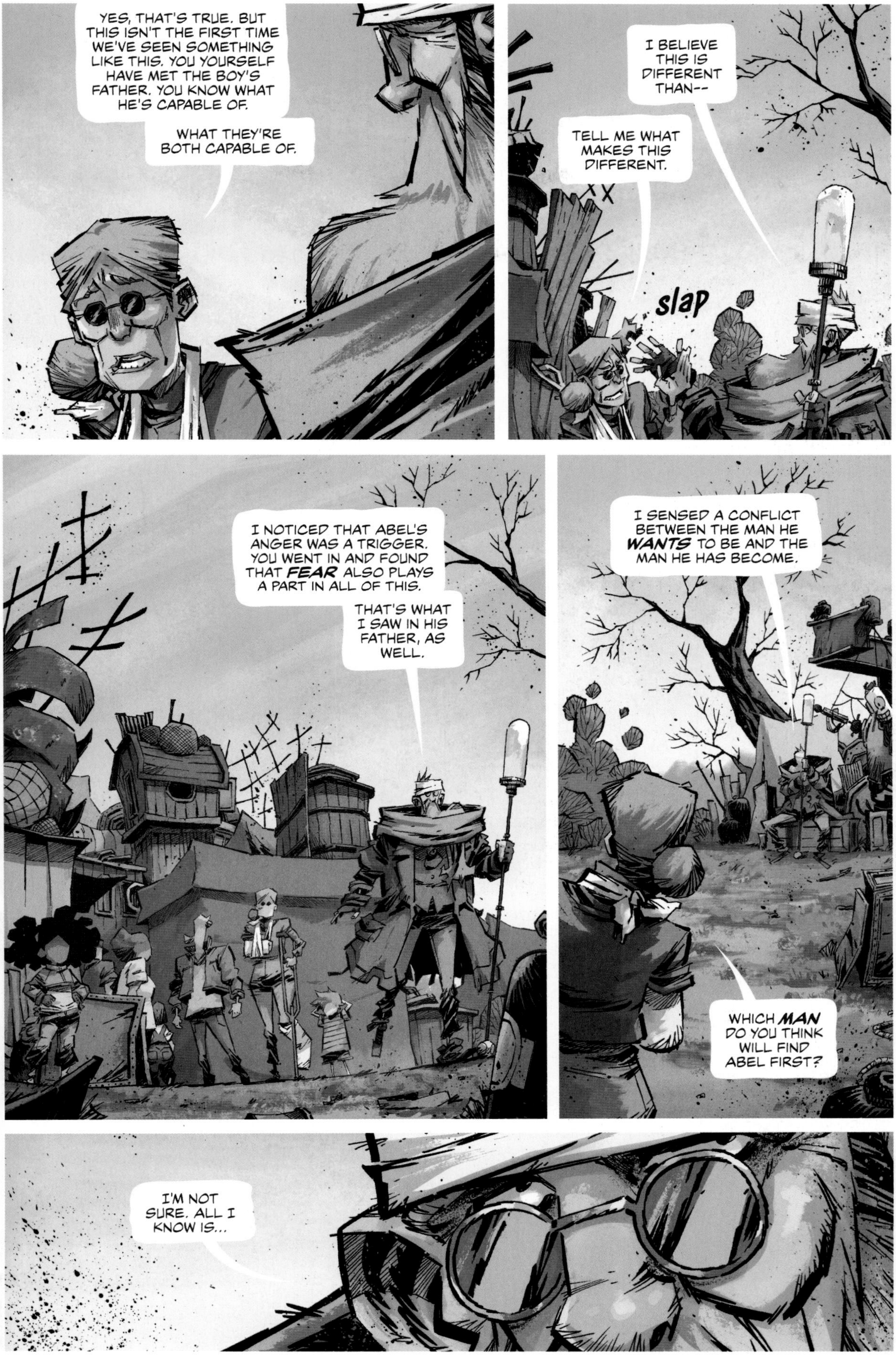
YES, THAT'S TRUE. BUT THIS ISN'T THE FIRST TIME WE'VE SEEN SOMETHING LIKE THIS. YOU YOURSELF HAVE MET THE BOY'S FATHER. YOU KNOW WHAT HE'S CAPABLE OF.
WHAT THEY'RE BOTH CAPABLE OF.
I BELIEVE THIS IS DIFFERENT THAN--
TELL ME WHAT MAKES THIS DIFFERENT.
slap
I NOTICED THAT ABEL'S ANGER WAS A TRIGGER. YOU WENT IN AND FOUND THAT FEAR ALSO PLAYS A PART IN ALL OF THIS.
THAT'S WHAT I SAW IN HIS FATHER, AS WELL.
I SENSED A CONFLICT BETWEEN THE MAN HE WANTS TO BE AND THE MAN HE HAS BECOME.
WHICH MAN DO YOU THINK WILL FIND ABEL FIRST?
I'M NOT SURE. ALL I KNOW IS...

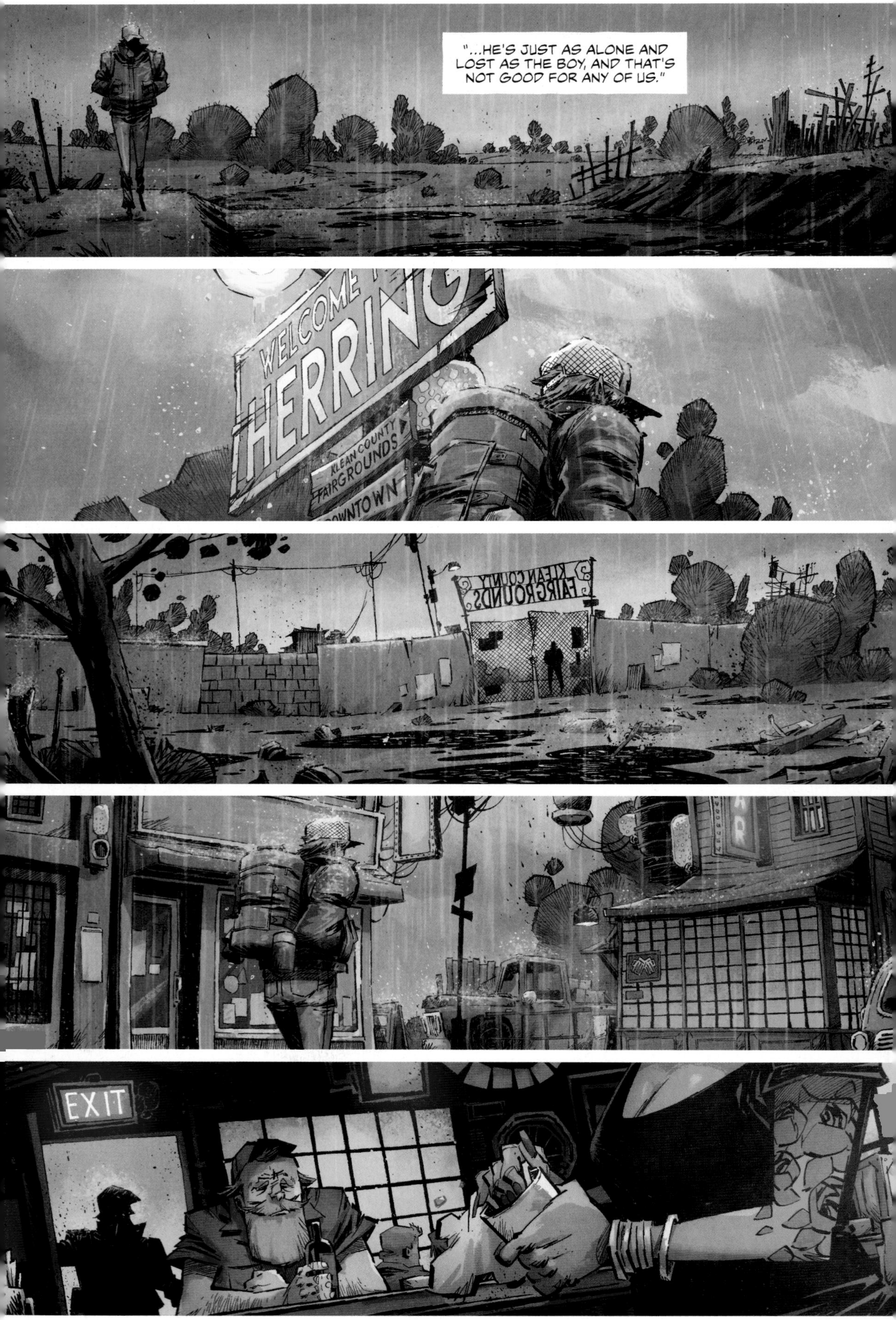
"...HE'S JUST AS ALONE AND LOST AS THE BOY, AND THAT'S NOT GOOD FOR ANY OF US."
WELCOME
HERRIN
KLEAN COUNTY FAIRGROUNDS
EXIT

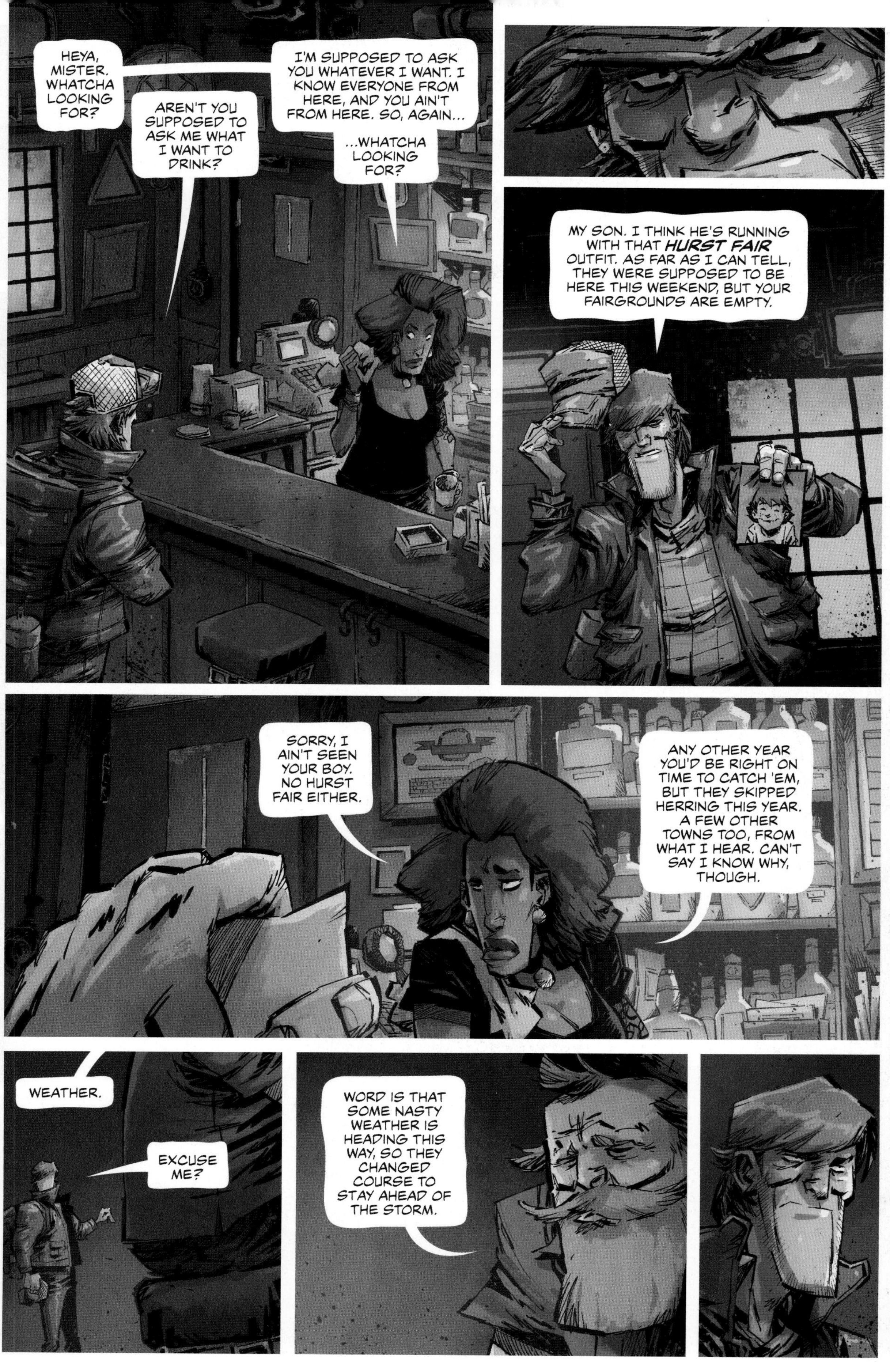
HEYA, MISTER. WHATCHA LOOKING FOR?
AREN'T YOU SUPPOSED TO ASK ME WHAT I WANT TO DRINK?
I'M SUPPOSED TO ASK YOU WHATEVER I WANT. I KNOW EVERYONE FROM HERE, AND YOU AIN'T FROM HERE. SO, AGAIN...
...WHATCHA LOOKING FOR?
MY SON. I THINK HE'S RUNNING WITH THAT HURST FAIR OUTFIT. AS FAR AS I CAN TELL, THEY WERE SUPPOSED TO BE HERE THIS WEEKEND, BUT YOUR FAIRGROUNDS ARE EMPTY.
SORRY, I AIN'T SEEN YOUR BOY. NO HURST FAIR EITHER.
ANY OTHER YEAR YOU'D BE RIGHT ON TIME TO CATCH 'EM, BUT THEY SKIPPED HERRING THIS YEAR. A FEW OTHER TOWNS TOO, FROM WHAT I HEAR. CAN'T SAY I KNOW WHY, THOUGH.
WEATHER.
EXCUSE ME?
WORD IS THAT SOME NASTY WEATHER IS HEADING THIS WAY, SO THEY CHANGED COURSE TO STAY AHEAD OF THE STORM.

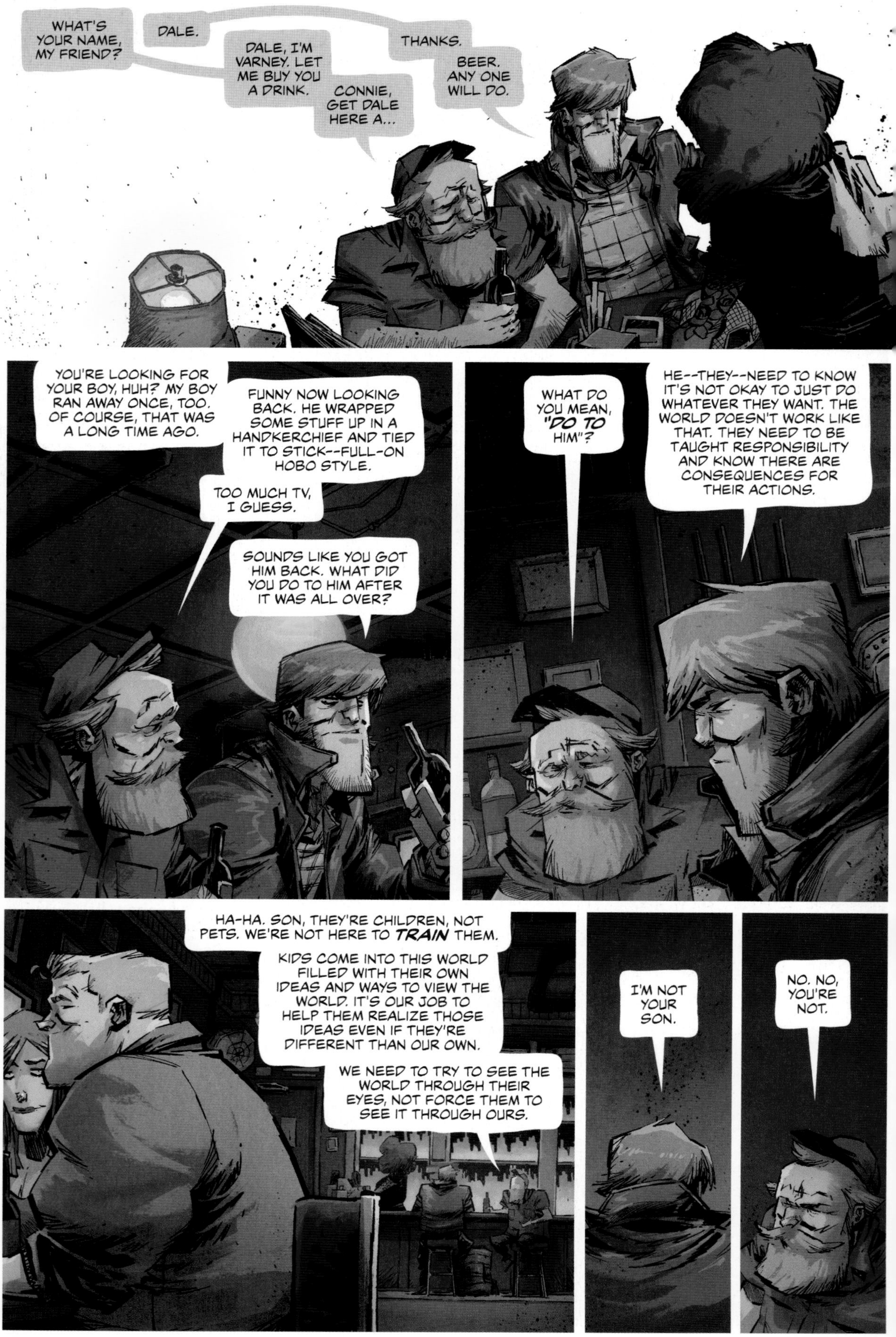
WHAT'S YOUR NAME, MY FRIEND?
DALE.
DALE, I'M VARNEY. LET ME BUY YOU A DRINK.
THANKS.
CONNIE, GET DALE HERE A...
BEER. ANY ONE WILL DO.
YOU'RE LOOKING FOR YOUR BOY, HUH? MY BOY RAN AWAY ONCE, TOO. OF COURSE, THAT WAS A LONG TIME AGO.
FUNNY NOW LOOKING BACK. HE WRAPPED SOME STUFF UP IN A HANDKERCHIEF AND TIED IT TO STICK--FULL-ON HOBO STYLE.
TOO MUCH TV, I GUESS.
SOUNDS LIKE YOU GOT HIM BACK. WHAT DID YOU DO TO HIM AFTER IT WAS ALL OVER?
WHAT DO YOU MEAN, "DO TO HIM"?
HE--THEY--NEED TO KNOW IT'S NOT OKAY TO JUST DO WHATEVER THEY WANT. THE WORLD DOESN'T WORK LIKE THAT. THEY NEED TO BE TAUGHT RESPONSIBILITY AND KNOW THERE ARE CONSEQUENCES FOR THEIR ACTIONS.
HA-HA. SON, THEY'RE CHILDREN, NOT PETS. WE'RE NOT HERE TO TRAIN THEM.
KIDS COME INTO THIS WORLD FILLED WITH THEIR OWN IDEAS AND WAYS TO VIEW THE WORLD. IT'S OUR JOB TO HELP THEM REALIZE THOSE IDEAS EVEN IF THEY'RE DIFFERENT THAN OUR OWN.
WE NEED TO TRY TO SEE THE WORLD THROUGH THEIR EYES, NOT FORCE THEM TO SEE IT THROUGH OURS.
I'M NOT YOUR SON.
NO. NO, YOU'RE NOT.

I APPRECIATE THE BEER, VARNEY, BUT I THINK I'VE GOT A HANDLE ON HOW TO RAISE MY KID.

I'M SURE YOU DO. THEN AGAIN, YOU'RE HERE IN A BAR, WHICH I'M GUESSING IS PRETTY FAR FROM YOUR HOME, LOOKING FOR YOUR BOY.

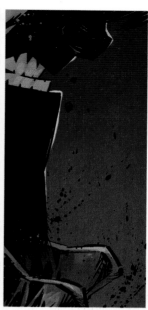

AND BASED ON THE GRIP YOU GOT ON THAT BOTTLE, I'D BET HE DIDN'T RUN AWAY BECAUSE HE WAS UPSET OVER GETTIN' TOO MANY HUGS.

KSSHHH

YOU DON'T KNOW SHIT ABOUT ME, OLD MAN. FUCK YOU AND YOUR BARSTOOL PSYCHOLOGY.

BEFORE YOU OPEN YOUR MOUTH ABOUT ME OR MY SON, I SUGGEST--

HEY, GUY...

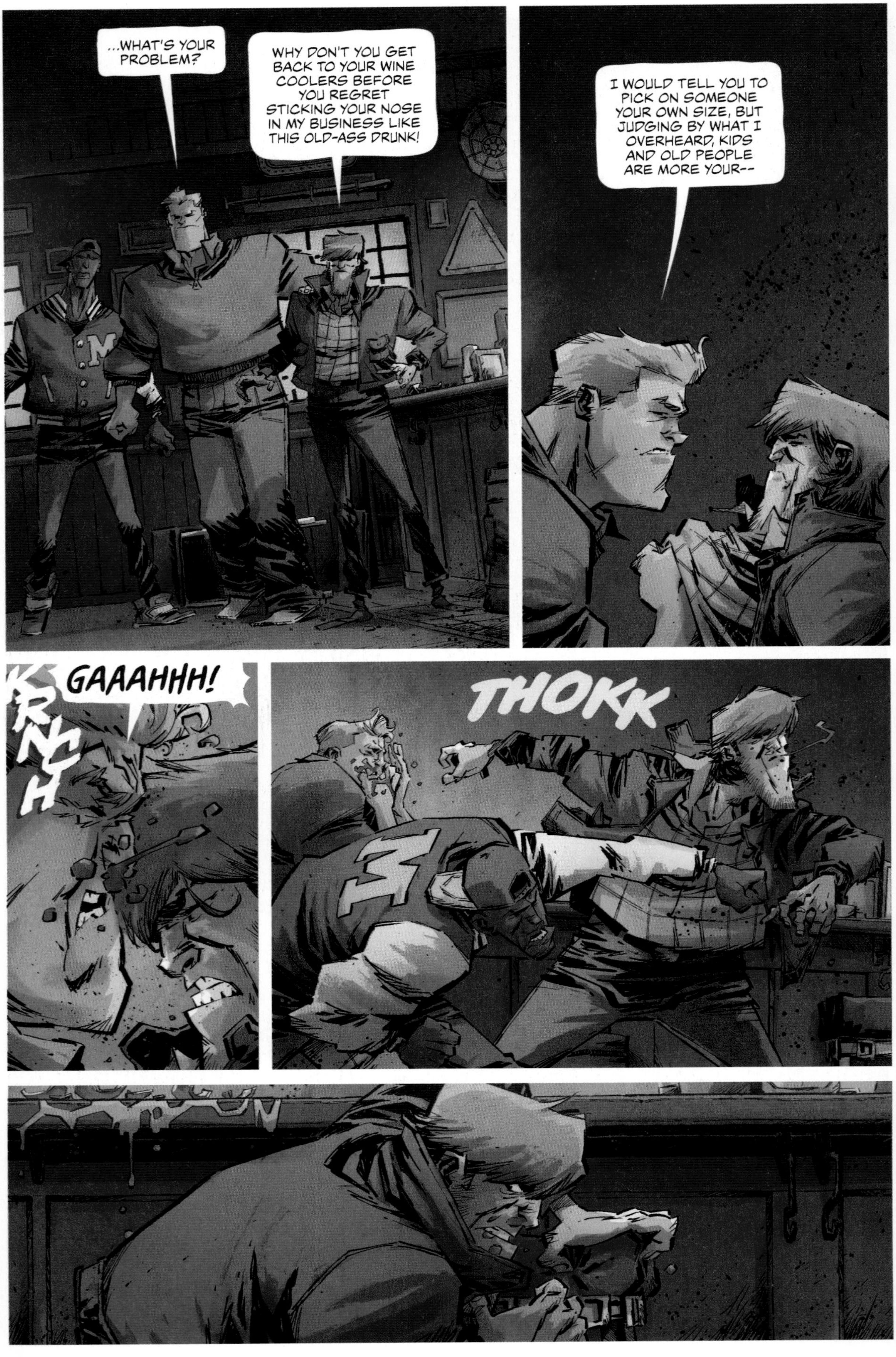
...WHAT'S YOUR PROBLEM?
WHY DON'T YOU GET BACK TO YOUR WINE COOLERS BEFORE YOU REGRET STICKING YOUR NOSE IN MY BUSINESS LIKE THIS OLD-ASS DRUNK!
I WOULD TELL YOU TO PICK ON SOMEONE YOUR OWN SIZE, BUT JUDGING BY WHAT I OVERHEARD, KIDS AND OLD PEOPLE ARE MORE YOUR--
GAAAHHH!
THOKK

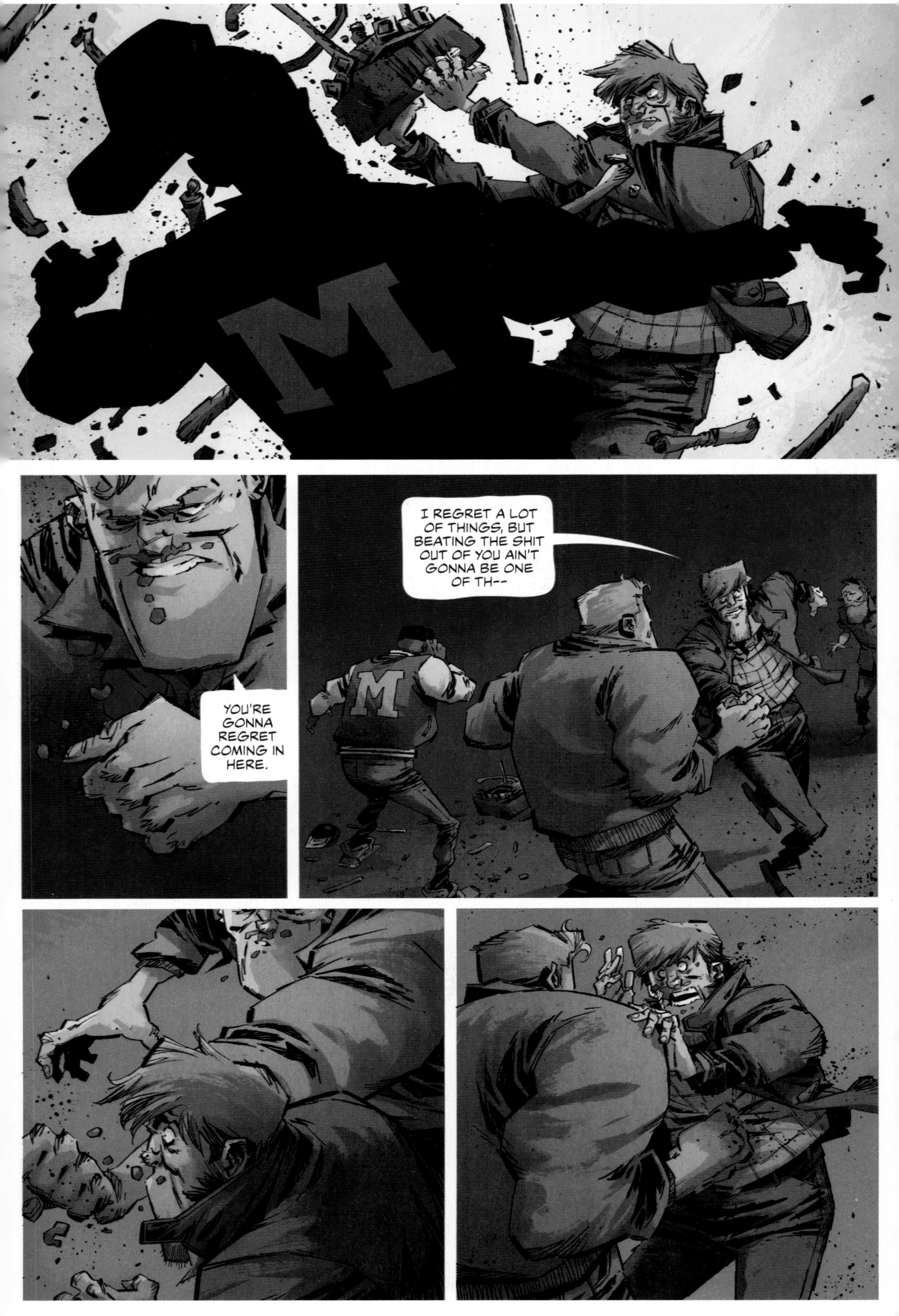
YOU'RE GONNA REGRET COMING IN HERE.
I REGRET A LOT OF THINGS, BUT BEATING THE SHIT OUT OF YOU AIN'T GONNA BE ONE OF TH--

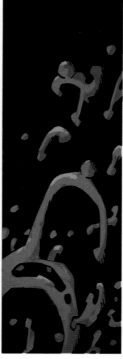

OKAY, BOYS. THAT'S ENOUGH.

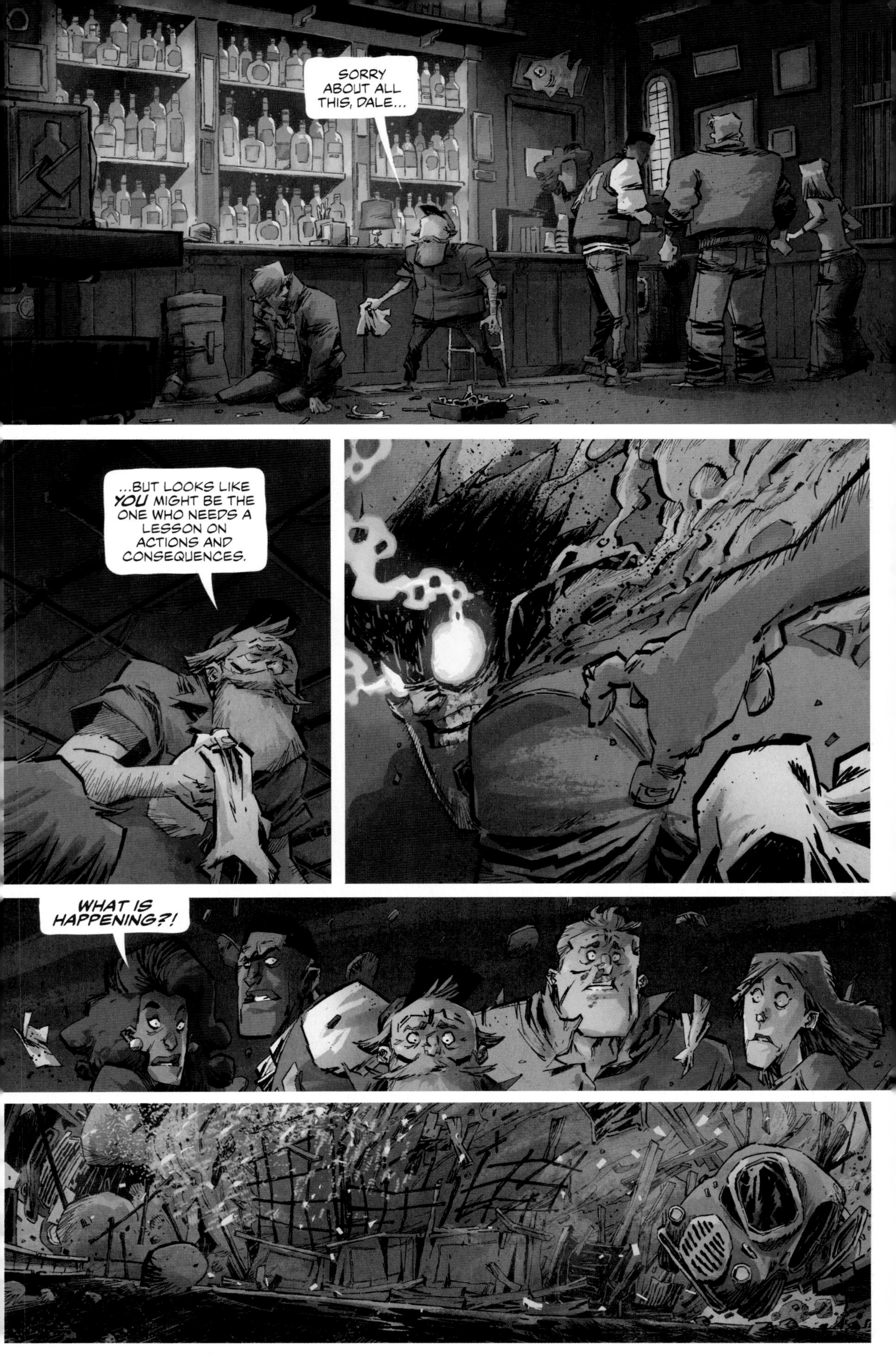
SORRY ABOUT ALL THIS, DALE...
...BUT LOOKS LIKE *YOU* MIGHT BE THE ONE WHO NEEDS A LESSON ON ACTIONS AND CONSEQUENCES.
WHAT IS HAPPENING?!

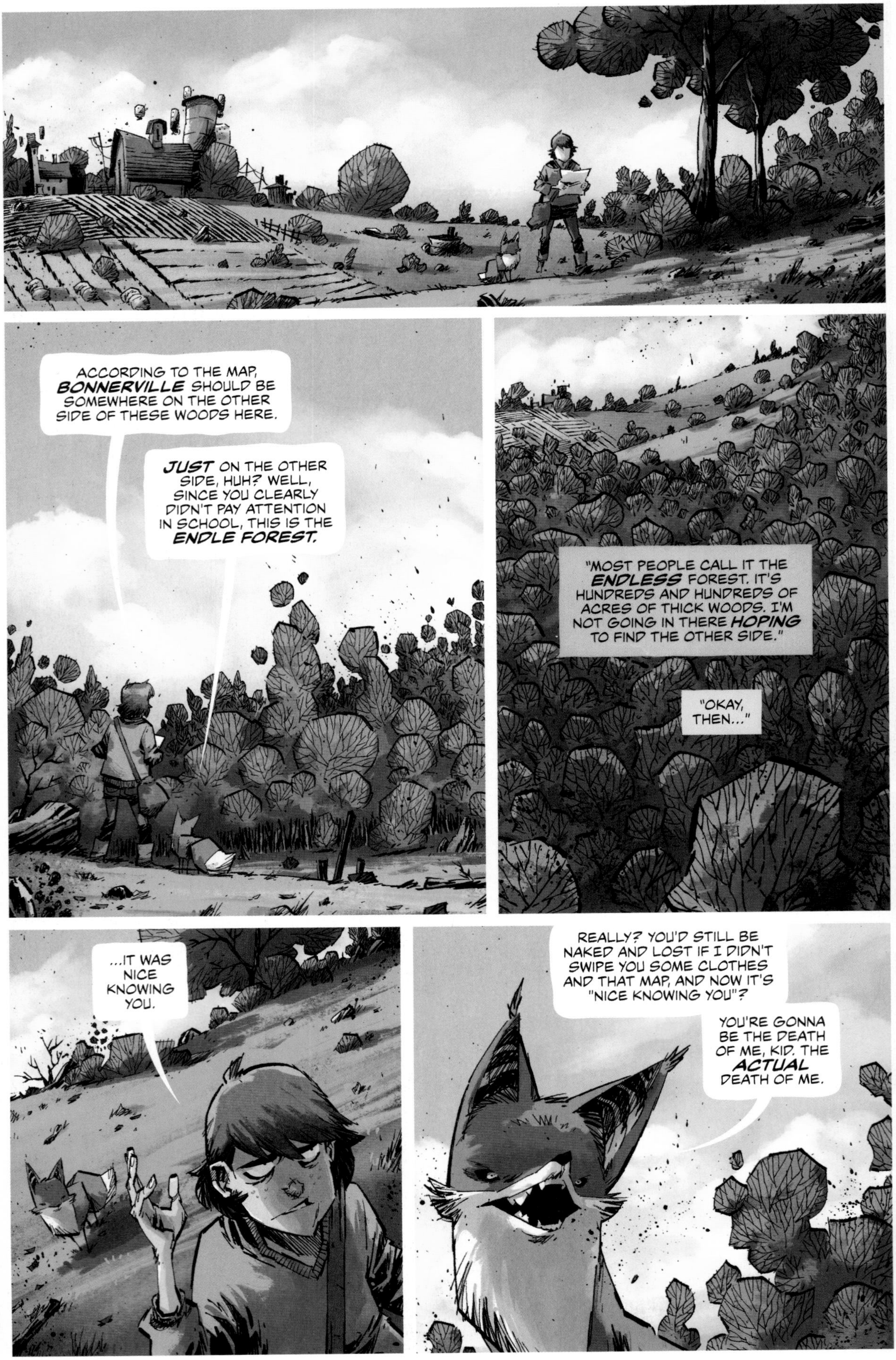
ACCORDING TO THE MAP, BONNERVILLE SHOULD BE SOMEWHERE ON THE OTHER SIDE OF THESE WOODS HERE.
JUST ON THE OTHER SIDE, HUH? WELL, SINCE YOU CLEARLY DIDN'T PAY ATTENTION IN SCHOOL, THIS IS THE ENDLE FOREST.
"MOST PEOPLE CALL IT THE ENDLESS FOREST. IT'S HUNDREDS AND HUNDREDS OF ACRES OF THICK WOODS. I'M NOT GOING IN THERE HOPING TO FIND THE OTHER SIDE."
"OKAY, THEN..."
...IT WAS NICE KNOWING YOU.
REALLY? YOU'D STILL BE NAKED AND LOST IF I DIDN'T SWIPE YOU SOME CLOTHES AND THAT MAP, AND NOW IT'S "NICE KNOWING YOU"?
YOU'RE GONNA BE THE DEATH OF ME, KID. THE ACTUAL DEATH OF ME.

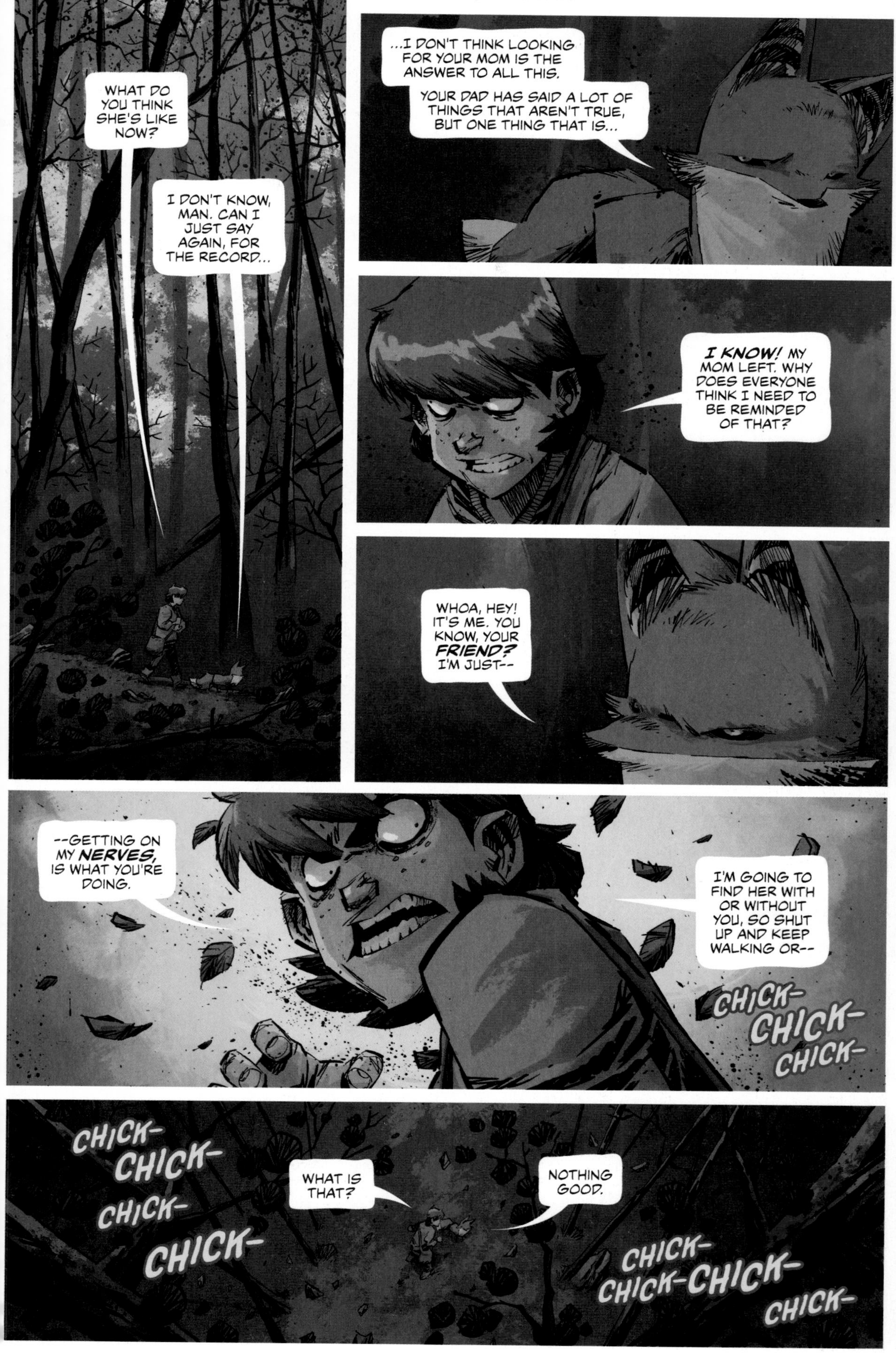

WHAT DO YOU THINK SHE'S LIKE NOW?
I DON'T KNOW, MAN. CAN I JUST SAY AGAIN, FOR THE RECORD...
...I DON'T THINK LOOKING FOR YOUR MOM IS THE ANSWER TO ALL THIS.
YOUR DAD HAS SAID A LOT OF THINGS THAT AREN'T TRUE, BUT ONE THING THAT IS...
I KNOW! MY MOM LEFT. WHY DOES EVERYONE THINK I NEED TO BE REMINDED OF THAT?
WHOA, HEY! IT'S ME. YOU KNOW, YOUR FRIEND? I'M JUST--
--GETTING ON MY NERVES, IS WHAT YOU'RE DOING.
I'M GOING TO FIND HER WITH OR WITHOUT YOU, SO SHUT UP AND KEEP WALKING OR--
CHICK-
CHICK-
CHICK-
CHICK-
CHICK-
CHICK-
CHICK-
WHAT IS THAT?
NOTHING GOOD.
CHICK-
CHICK-CHICK-
CHICK-

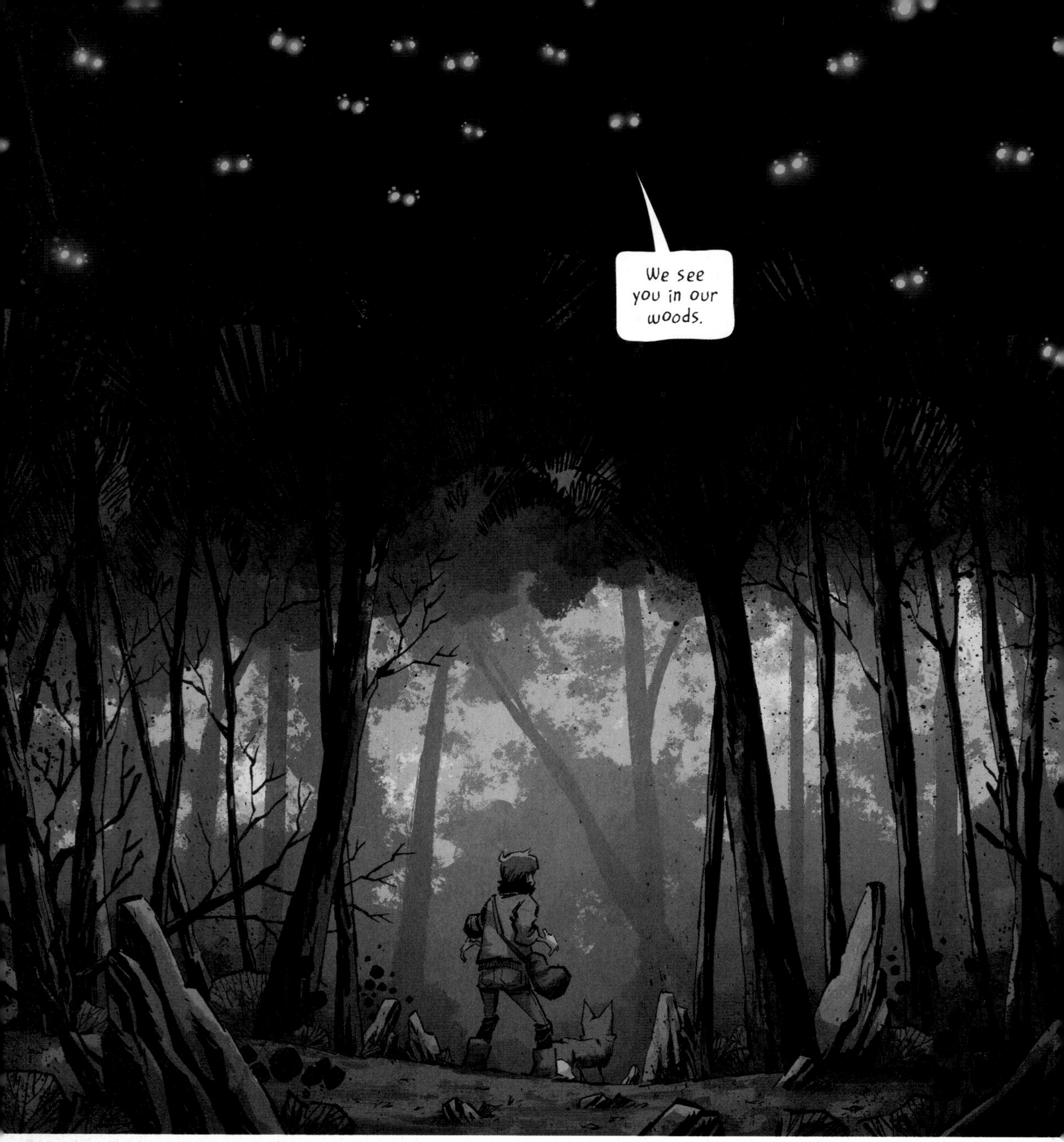
We see you in our woods.

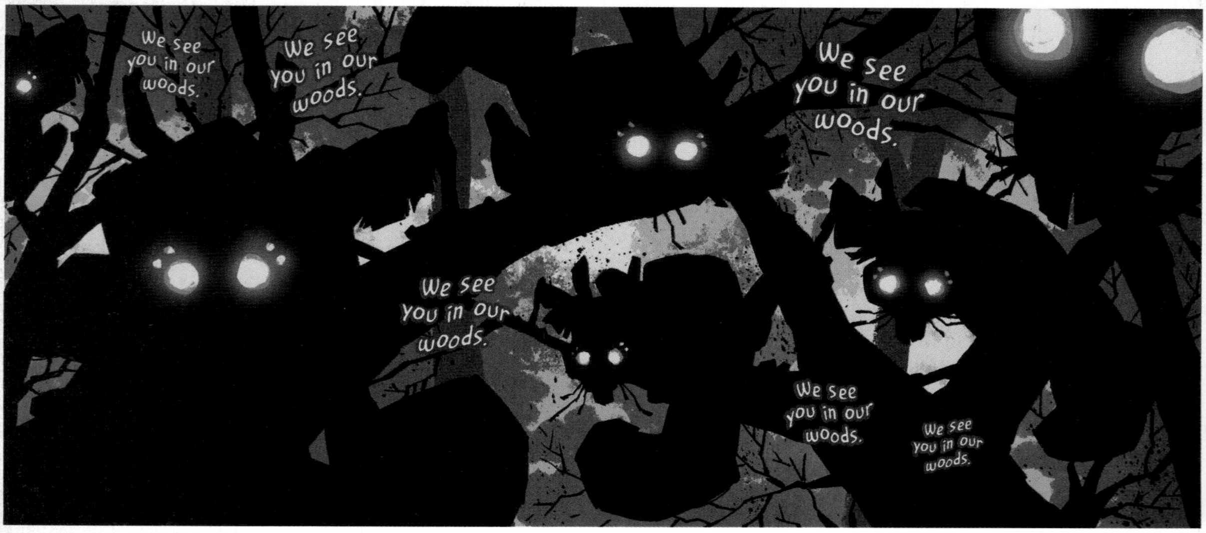
We see you in our woods.
We see you in our woods.
We see you in our woods.
We see you in our woods.
We see you in our woods.
We see you in our woods.

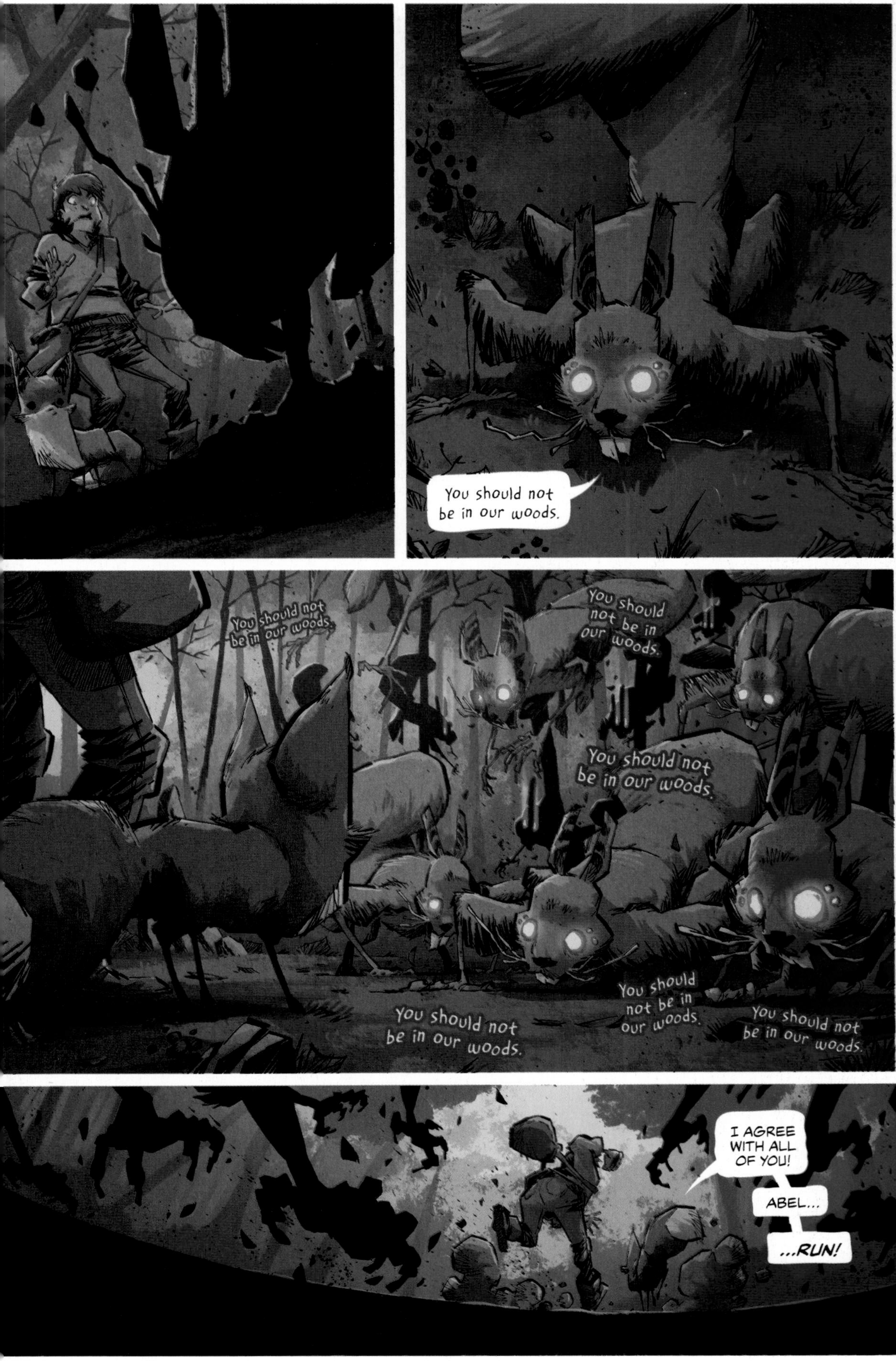
You should not be in our woods.
You should not be in our woods.
You should not be in our woods.
You should not be in our woods.
You should not be in our woods.
You should not be in our woods.
You should not be in our woods.
I AGREE WITH ALL OF YOU!
ABEL...
...RUN!

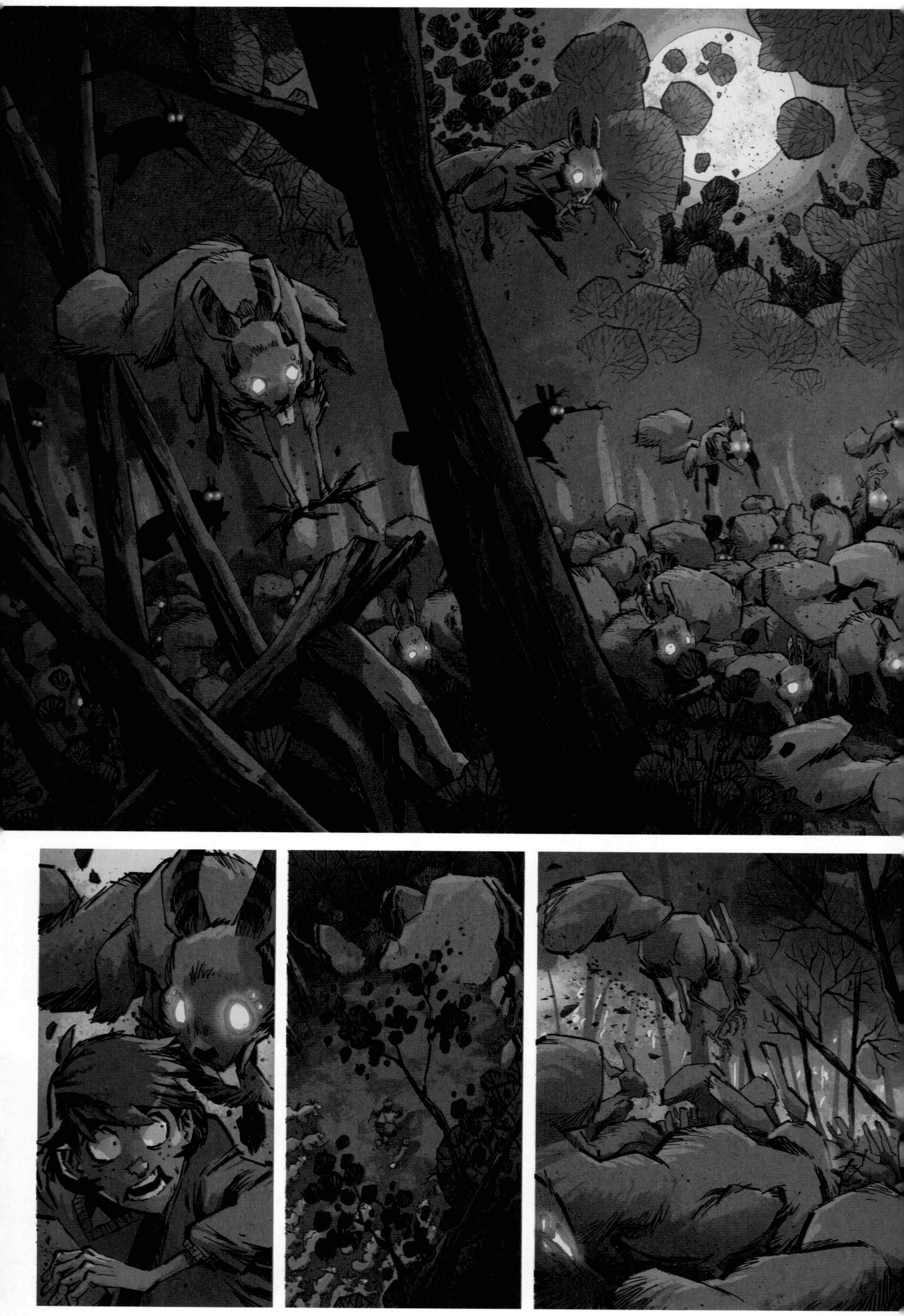

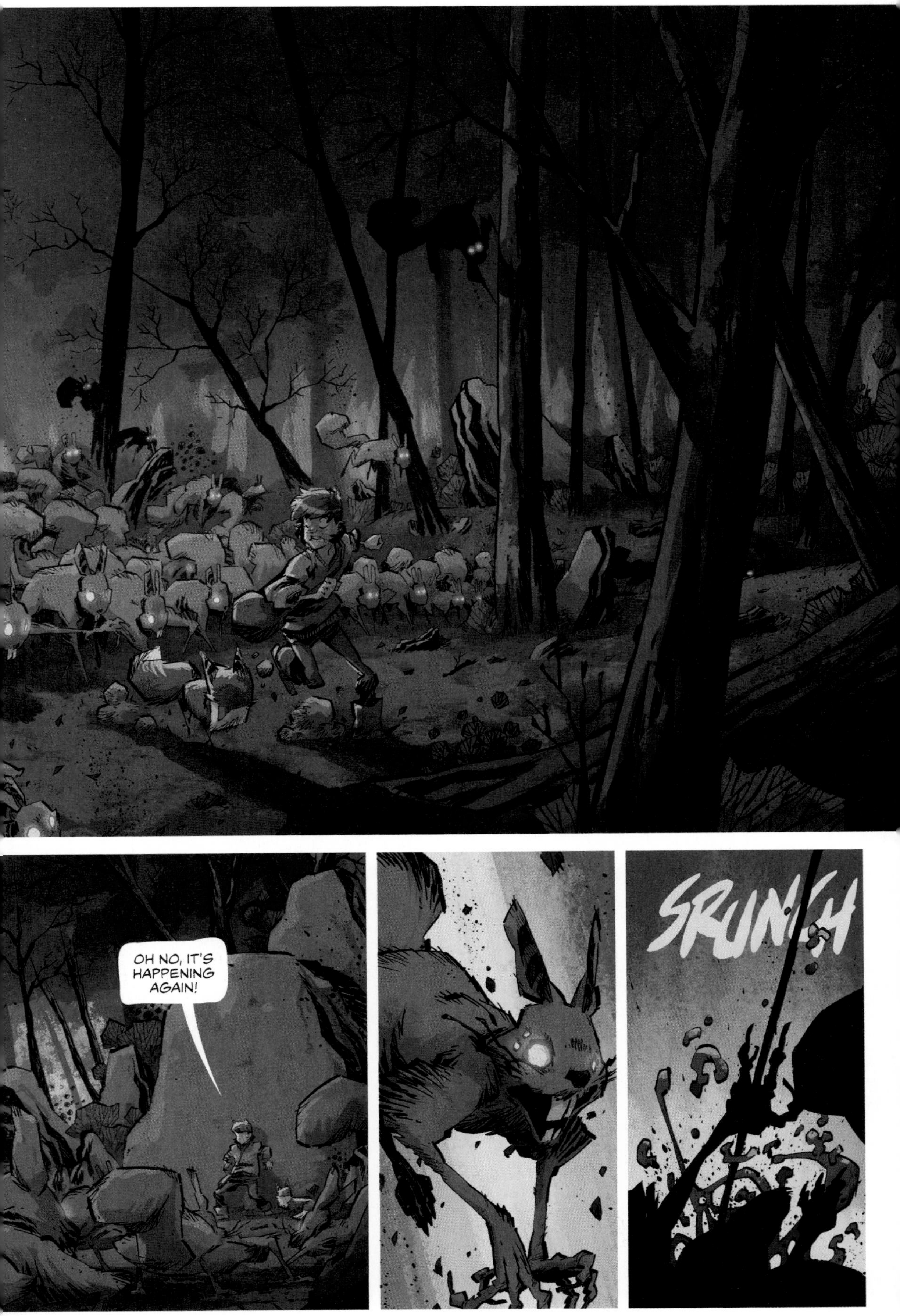
OH NO, IT'S HAPPENING AGAIN!
SRUNCH

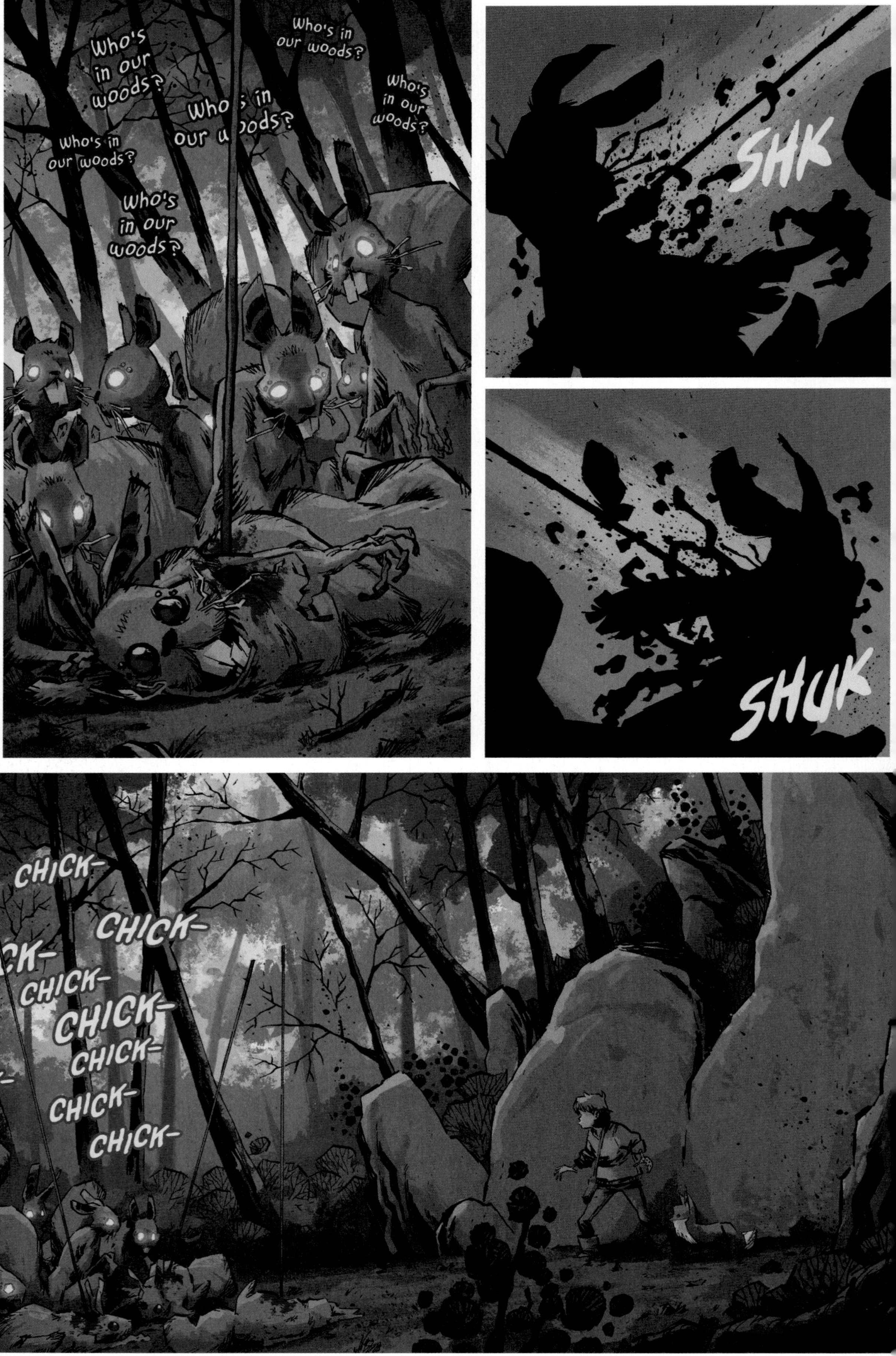
Who's in our woods?
Who's in our woods?
Who's in our woods?
Who's in our woods?
Who's in our woods?
Who's in our woods?
SHK
SHUK
CHICK-
CHICK-
ICK-
CHICK-
CHICK-
CHICK-
CK-
CHICK-
CHICK-

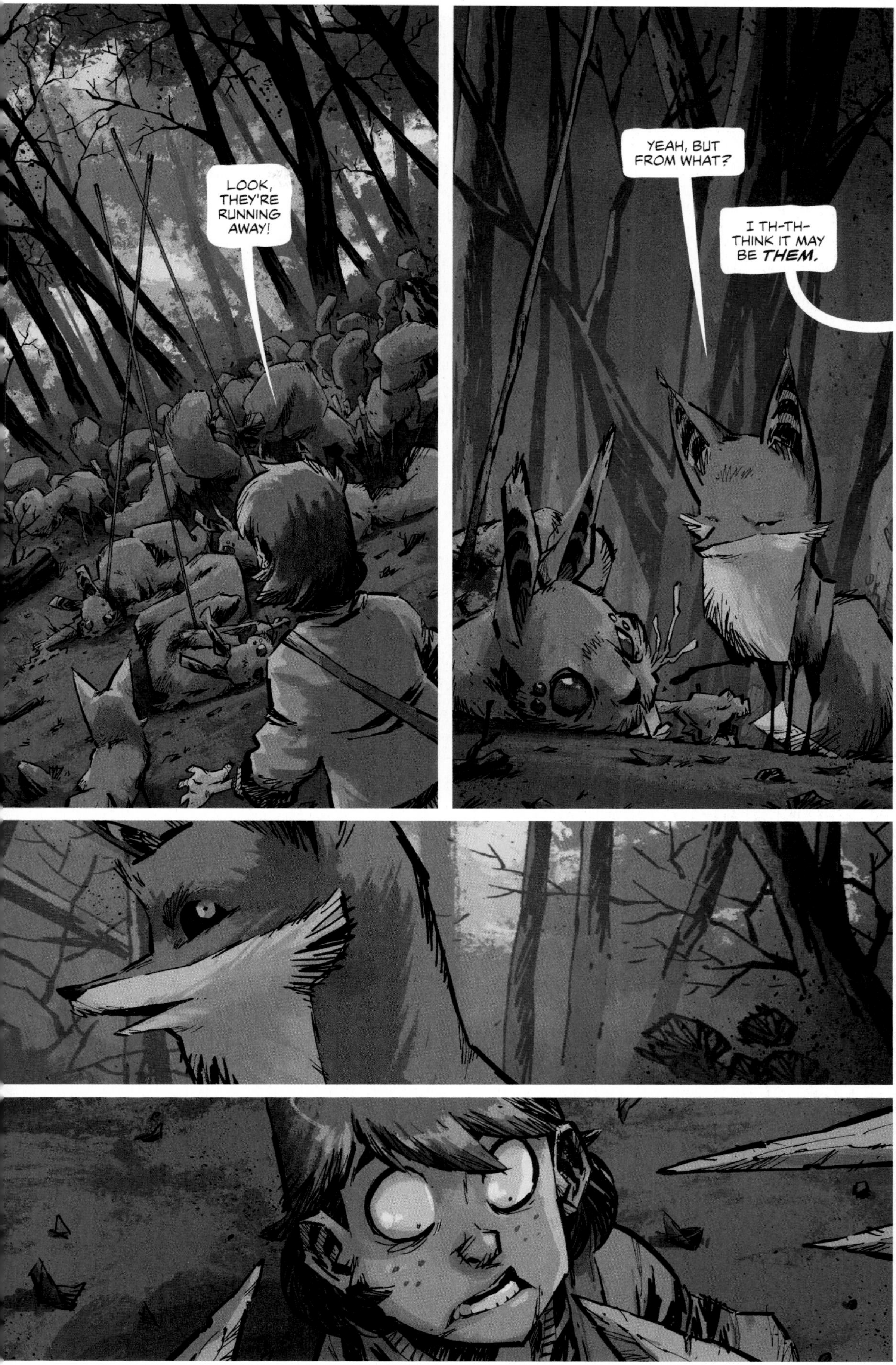
LOOK, THEY'RE RUNNING AWAY!
YEAH, BUT FROM WHAT?
I TH-TH-THINK IT MAY BE ***THEM.***

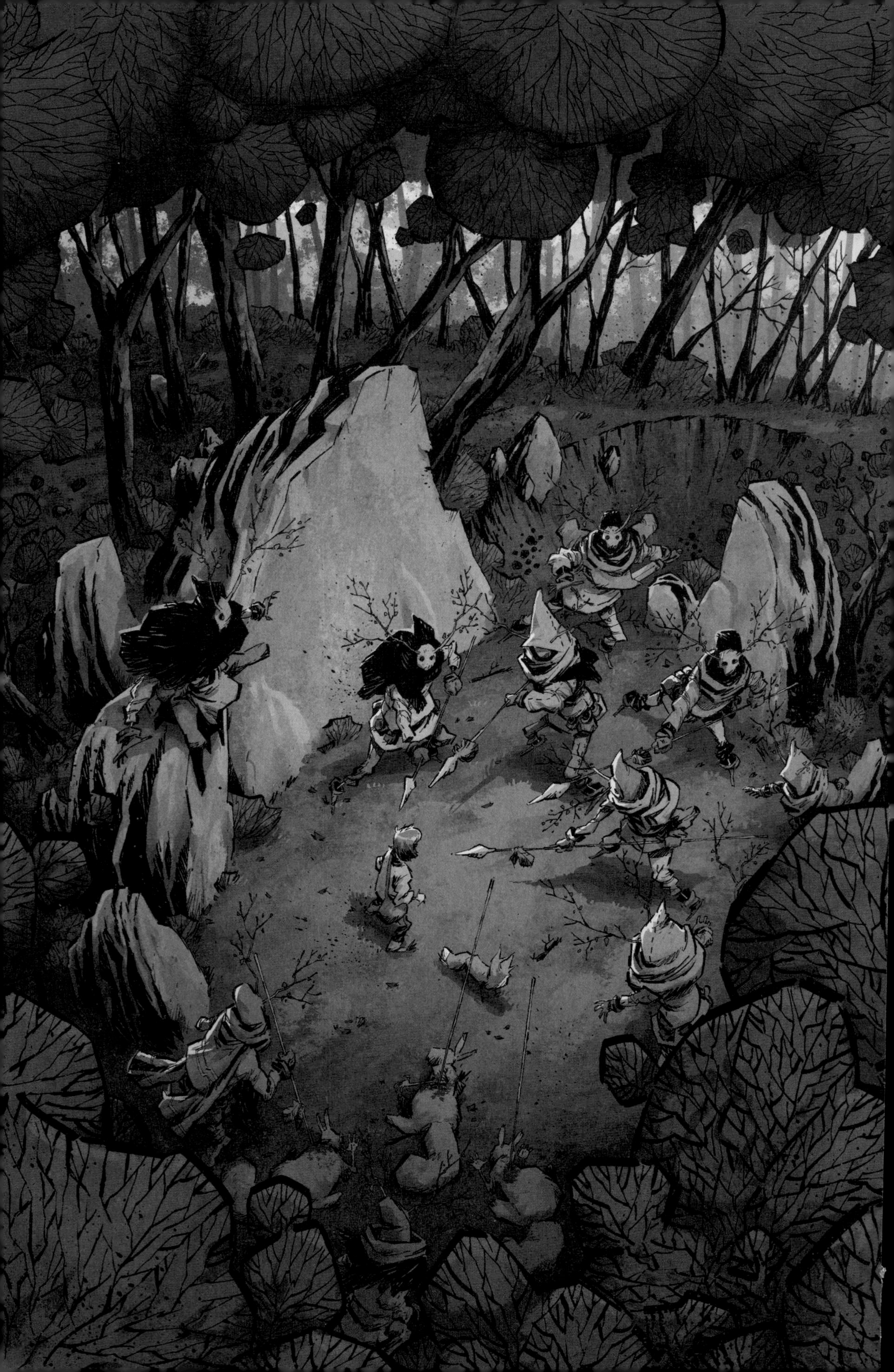

CHAPTER
NINE

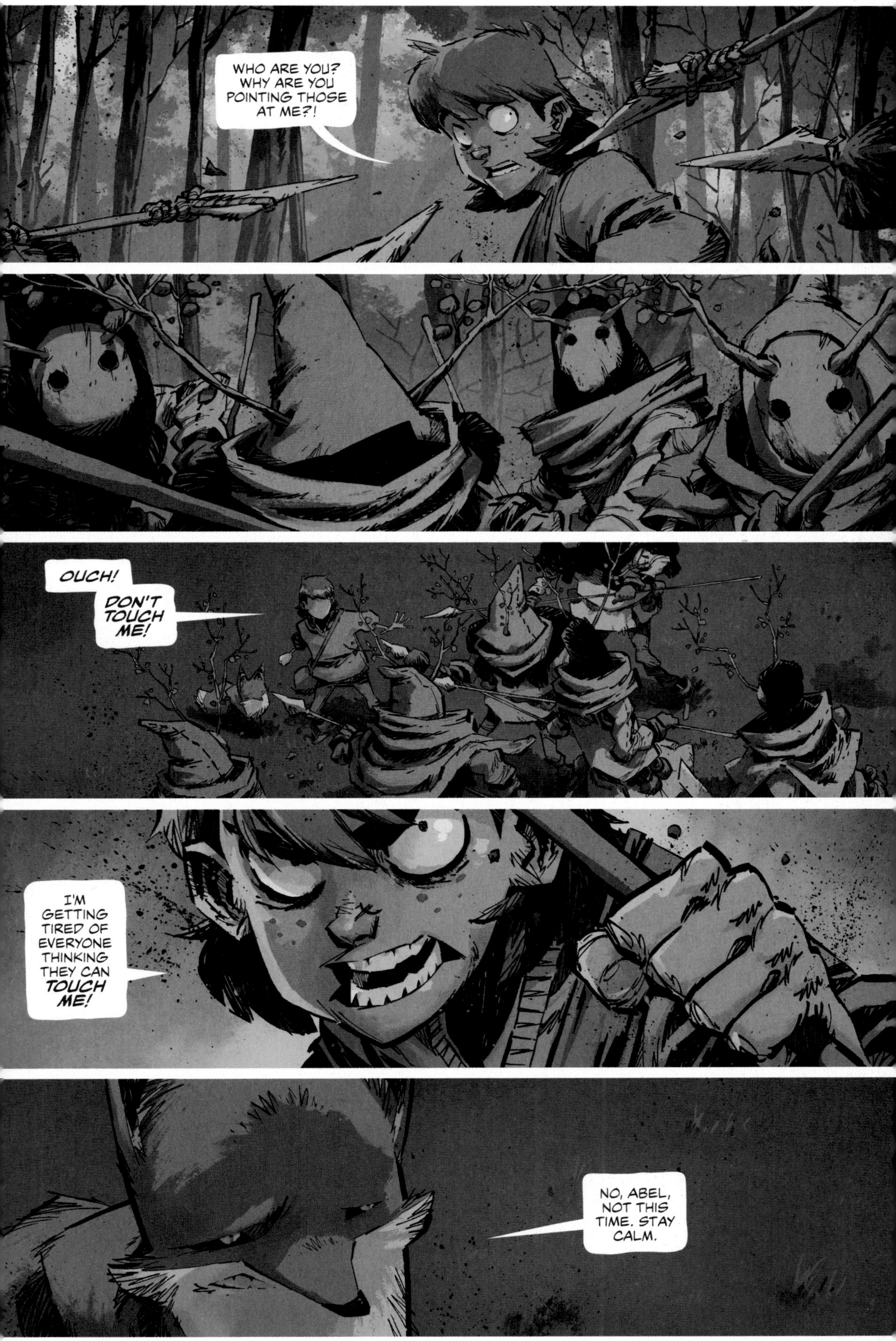
WHO ARE YOU? WHY ARE YOU POINTING THOSE AT ME?!
OUCH!
DON'T TOUCH ME!
I'M GETTING TIRED OF EVERYONE THINKING THEY CAN TOUCH ME!
NO, ABEL, NOT THIS TIME. STAY CALM.

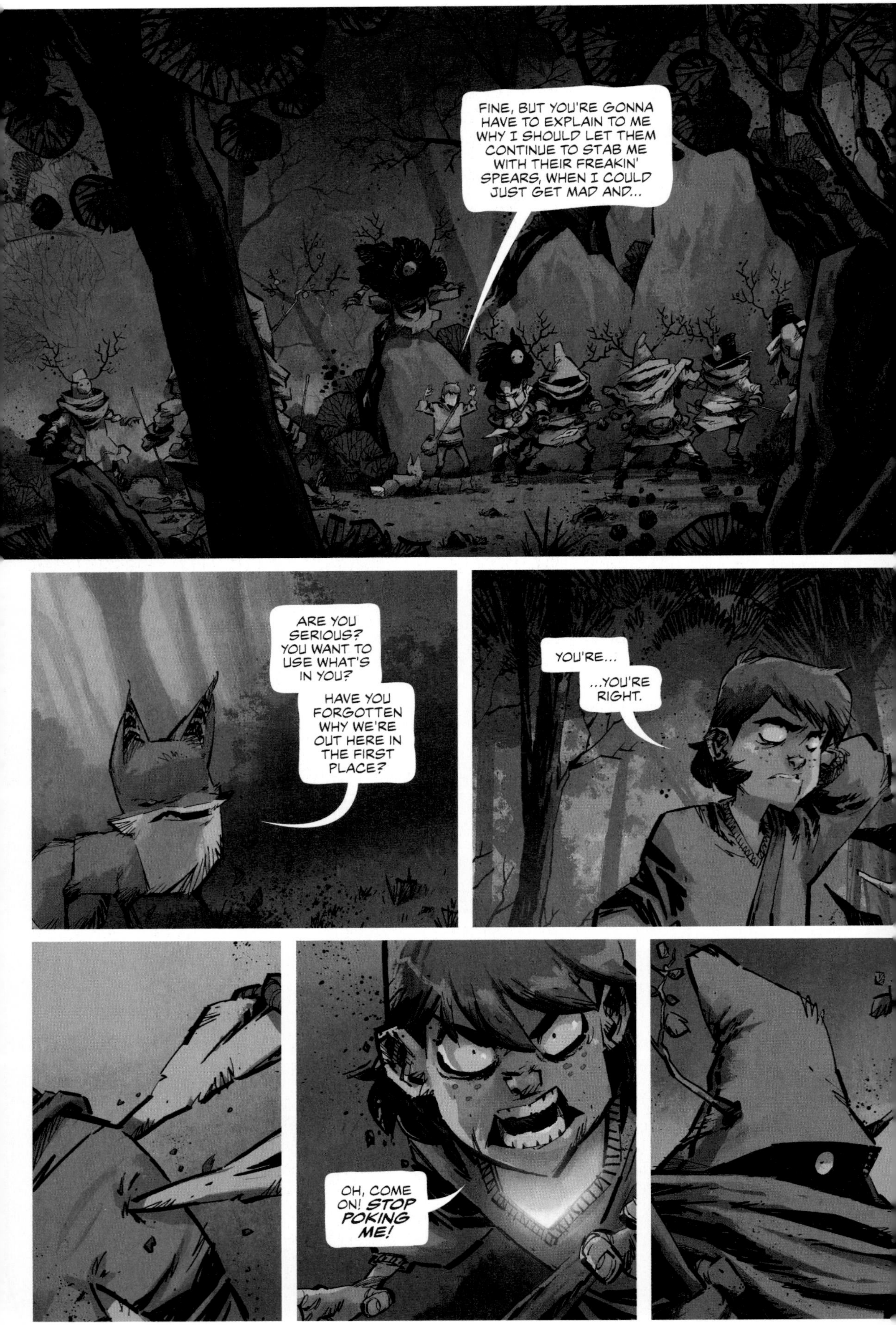
FINE, BUT YOU'RE GONNA HAVE TO EXPLAIN TO ME WHY I SHOULD LET THEM CONTINUE TO STAB ME WITH THEIR FREAKIN' SPEARS, WHEN I COULD JUST GET MAD AND...
ARE YOU SERIOUS? YOU WANT TO USE WHAT'S IN YOU?
HAVE YOU FORGOTTEN WHY WE'RE OUT HERE IN THE FIRST PLACE?
YOU'RE...
...YOU'RE RIGHT.
OH, COME ON! ***STOP POKING ME!***

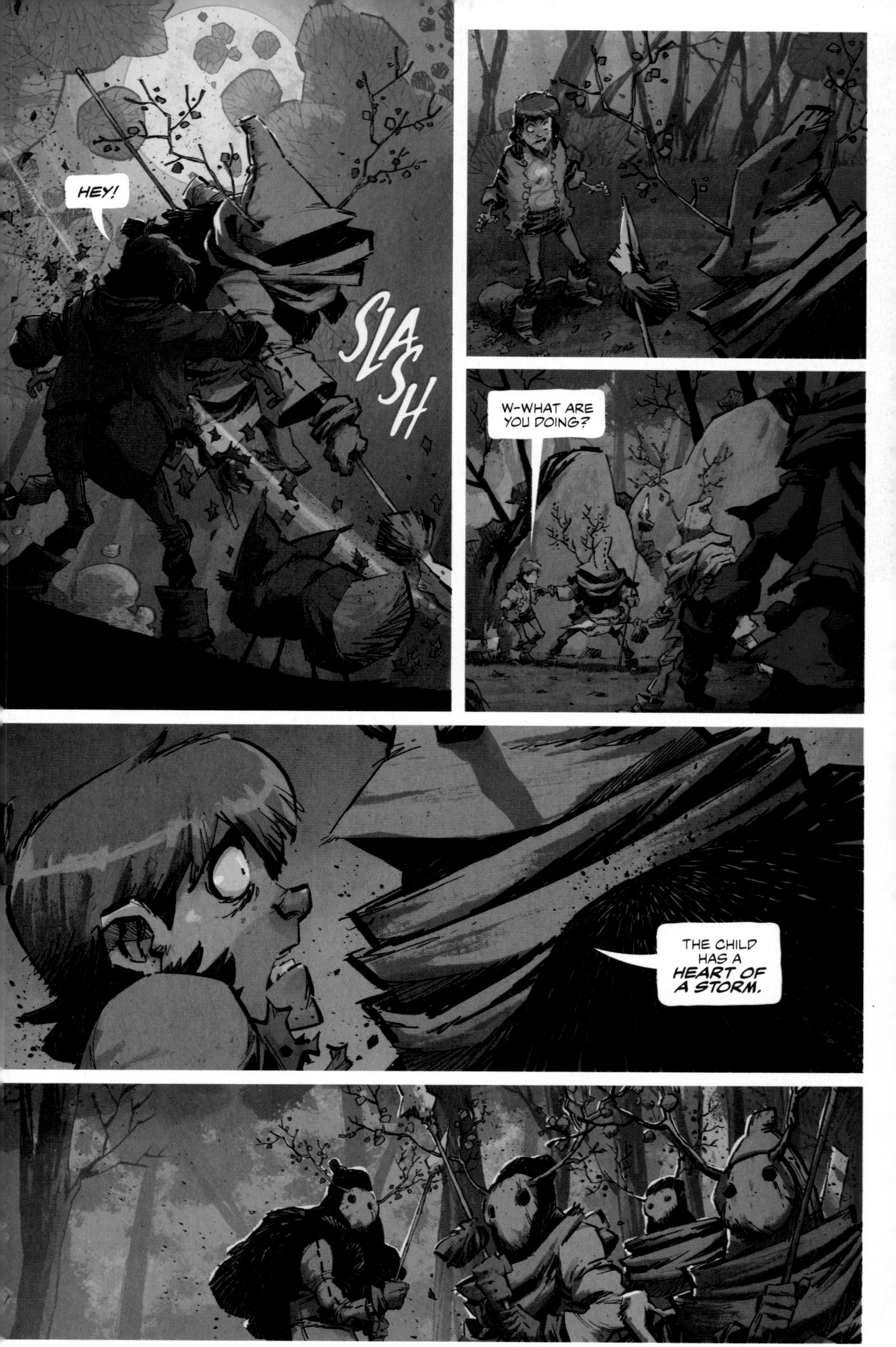
HEY!
SLASH
W-WHAT ARE YOU DOING?
THE CHILD HAS A HEART OF A STORM.

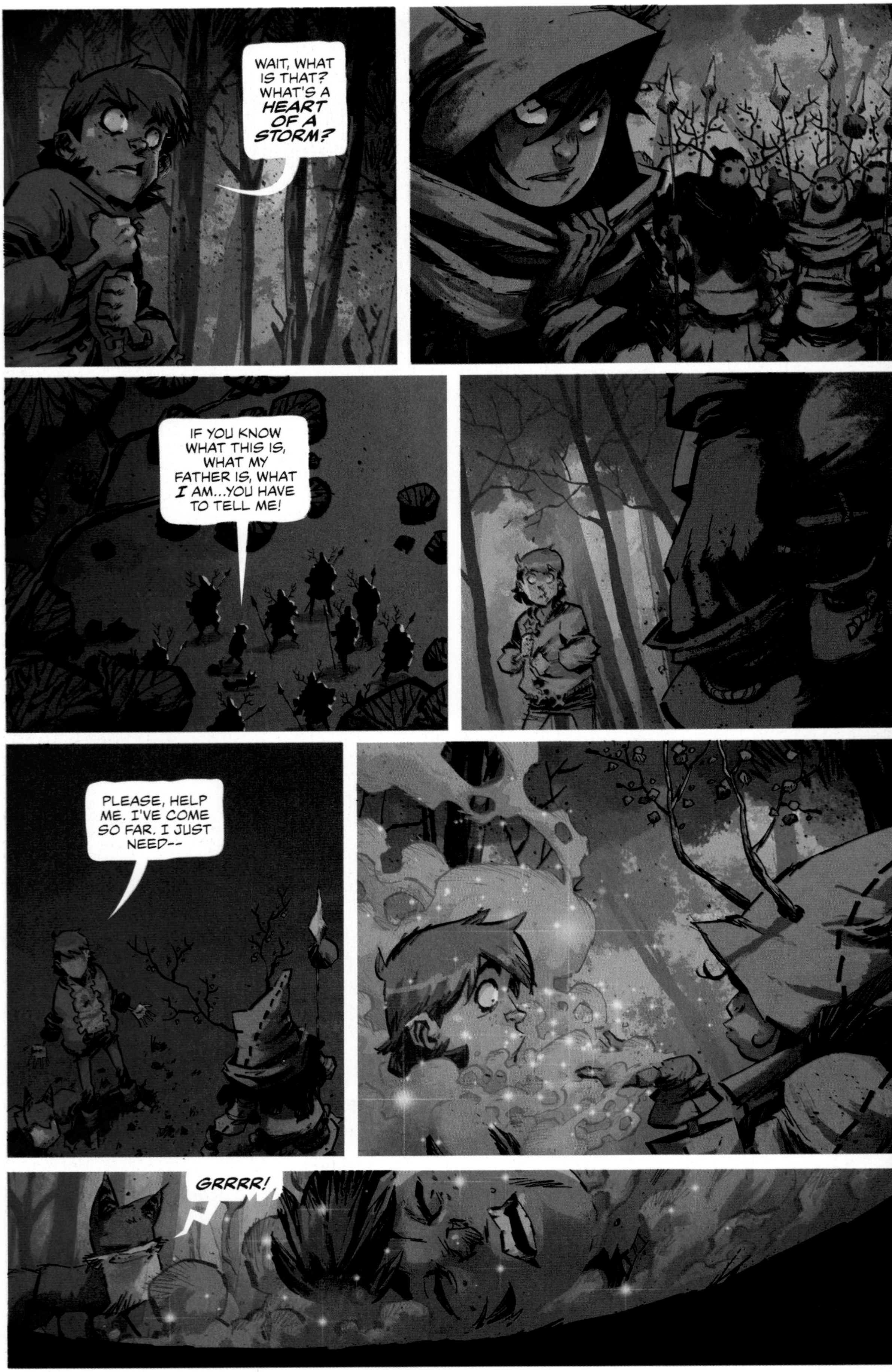
WAIT, WHAT IS THAT? WHAT'S A HEART OF A STORM?
IF YOU KNOW WHAT THIS IS, WHAT MY FATHER IS, WHAT I AM...YOU HAVE TO TELL ME!
PLEASE, HELP ME. I'VE COME SO FAR. I JUST NEED--
GRRRR!

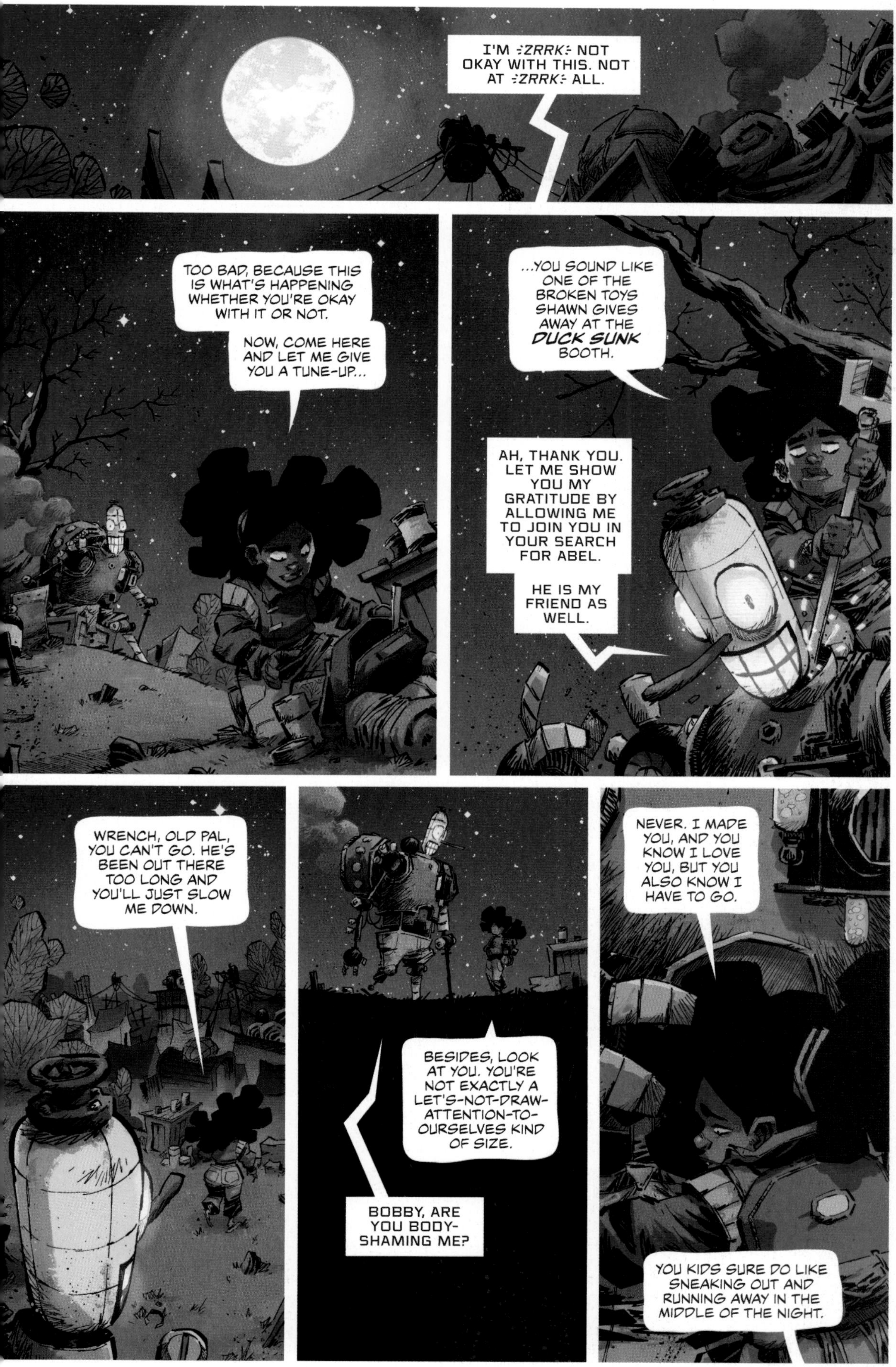
I'M -ZRRK- NOT OKAY WITH THIS. NOT AT -ZRRK- ALL.
TOO BAD, BECAUSE THIS IS WHAT'S HAPPENING WHETHER YOU'RE OKAY WITH IT OR NOT.
NOW, COME HERE AND LET ME GIVE YOU A TUNE-UP...
...YOU SOUND LIKE ONE OF THE BROKEN TOYS SHAWN GIVES AWAY AT THE DUCK SUNK BOOTH.
AH, THANK YOU. LET ME SHOW YOU MY GRATITUDE BY ALLOWING ME TO JOIN YOU IN YOUR SEARCH FOR ABEL.
HE IS MY FRIEND AS WELL.
WRENCH, OLD PAL, YOU CAN'T GO. HE'S BEEN OUT THERE TOO LONG AND YOU'LL JUST SLOW ME DOWN.
BESIDES, LOOK AT YOU. YOU'RE NOT EXACTLY A LET'S-NOT-DRAW-ATTENTION-TO-OURSELVES KIND OF SIZE.
BOBBY, ARE YOU BODY-SHAMING ME?
NEVER. I MADE YOU, AND YOU KNOW I LOVE YOU, BUT YOU ALSO KNOW I HAVE TO GO.
YOU KIDS SURE DO LIKE SNEAKING OUT AND RUNNING AWAY IN THE MIDDLE OF THE NIGHT.

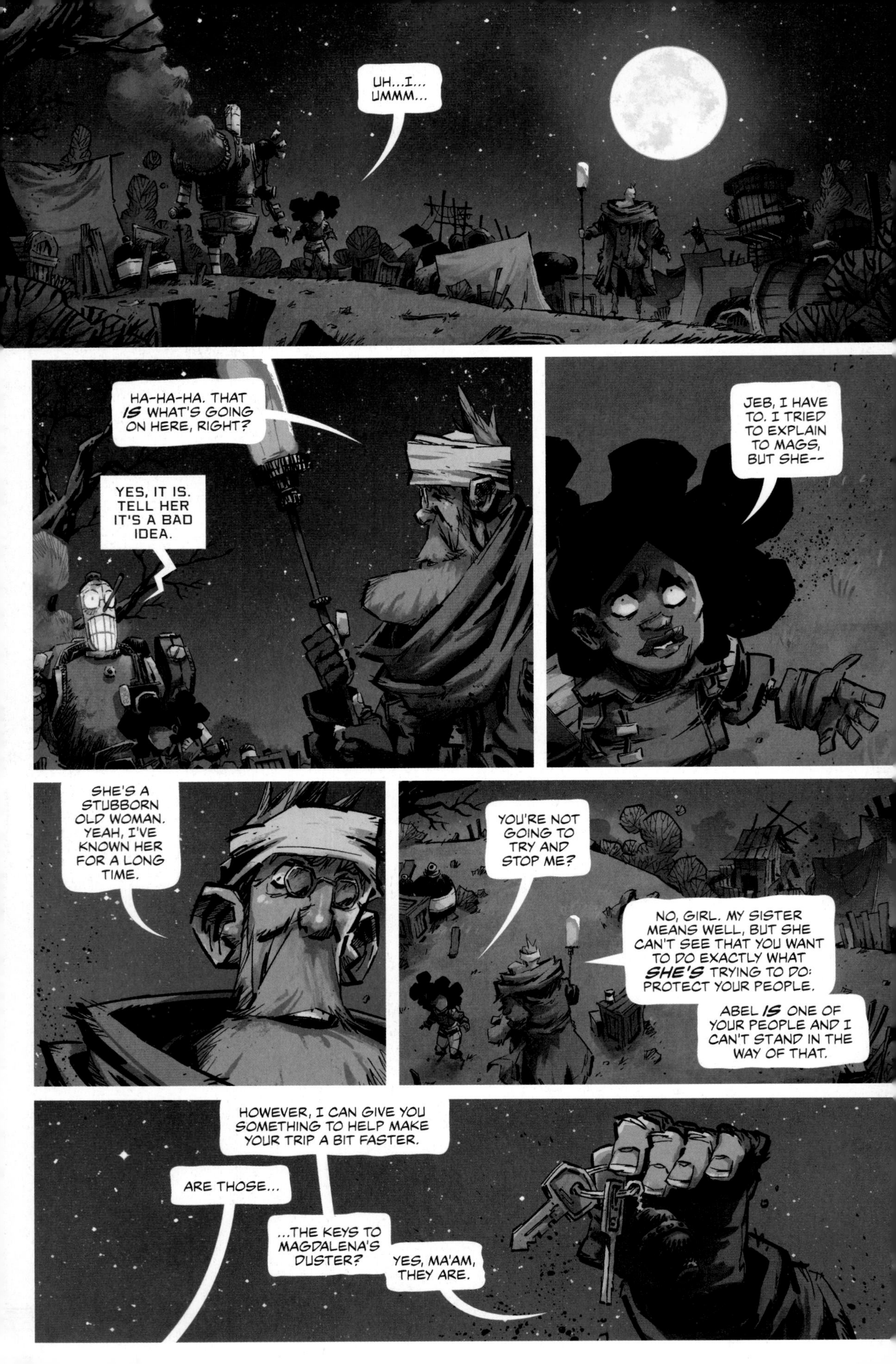
UH...I...
UMMM...
HA-HA-HA. THAT IS WHAT'S GOING ON HERE, RIGHT?
YES, IT IS. TELL HER IT'S A BAD IDEA.
JEB, I HAVE TO. I TRIED TO EXPLAIN TO MAGS, BUT SHE--
SHE'S A STUBBORN OLD WOMAN. YEAH, I'VE KNOWN HER FOR A LONG TIME.
YOU'RE NOT GOING TO TRY AND STOP ME?
NO, GIRL. MY SISTER MEANS WELL, BUT SHE CAN'T SEE THAT YOU WANT TO DO EXACTLY WHAT SHE'S TRYING TO DO: PROTECT YOUR PEOPLE.
ABEL IS ONE OF YOUR PEOPLE AND I CAN'T STAND IN THE WAY OF THAT.
HOWEVER, I CAN GIVE YOU SOMETHING TO HELP MAKE YOUR TRIP A BIT FASTER.
ARE THOSE...
...THE KEYS TO MAGDALENA'S DUSTER?
YES, MA'AM, THEY ARE.

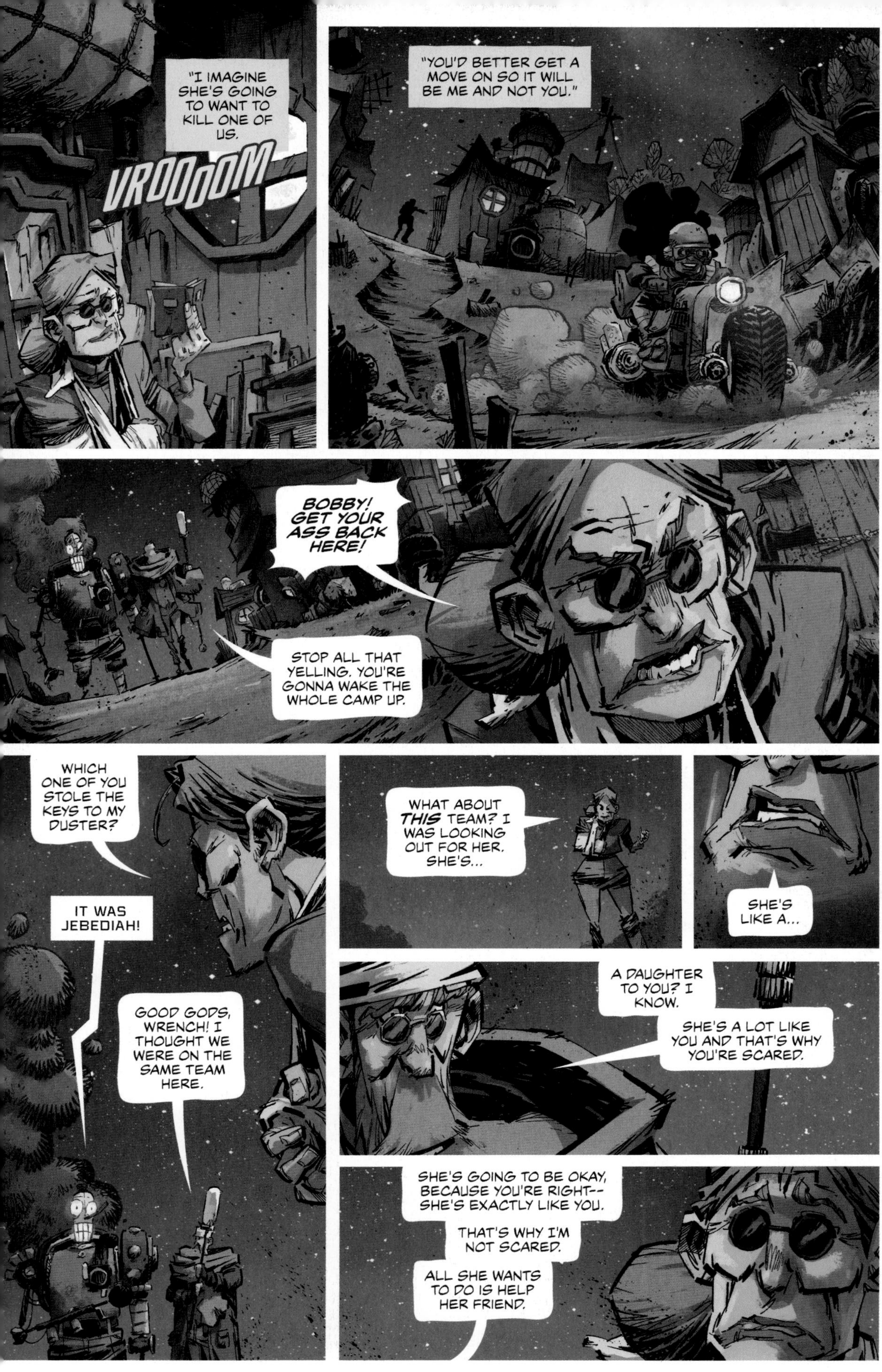
"I IMAGINE SHE'S GOING TO WANT TO KILL ONE OF US.
VROOOOOM
"YOU'D BETTER GET A MOVE ON SO IT WILL BE ME AND NOT YOU."
BOBBY! GET YOUR ASS BACK HERE!
STOP ALL THAT YELLING. YOU'RE GONNA WAKE THE WHOLE CAMP UP.
WHICH ONE OF YOU STOLE THE KEYS TO MY DUSTER?
IT WAS JEBEDIAH!
GOOD GODS, WRENCH! I THOUGHT WE WERE ON THE SAME TEAM HERE.
WHAT ABOUT THIS TEAM? I WAS LOOKING OUT FOR HER. SHE'S...
SHE'S LIKE A...
A DAUGHTER TO YOU? I KNOW.
SHE'S A LOT LIKE YOU AND THAT'S WHY YOU'RE SCARED.
SHE'S GOING TO BE OKAY, BECAUSE YOU'RE RIGHT-- SHE'S EXACTLY LIKE YOU.
THAT'S WHY I'M NOT SCARED.
ALL SHE WANTS TO DO IS HELP HER FRIEND.

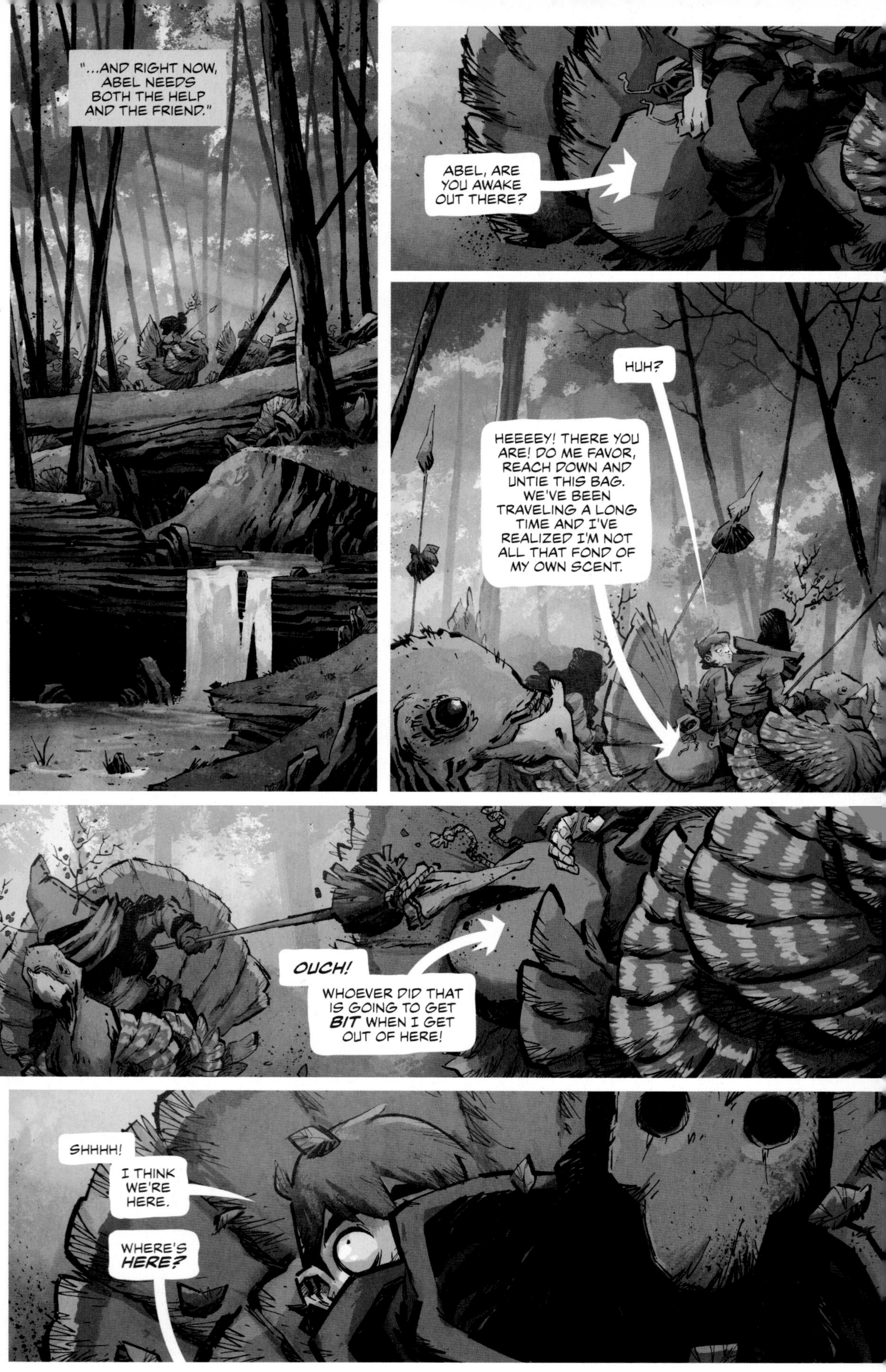
"...AND RIGHT NOW, ABEL NEEDS BOTH THE HELP AND THE FRIEND."
ABEL, ARE YOU AWAKE OUT THERE?
HUH?
HEEEEY! THERE YOU ARE! DO ME FAVOR, REACH DOWN AND UNTIE THIS BAG. WE'VE BEEN TRAVELING A LONG TIME AND I'VE REALIZED I'M NOT ALL THAT FOND OF MY OWN SCENT.
OUCH!
WHOEVER DID THAT IS GOING TO GET BIT WHEN I GET OUT OF HERE!
SHHHH!
I THINK WE'RE HERE.
WHERE'S HERE?

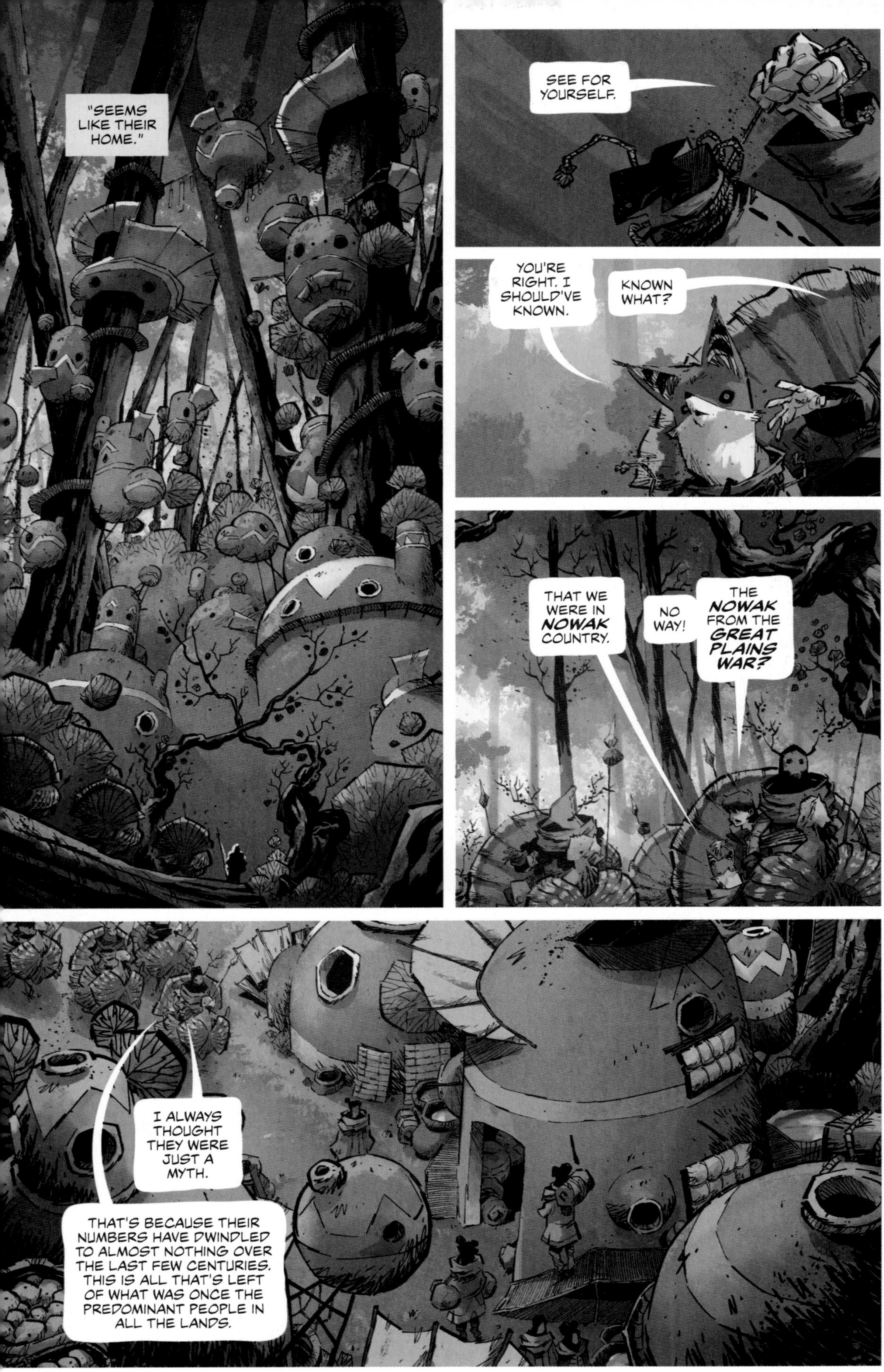
"SEEMS LIKE THEIR HOME."
SEE FOR YOURSELF.
YOU'RE RIGHT. I SHOULD'VE KNOWN.
KNOWN WHAT?
THAT WE WERE IN **NOWAK** COUNTRY.
NO WAY!
THE **NOWAK** FROM THE **GREAT PLAINS WAR?**
I ALWAYS THOUGHT THEY WERE JUST A MYTH.
THAT'S BECAUSE THEIR NUMBERS HAVE DWINDLED TO ALMOST NOTHING OVER THE LAST FEW CENTURIES. THIS IS ALL THAT'S LEFT OF WHAT WAS ONCE THE PREDOMINANT PEOPLE IN ALL THE LANDS.

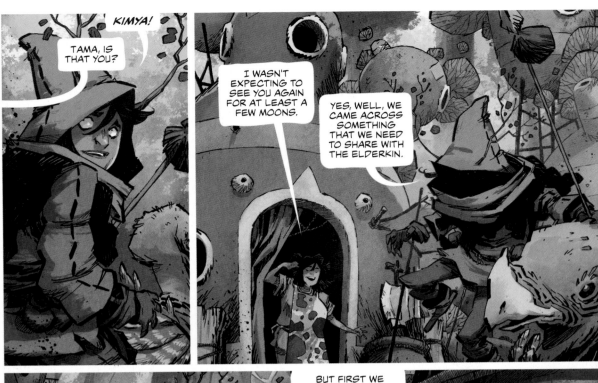

KIMYA!

TAMA, IS THAT YOU?

I WASN'T EXPECTING TO SEE YOU AGAIN FOR AT LEAST A FEW MOONS.

YES, WELL, WE CAME ACROSS SOMETHING THAT WE NEED TO SHARE WITH THE ELDERKIN.

BUT FIRST WE BROUGHT YOU A GIFT. WE FOUND OURSELVES HAVING TO SEND A FEW SQUIRKS ON TO THE *NEXT PLAIN.*

AH, PRAISE *THE ANTLERS* FOR THIS BLESSING. I WILL BEGIN CURING THEM TONIGHT!

WAIT...THAT WAS MEAT FROM THOSE CREATURES THEY KILLED?

YEAH. THE NOWAK BELIEVE IN THE LIFE CYCLE. NOTHING GETS LEFT BEHIND OR GOES UNUSED.

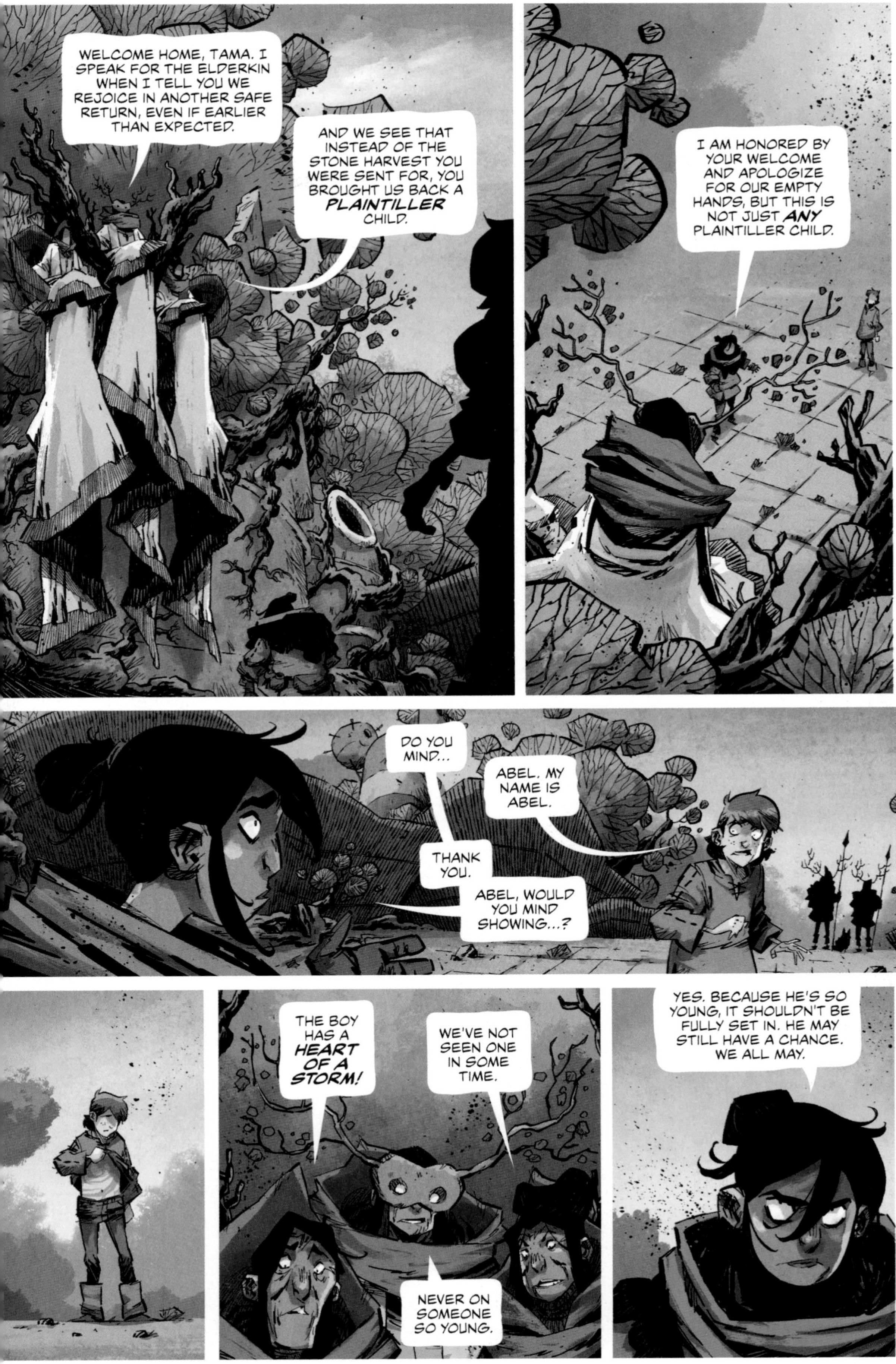
WELCOME HOME, TAMA. I SPEAK FOR THE ELDERKIN WHEN I TELL YOU WE REJOICE IN ANOTHER SAFE RETURN, EVEN IF EARLIER THAN EXPECTED.
AND WE SEE THAT INSTEAD OF THE STONE HARVEST YOU WERE SENT FOR, YOU BROUGHT US BACK A PLAINTILLER CHILD.
I AM HONORED BY YOUR WELCOME AND APOLOGIZE FOR OUR EMPTY HANDS, BUT THIS IS NOT JUST ANY PLAINTILLER CHILD.
DO YOU MIND...
ABEL. MY NAME IS ABEL.
THANK YOU.
ABEL, WOULD YOU MIND SHOWING...?
THE BOY HAS A HEART OF A STORM!
WE'VE NOT SEEN ONE IN SOME TIME.
NEVER ON SOMEONE SO YOUNG.
YES. BECAUSE HE'S SO YOUNG, IT SHOULDN'T BE FULLY SET IN. HE MAY STILL HAVE A CHANCE. WE ALL MAY.

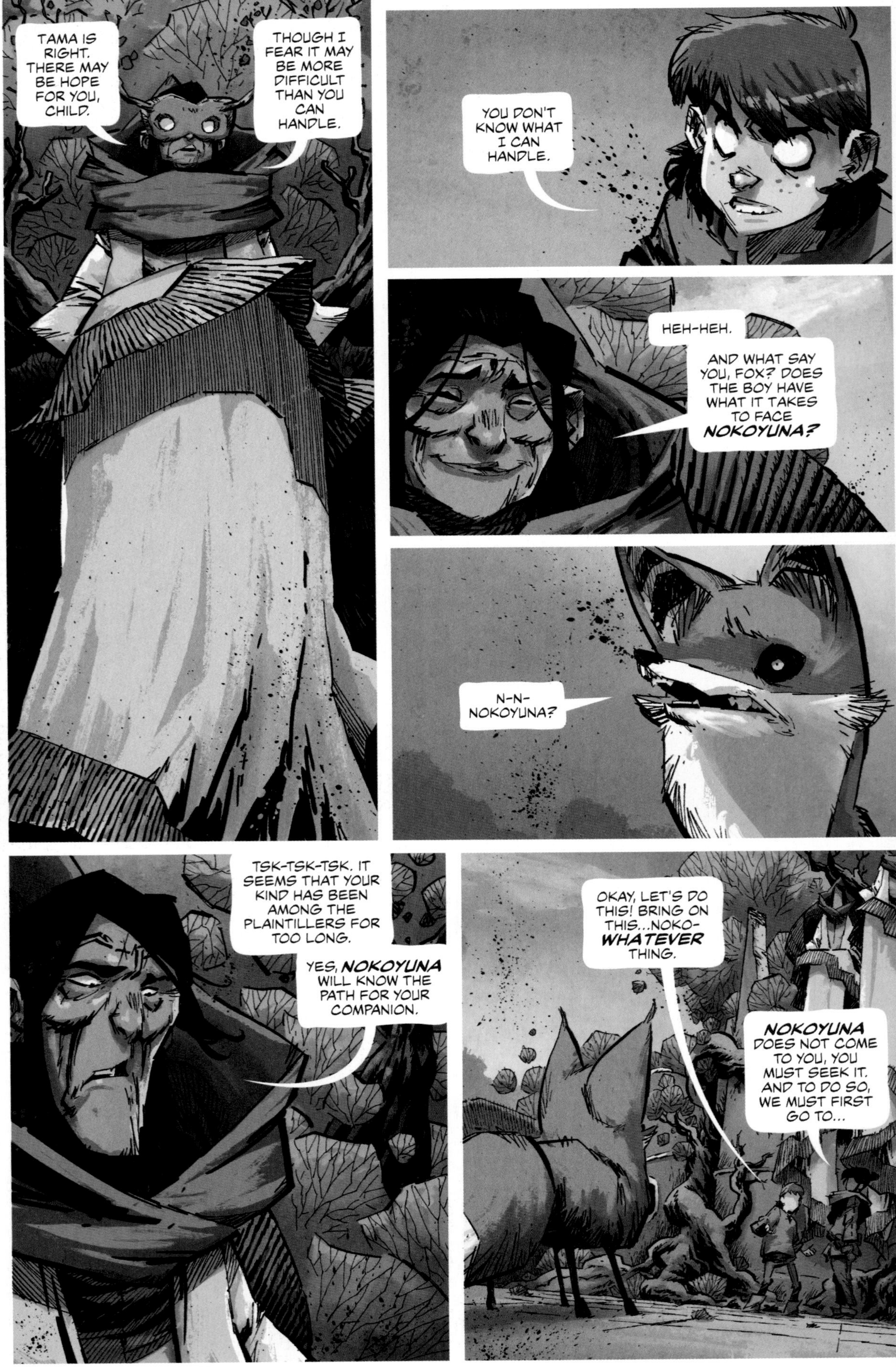
TAMA IS RIGHT. THERE MAY BE HOPE FOR YOU, CHILD.
THOUGH I FEAR IT MAY BE MORE DIFFICULT THAN YOU CAN HANDLE.
YOU DON'T KNOW WHAT I CAN HANDLE.
HEH-HEH.
AND WHAT SAY YOU, FOX? DOES THE BOY HAVE WHAT IT TAKES TO FACE ***NOKOYUNA?***
N-N-NOKOYUNA?
TSK-TSK-TSK. IT SEEMS THAT YOUR KIND HAS BEEN AMONG THE PLAINTILLERS FOR TOO LONG.
YES, ***NOKOYUNA*** WILL KNOW THE PATH FOR YOUR COMPANION.
OKAY, LET'S DO THIS! BRING ON THIS...NOKO-***WHATEVER*** THING.
NOKOYUNA DOES NOT COME TO YOU, YOU MUST SEEK IT. AND TO DO SO, WE MUST FIRST GO TO...

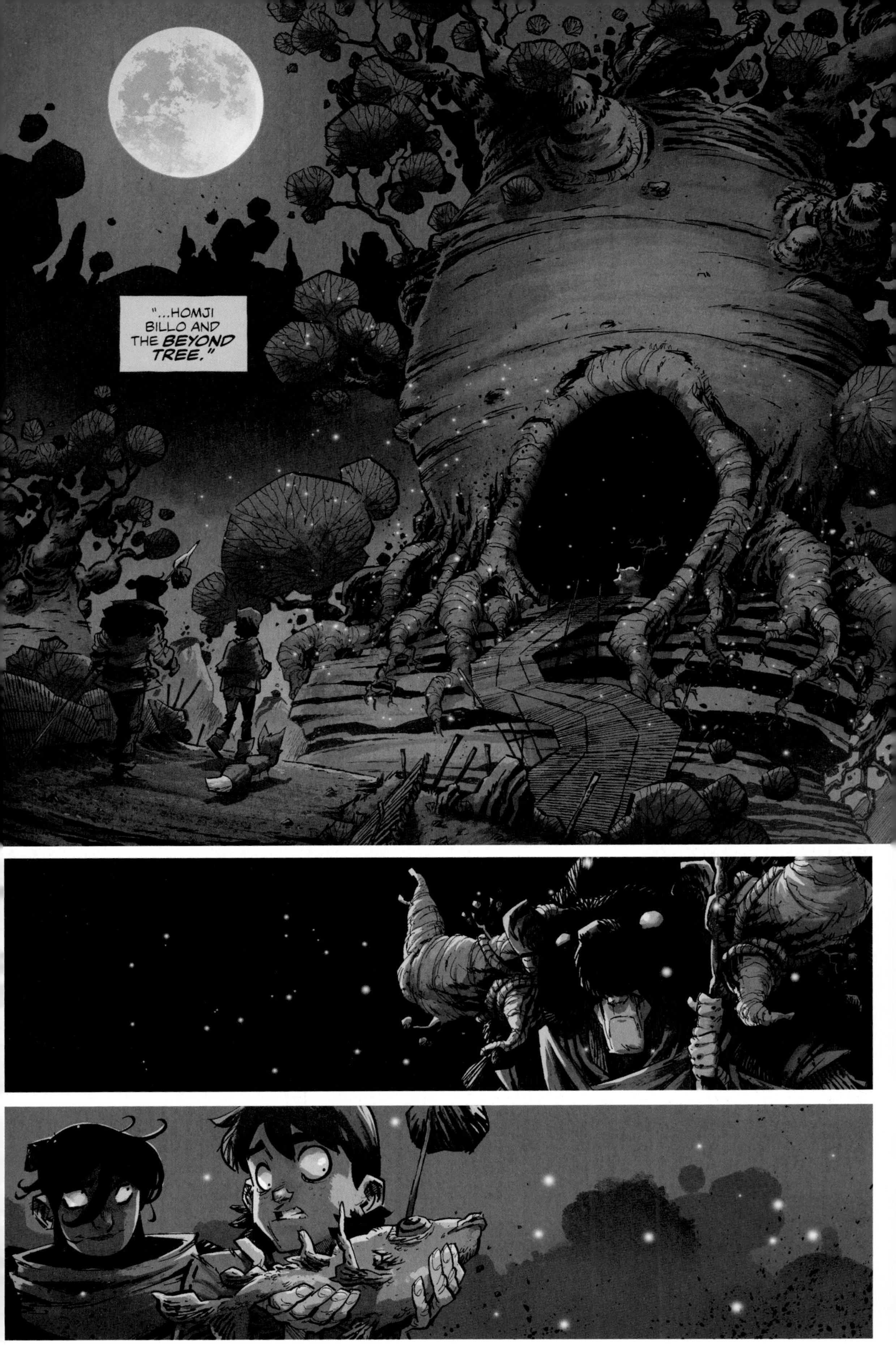
"...HOMJI BILLO AND THE BEYOND TREE."

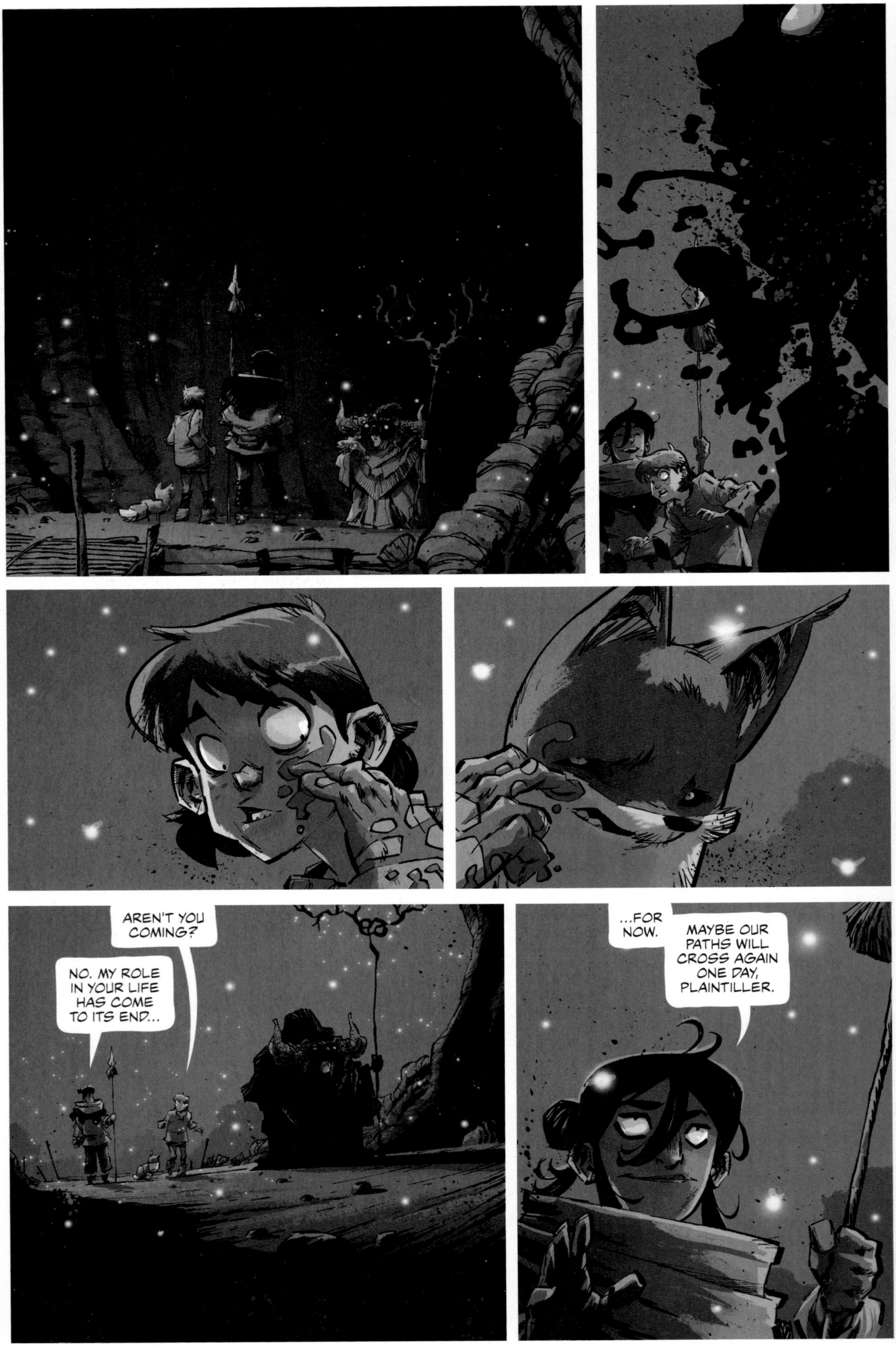
AREN'T YOU COMING?
NO. MY ROLE IN YOUR LIFE HAS COME TO ITS END...
...FOR NOW.
MAYBE OUR PATHS WILL CROSS AGAIN ONE DAY, PLAINTILLER.

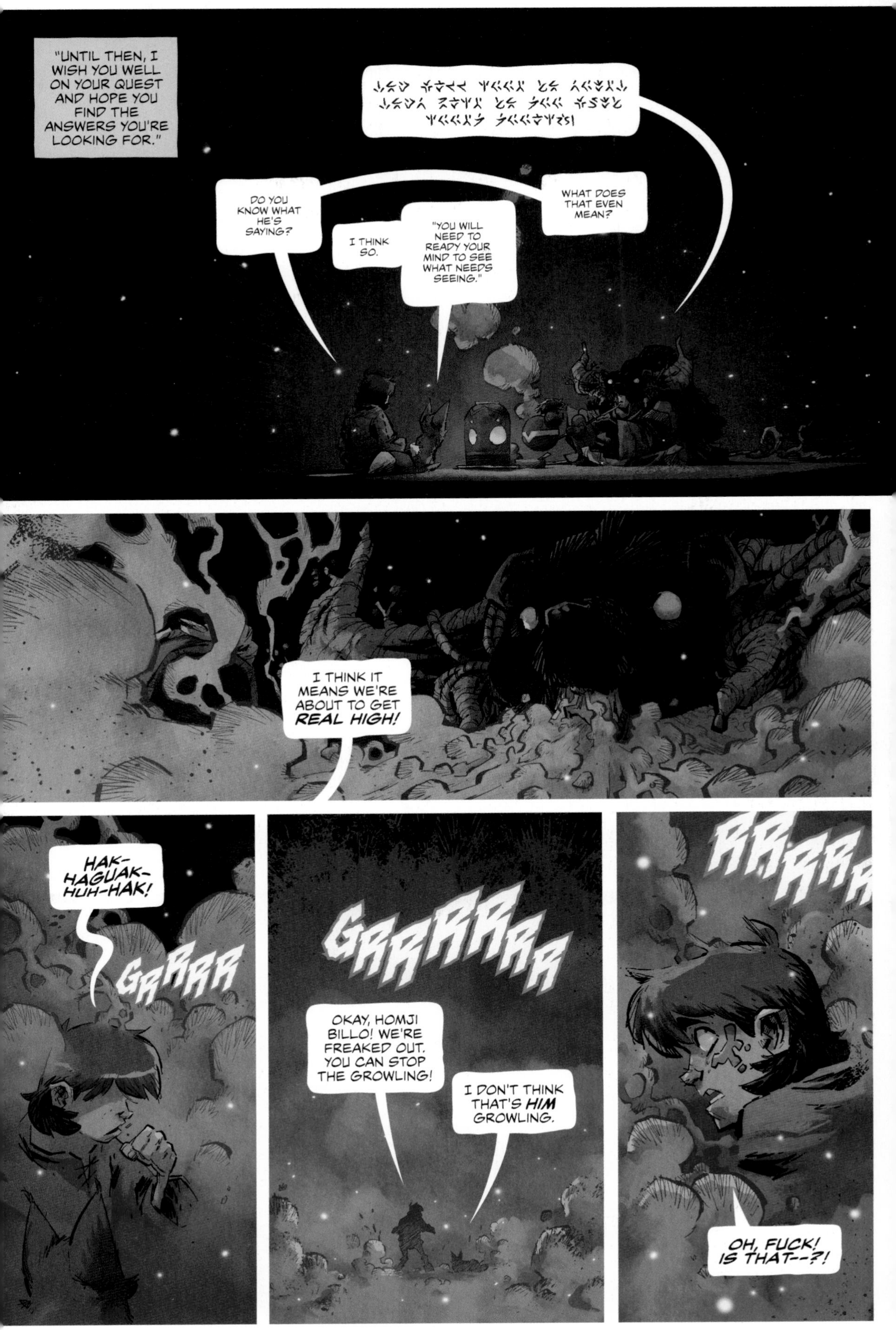
"UNTIL THEN, I WISH YOU WELL ON YOUR QUEST AND HOPE YOU FIND THE ANSWERS YOU'RE LOOKING FOR."
DO YOU KNOW WHAT HE'S SAYING?
I THINK SO.
"YOU WILL NEED TO READY YOUR MIND TO SEE WHAT NEEDS SEEING."
WHAT DOES THAT EVEN MEAN?
I THINK IT MEANS WE'RE ABOUT TO GET REAL HIGH!
HAK-HAGUAK-HUH-HAK!
GRRRR
GRRRRRRR
OKAY, HOMJI BILLO! WE'RE FREAKED OUT. YOU CAN STOP THE GROWLING!
I DON'T THINK THAT'S HIM GROWLING.
RRRRRR
OH, FUCK! IS THAT--?!

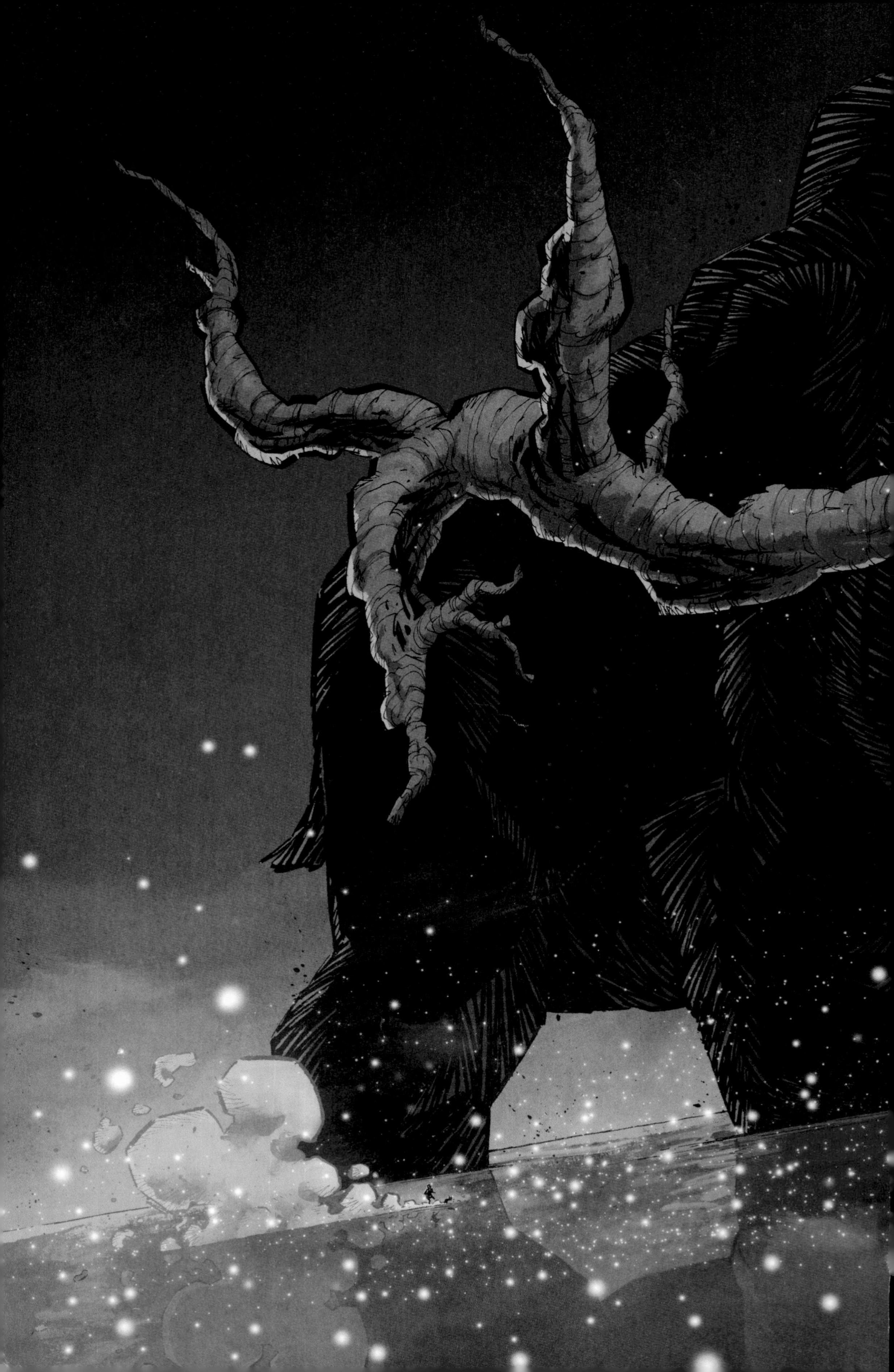

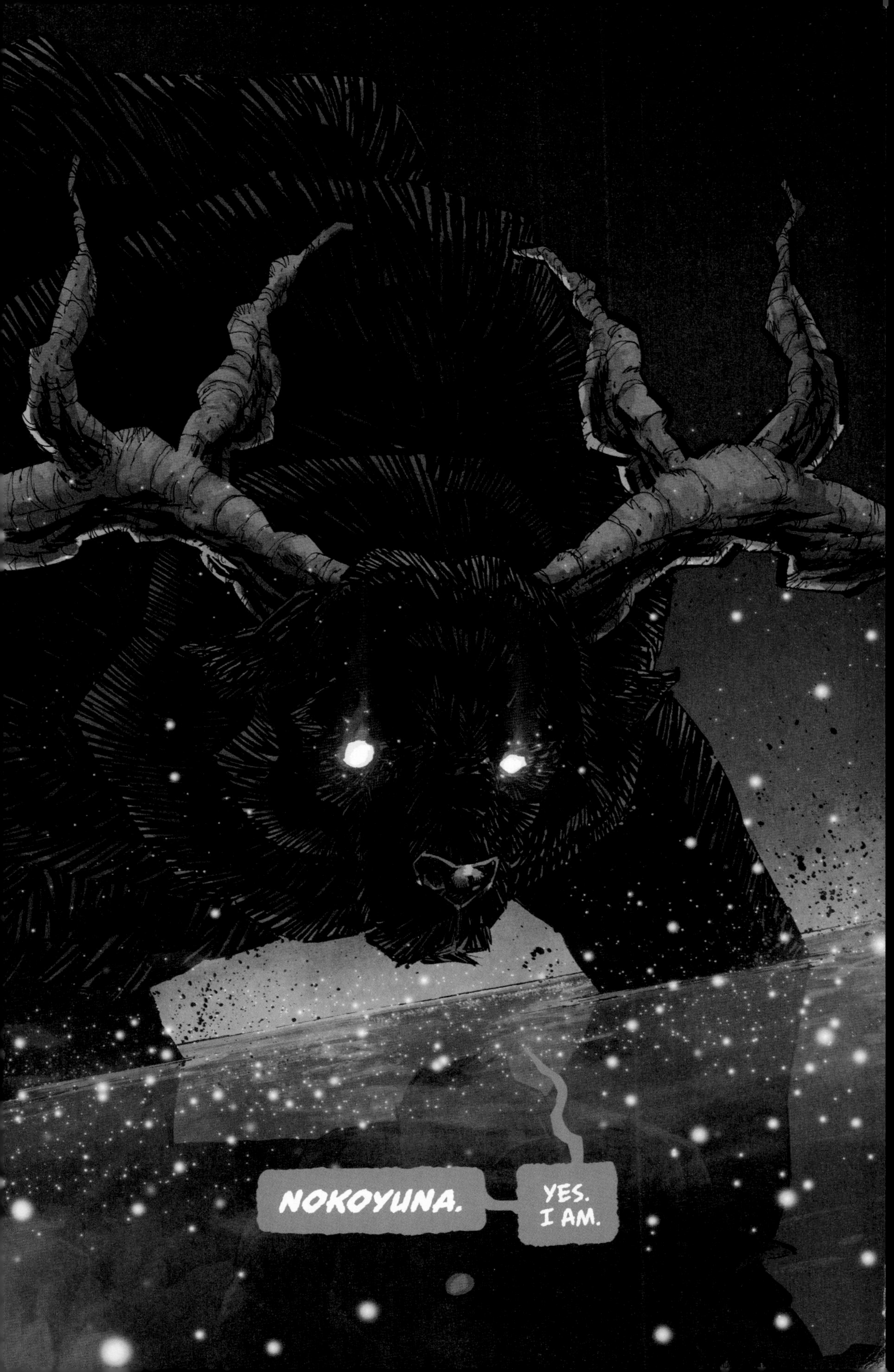
NOKOYUNA.
YES. I AM.

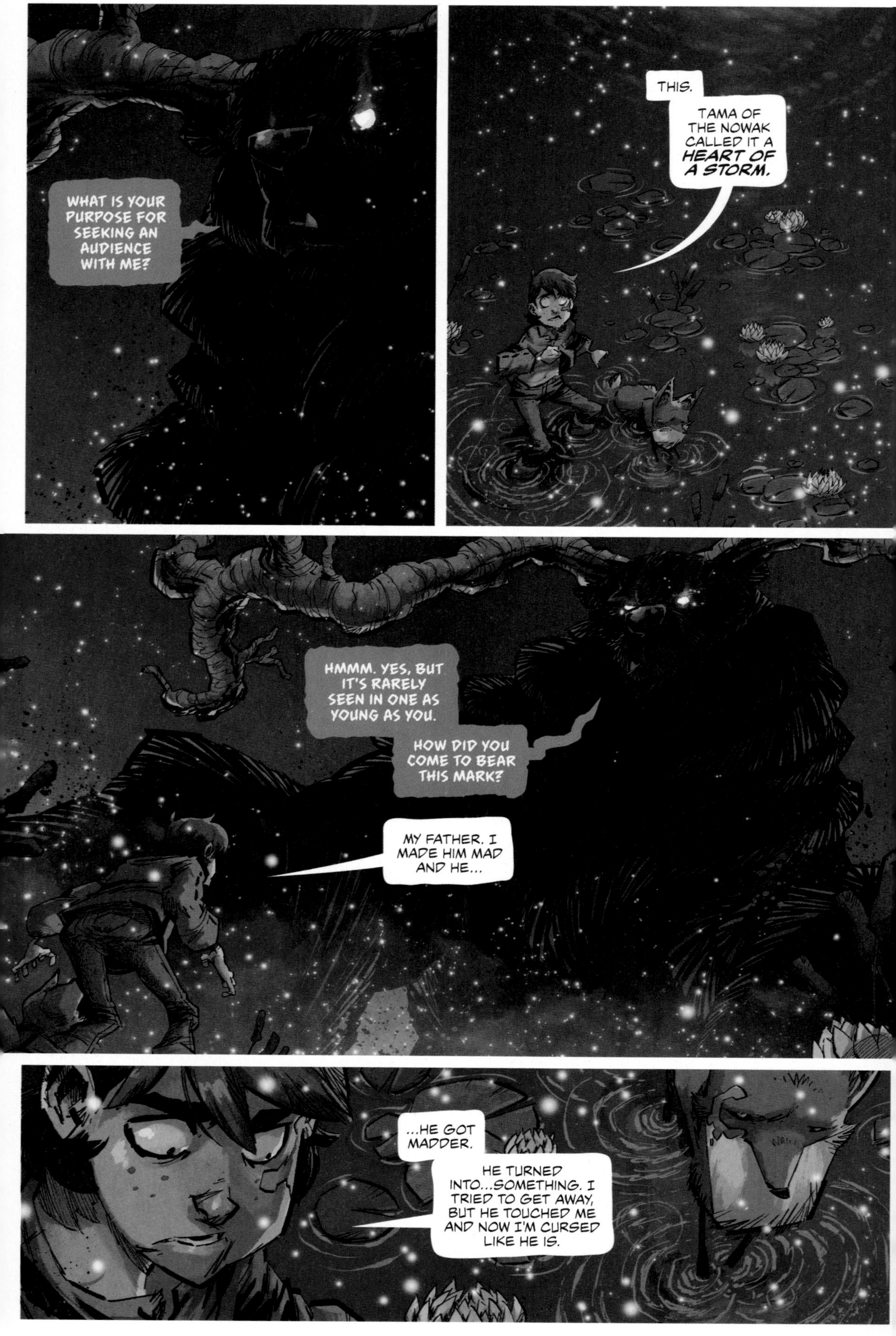

WHAT IS YOUR PURPOSE FOR SEEKING AN AUDIENCE WITH ME?
THIS.
TAMA OF THE NOWAK CALLED IT A **HEART OF A STORM.**
HMMM. YES, BUT IT'S RARELY SEEN IN ONE AS YOUNG AS YOU.
HOW DID YOU COME TO BEAR THIS MARK?
MY FATHER. I MADE HIM MAD AND HE...
...HE GOT MADDER.
HE TURNED INTO...SOMETHING. I TRIED TO GET AWAY, BUT HE TOUCHED ME AND NOW I'M CURSED LIKE HE IS.

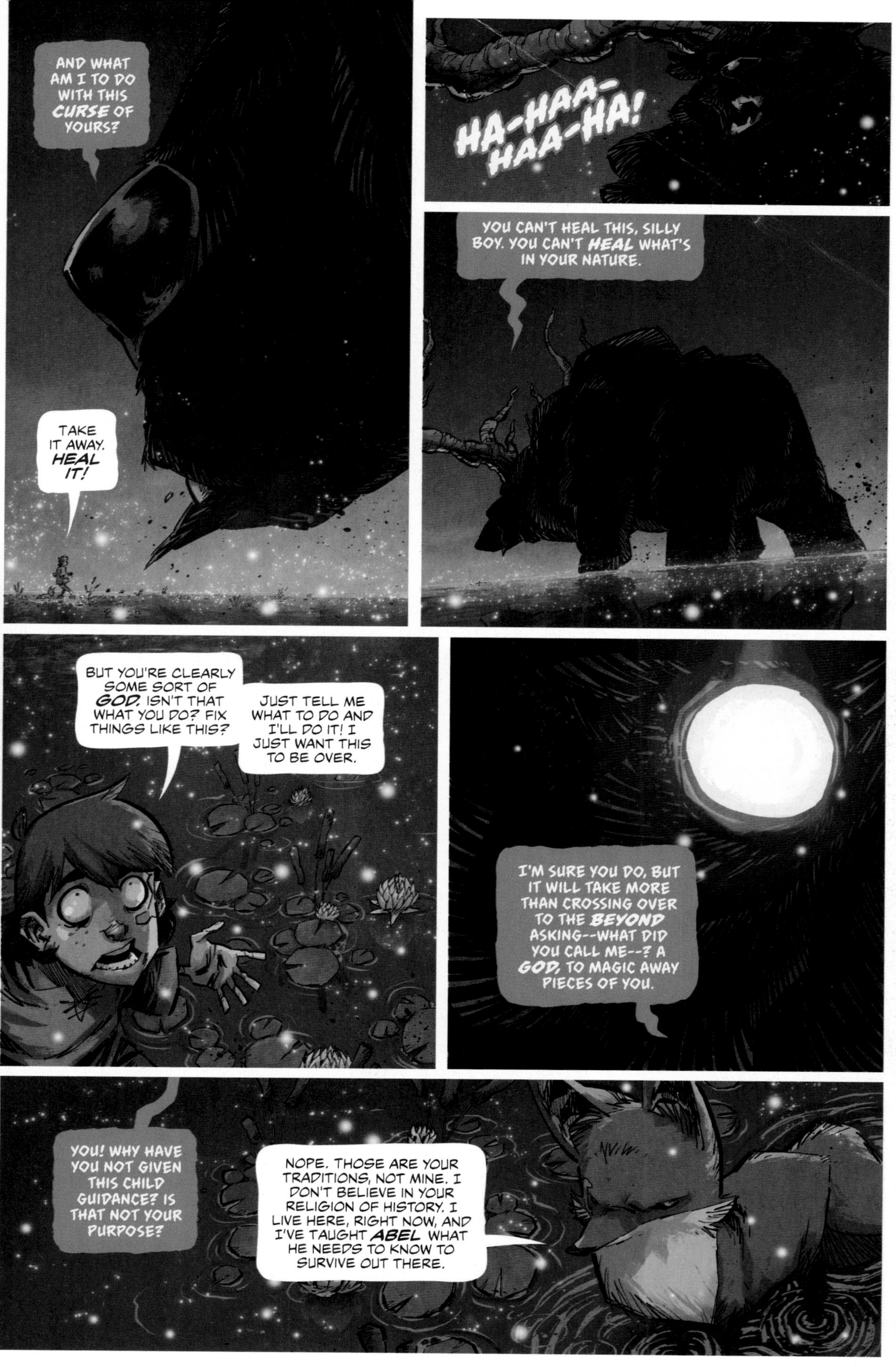
AND WHAT AM I TO DO WITH THIS CURSE OF YOURS?
TAKE IT AWAY. HEAL IT!
HA-HAA-HAA-HA!
YOU CAN'T HEAL THIS, SILLY BOY. YOU CAN'T HEAL WHAT'S IN YOUR NATURE.
BUT YOU'RE CLEARLY SOME SORT OF GOD, ISN'T THAT WHAT YOU DO? FIX THINGS LIKE THIS?
JUST TELL ME WHAT TO DO AND I'LL DO IT! I JUST WANT THIS TO BE OVER.
I'M SURE YOU DO, BUT IT WILL TAKE MORE THAN CROSSING OVER TO THE BEYOND ASKING--WHAT DID YOU CALL ME--? A GOD, TO MAGIC AWAY PIECES OF YOU.
YOU! WHY HAVE YOU NOT GIVEN THIS CHILD GUIDANCE? IS THAT NOT YOUR PURPOSE?
NOPE. THOSE ARE YOUR TRADITIONS, NOT MINE. I DON'T BELIEVE IN YOUR RELIGION OF HISTORY. I LIVE HERE, RIGHT NOW, AND I'VE TAUGHT ABEL WHAT HE NEEDS TO KNOW TO SURVIVE OUT THERE.

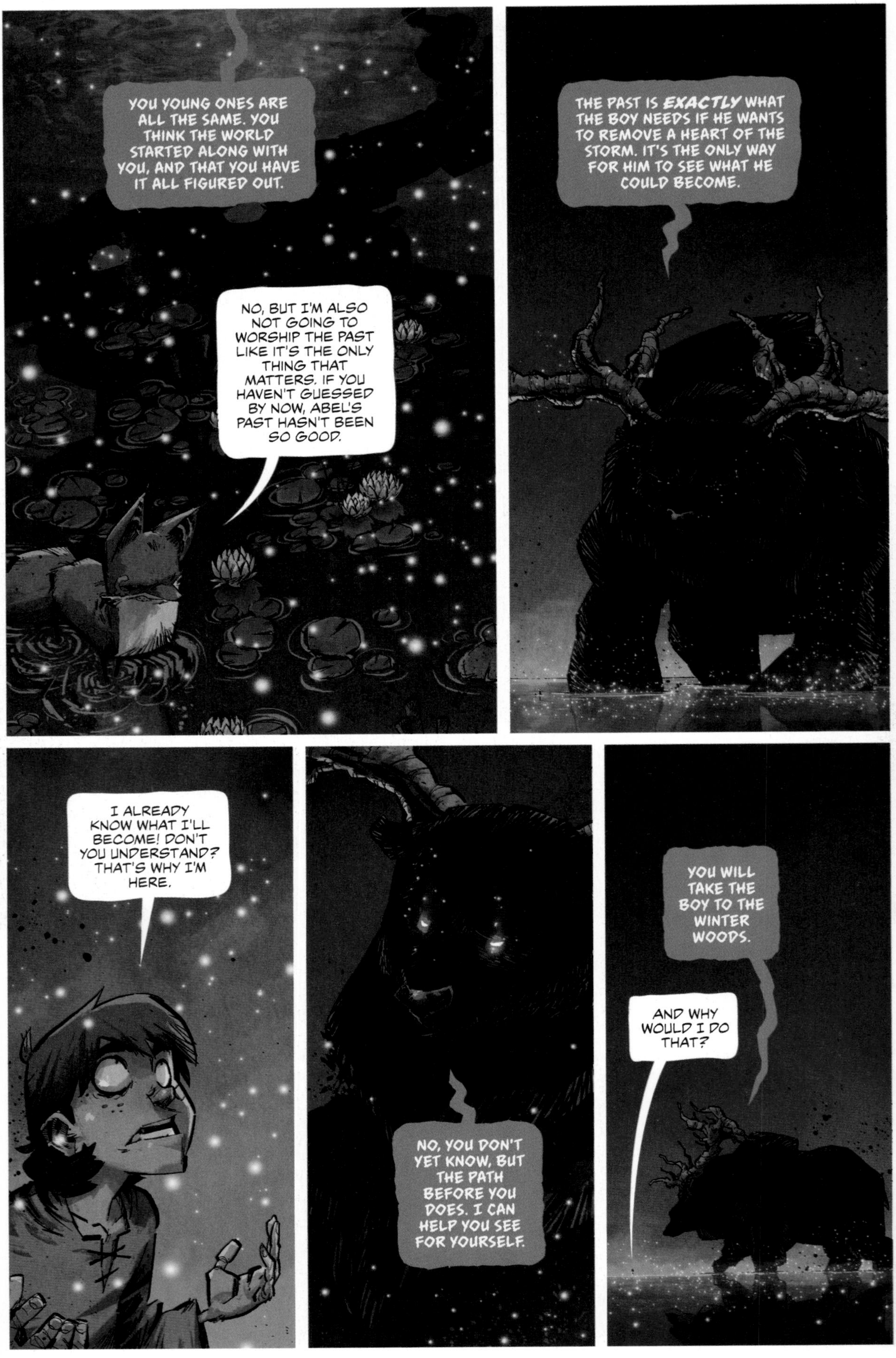
YOU YOUNG ONES ARE ALL THE SAME. YOU THINK THE WORLD STARTED ALONG WITH YOU, AND THAT YOU HAVE IT ALL FIGURED OUT.
NO, BUT I'M ALSO NOT GOING TO WORSHIP THE PAST LIKE IT'S THE ONLY THING THAT MATTERS. IF YOU HAVEN'T GUESSED BY NOW, ABEL'S PAST HASN'T BEEN SO GOOD.
THE PAST IS EXACTLY WHAT THE BOY NEEDS IF HE WANTS TO REMOVE A HEART OF THE STORM. IT'S THE ONLY WAY FOR HIM TO SEE WHAT HE COULD BECOME.
I ALREADY KNOW WHAT I'LL BECOME! DON'T YOU UNDERSTAND? THAT'S WHY I'M HERE.
NO, YOU DON'T YET KNOW, BUT THE PATH BEFORE YOU DOES. I CAN HELP YOU SEE FOR YOURSELF.
YOU WILL TAKE THE BOY TO THE WINTER WOODS.
AND WHY WOULD I DO THAT?

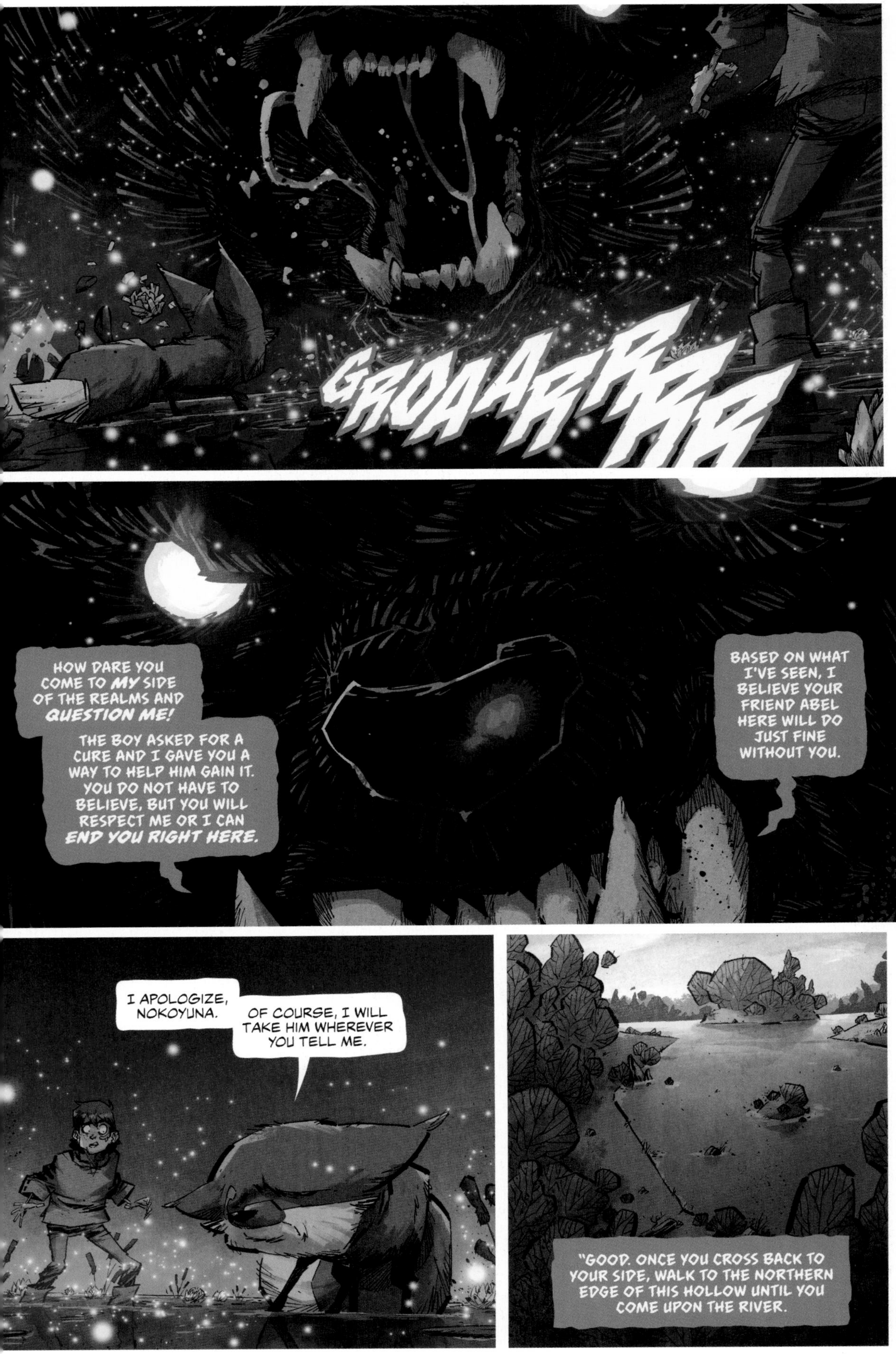
GROAARRRR
HOW DARE YOU COME TO MY SIDE OF THE REALMS AND QUESTION ME!
THE BOY ASKED FOR A CURE AND I GAVE YOU A WAY TO HELP HIM GAIN IT. YOU DO NOT HAVE TO BELIEVE, BUT YOU WILL RESPECT ME OR I CAN END YOU RIGHT HERE.
BASED ON WHAT I'VE SEEN, I BELIEVE YOUR FRIEND ABEL HERE WILL DO JUST FINE WITHOUT YOU.
I APOLOGIZE, NOKOYUNA.
OF COURSE, I WILL TAKE HIM WHEREVER YOU TELL ME.
"GOOD. ONCE YOU CROSS BACK TO YOUR SIDE, WALK TO THE NORTHERN EDGE OF THIS HOLLOW UNTIL YOU COME UPON THE RIVER.

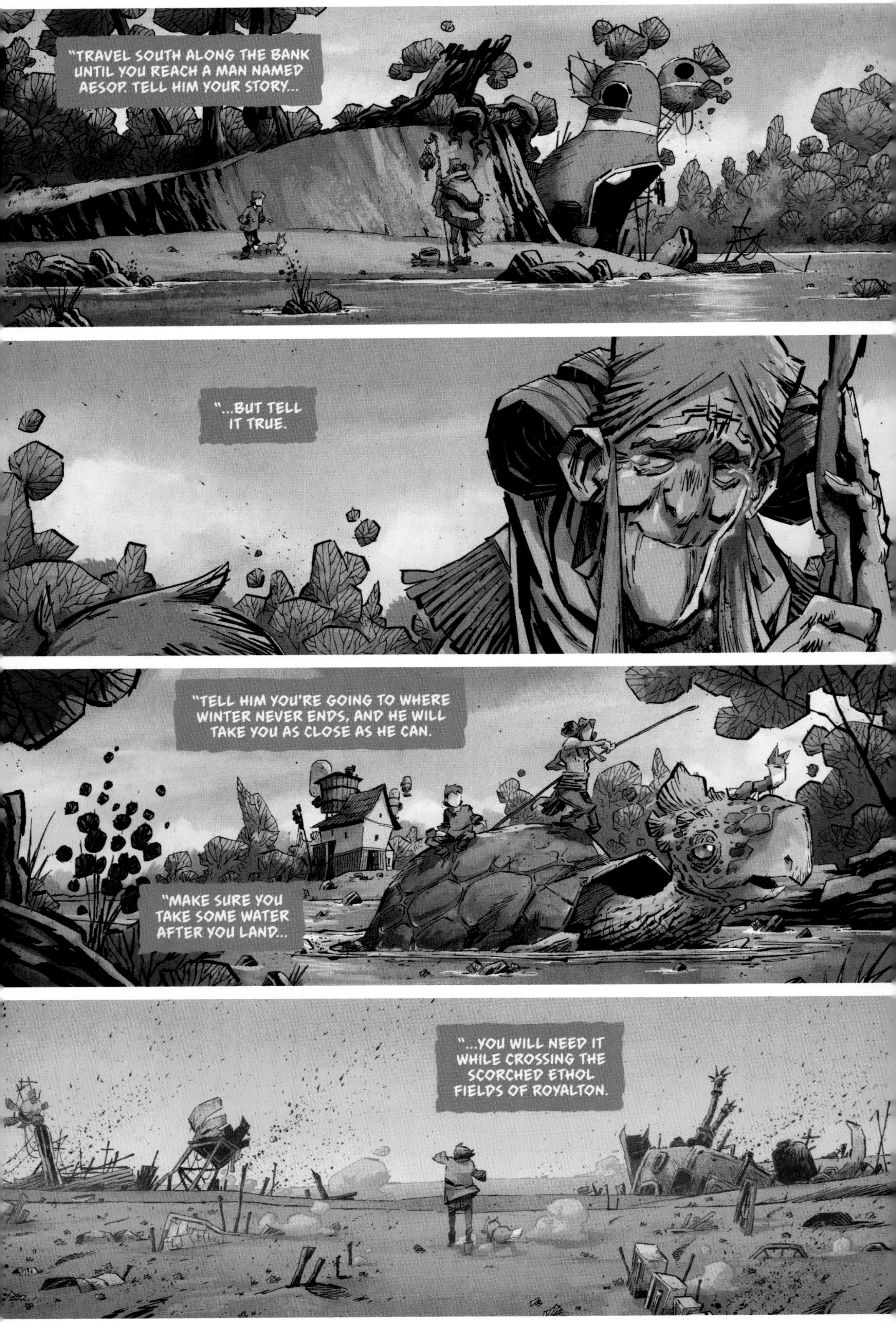
"TRAVEL SOUTH ALONG THE BANK UNTIL YOU REACH A MAN NAMED AESOP. TELL HIM YOUR STORY...
"...BUT TELL IT TRUE.
"TELL HIM YOU'RE GOING TO WHERE WINTER NEVER ENDS, AND HE WILL TAKE YOU AS CLOSE AS HE CAN.
"MAKE SURE YOU TAKE SOME WATER AFTER YOU LAND...
"...YOU WILL NEED IT WHILE CROSSING THE SCORCHED ETHOL FIELDS OF ROYALTON.

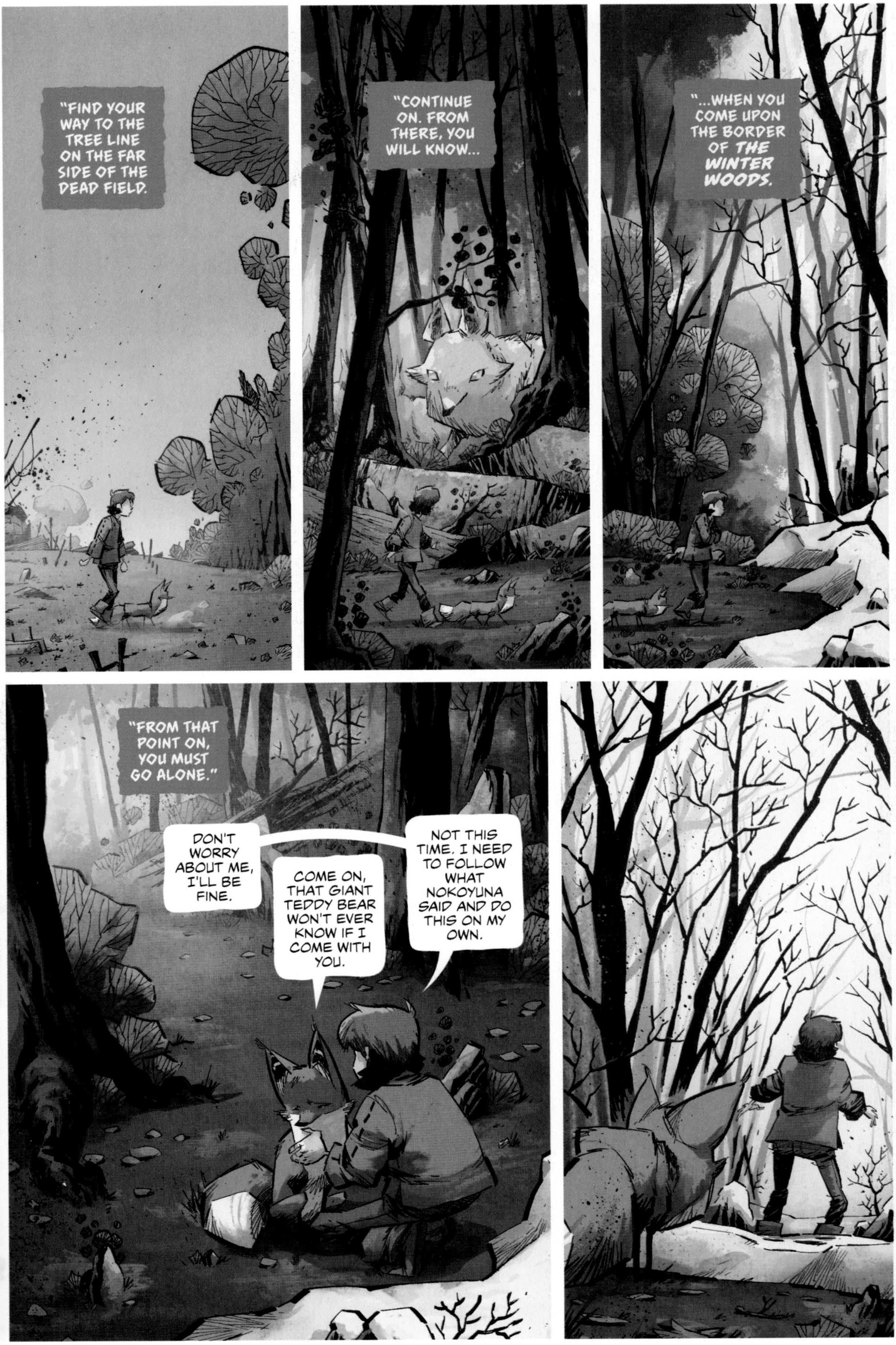

"FIND YOUR WAY TO THE TREE LINE ON THE FAR SIDE OF THE DEAD FIELD.
"CONTINUE ON. FROM THERE, YOU WILL KNOW...
"...WHEN YOU COME UPON THE BORDER OF *THE WINTER WOODS.*
"FROM THAT POINT ON, YOU MUST GO ALONE."
COME ON, THAT GIANT TEDDY BEAR WON'T EVER KNOW IF I COME WITH YOU.
NOT THIS TIME. I NEED TO FOLLOW WHAT NOKOYUNA SAID AND DO THIS ON MY OWN.
DON'T WORRY ABOUT ME, I'LL BE FINE.

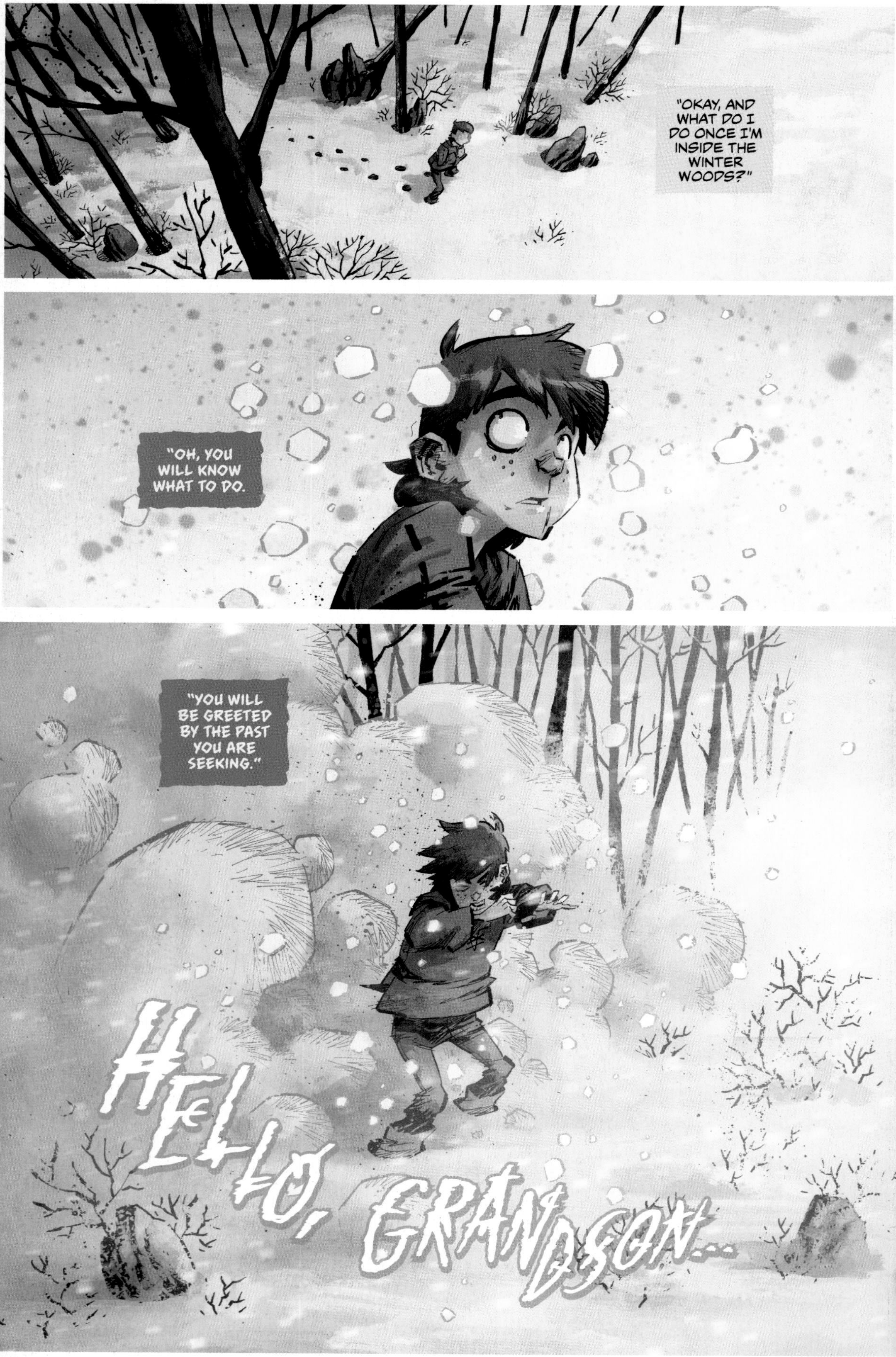
"OKAY, AND WHAT DO I DO ONCE I'M INSIDE THE WINTER WOODS?"
"OH, YOU WILL KNOW WHAT TO DO.
"YOU WILL BE GREETED BY THE PAST YOU ARE SEEKING."
HELLO, GRANDSON...

CHAPTER
TEN

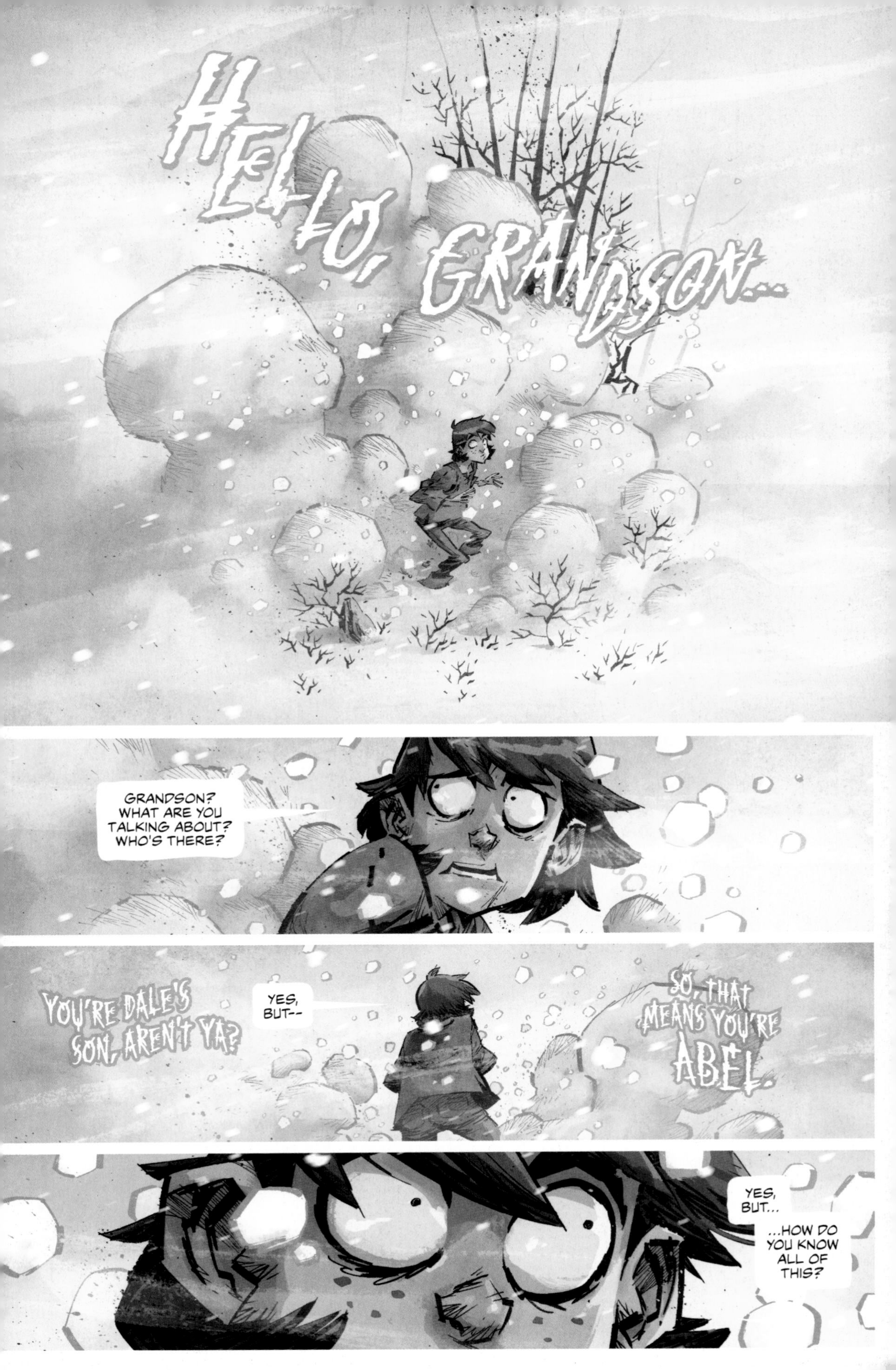
HELLO, GRANDSON...
GRANDSON? WHAT ARE YOU TALKING ABOUT? WHO'S THERE?
YOU'RE DALE'S SON, AREN'T YA?
YES, BUT--
SO, THAT MEANS YOU'RE ABEL.
YES, BUT...
...HOW DO YOU KNOW ALL OF THIS?

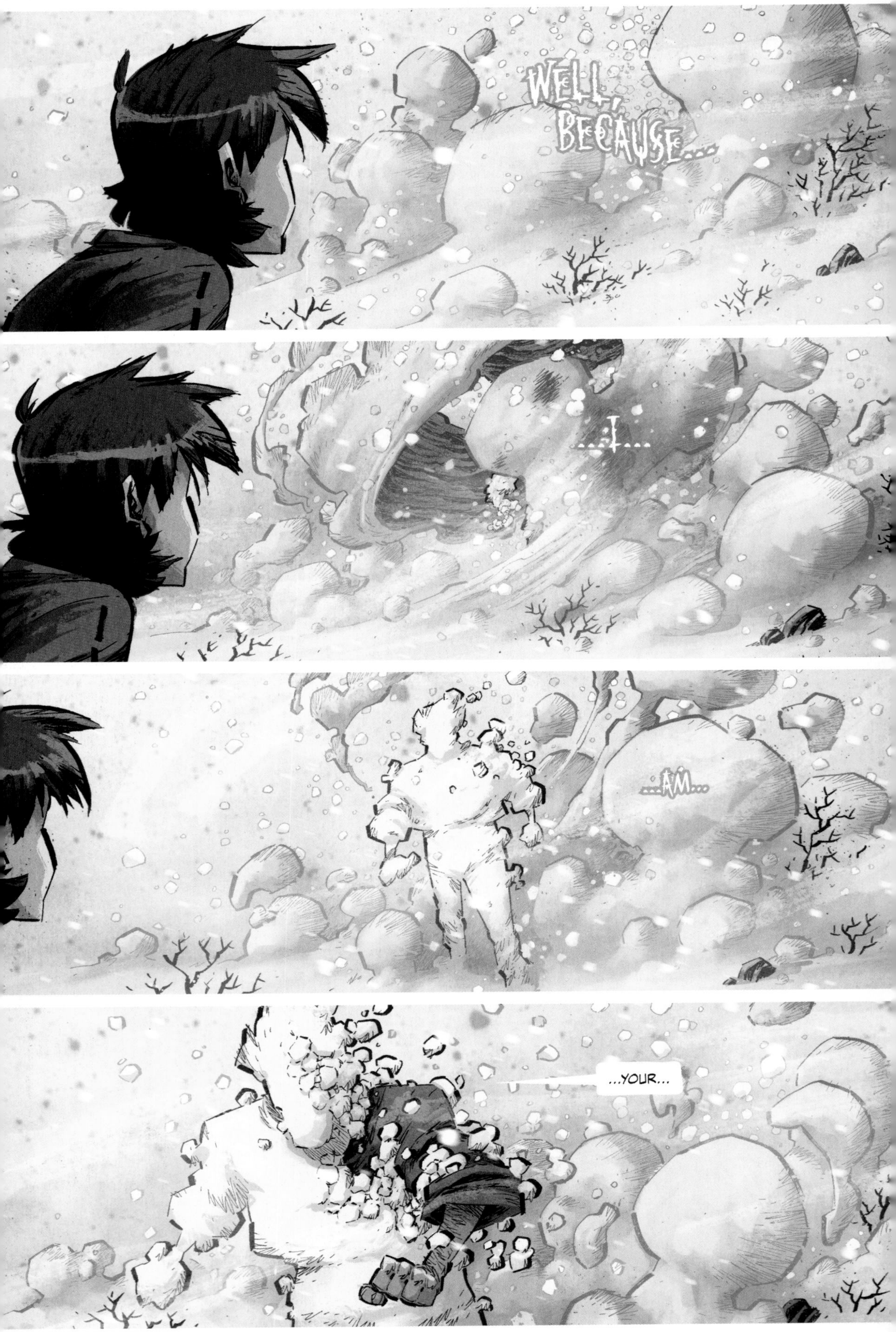
WELL, BECAUSE...
...I...
...AM...
...YOUR...

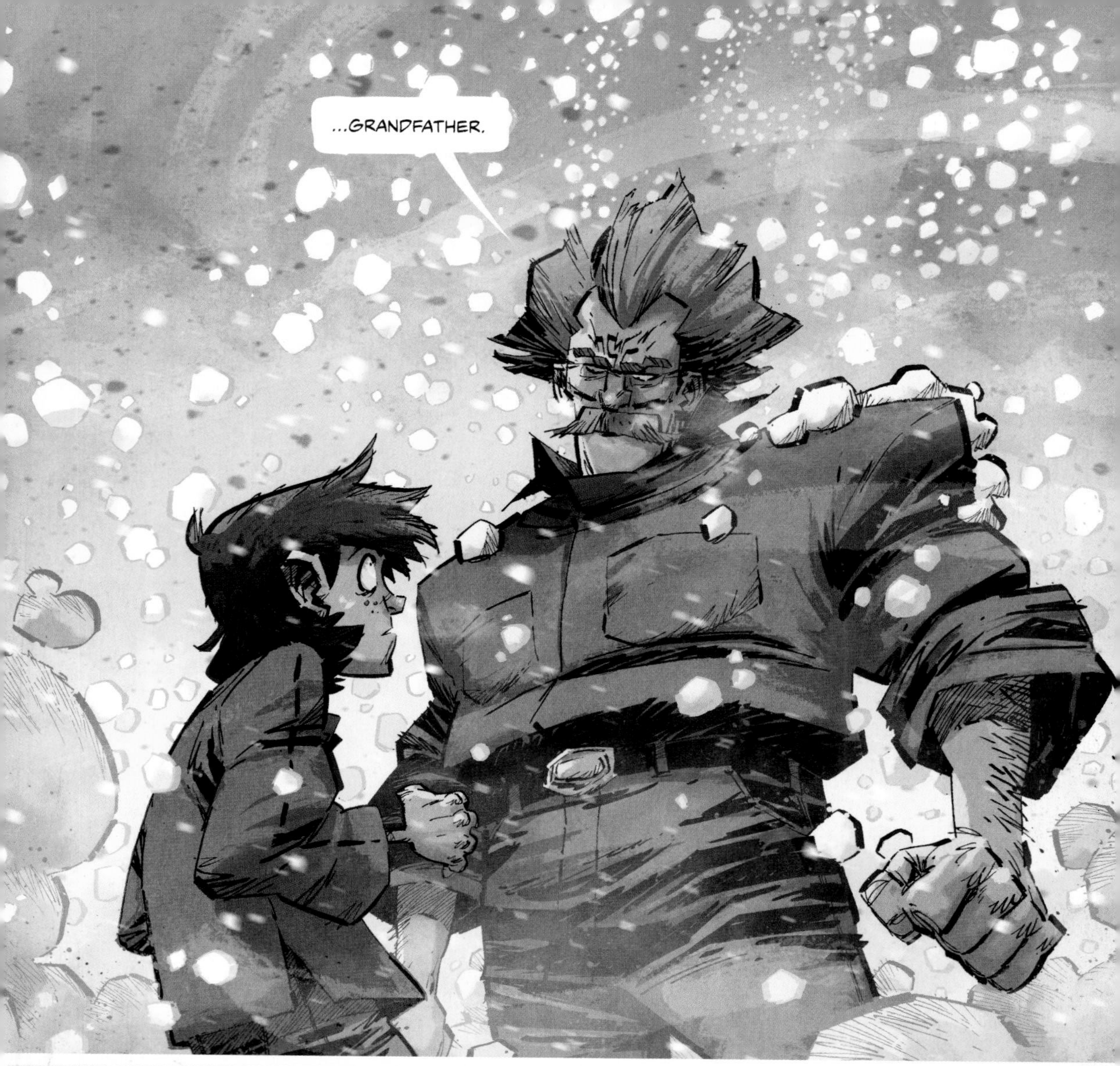
...GRANDFATHER.

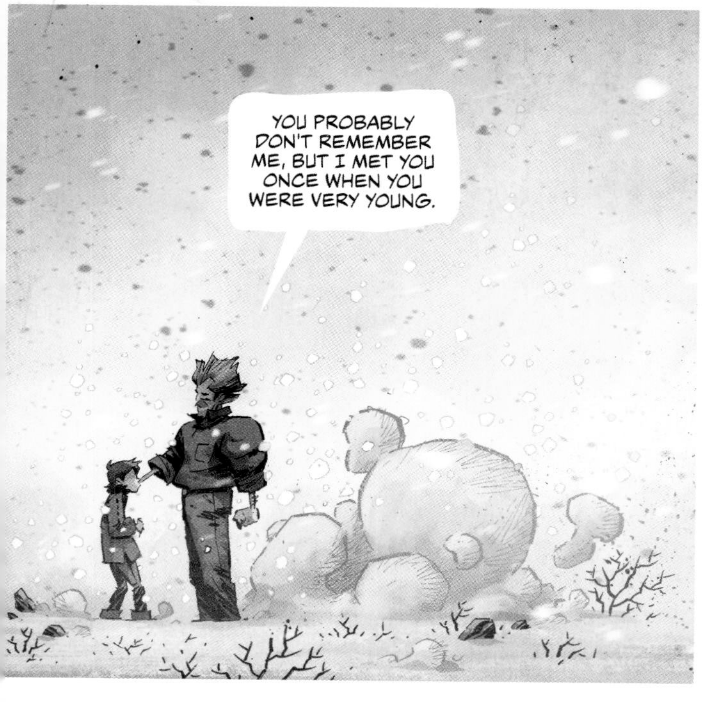
YOU PROBABLY DON'T REMEMBER ME, BUT I MET YOU ONCE WHEN YOU WERE VERY YOUNG.

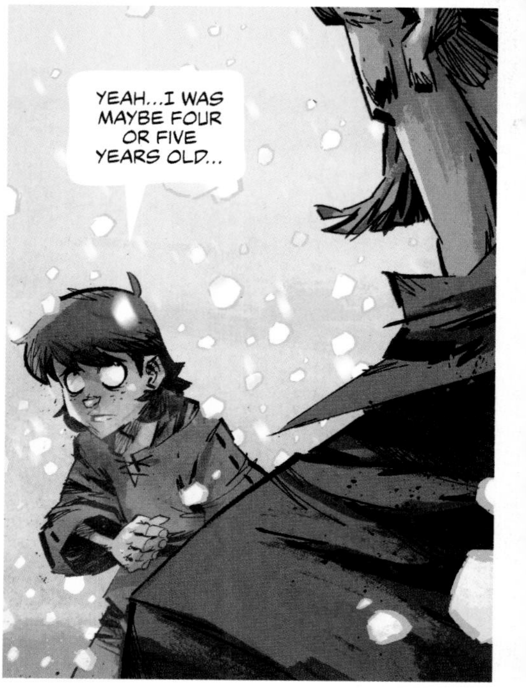
YEAH...I WAS MAYBE FOUR OR FIVE YEARS OLD...

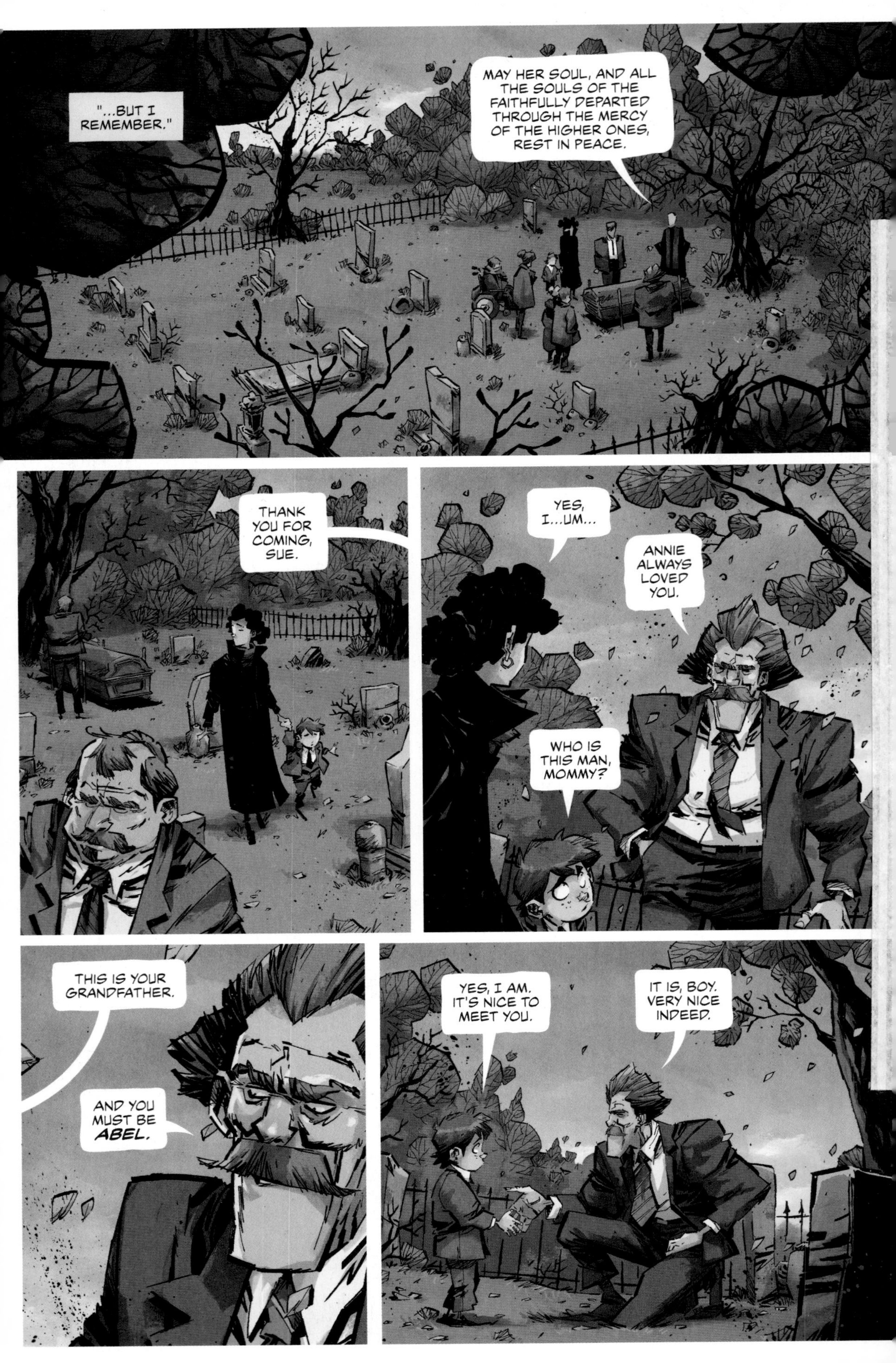

"...BUT I REMEMBER."
MAY HER SOUL, AND ALL THE SOULS OF THE FAITHFULLY DEPARTED THROUGH THE MERCY OF THE HIGHER ONES, REST IN PEACE.
THANK YOU FOR COMING, SUE.
YES, I...UM...
ANNIE ALWAYS LOVED YOU.
WHO IS THIS MAN, MOMMY?
THIS IS YOUR GRANDFATHER.
AND YOU MUST BE ABEL.
YES, I AM. IT'S NICE TO MEET YOU.
IT IS, BOY. VERY NICE INDEED.

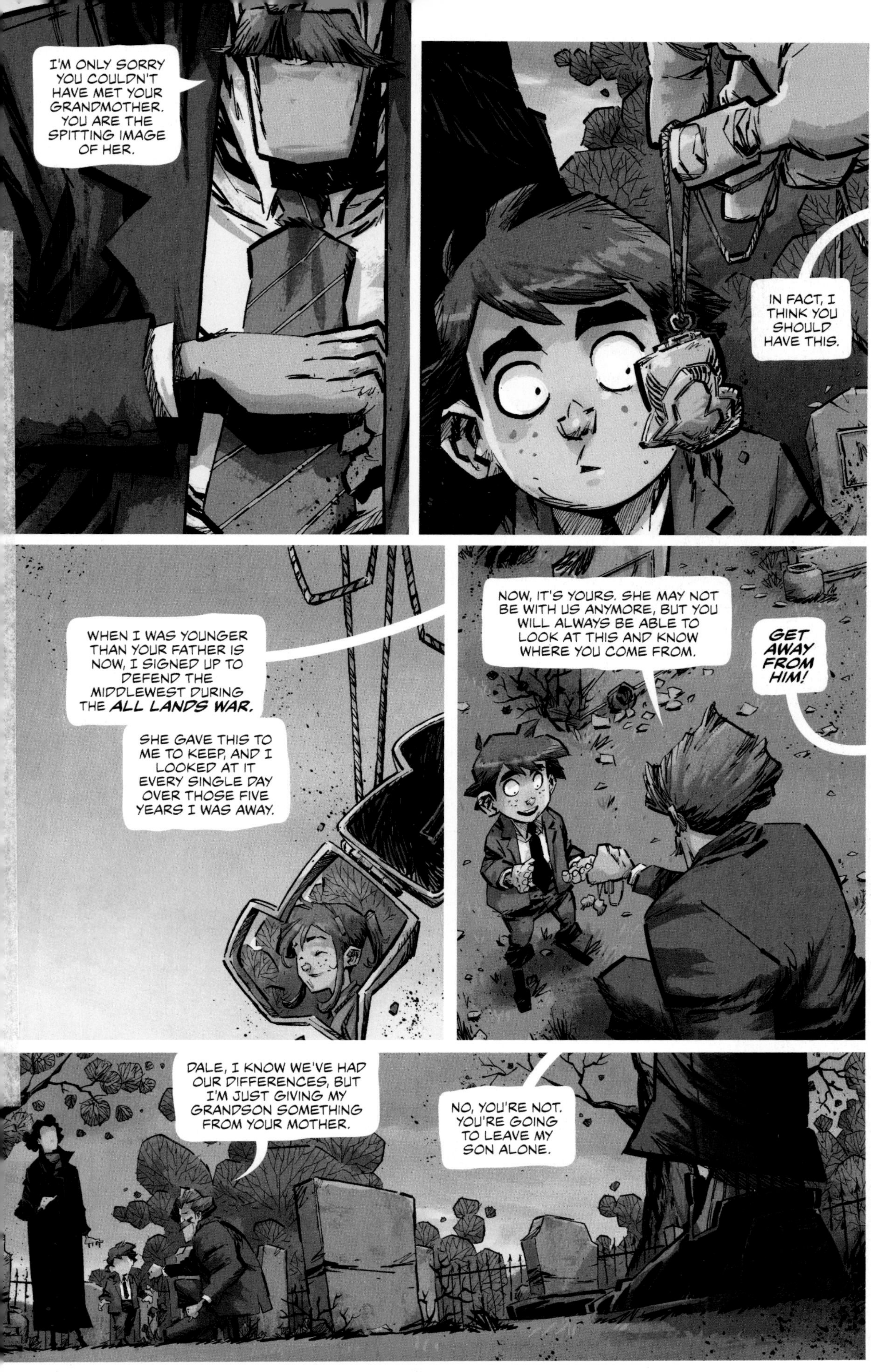
I'M ONLY SORRY YOU COULDN'T HAVE MET YOUR GRANDMOTHER. YOU ARE THE SPITTING IMAGE OF HER.
IN FACT, I THINK YOU SHOULD HAVE THIS.
WHEN I WAS YOUNGER THAN YOUR FATHER IS NOW, I SIGNED UP TO DEFEND THE MIDDLEWEST DURING THE ALL LANDS WAR.
SHE GAVE THIS TO ME TO KEEP, AND I LOOKED AT IT EVERY SINGLE DAY OVER THOSE FIVE YEARS I WAS AWAY.
NOW, IT'S YOURS. SHE MAY NOT BE WITH US ANYMORE, BUT YOU WILL ALWAYS BE ABLE TO LOOK AT THIS AND KNOW WHERE YOU COME FROM.
GET AWAY FROM HIM!
DALE, I KNOW WE'VE HAD OUR DIFFERENCES, BUT I'M JUST GIVING MY GRANDSON SOMETHING FROM YOUR MOTHER.
NO, YOU'RE NOT. YOU'RE GOING TO LEAVE MY SON ALONE.

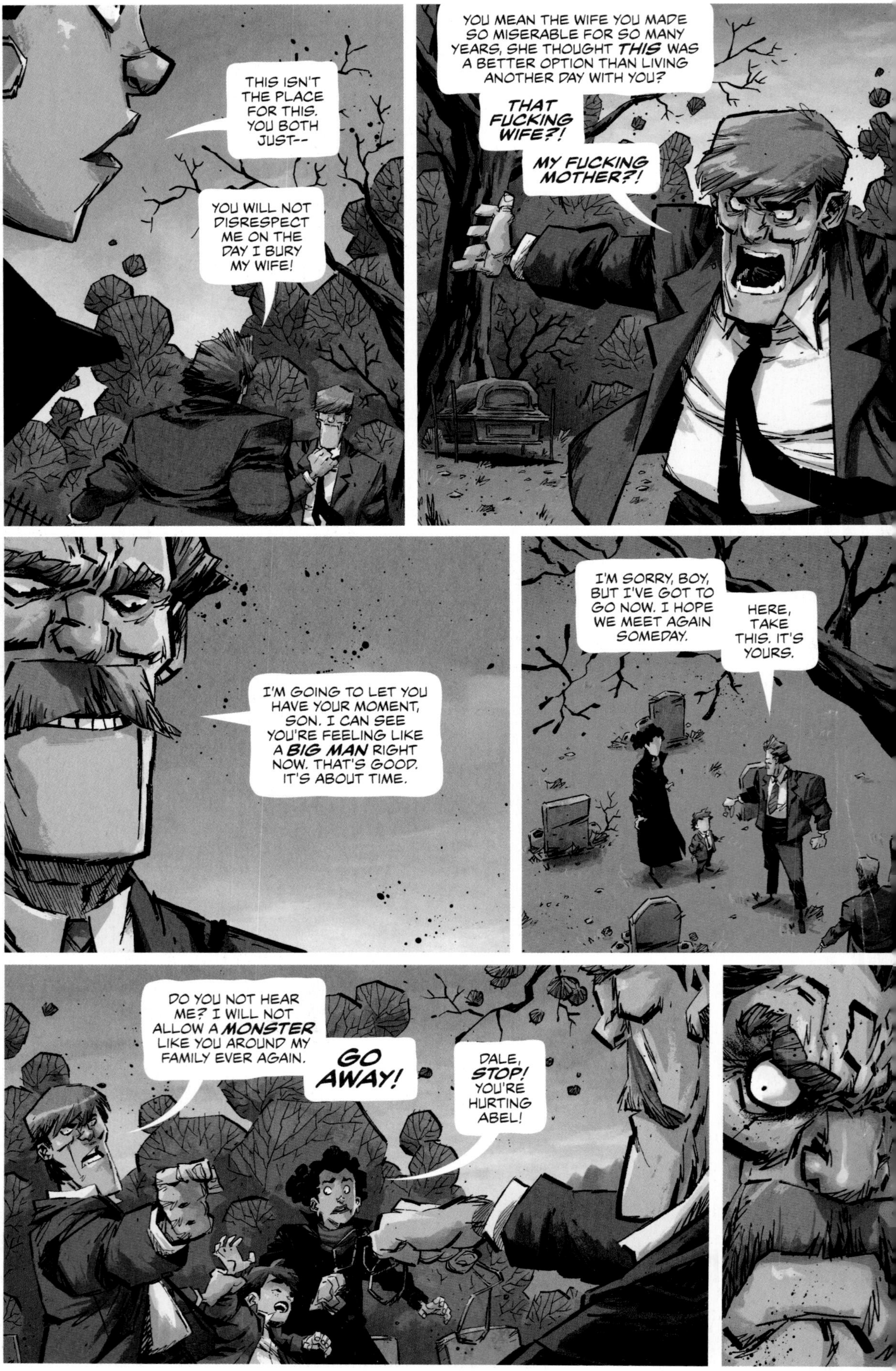
THIS ISN'T THE PLACE FOR THIS. YOU BOTH JUST--
YOU WILL NOT DISRESPECT ME ON THE DAY I BURY MY WIFE!
YOU MEAN THE WIFE YOU MADE SO MISERABLE FOR SO MANY YEARS, SHE THOUGHT THIS WAS A BETTER OPTION THAN LIVING ANOTHER DAY WITH YOU?
THAT FUCKING WIFE?!
MY FUCKING MOTHER?!
I'M GOING TO LET YOU HAVE YOUR MOMENT, SON. I CAN SEE YOU'RE FEELING LIKE A BIG MAN RIGHT NOW. THAT'S GOOD. IT'S ABOUT TIME.
I'M SORRY, BOY, BUT I'VE GOT TO GO NOW. I HOPE WE MEET AGAIN SOMEDAY.
HERE, TAKE THIS. IT'S YOURS.
DO YOU NOT HEAR ME? I WILL NOT ALLOW A MONSTER LIKE YOU AROUND MY FAMILY EVER AGAIN.
GO AWAY!
DALE, STOP! YOU'RE HURTING ABEL!

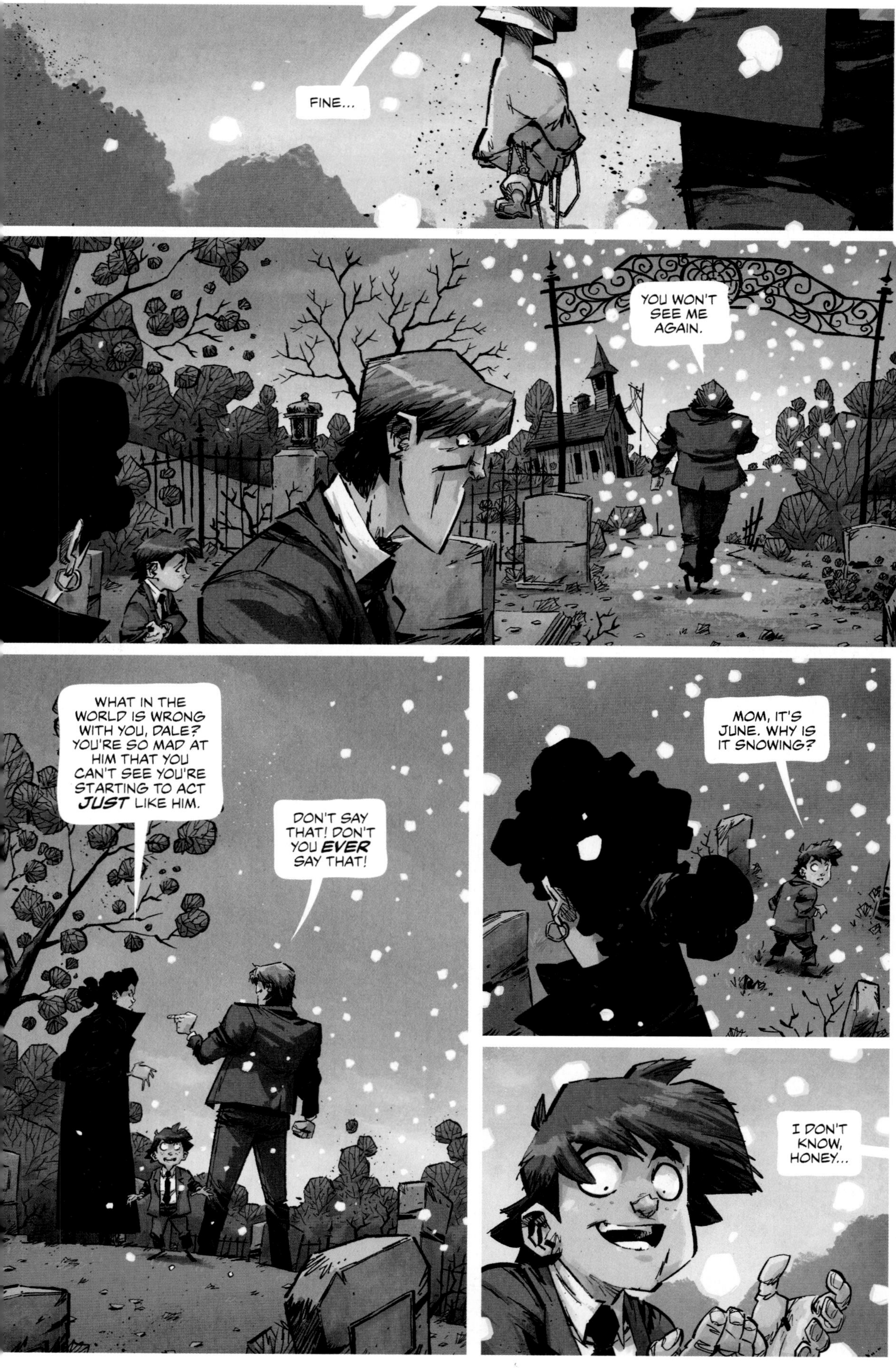
FINE...
YOU WON'T SEE ME AGAIN.
WHAT IN THE WORLD IS WRONG WITH YOU, DALE? YOU'RE SO MAD AT HIM THAT YOU CAN'T SEE YOU'RE STARTING TO ACT JUST LIKE HIM.
DON'T SAY THAT! DON'T YOU EVER SAY THAT!
MOM, IT'S JUNE. WHY IS IT SNOWING?
I DON'T KNOW, HONEY...

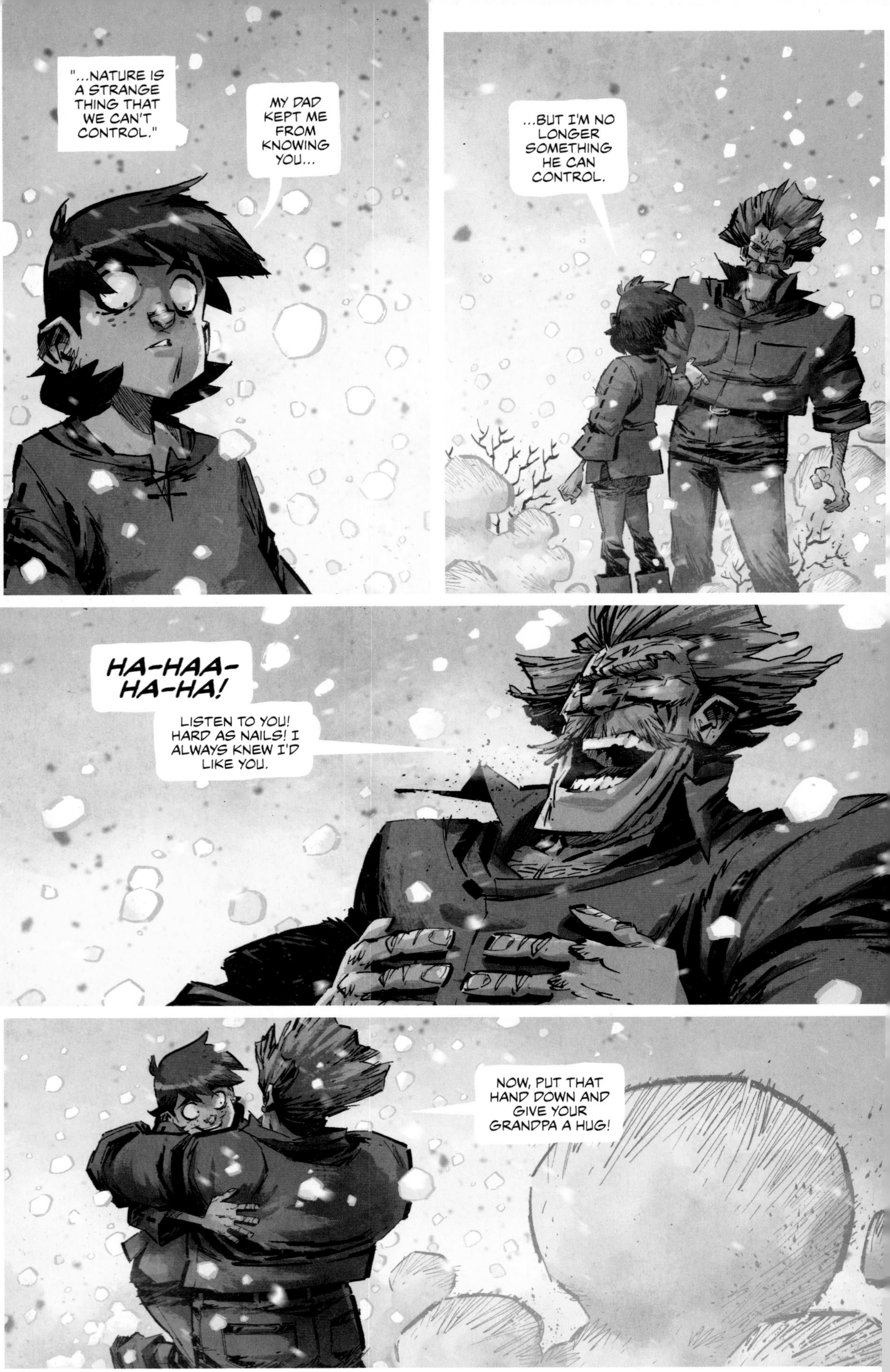
"...NATURE IS A STRANGE THING THAT WE CAN'T CONTROL."
MY DAD KEPT ME FROM KNOWING YOU...
...BUT I'M NO LONGER SOMETHING HE CAN CONTROL.
HA-HAA-HA-HA!
LISTEN TO YOU! HARD AS NAILS! I ALWAYS KNEW I'D LIKE YOU.
NOW, PUT THAT HAND DOWN AND GIVE YOUR GRANDPA A HUG!

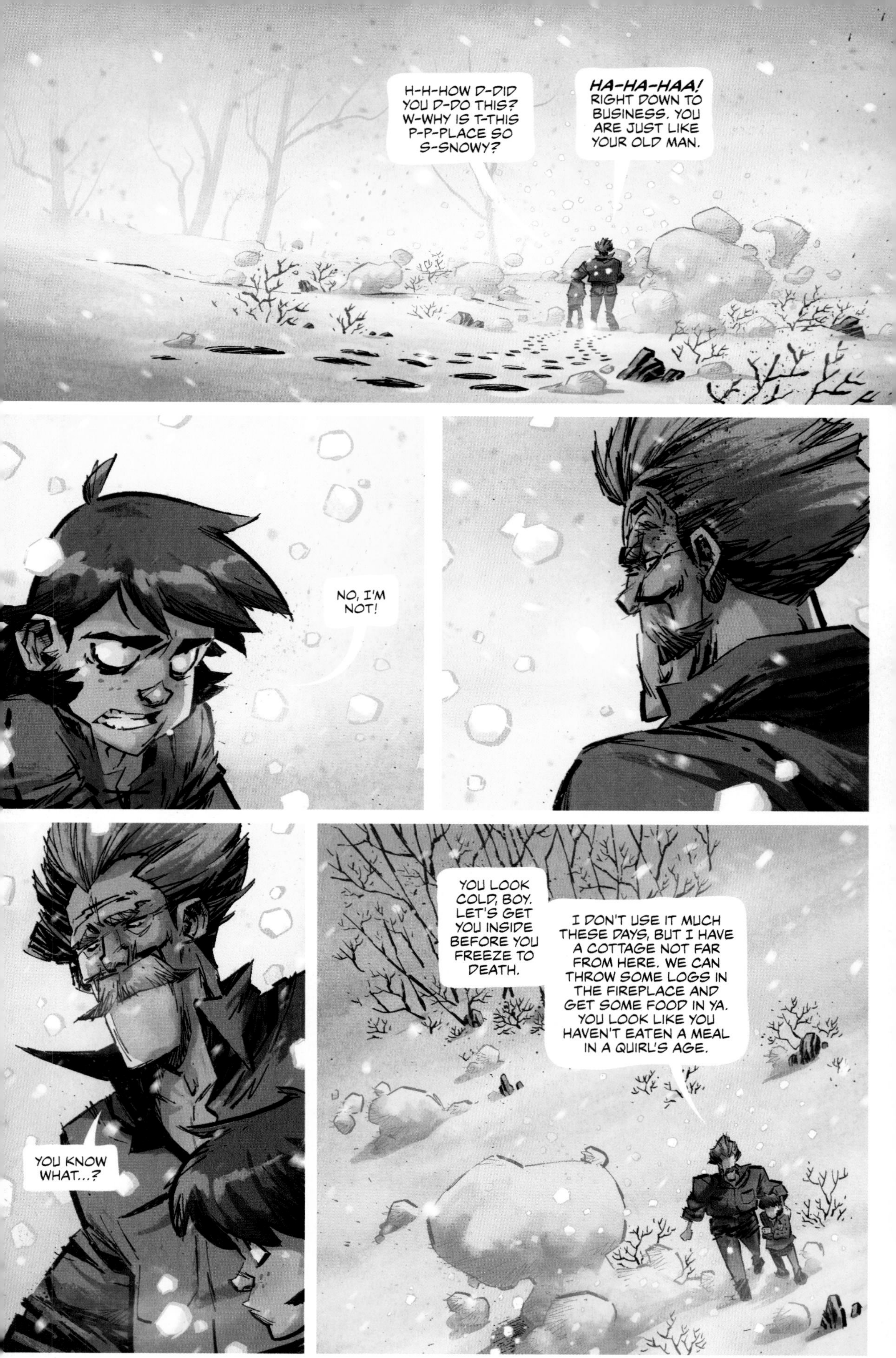
H-H-HOW D-DID YOU D-DO THIS? W-WHY IS T-THIS P-P-PLACE SO S-SNOWY?
HA-HA-HAA! RIGHT DOWN TO BUSINESS. YOU ARE JUST LIKE YOUR OLD MAN.
NO, I'M NOT!
YOU KNOW WHAT...?
YOU LOOK COLD, BOY. LET'S GET YOU INSIDE BEFORE YOU FREEZE TO DEATH.
I DON'T USE IT MUCH THESE DAYS, BUT I HAVE A COTTAGE NOT FAR FROM HERE. WE CAN THROW SOME LOGS IN THE FIREPLACE AND GET SOME FOOD IN YA. YOU LOOK LIKE YOU HAVEN'T EATEN A MEAL IN A QUIRL'S AGE.

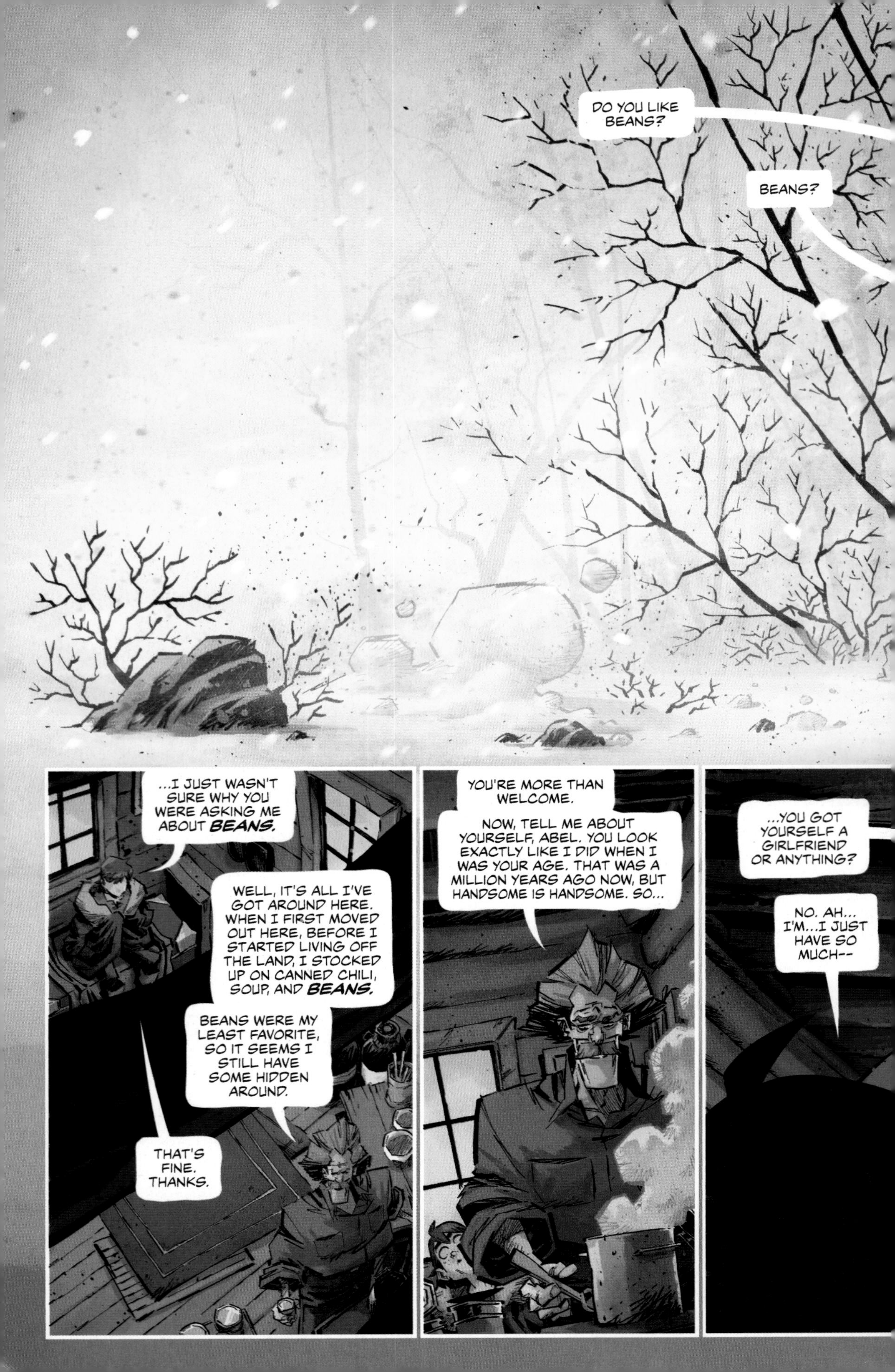
DO YOU LIKE BEANS?
BEANS?
...I JUST WASN'T SURE WHY YOU WERE ASKING ME ABOUT **BEANS.**
WELL, IT'S ALL I'VE GOT AROUND HERE. WHEN I FIRST MOVED OUT HERE, BEFORE I STARTED LIVING OFF THE LAND, I STOCKED UP ON CANNED CHILI, SOUP, AND **BEANS.**
BEANS WERE MY LEAST FAVORITE, SO IT SEEMS I STILL HAVE SOME HIDDEN AROUND.
THAT'S FINE. THANKS.
YOU'RE MORE THAN WELCOME.
NOW, TELL ME ABOUT YOURSELF, ABEL. YOU LOOK EXACTLY LIKE I DID WHEN I WAS YOUR AGE. THAT WAS A MILLION YEARS AGO NOW, BUT HANDSOME IS HANDSOME. SO...
...YOU GOT YOURSELF A GIRLFRIEND OR ANYTHING?
NO. AH... I'M...I JUST HAVE SO MUCH--

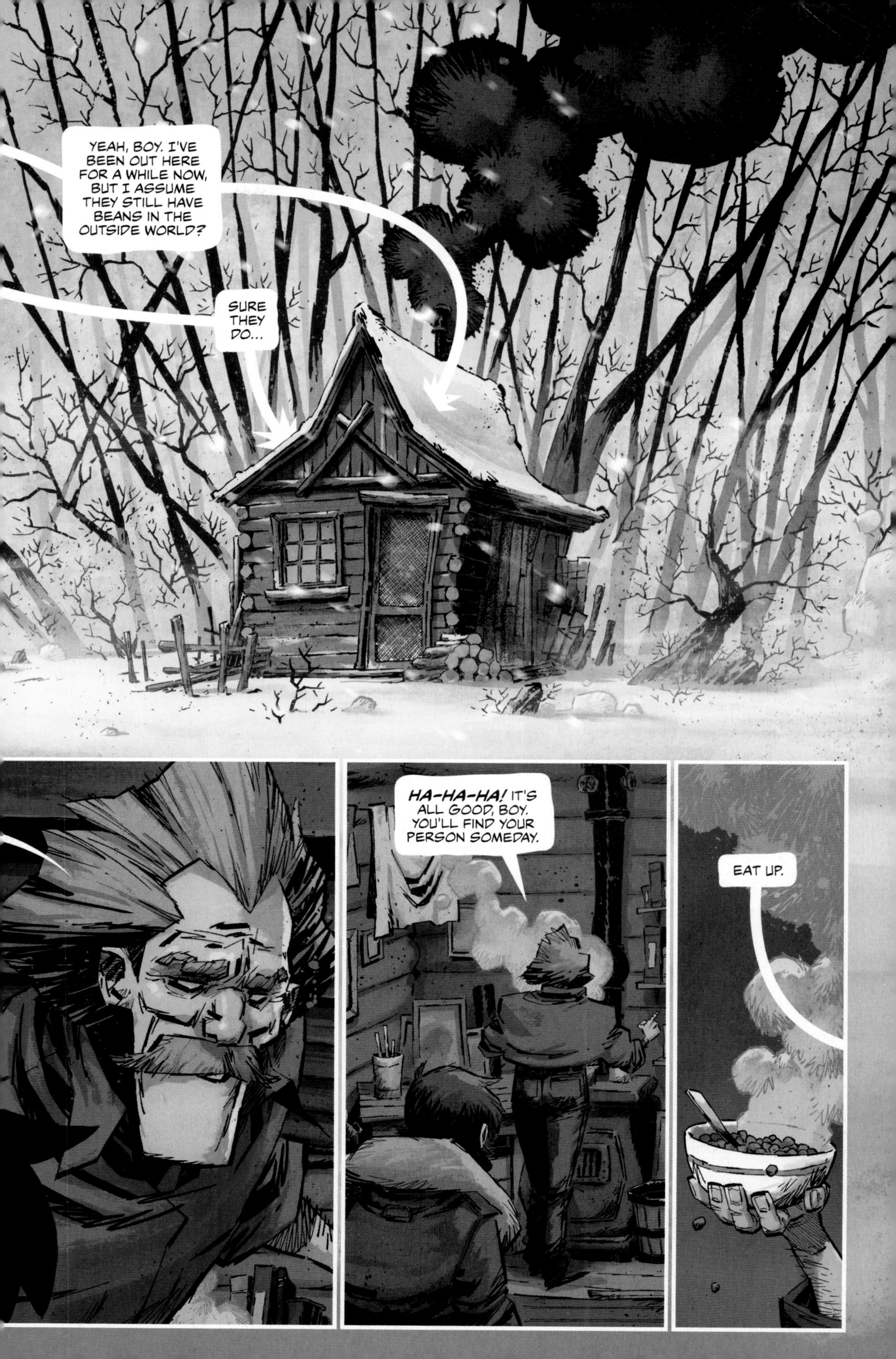
YEAH, BOY. I'VE BEEN OUT HERE FOR A WHILE NOW, BUT I ASSUME THEY STILL HAVE BEANS IN THE OUTSIDE WORLD?
SURE THEY DO...
HA-HA-HA! IT'S ALL GOOD, BOY. YOU'LL FIND YOUR PERSON SOMEDAY.
EAT UP.

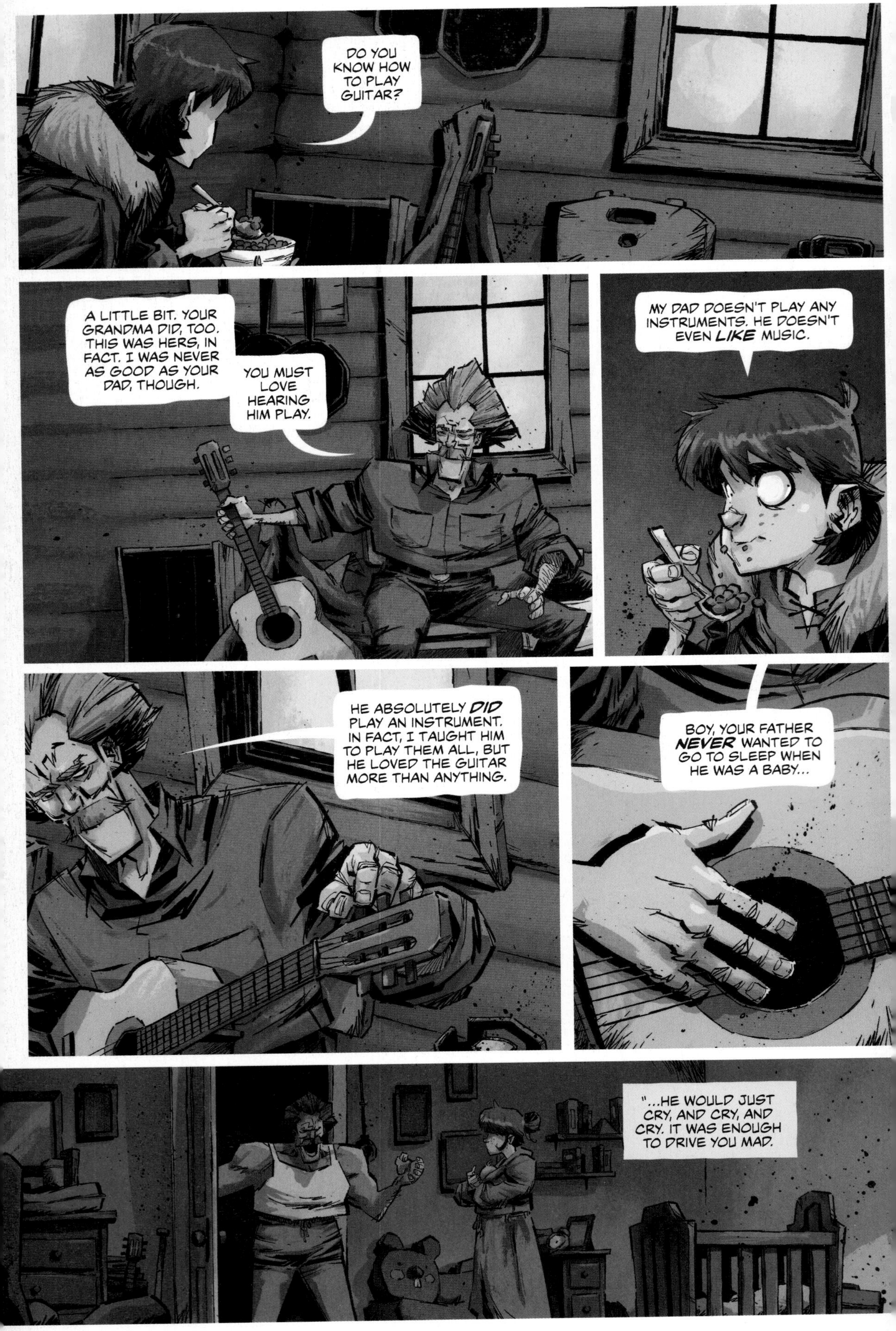
DO YOU KNOW HOW TO PLAY GUITAR?
A LITTLE BIT. YOUR GRANDMA DID, TOO. THIS WAS HERS, IN FACT. I WAS NEVER AS GOOD AS YOUR DAD, THOUGH.
YOU MUST LOVE HEARING HIM PLAY.
MY DAD DOESN'T PLAY ANY INSTRUMENTS. HE DOESN'T EVEN LIKE MUSIC.
HE ABSOLUTELY DID PLAY AN INSTRUMENT. IN FACT, I TAUGHT HIM TO PLAY THEM ALL, BUT HE LOVED THE GUITAR MORE THAN ANYTHING.
BOY, YOUR FATHER NEVER WANTED TO GO TO SLEEP WHEN HE WAS A BABY...
"...HE WOULD JUST CRY, AND CRY, AND CRY. IT WAS ENOUGH TO DRIVE YOU MAD.

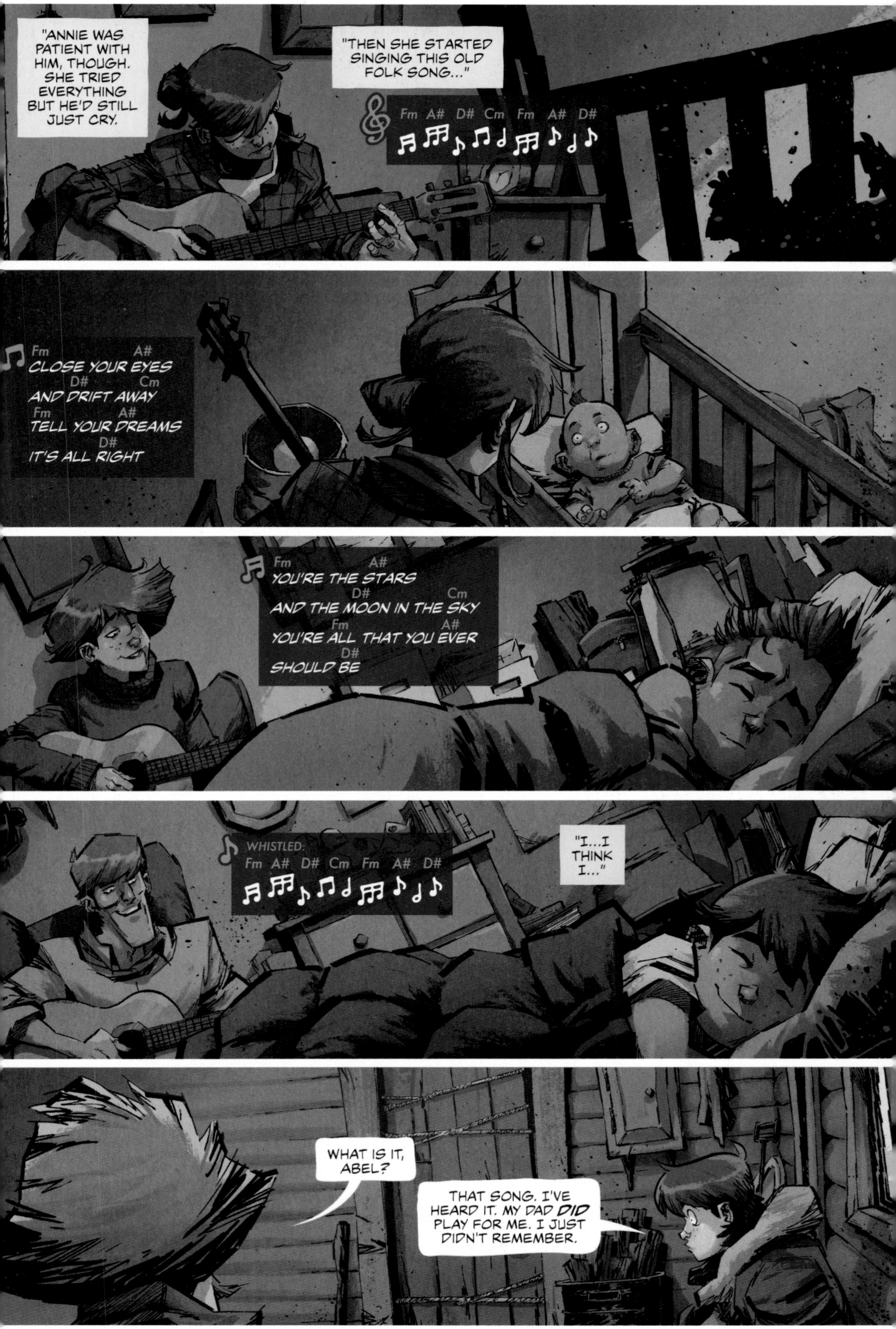
"ANNIE WAS PATIENT WITH HIM, THOUGH. SHE TRIED EVERYTHING BUT HE'D STILL JUST CRY.
"THEN SHE STARTED SINGING THIS OLD FOLK SONG..."
Fm A# D# Cm Fm A# D#
Fm A# CLOSE YOUR EYES
D# Cm AND DRIFT AWAY
Fm A# TELL YOUR DREAMS
D# IT'S ALL RIGHT
Fm A# YOU'RE THE STARS
D# Cm AND THE MOON IN THE SKY
Fm A# YOU'RE ALL THAT YOU EVER
D# SHOULD BE
WHISTLED:
Fm A# D# Cm Fm A# D#
"I...I THINK I..."
WHAT IS IT, ABEL?
THAT SONG. I'VE HEARD IT. MY DAD DID PLAY FOR ME. I JUST DIDN'T REMEMBER.

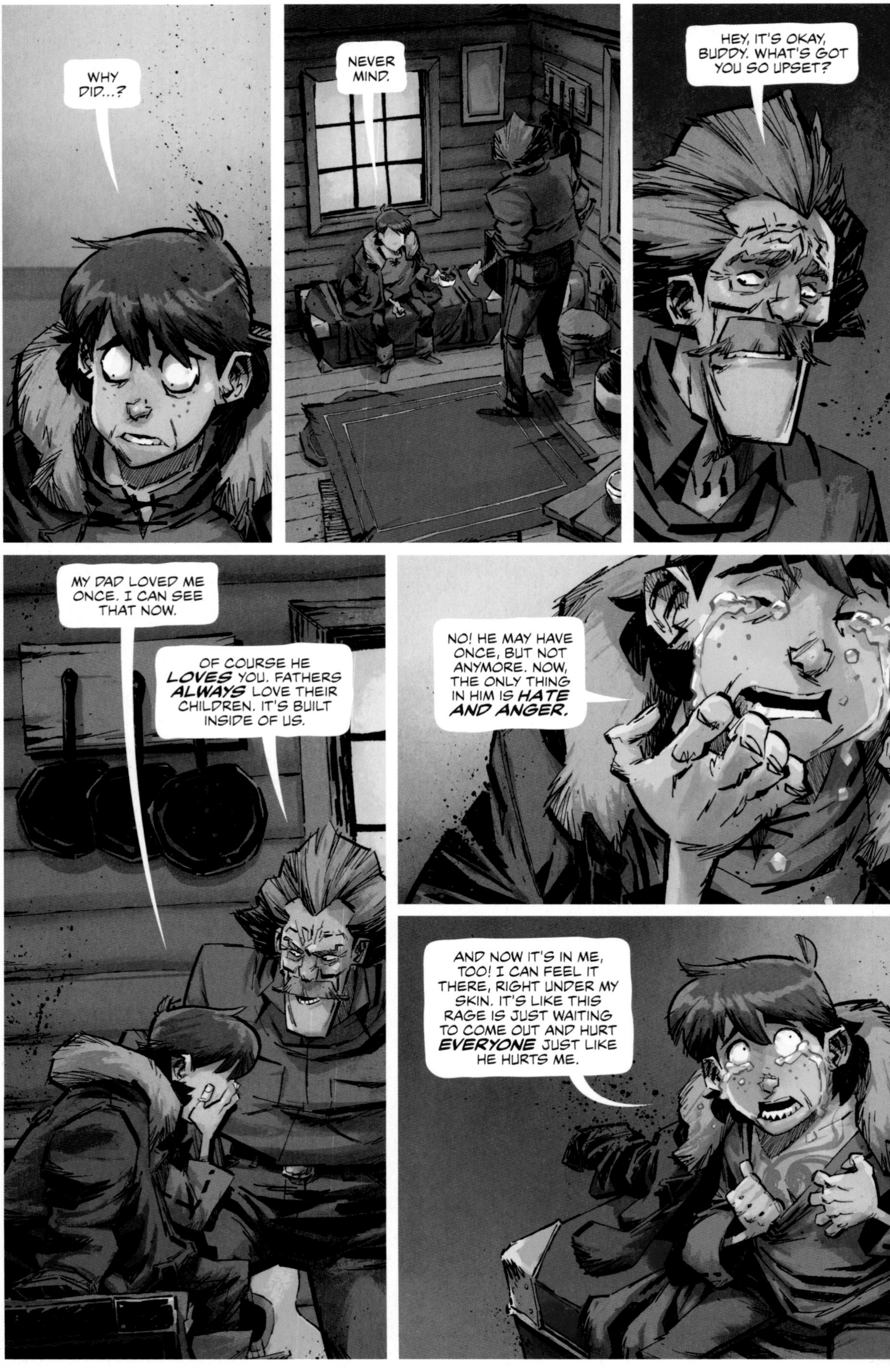
WHY DID...?
NEVER MIND.
HEY, IT'S OKAY, BUDDY. WHAT'S GOT YOU SO UPSET?
MY DAD LOVED ME ONCE. I CAN SEE THAT NOW.
OF COURSE HE **LOVES** YOU. FATHERS **ALWAYS** LOVE THEIR CHILDREN. IT'S BUILT INSIDE OF US.
NO! HE MAY HAVE ONCE, BUT NOT ANYMORE. NOW, THE ONLY THING IN HIM IS **HATE AND ANGER.**
AND NOW IT'S IN ME, TOO! I CAN FEEL IT THERE, RIGHT UNDER MY SKIN. IT'S LIKE THIS RAGE IS JUST WAITING TO COME OUT AND HURT **EVERYONE** JUST LIKE HE HURTS ME.

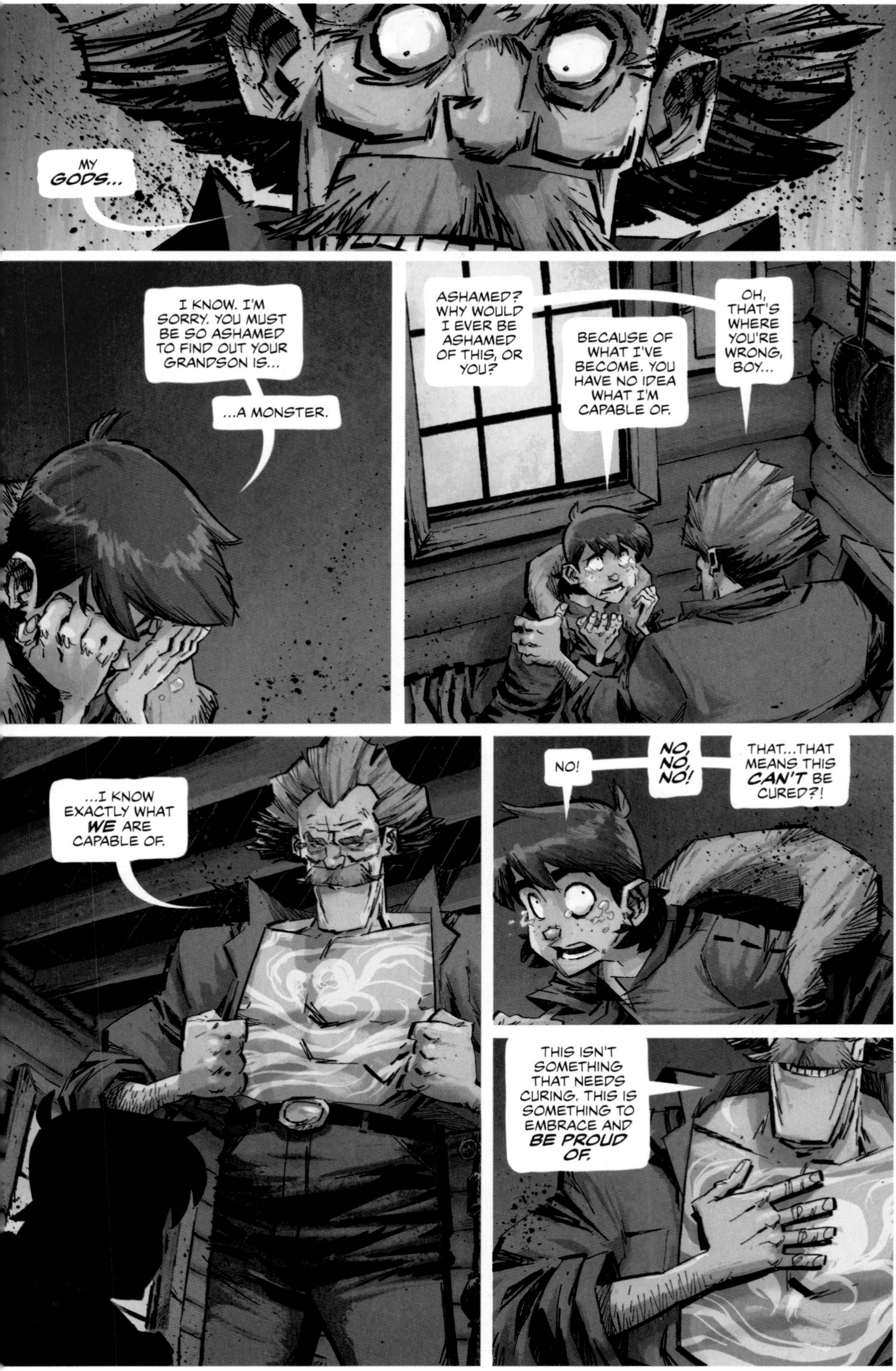
MY GODS...
I KNOW. I'M SORRY. YOU MUST BE SO ASHAMED TO FIND OUT YOUR GRANDSON IS...
...A MONSTER.
ASHAMED? WHY WOULD I EVER BE ASHAMED OF THIS, OR YOU?
BECAUSE OF WHAT I'VE BECOME. YOU HAVE NO IDEA WHAT I'M CAPABLE OF.
OH, THAT'S WHERE YOU'RE WRONG, BOY...
...I KNOW EXACTLY WHAT WE ARE CAPABLE OF.
NO!
NO, NO, NO!
THAT...THAT MEANS THIS CAN'T BE CURED?!
THIS ISN'T SOMETHING THAT NEEDS CURING. THIS IS SOMETHING TO EMBRACE AND BE PROUD OF.

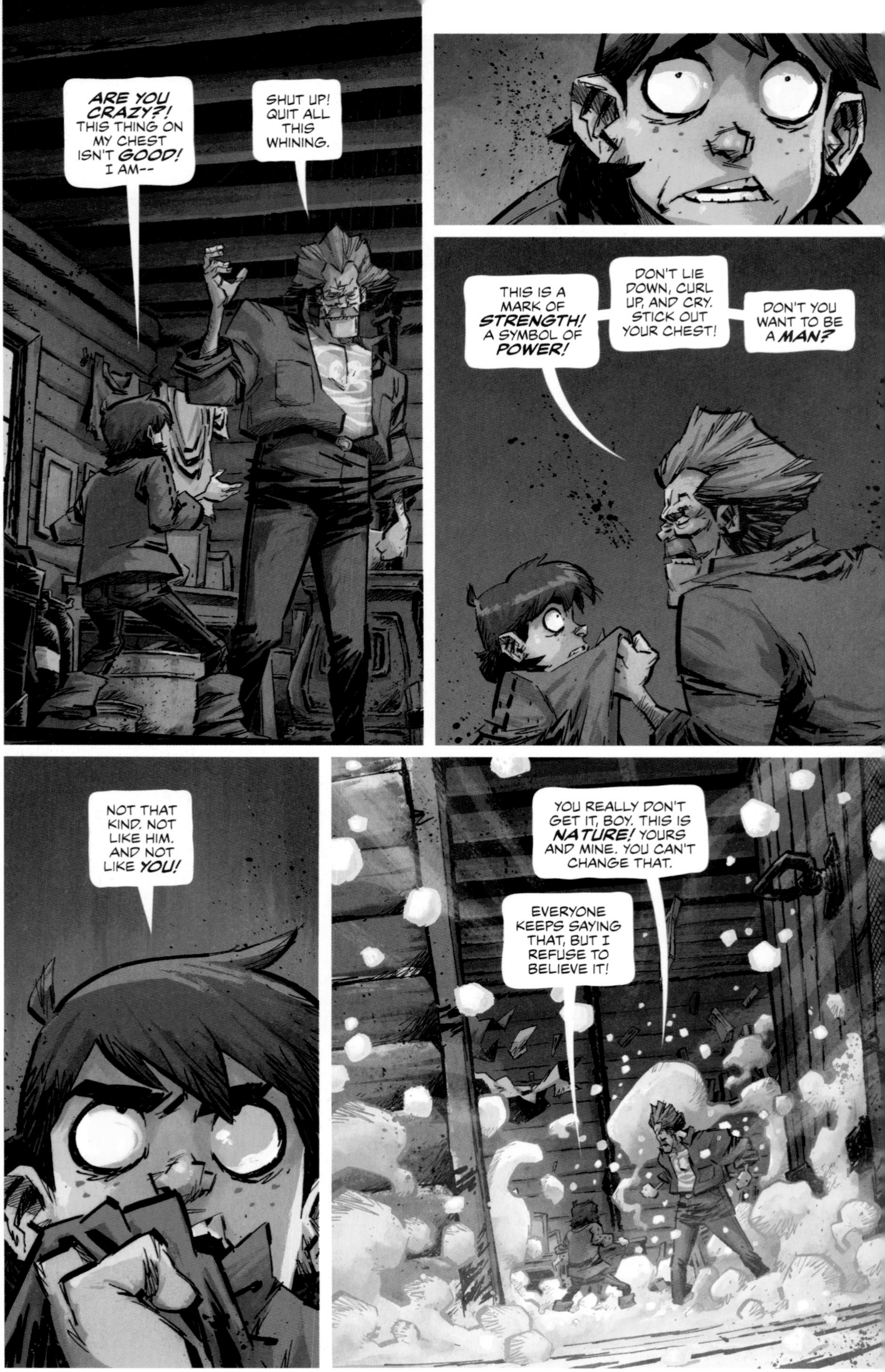

ARE YOU CRAZY?! THIS THING ON MY CHEST ISN'T *GOOD!* I AM--
SHUT UP! QUIT ALL THIS WHINING.
THIS IS A MARK OF *STRENGTH!* A SYMBOL OF *POWER!*
DON'T LIE DOWN, CURL UP, AND CRY. STICK OUT YOUR CHEST!
DON'T YOU WANT TO BE A *MAN?*
NOT THAT KIND. NOT LIKE HIM. AND NOT LIKE *YOU!*
YOU REALLY DON'T GET IT, BOY. THIS IS *NATURE!* YOURS AND MINE. YOU CAN'T CHANGE THAT.
EVERYONE KEEPS SAYING THAT, BUT I REFUSE TO BELIEVE IT!

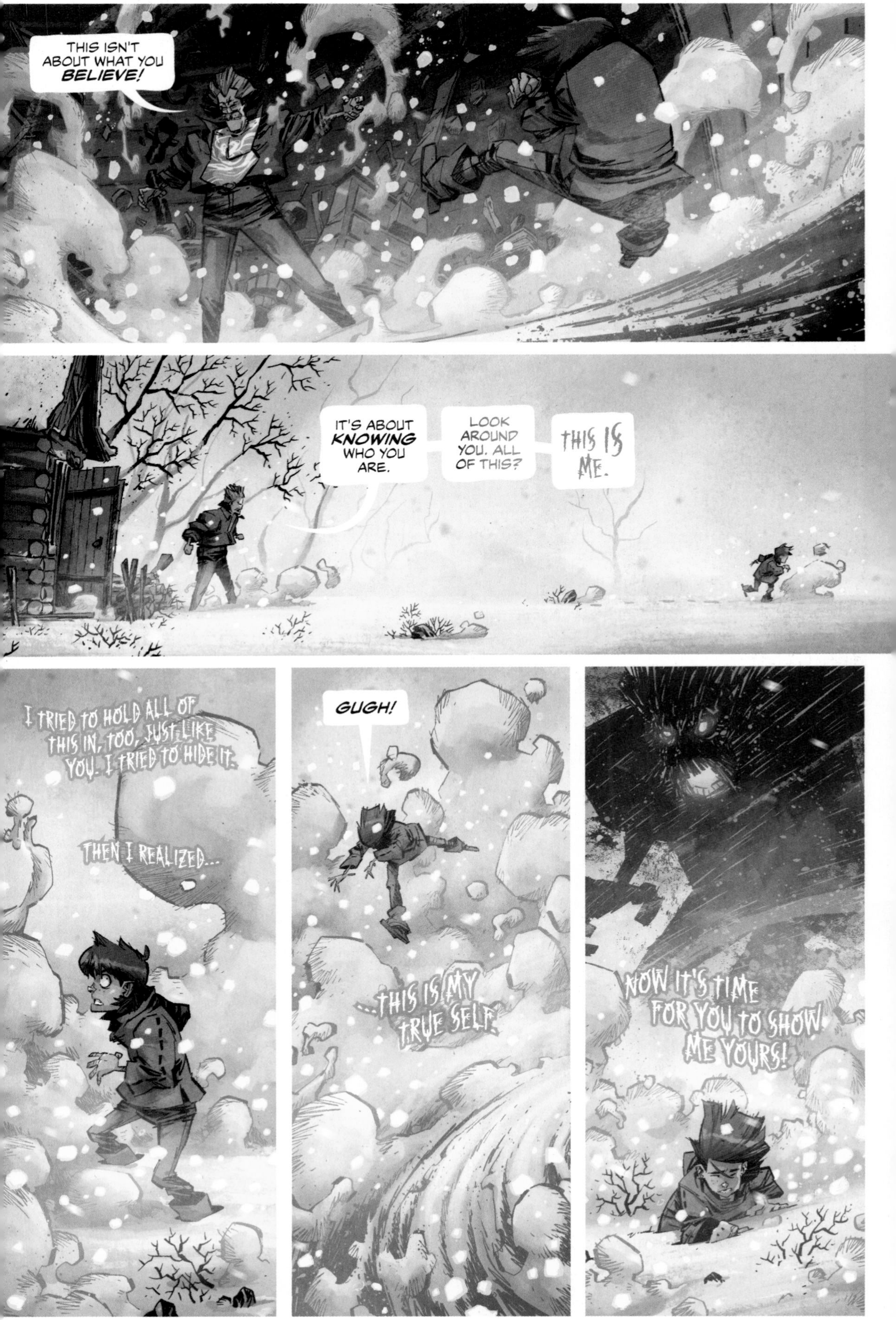
THIS ISN'T ABOUT WHAT YOU BELIEVE!
IT'S ABOUT KNOWING WHO YOU ARE.
LOOK AROUND YOU. ALL OF THIS?
THIS IS ME.
I TRIED TO HOLD ALL OF THIS IN, TOO, JUST LIKE YOU. I TRIED TO HIDE IT.
THEN I REALIZED...
GUGH!
...THIS IS MY TRUE SELF.
NOW IT'S TIME FOR YOU TO SHOW ME YOURS!

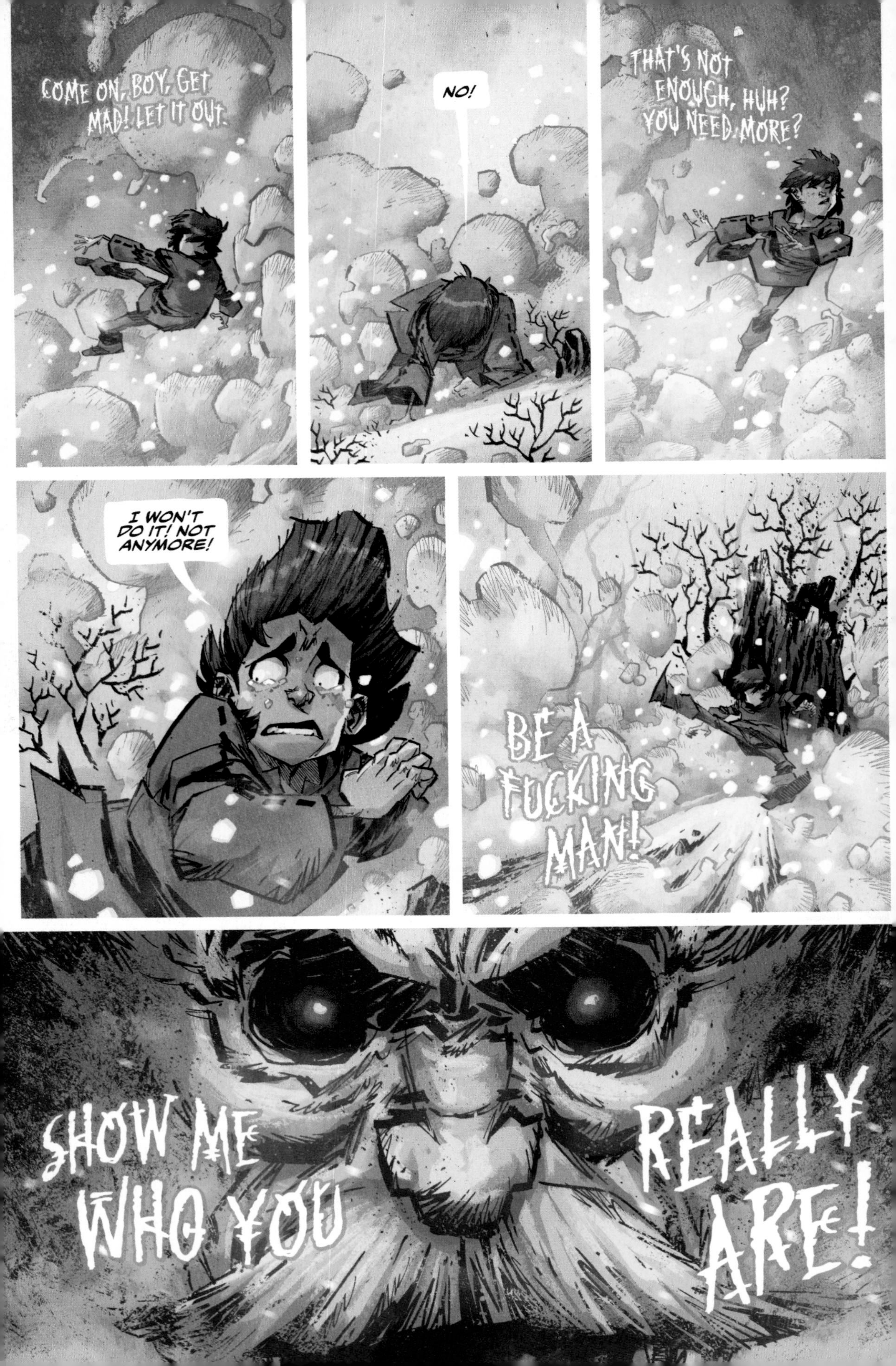
COME ON, BOY, GET MAD! LET IT OUT.
NO!
THAT'S NOT ENOUGH, HUH? YOU NEED MORE?
I WON'T DO IT! NOT ANYMORE!
BE A FUCKING MAN!
SHOW ME WHO YOU REALLY ARE!

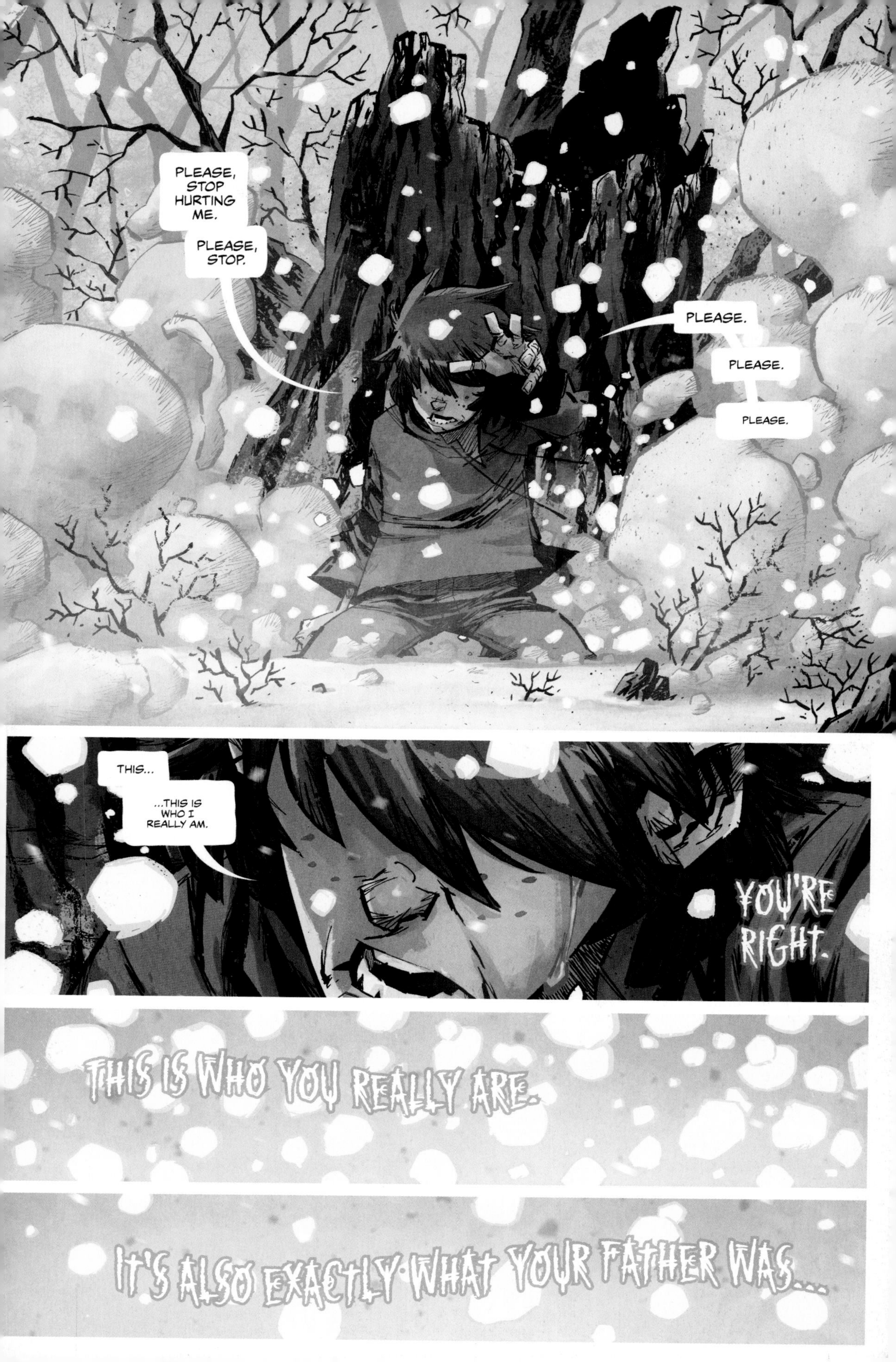
PLEASE, STOP HURTING ME.
PLEASE, STOP.
PLEASE.
PLEASE.
PLEASE.
THIS...
...THIS IS WHO I REALLY AM.
YOU'RE RIGHT.
THIS IS WHO YOU REALLY ARE.
IT'S ALSO EXACTLY WHAT YOUR FATHER WAS...

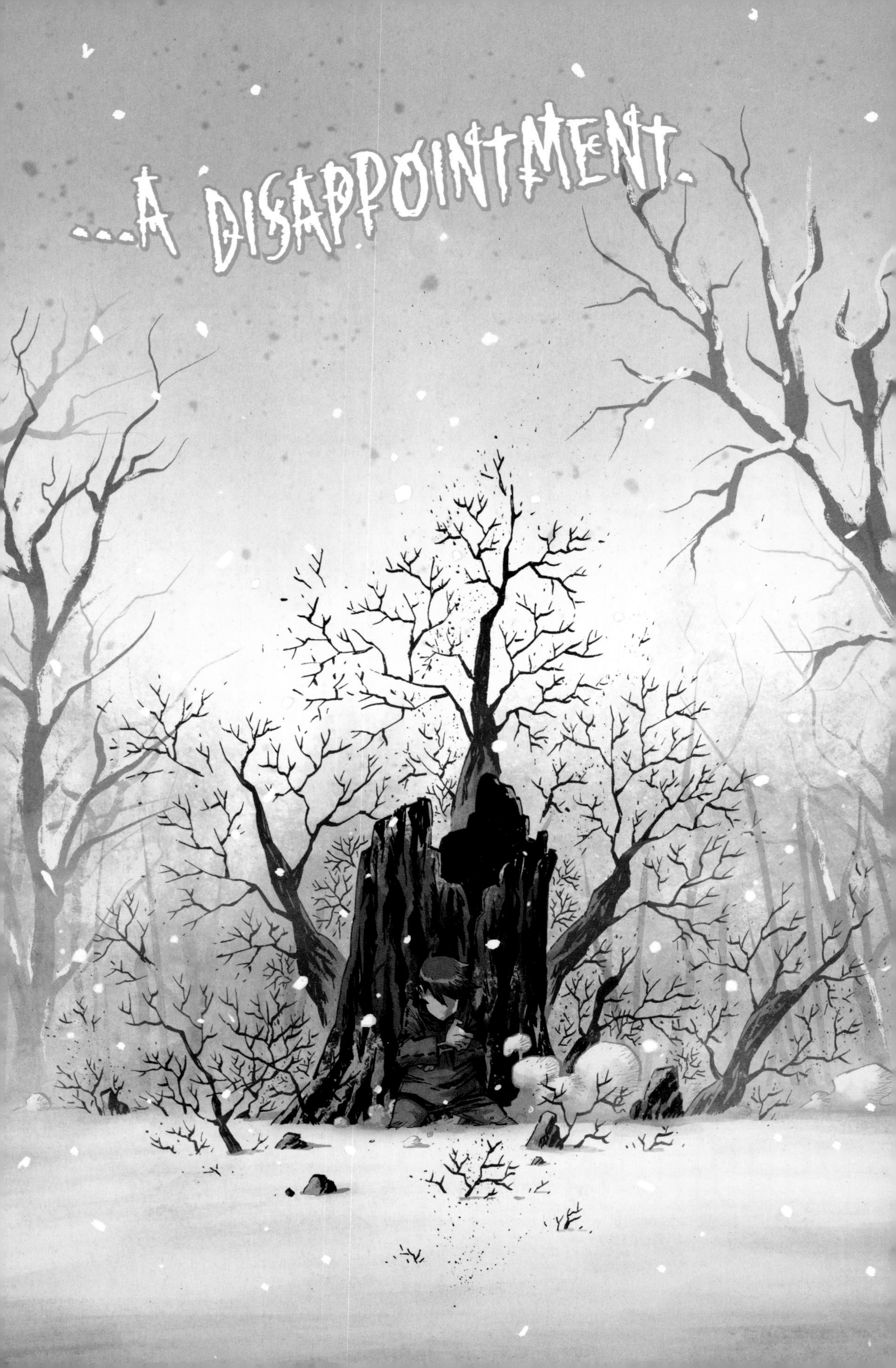
...A DISAPPOINTMENT.

CHAPTER
ELEVEN

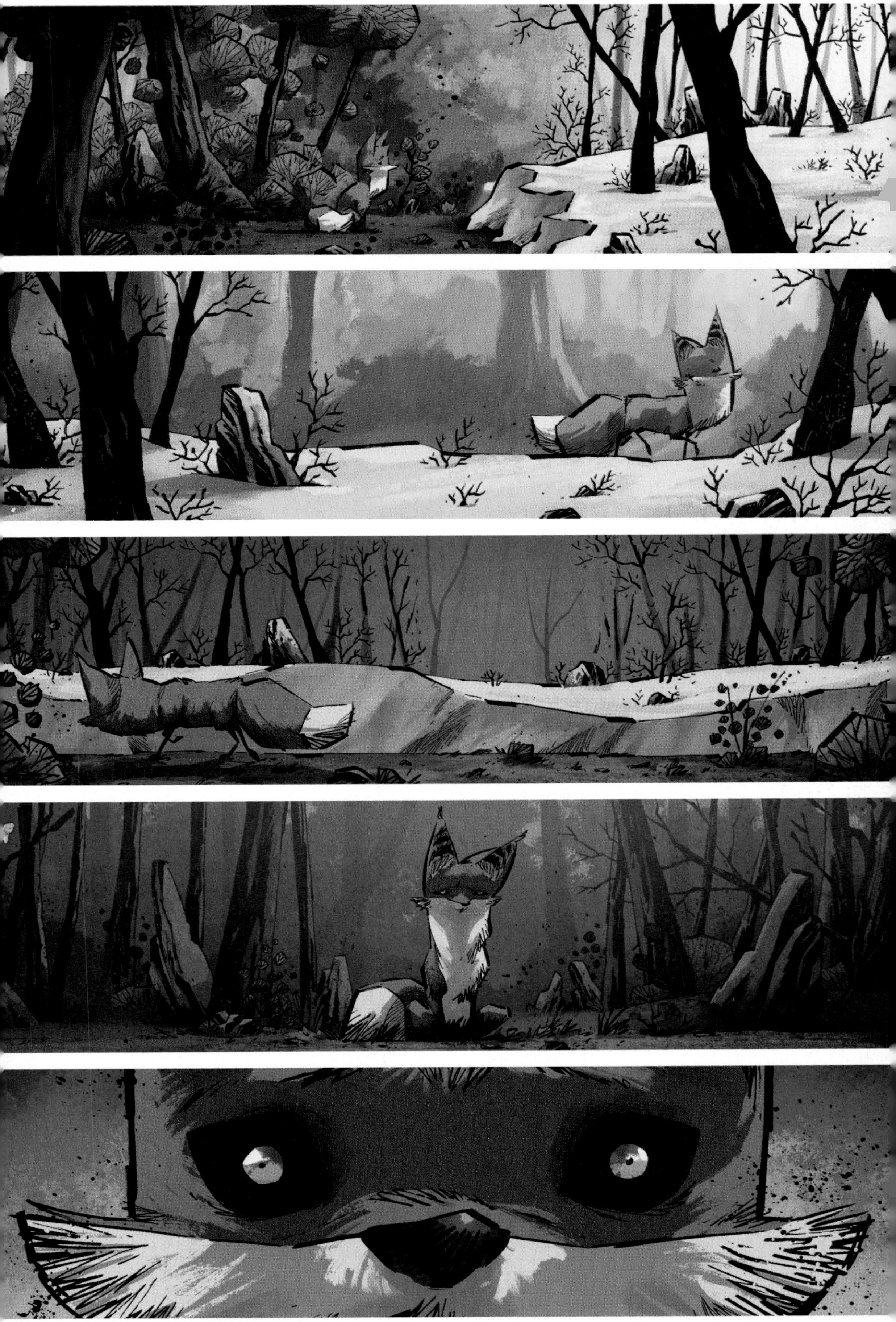

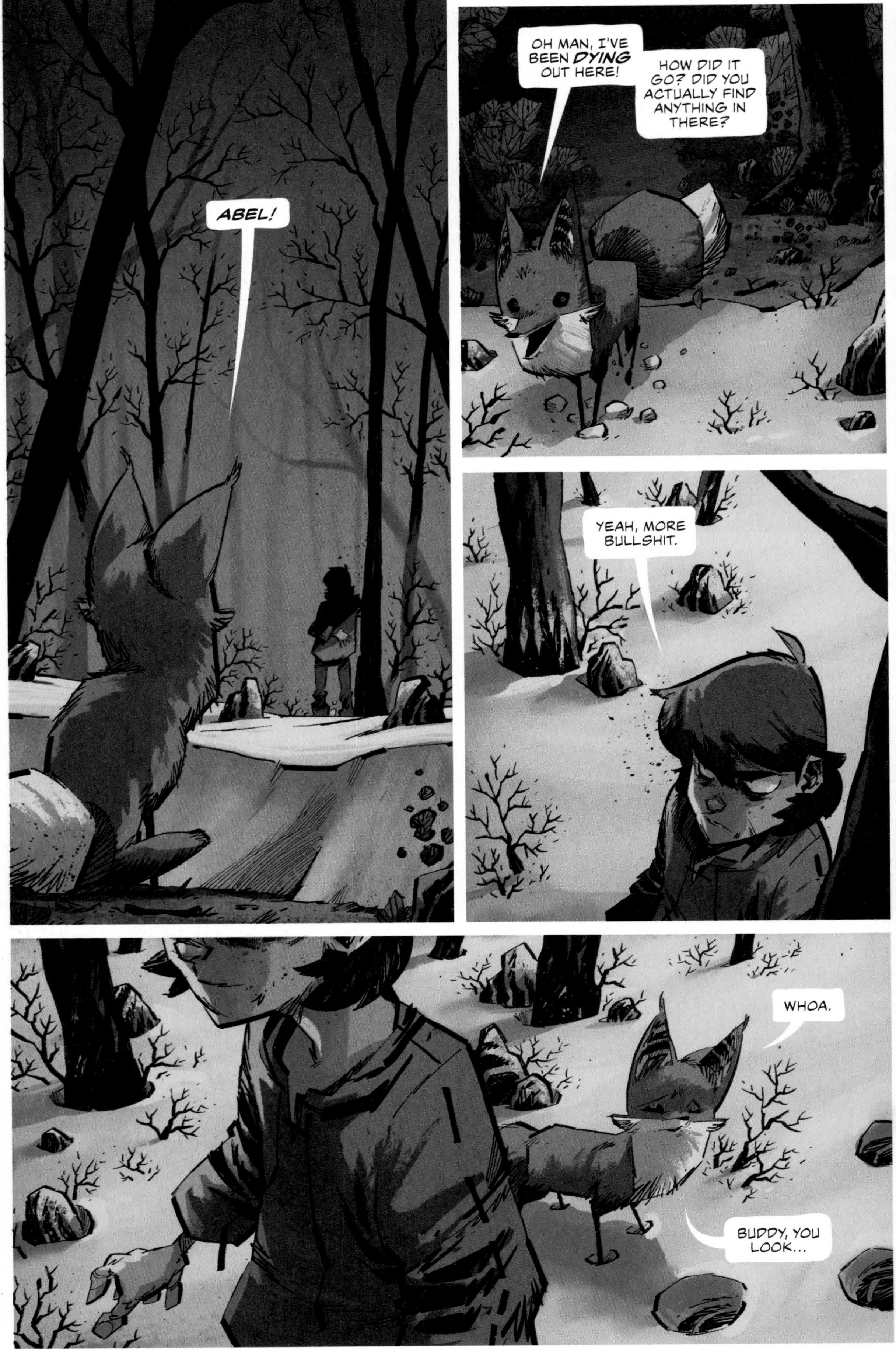
ABEL!
OH MAN, I'VE BEEN DYING OUT HERE!
HOW DID IT GO? DID YOU ACTUALLY FIND ANYTHING IN THERE?
YEAH, MORE BULLSHIT.
WHOA.
BUDDY, YOU LOOK...

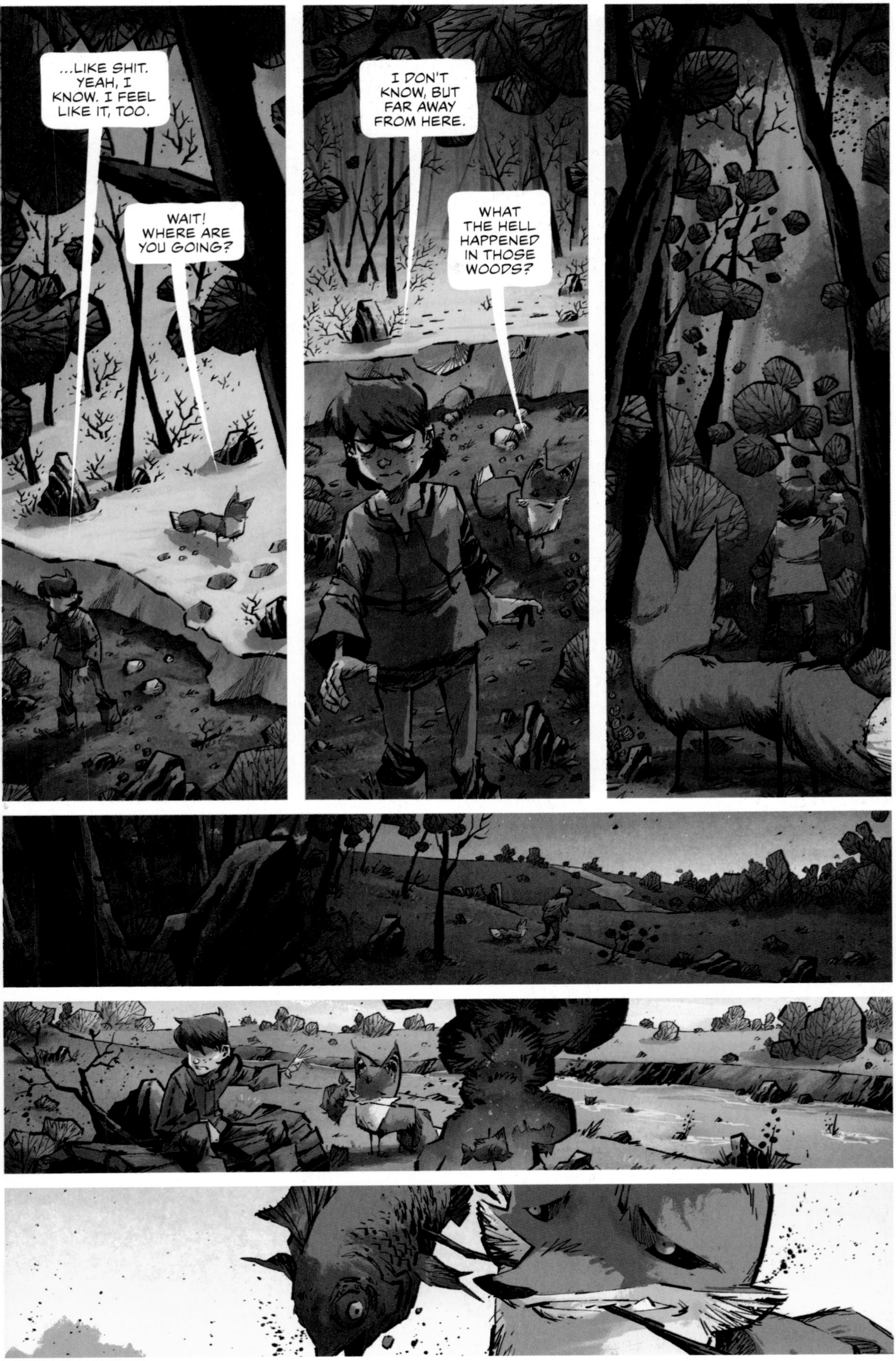

...LIKE SHIT. YEAH, I KNOW. I FEEL LIKE IT, TOO.
WAIT! WHERE ARE YOU GOING?
I DON'T KNOW, BUT FAR AWAY FROM HERE.
WHAT THE HELL HAPPENED IN THOSE WOODS?

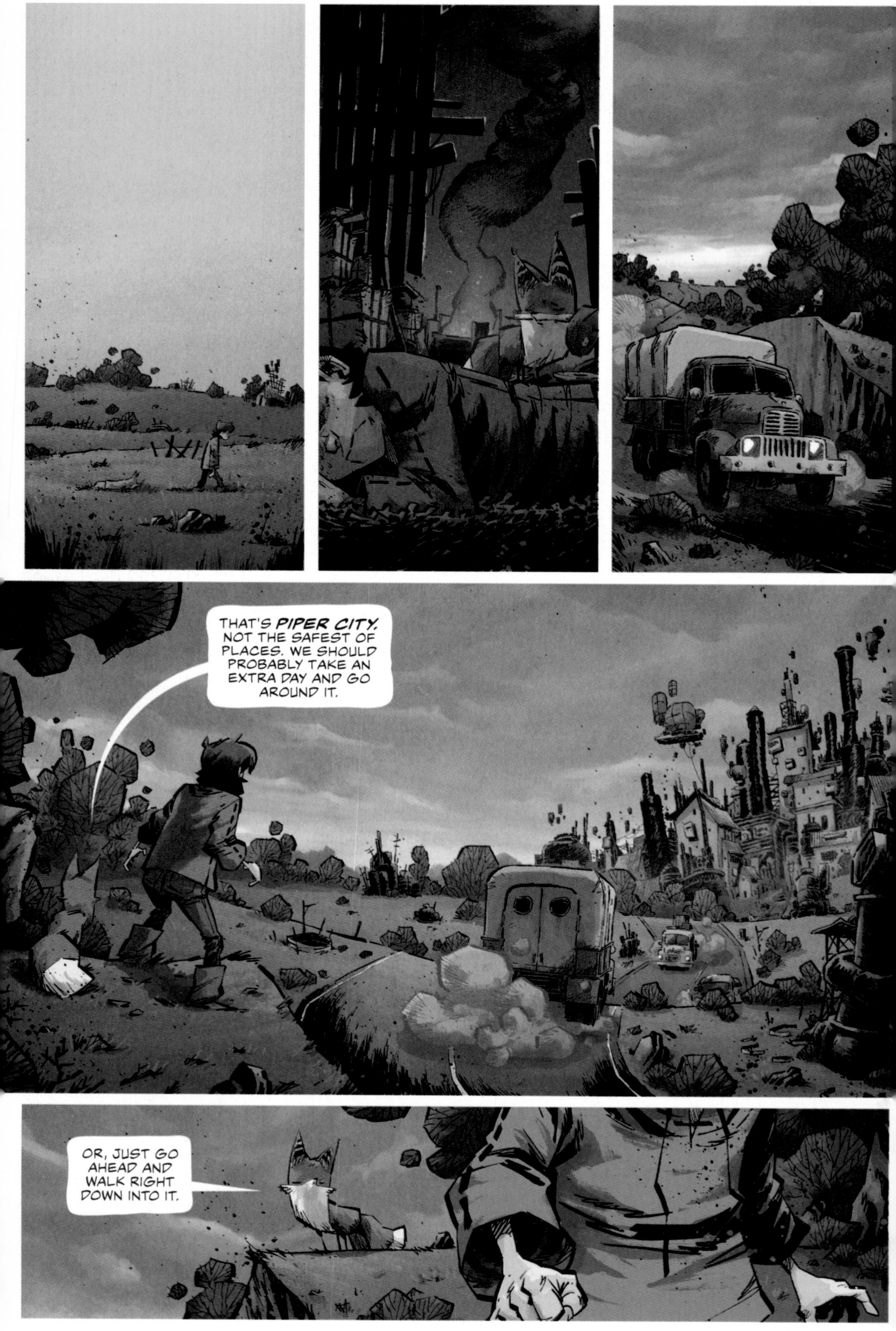
THAT'S PIPER CITY. NOT THE SAFEST OF PLACES. WE SHOULD PROBABLY TAKE AN EXTRA DAY AND GO AROUND IT.
OR, JUST GO AHEAD AND WALK RIGHT DOWN INTO IT.

IT'S SAD WHAT THIS PLACE HAS BECOME. THIS USED TO BE *THE* CITY TO COME TO, LIVE IN, AND EXPERIENCE.

THEN, *CENTIPEDE CORP* DECIDED TO PACK UP, LEAVE TOWN, AND TAKE EVERY JOB THIS PLACE HAD WITH IT.

NOW IT'S JUST A RUSTY OLD CORPSE.

BUT, THERE'S AN UPSIDE FOR US: HARD TIMES OR NOT...

...PEOPLE IN CITIES THROW OUT THE BEST FOOD!

PIZZA?

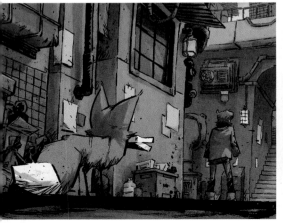

OH, COME ON!

WHAT THE HELL IS GOING ON WITH YOU?

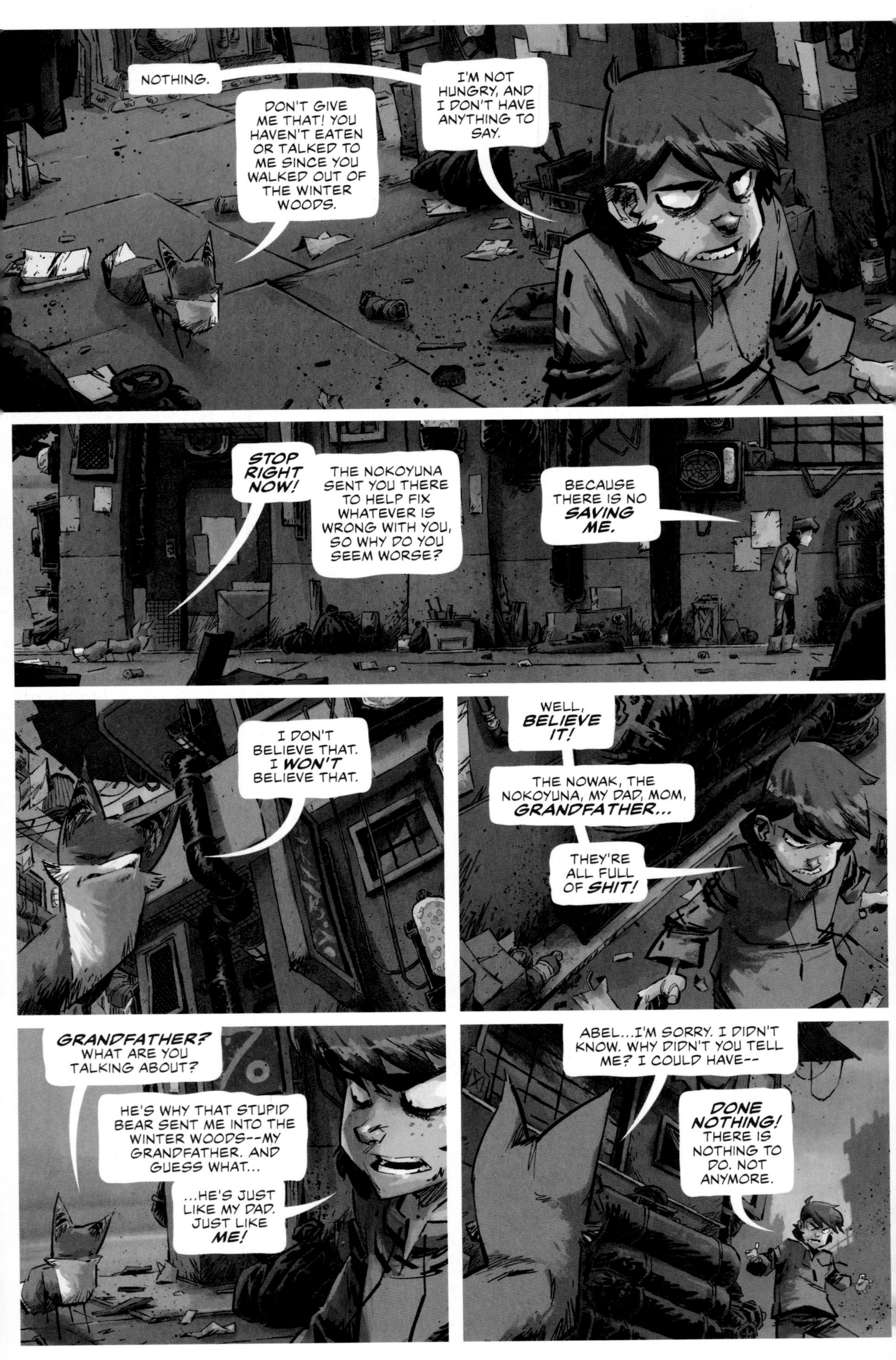
I'M NOT HUNGRY, AND I DON'T HAVE ANYTHING TO SAY.
NOTHING.
DON'T GIVE ME THAT! YOU HAVEN'T EATEN OR TALKED TO ME SINCE YOU WALKED OUT OF THE WINTER WOODS.
STOP RIGHT NOW!
THE NOKOYUNA SENT YOU THERE TO HELP FIX WHATEVER IS WRONG WITH YOU, SO WHY DO YOU SEEM WORSE?
BECAUSE THERE IS NO SAVING ME.
I DON'T BELIEVE THAT. I WON'T BELIEVE THAT.
WELL, BELIEVE IT!
THE NOWAK, THE NOKOYUNA, MY DAD, MOM, GRANDFATHER...
THEY'RE ALL FULL OF SHIT!
GRANDFATHER? WHAT ARE YOU TALKING ABOUT?
HE'S WHY THAT STUPID BEAR SENT ME INTO THE WINTER WOODS--MY GRANDFATHER. AND GUESS WHAT...
...HE'S JUST LIKE MY DAD. JUST LIKE ME!
ABEL...I'M SORRY. I DIDN'T KNOW. WHY DIDN'T YOU TELL ME? I COULD HAVE--
DONE NOTHING! THERE IS NOTHING TO DO. NOT ANYMORE.

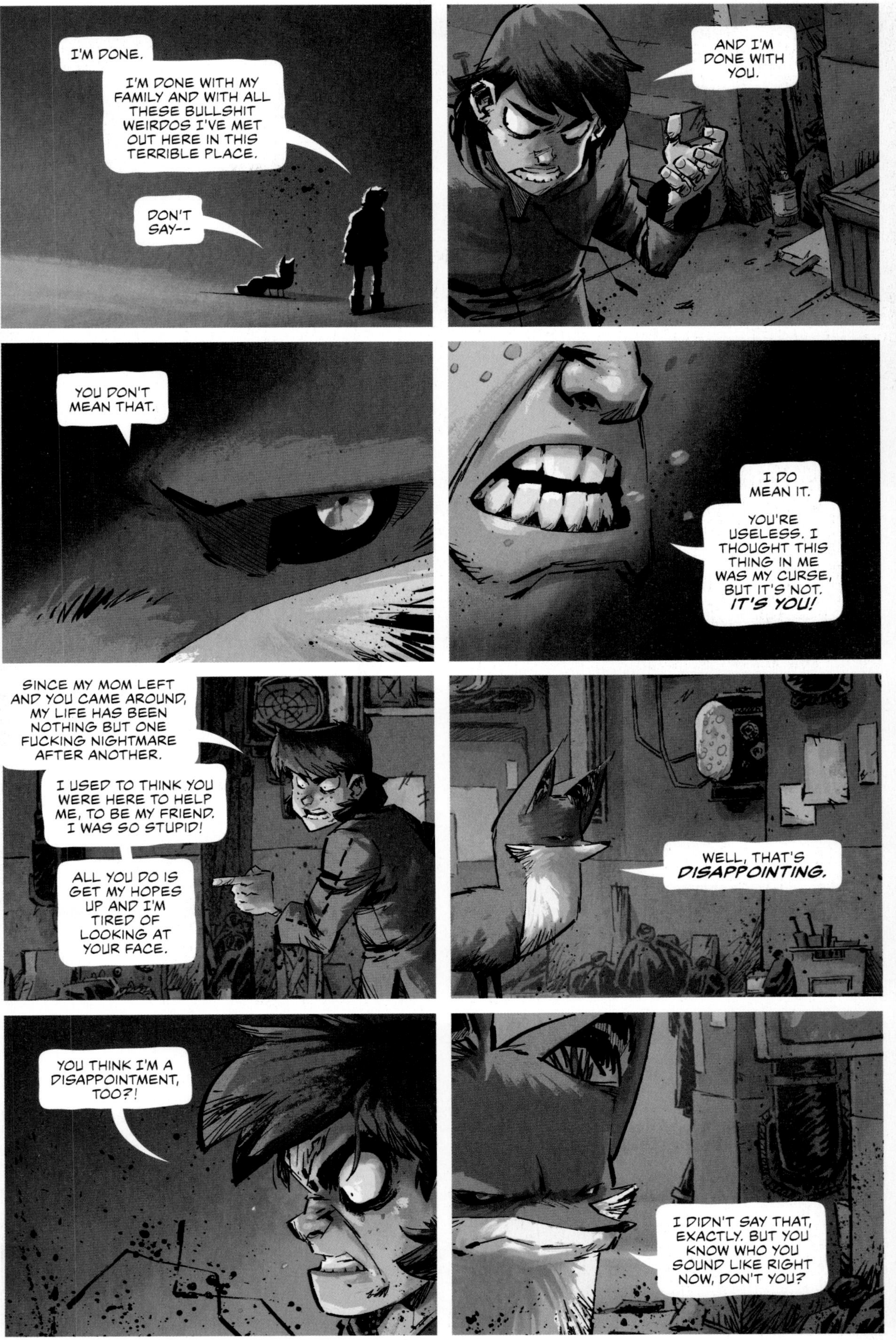
I'M DONE.
I'M DONE WITH MY FAMILY AND WITH ALL THESE BULLSHIT WEIRDOS I'VE MET OUT HERE IN THIS TERRIBLE PLACE.
DON'T SAY--
AND I'M DONE WITH YOU.
YOU DON'T MEAN THAT.
I DO MEAN IT.
YOU'RE USELESS. I THOUGHT THIS THING IN ME WAS MY CURSE, BUT IT'S NOT. IT'S YOU!
SINCE MY MOM LEFT AND YOU CAME AROUND, MY LIFE HAS BEEN NOTHING BUT ONE FUCKING NIGHTMARE AFTER ANOTHER.
I USED TO THINK YOU WERE HERE TO HELP ME, TO BE MY FRIEND. I WAS SO STUPID!
ALL YOU DO IS GET MY HOPES UP AND I'M TIRED OF LOOKING AT YOUR FACE.
WELL, THAT'S DISAPPOINTING.
YOU THINK I'M A DISAPPOINTMENT, TOO?!
I DIDN'T SAY THAT, EXACTLY. BUT YOU KNOW WHO YOU SOUND LIKE RIGHT NOW, DON'T YOU?

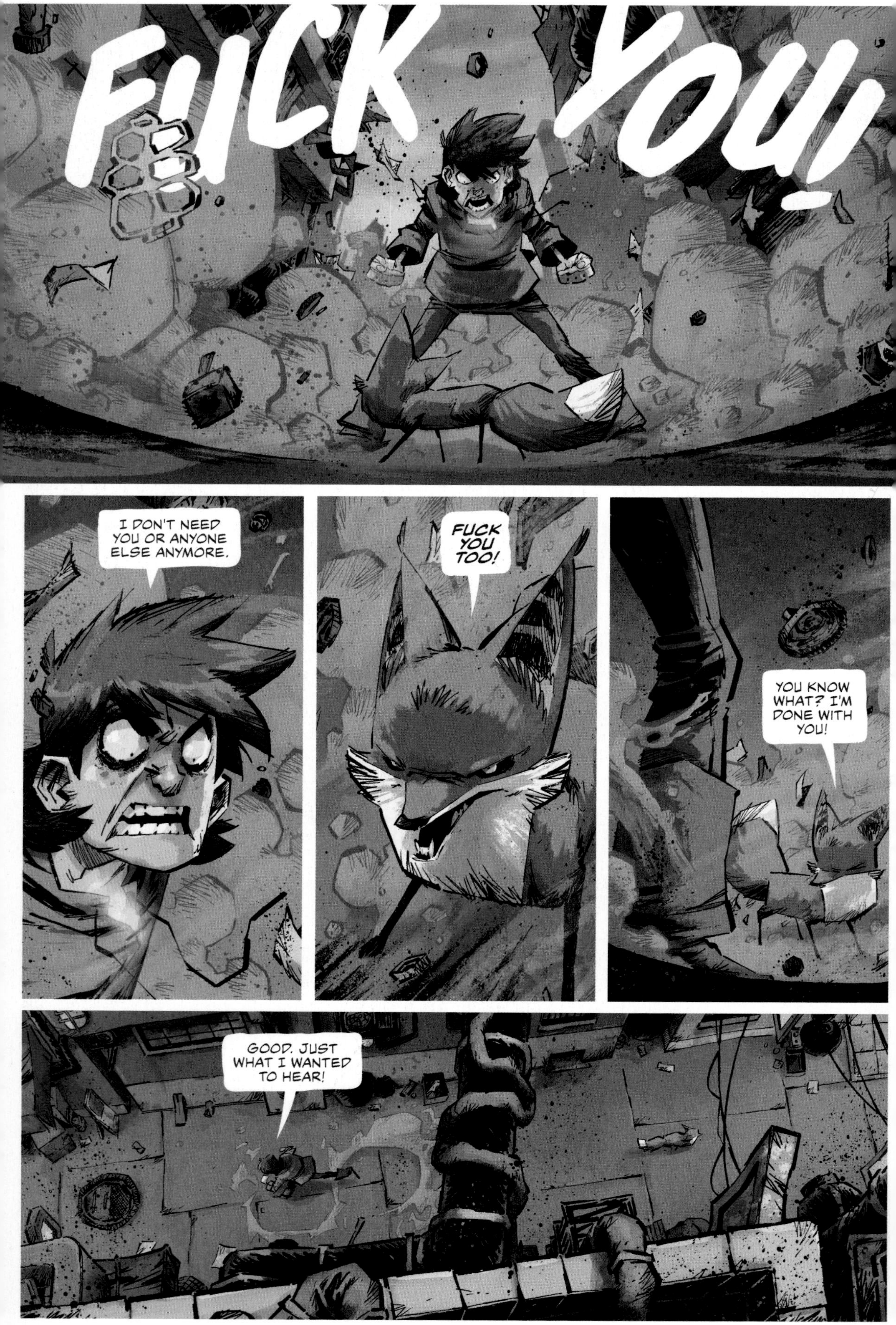
FUCK YOU!
I DON'T NEED YOU OR ANYONE ELSE ANYMORE.
FUCK YOU TOO!
YOU KNOW WHAT? I'M DONE WITH YOU!
GOOD. JUST WHAT I WANTED TO HEAR!

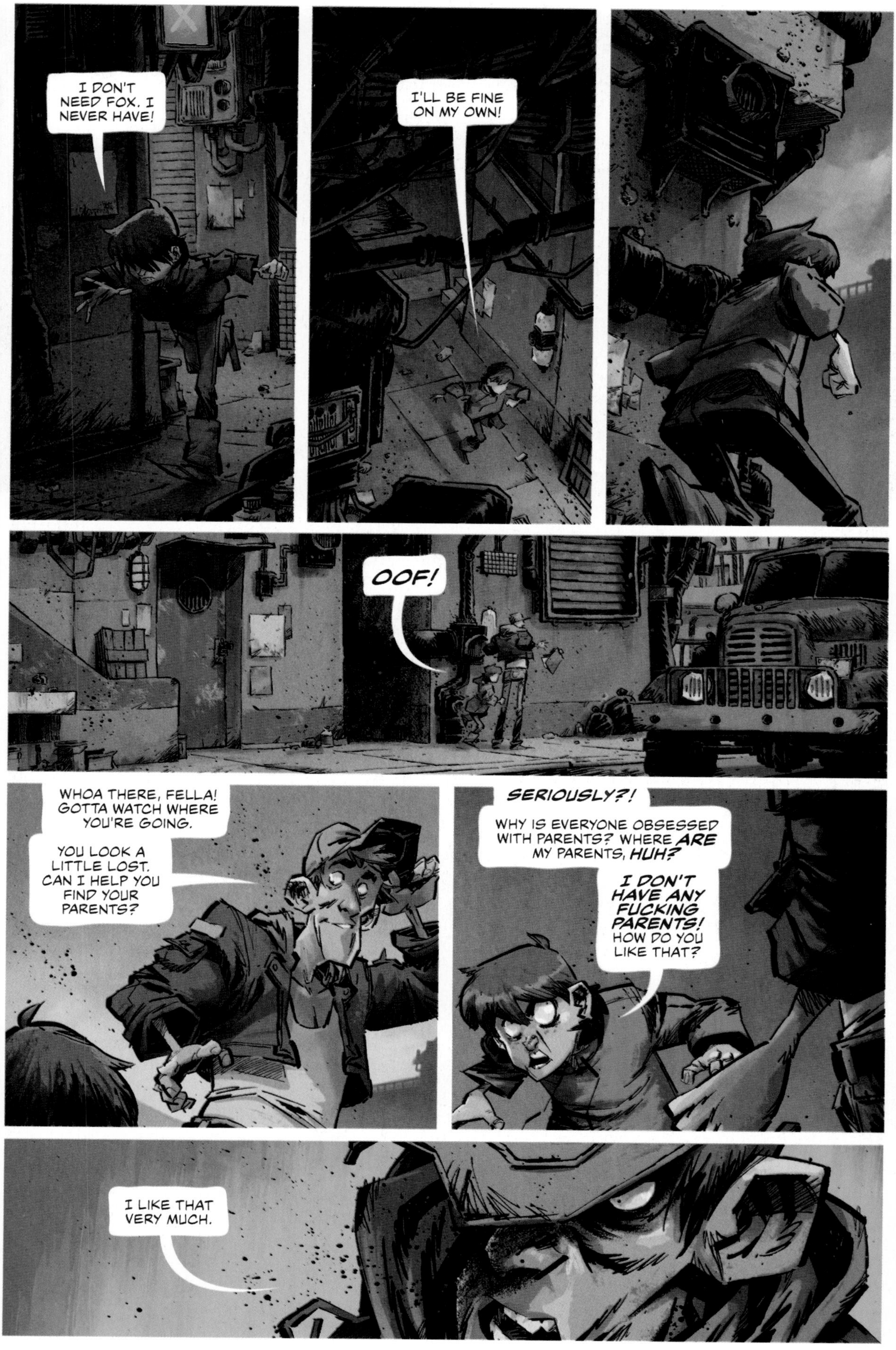
I DON'T NEED FOX. I NEVER HAVE!
I'LL BE FINE ON MY OWN!
OOF!
WHOA THERE, FELLA! GOTTA WATCH WHERE YOU'RE GOING.
YOU LOOK A LITTLE LOST. CAN I HELP YOU FIND YOUR PARENTS?
SERIOUSLY?!
WHY IS EVERYONE OBSESSED WITH PARENTS? WHERE ARE MY PARENTS, HUH?
I DON'T HAVE ANY FUCKING PARENTS! HOW DO YOU LIKE THAT?
I LIKE THAT VERY MUCH.

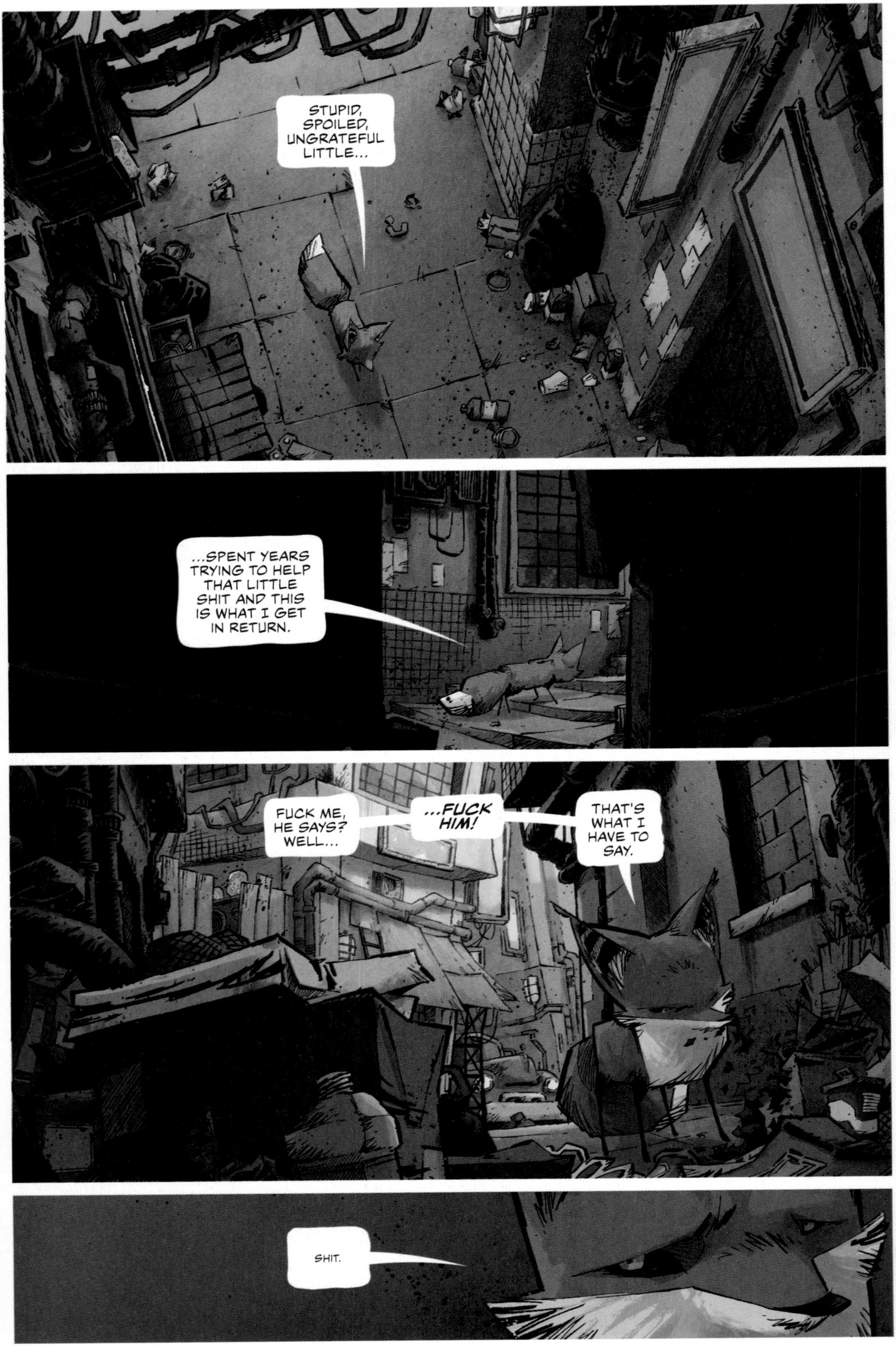
STUPID, SPOILED, UNGRATEFUL LITTLE...
...SPENT YEARS TRYING TO HELP THAT LITTLE SHIT AND THIS IS WHAT I GET IN RETURN.
FUCK ME, HE SAYS? WELL...
...FUCK HIM!
THAT'S WHAT I HAVE TO SAY.
SHIT.

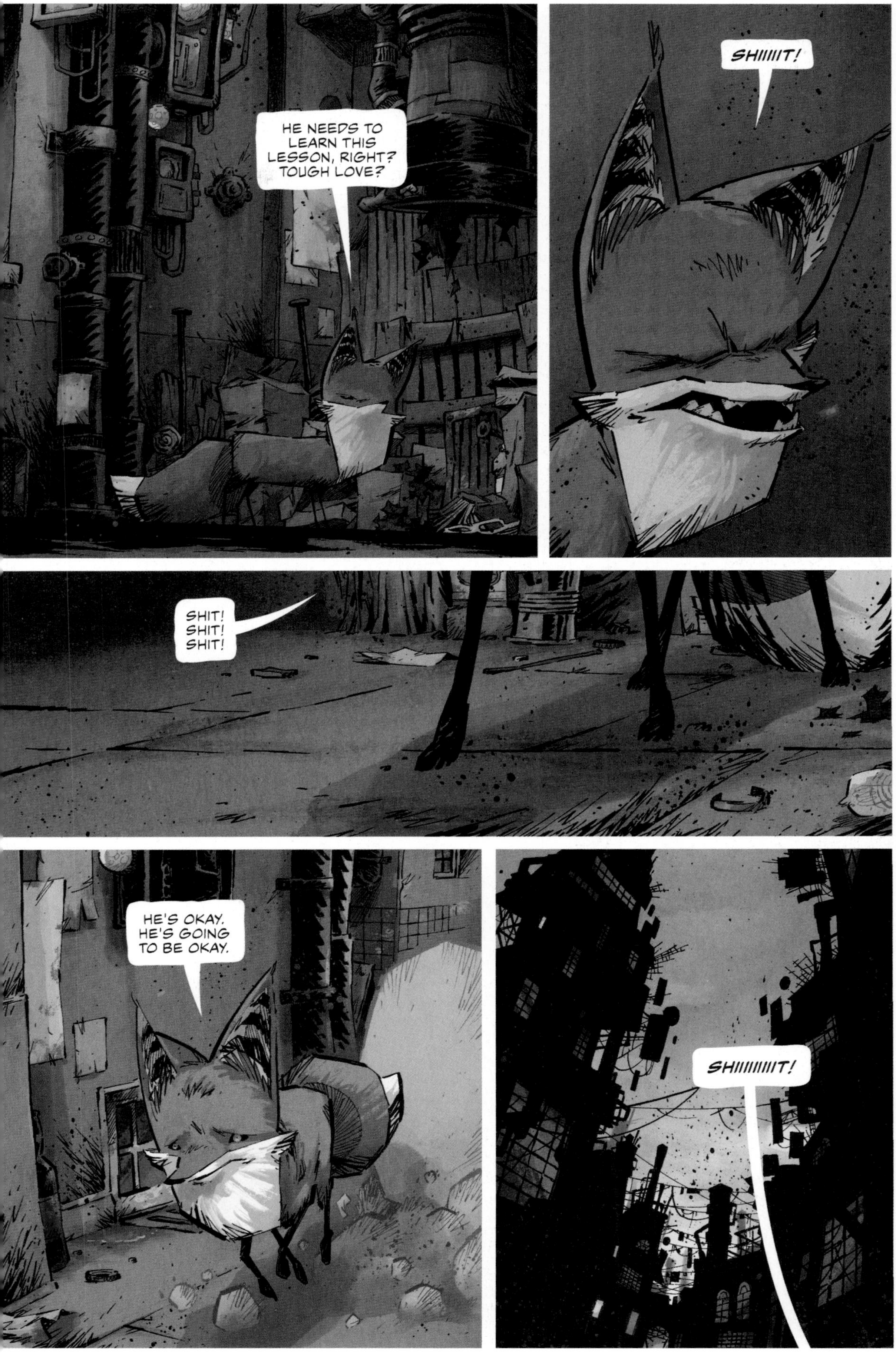
HE NEEDS TO LEARN THIS LESSON, RIGHT? TOUGH LOVE?
SHIIIIT!
SHIT! SHIT! SHIT!
HE'S OKAY. HE'S GOING TO BE OKAY.
SHIIIIIIIIT!

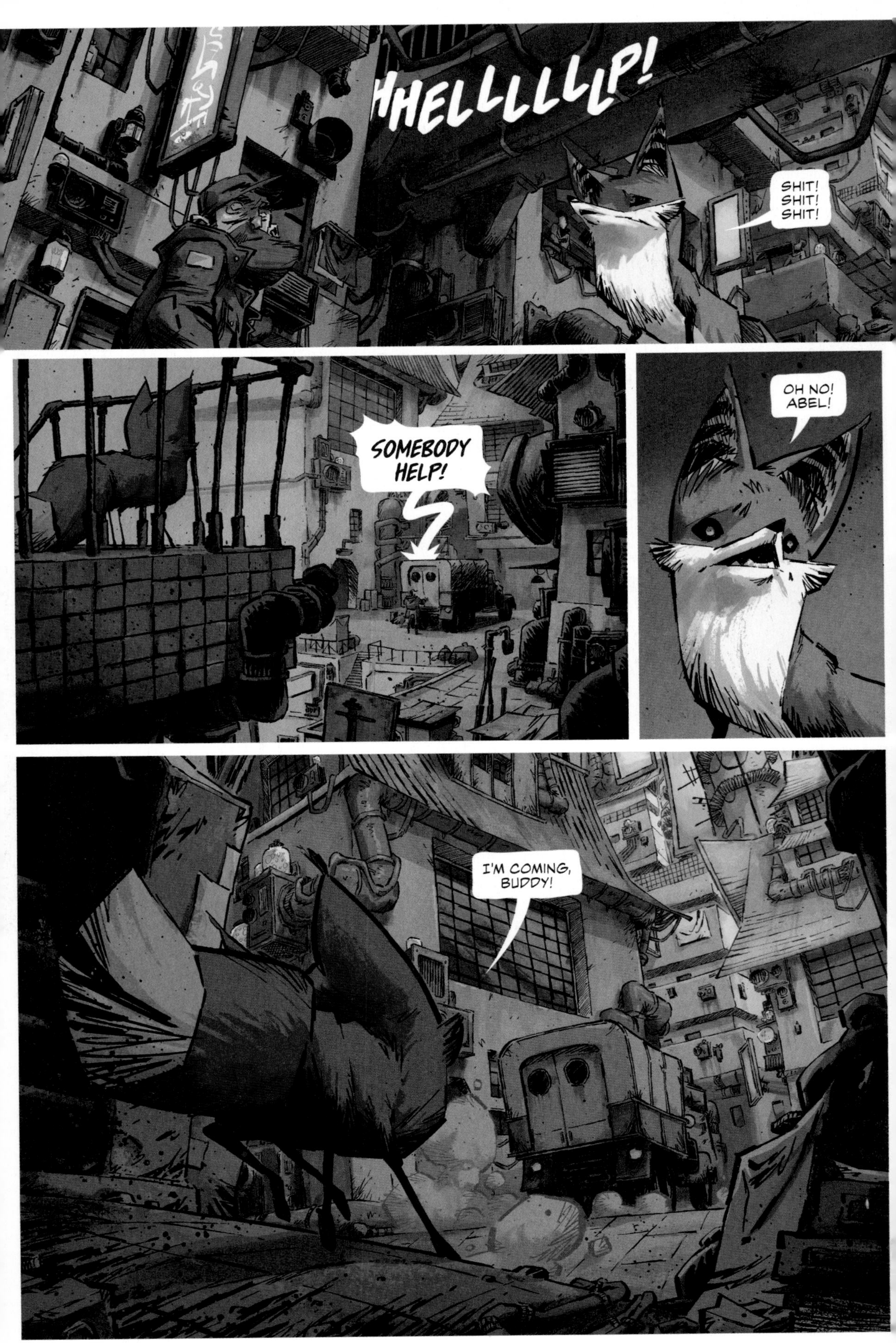
HHELLLLLLP!
SHIT! SHIT! SHIT!
SOMEBODY HELP!
OH NO! ABEL!
I'M COMING, BUDDY!

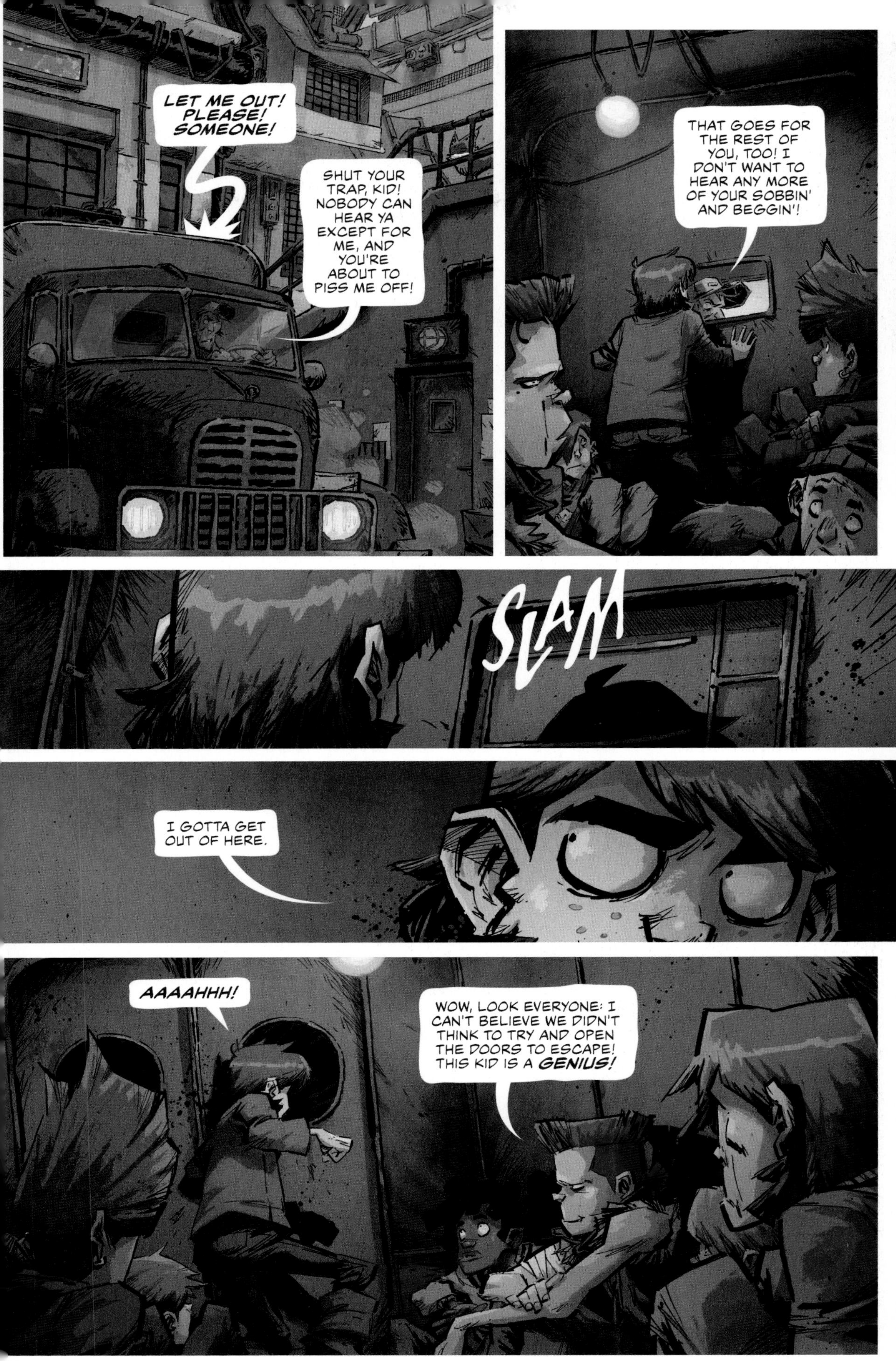
LET ME OUT! PLEASE! SOMEONE!
SHUT YOUR TRAP, KID! NOBODY CAN HEAR YA EXCEPT FOR ME, AND YOU'RE ABOUT TO PISS ME OFF!
THAT GOES FOR THE REST OF YOU, TOO! I DON'T WANT TO HEAR ANY MORE OF YOUR SOBBIN' AND BEGGIN'!
SLAM
I GOTTA GET OUT OF HERE.
AAAAHHH!
WOW, LOOK EVERYONE: I CAN'T BELIEVE WE DIDN'T THINK TO TRY AND OPEN THE DOORS TO ESCAPE! THIS KID IS A GENIUS!

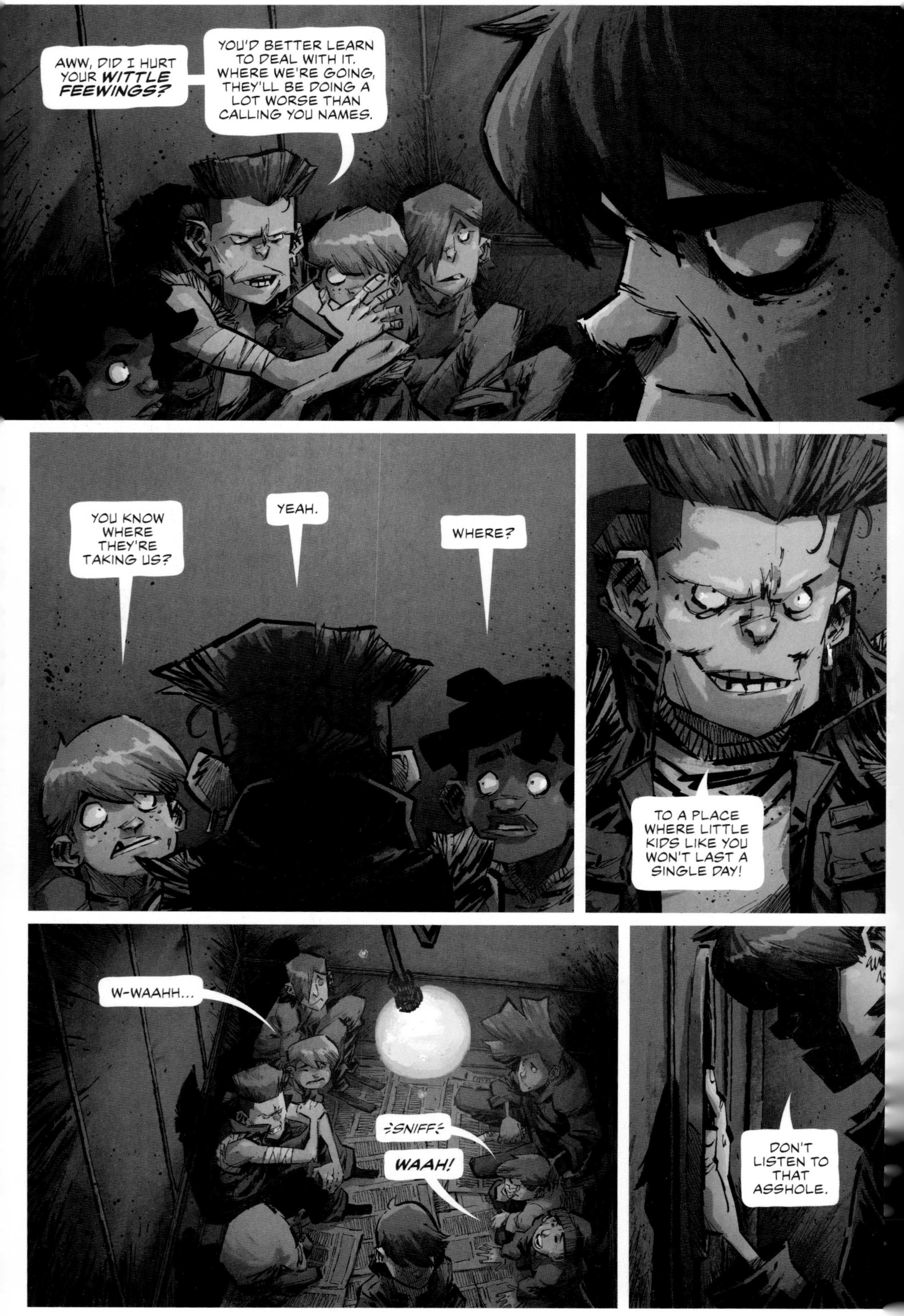
AWW, DID I HURT YOUR *WITTLE FEEWINGS?*
YOU'D BETTER LEARN TO DEAL WITH IT. WHERE WE'RE GOING, THEY'LL BE DOING A LOT WORSE THAN CALLING YOU NAMES.
YOU KNOW WHERE THEY'RE TAKING US?
YEAH.
WHERE?
TO A PLACE WHERE LITTLE KIDS LIKE YOU WON'T LAST A SINGLE DAY!
W-WAAHH...
SNIFF
WAAH!
DON'T LISTEN TO THAT ASSHOLE.

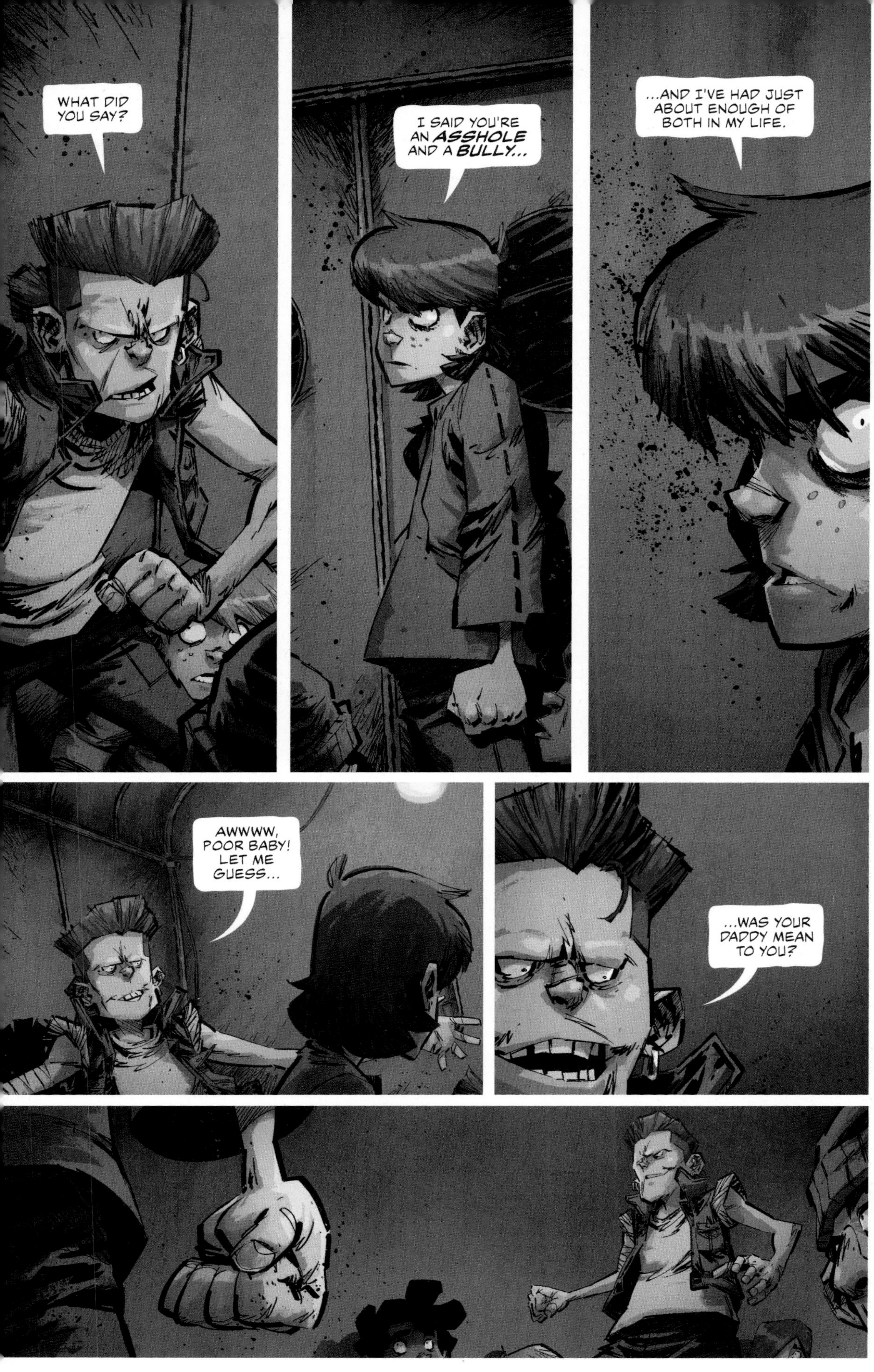
WHAT DID YOU SAY?
I SAID YOU'RE AN ASSHOLE AND A BULLY...
...AND I'VE HAD JUST ABOUT ENOUGH OF BOTH IN MY LIFE.
AWWWW, POOR BABY! LET ME GUESS...
...WAS YOUR DADDY MEAN TO YOU?

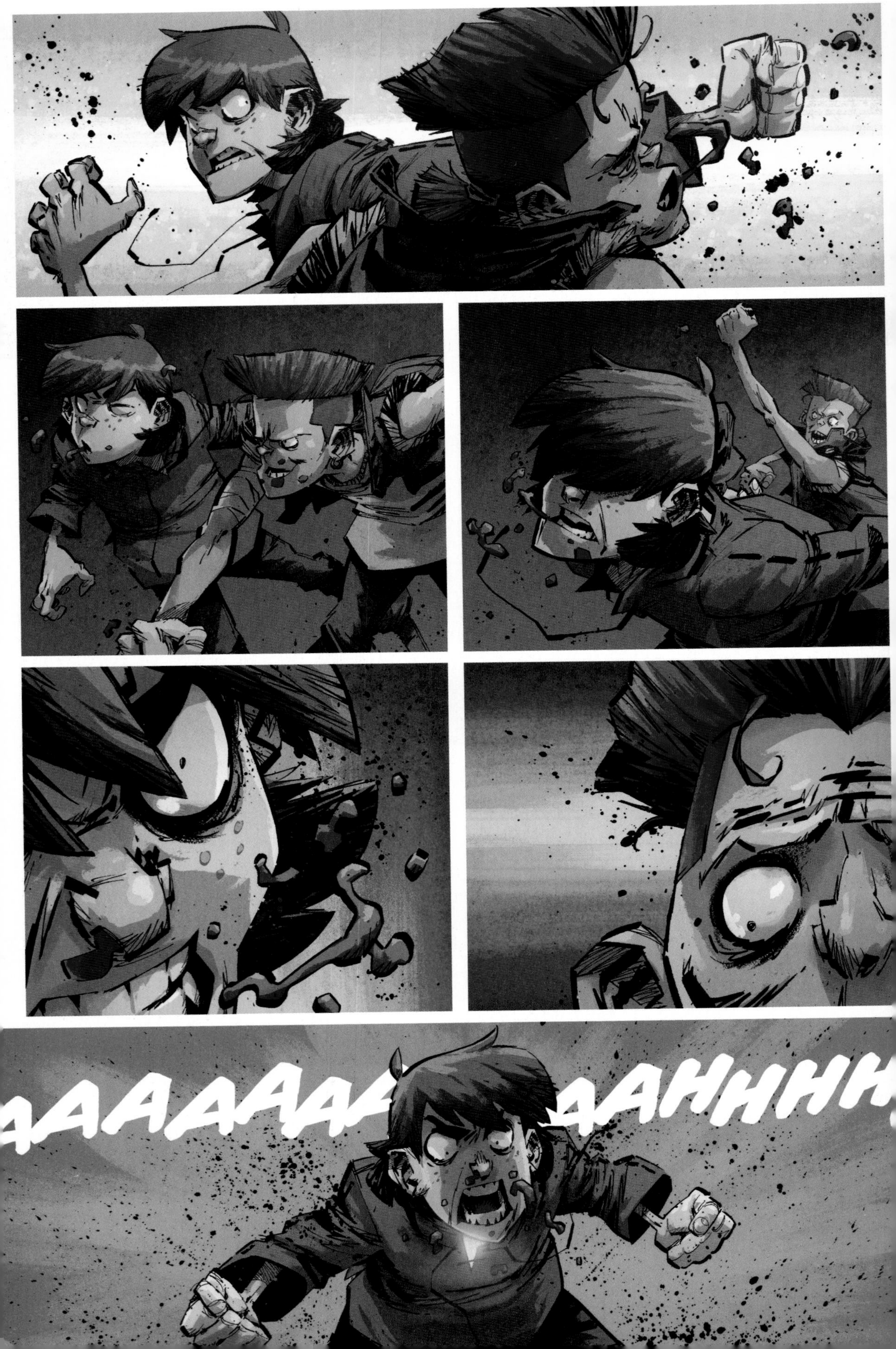
AAAAAA
AAHHHH

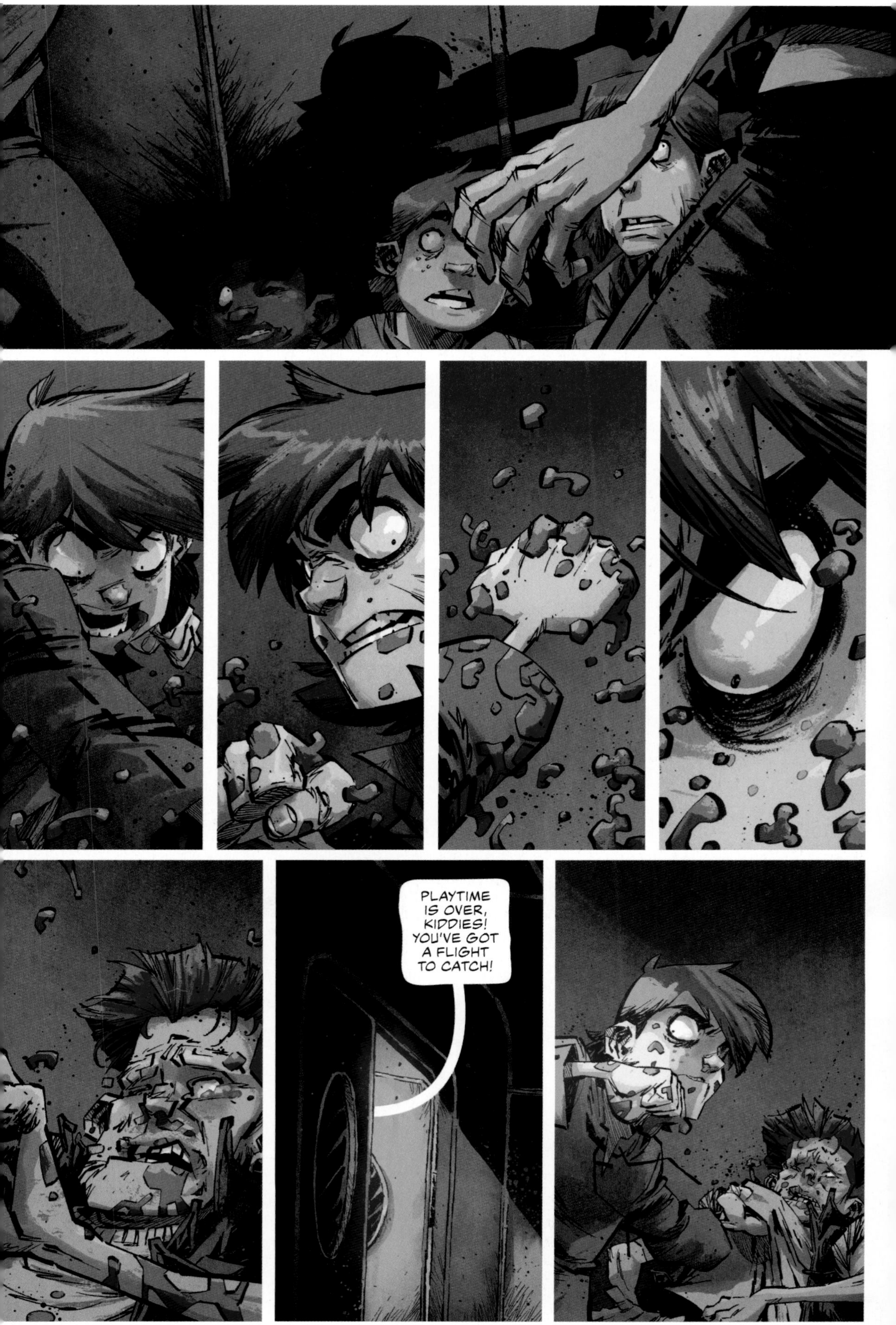
PLAYTIME IS OVER, KIDDIES! YOU'VE GOT A FLIGHT TO CATCH!

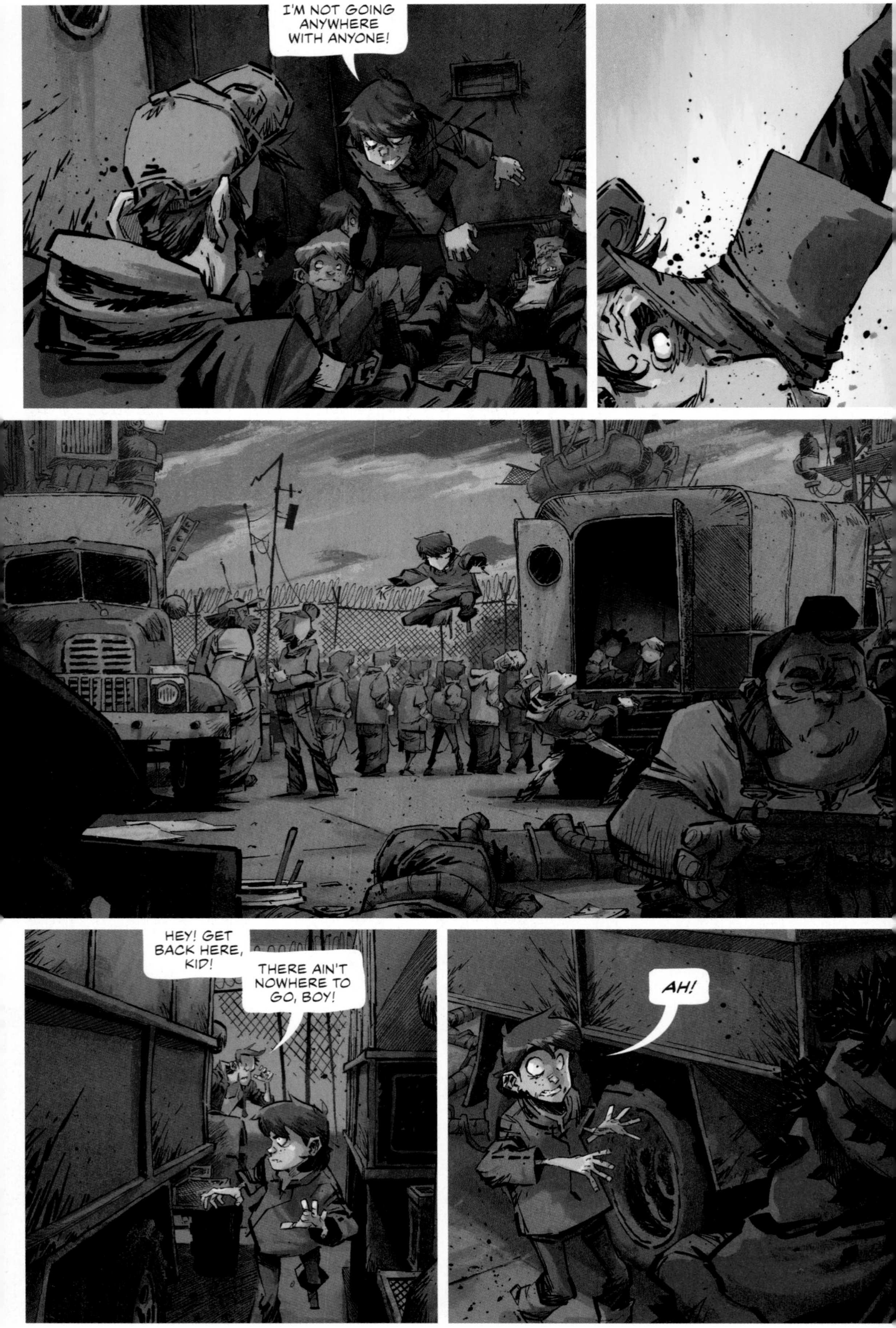
I'M NOT GOING ANYWHERE WITH ANYONE!
HEY! GET BACK HERE, KID!
THERE AIN'T NOWHERE TO GO, BOY!
AH!

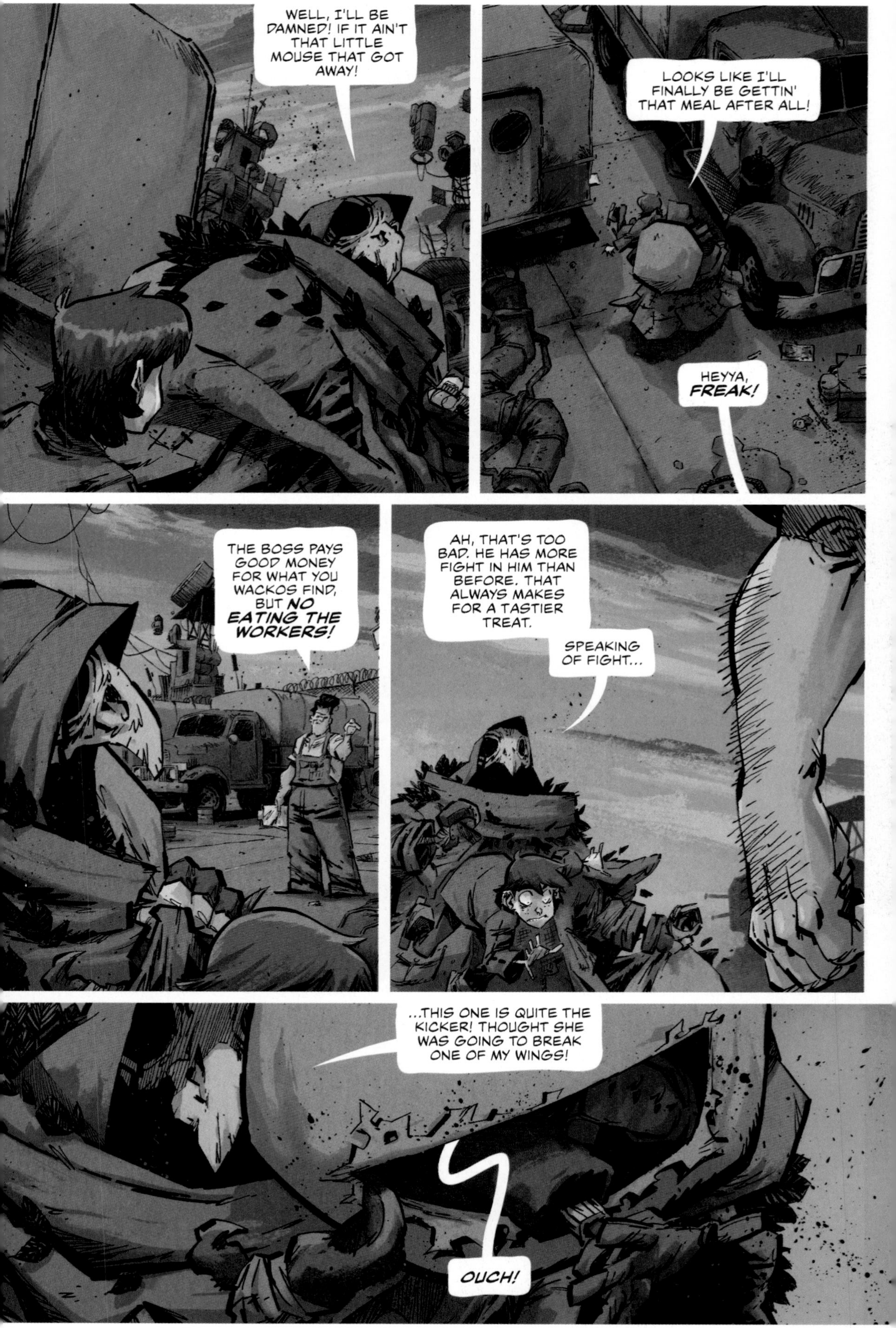

WELL, I'LL BE DAMNED! IF IT AIN'T THAT LITTLE MOUSE THAT GOT AWAY!
LOOKS LIKE I'LL FINALLY BE GETTIN' THAT MEAL AFTER ALL!
HEYYA, **FREAK!**
THE BOSS PAYS GOOD MONEY FOR WHAT YOU WACKOS FIND, BUT **NO EATING THE WORKERS!**
AH, THAT'S TOO BAD. HE HAS MORE FIGHT IN HIM THAN BEFORE. THAT ALWAYS MAKES FOR A TASTIER TREAT.
SPEAKING OF FIGHT...
...THIS ONE IS QUITE THE KICKER! THOUGHT SHE WAS GOING TO BREAK ONE OF MY WINGS!
OUCH!

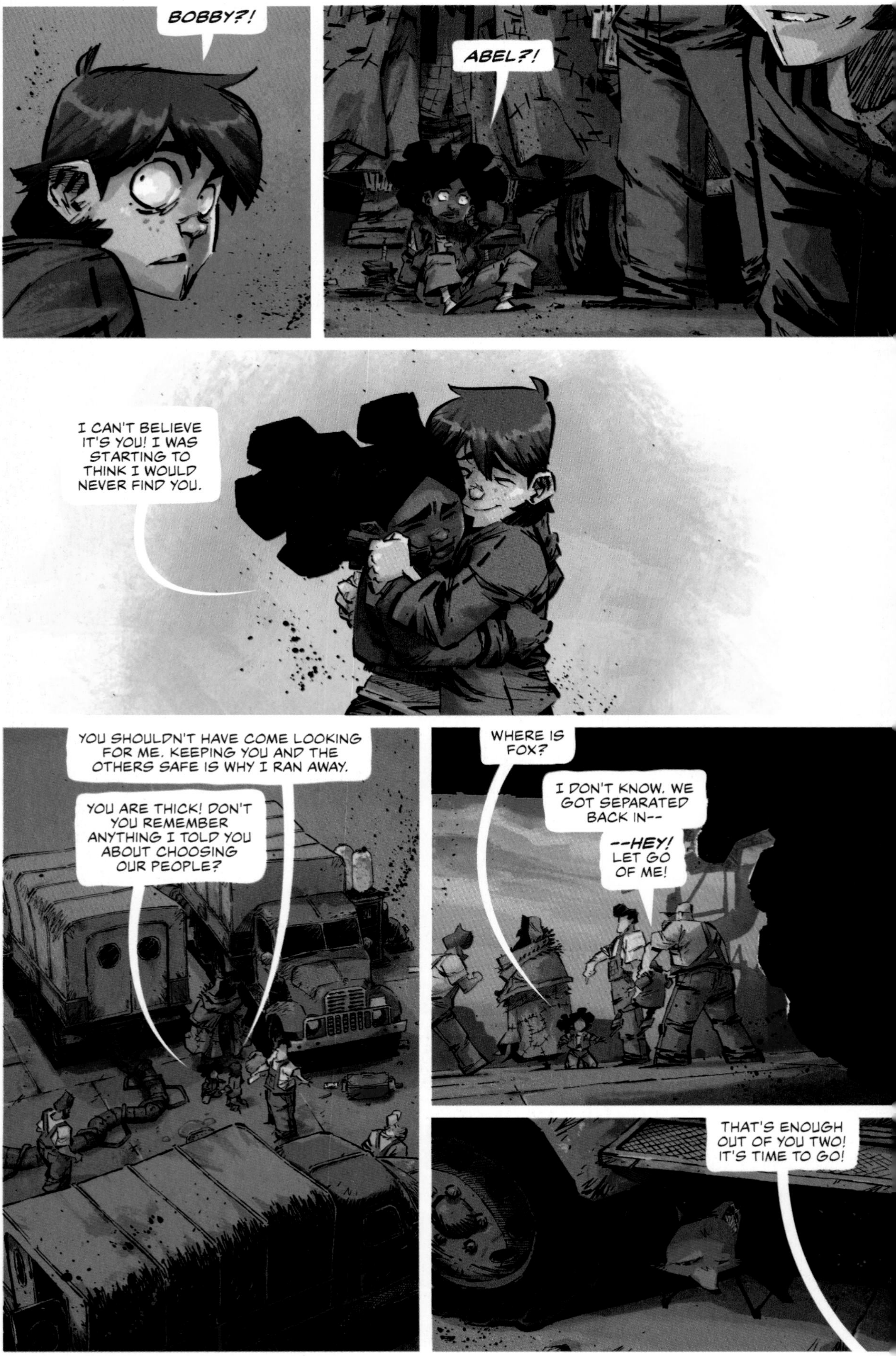
BOBBY?!
ABEL?!
I CAN'T BELIEVE IT'S YOU! I WAS STARTING TO THINK I WOULD NEVER FIND YOU.
YOU SHOULDN'T HAVE COME LOOKING FOR ME. KEEPING YOU AND THE OTHERS SAFE IS WHY I RAN AWAY.
YOU ARE THICK! DON'T YOU REMEMBER ANYTHING I TOLD YOU ABOUT CHOOSING OUR PEOPLE?
WHERE IS FOX?
I DON'T KNOW. WE GOT SEPARATED BACK IN--
--HEY! LET GO OF ME!
THAT'S ENOUGH OUT OF YOU TWO! IT'S TIME TO GO!

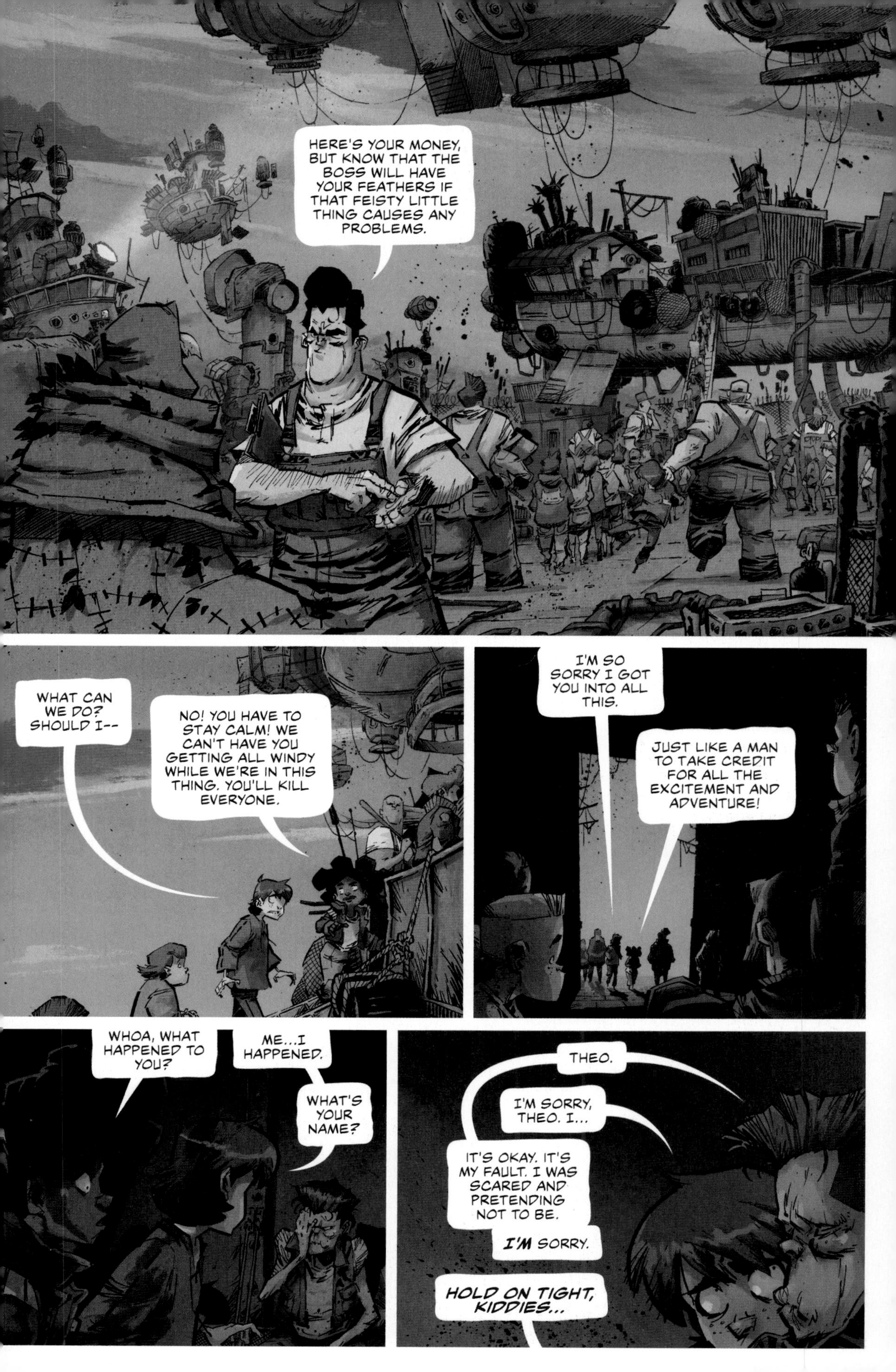
HERE'S YOUR MONEY, BUT KNOW THAT THE BOSS WILL HAVE YOUR FEATHERS IF THAT FEISTY LITTLE THING CAUSES ANY PROBLEMS.
WHAT CAN WE DO? SHOULD I--
NO! YOU HAVE TO STAY CALM! WE CAN'T HAVE YOU GETTING ALL WINDY WHILE WE'RE IN THIS THING. YOU'LL KILL EVERYONE.
I'M SO SORRY I GOT YOU INTO ALL THIS.
JUST LIKE A MAN TO TAKE CREDIT FOR ALL THE EXCITEMENT AND ADVENTURE!
WHOA, WHAT HAPPENED TO YOU?
ME...I HAPPENED.
WHAT'S YOUR NAME?
THEO.
I'M SORRY, THEO. I...
IT'S OKAY. IT'S MY FAULT. I WAS SCARED AND PRETENDING NOT TO BE.
I'M SORRY.
HOLD ON TIGHT, KIDDIES...

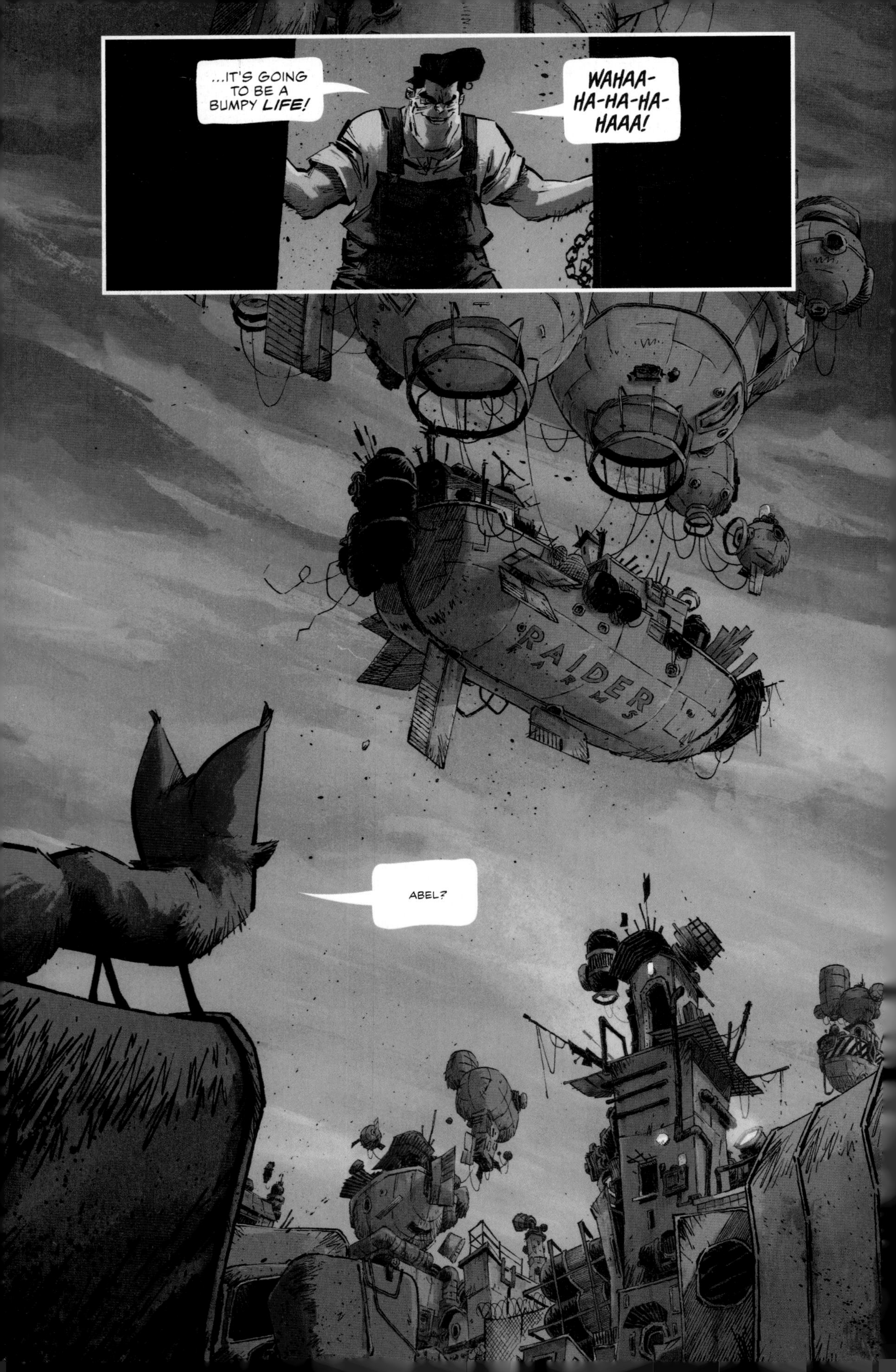
...IT'S GOING TO BE A BUMPY LIFE!
WAHAA-HA-HA-HA-HAAA!
RAIDER
ARMS
ABEL?

CHAPTER
TWELVE

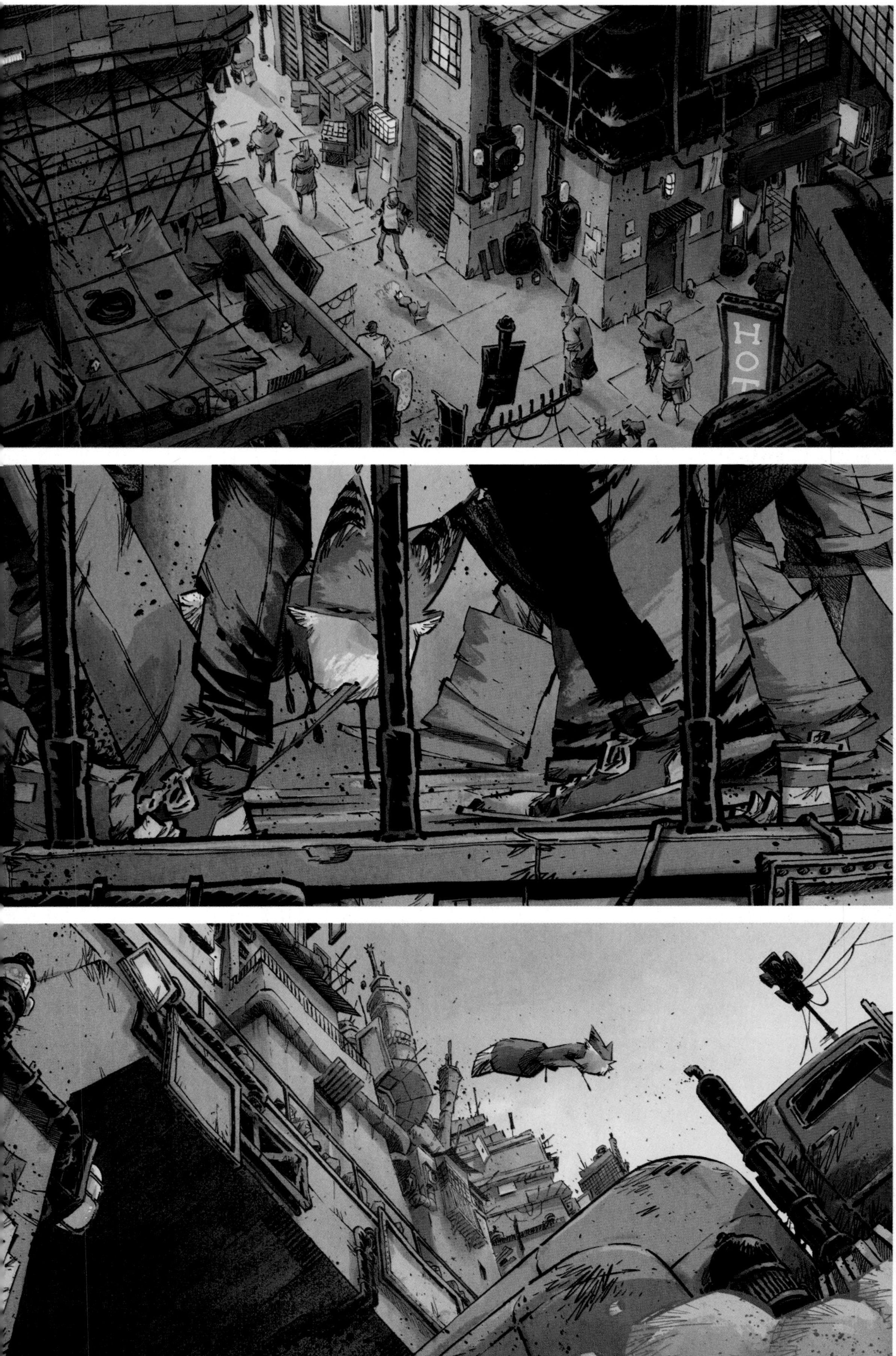
HO

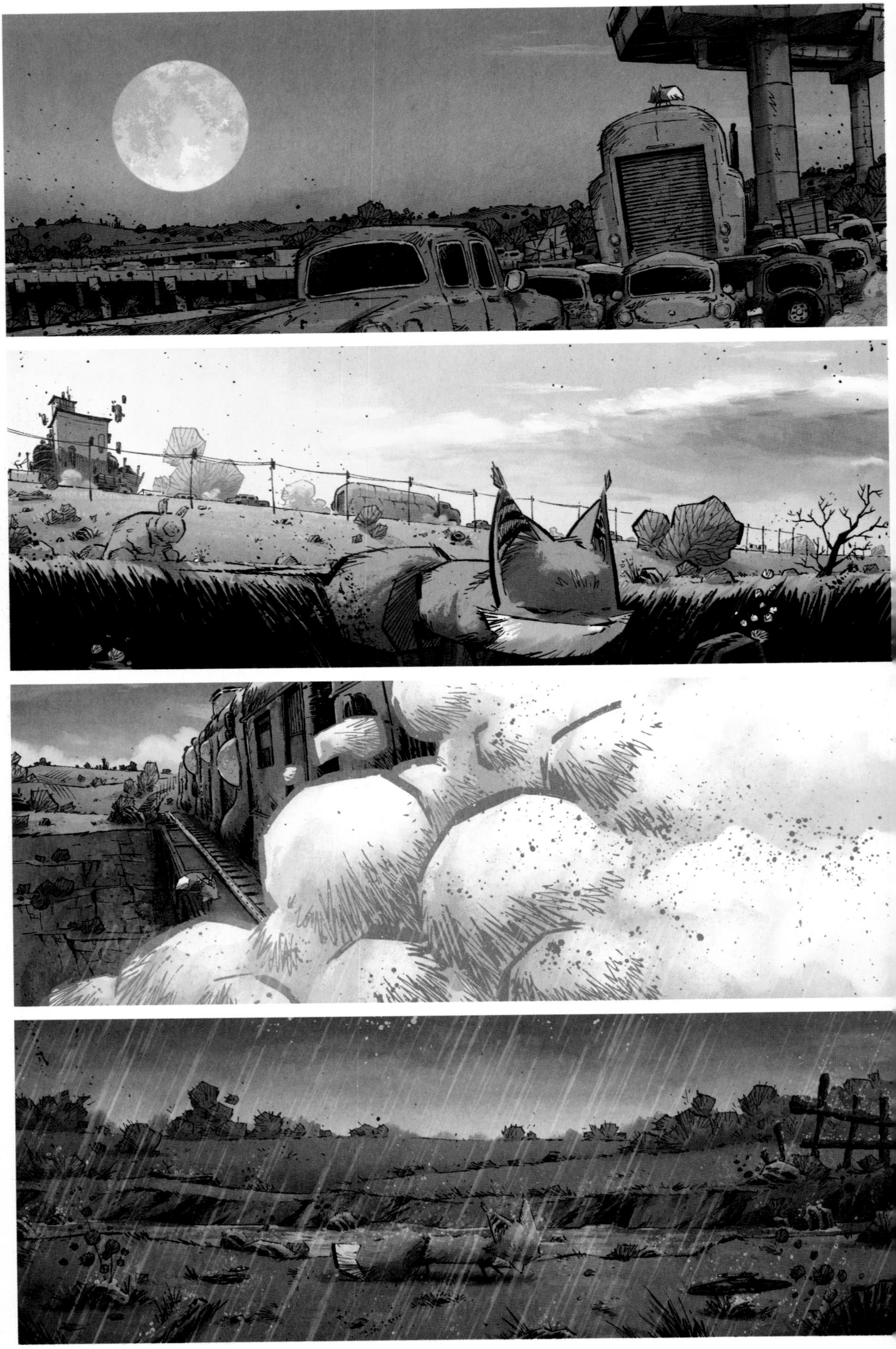

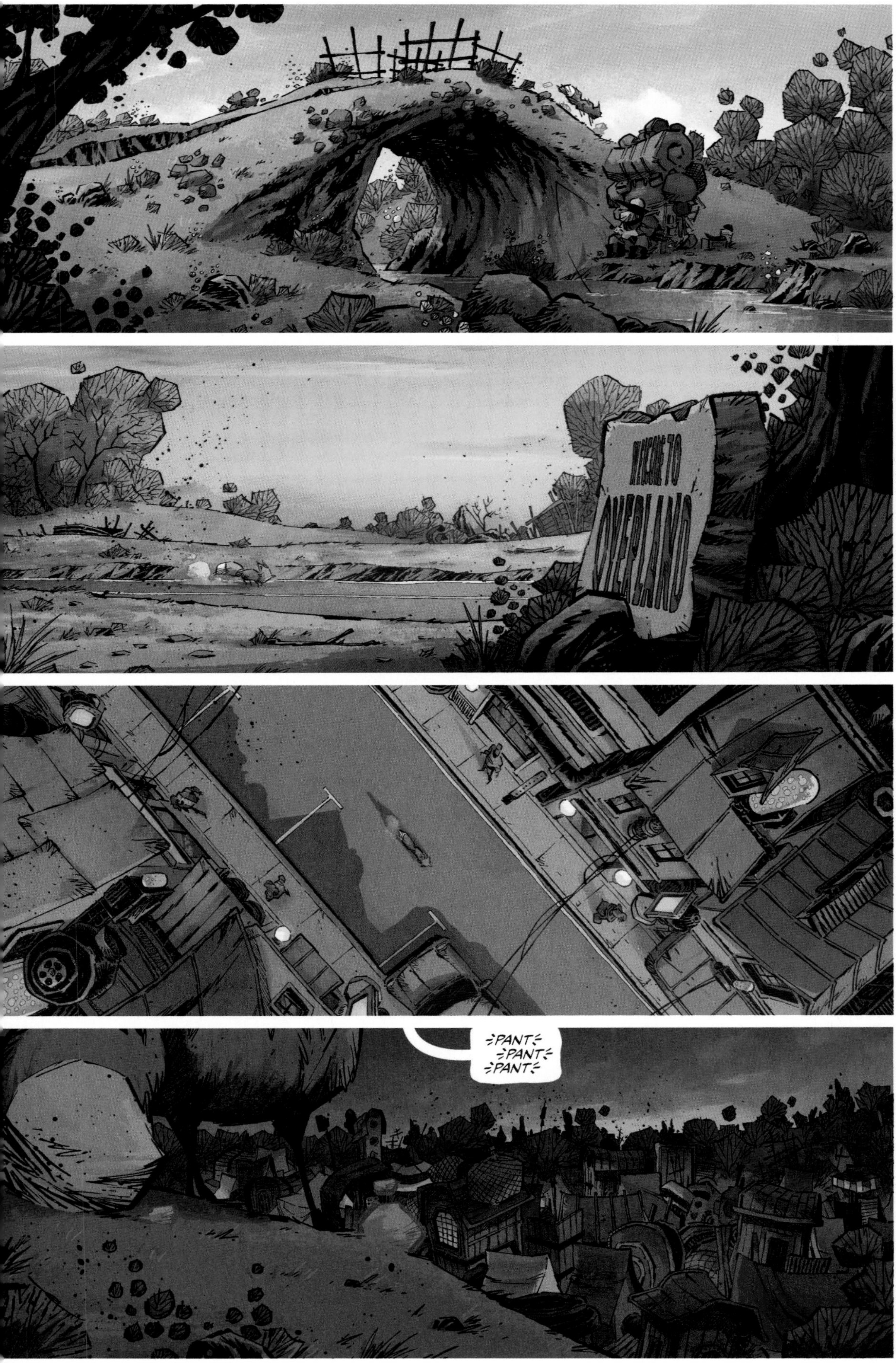
WELCOME TO
OVERLAND
PANT PANT PANT

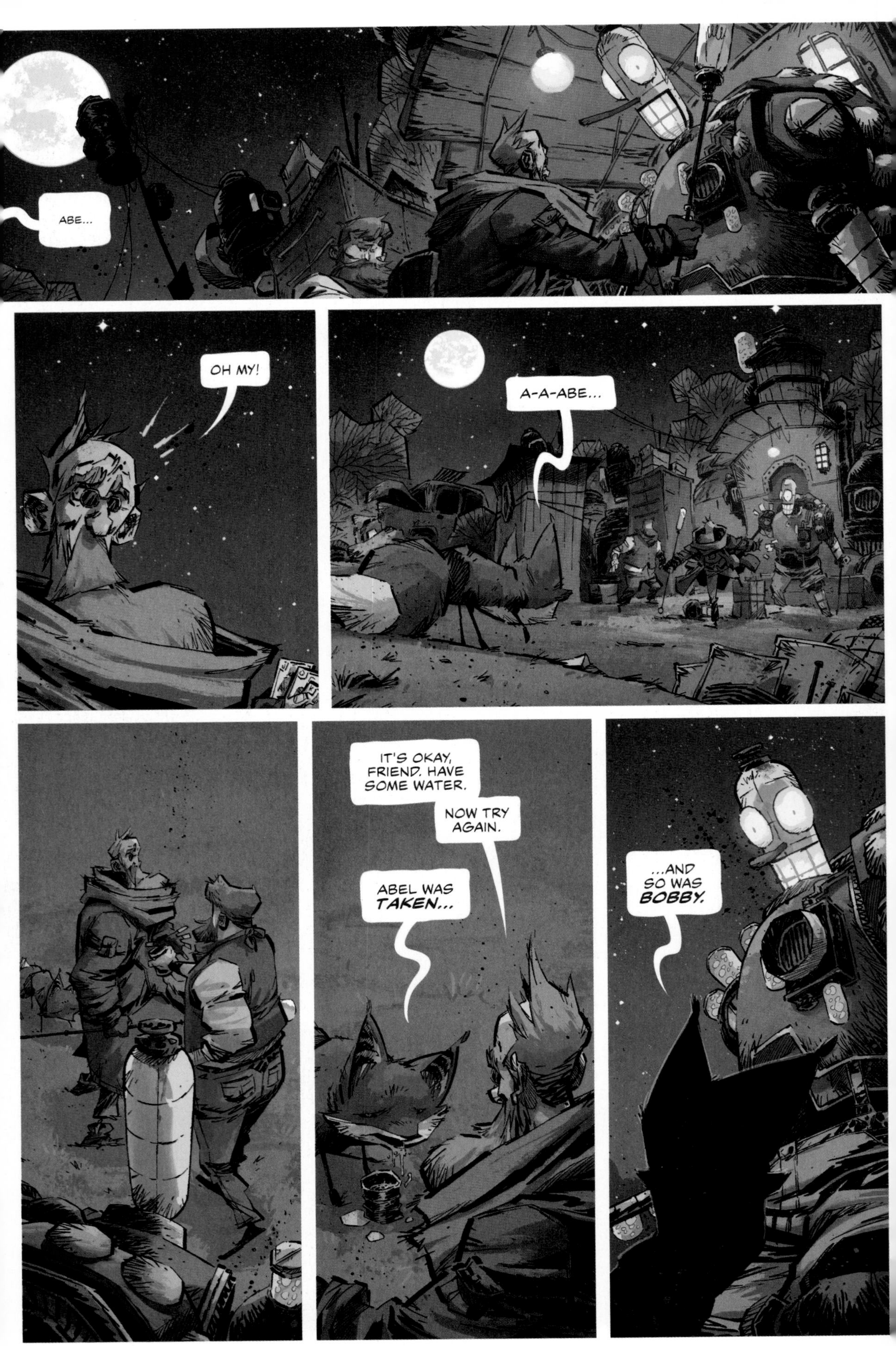
ABE...
OH MY!
A-A-ABE...
IT'S OKAY, FRIEND. HAVE SOME WATER.
NOW TRY AGAIN.
ABEL WAS *TAKEN...*
...AND SO WAS *BOBBY.*

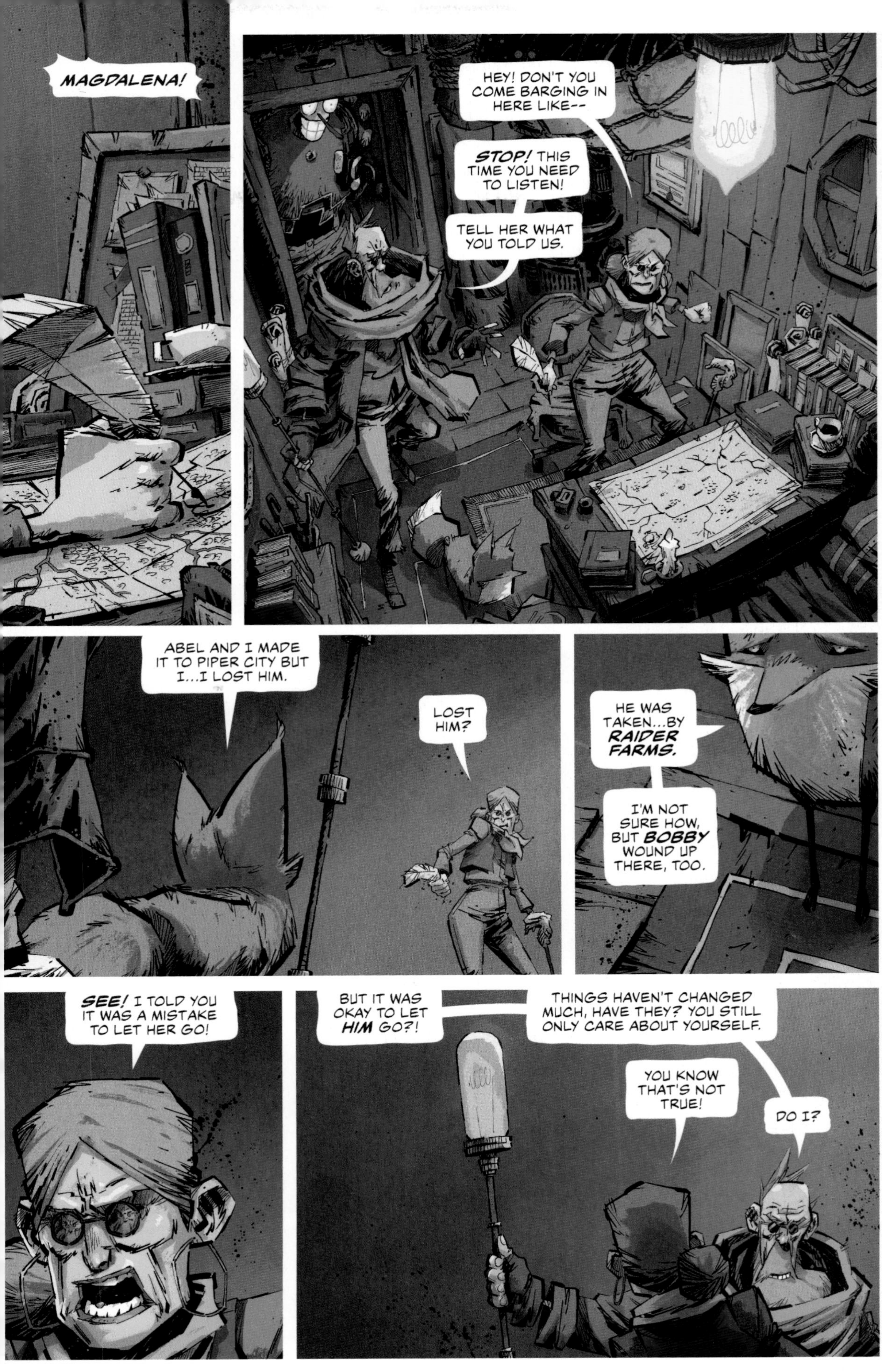
MAGDALENA!
HEY! DON'T YOU COME BARGING IN HERE LIKE--
STOP! THIS TIME YOU NEED TO LISTEN!
TELL HER WHAT YOU TOLD US.
ABEL AND I MADE IT TO PIPER CITY BUT I...I LOST HIM.
LOST HIM?
HE WAS TAKEN...BY RAIDER FARMS.
I'M NOT SURE HOW, BUT BOBBY WOUND UP THERE, TOO.
SEE! I TOLD YOU IT WAS A MISTAKE TO LET HER GO!
BUT IT WAS OKAY TO LET HIM GO?!
THINGS HAVEN'T CHANGED MUCH, HAVE THEY? YOU STILL ONLY CARE ABOUT YOURSELF.
YOU KNOW THAT'S NOT TRUE!
DO I?

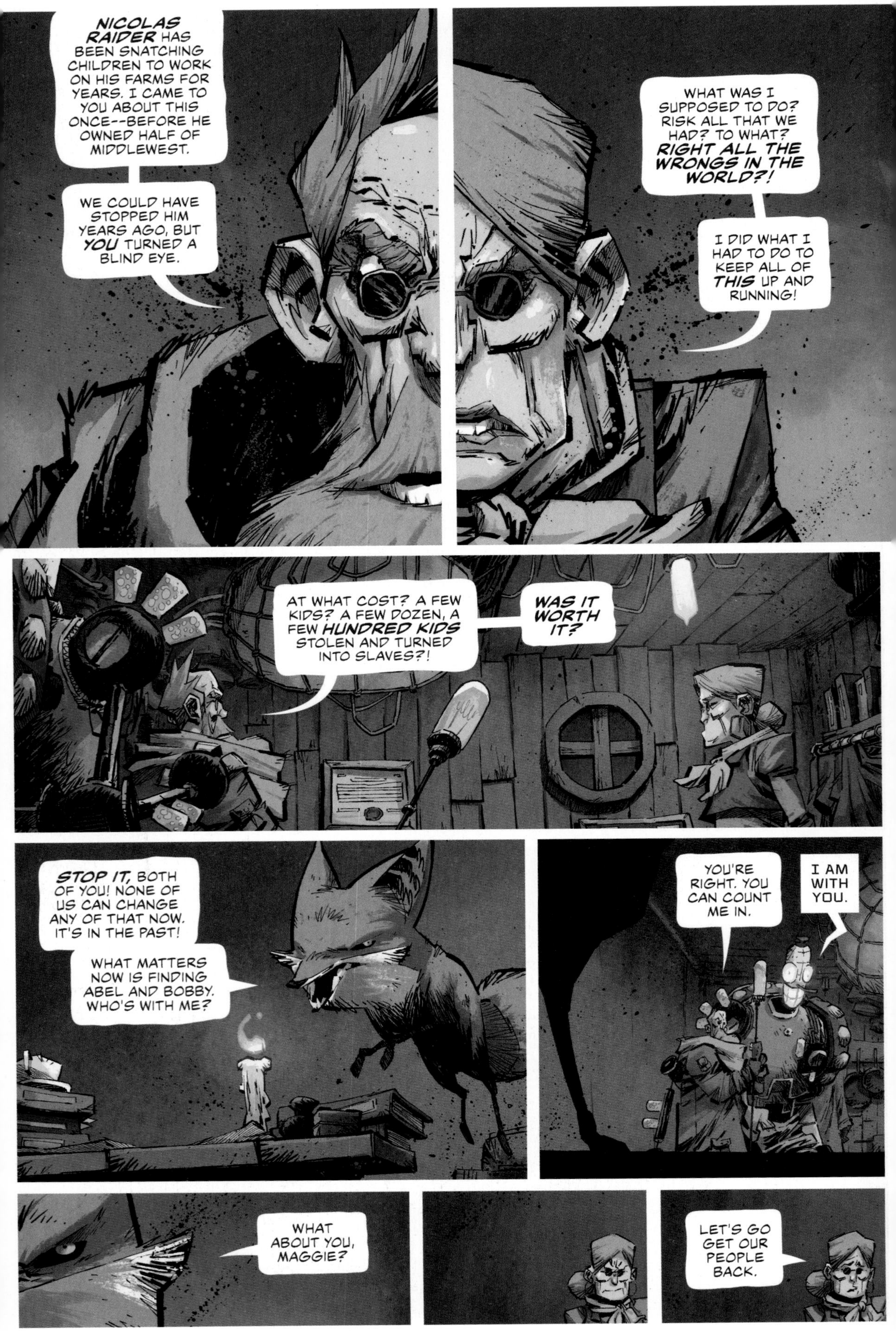
NICOLAS RAIDER HAS BEEN SNATCHING CHILDREN TO WORK ON HIS FARMS FOR YEARS. I CAME TO YOU ABOUT THIS ONCE--BEFORE HE OWNED HALF OF MIDDLEWEST.
WE COULD HAVE STOPPED HIM YEARS AGO, BUT ***YOU*** TURNED A BLIND EYE.
WHAT WAS I SUPPOSED TO DO? RISK ALL THAT WE HAD? TO WHAT? ***RIGHT ALL THE WRONGS IN THE WORLD?!***
I DID WHAT I HAD TO DO TO KEEP ALL OF ***THIS*** UP AND RUNNING!
AT WHAT COST? A FEW KIDS? A FEW DOZEN, A FEW ***HUNDRED KIDS*** STOLEN AND TURNED INTO SLAVES?!
WAS IT WORTH IT?
STOP IT, BOTH OF YOU! NONE OF US CAN CHANGE ANY OF THAT NOW. IT'S IN THE PAST!
WHAT MATTERS NOW IS FINDING ABEL AND BOBBY. WHO'S WITH ME?
YOU'RE RIGHT. YOU CAN COUNT ME IN.
I AM WITH YOU.
WHAT ABOUT YOU, MAGGIE?
LET'S GO GET OUR PEOPLE BACK.

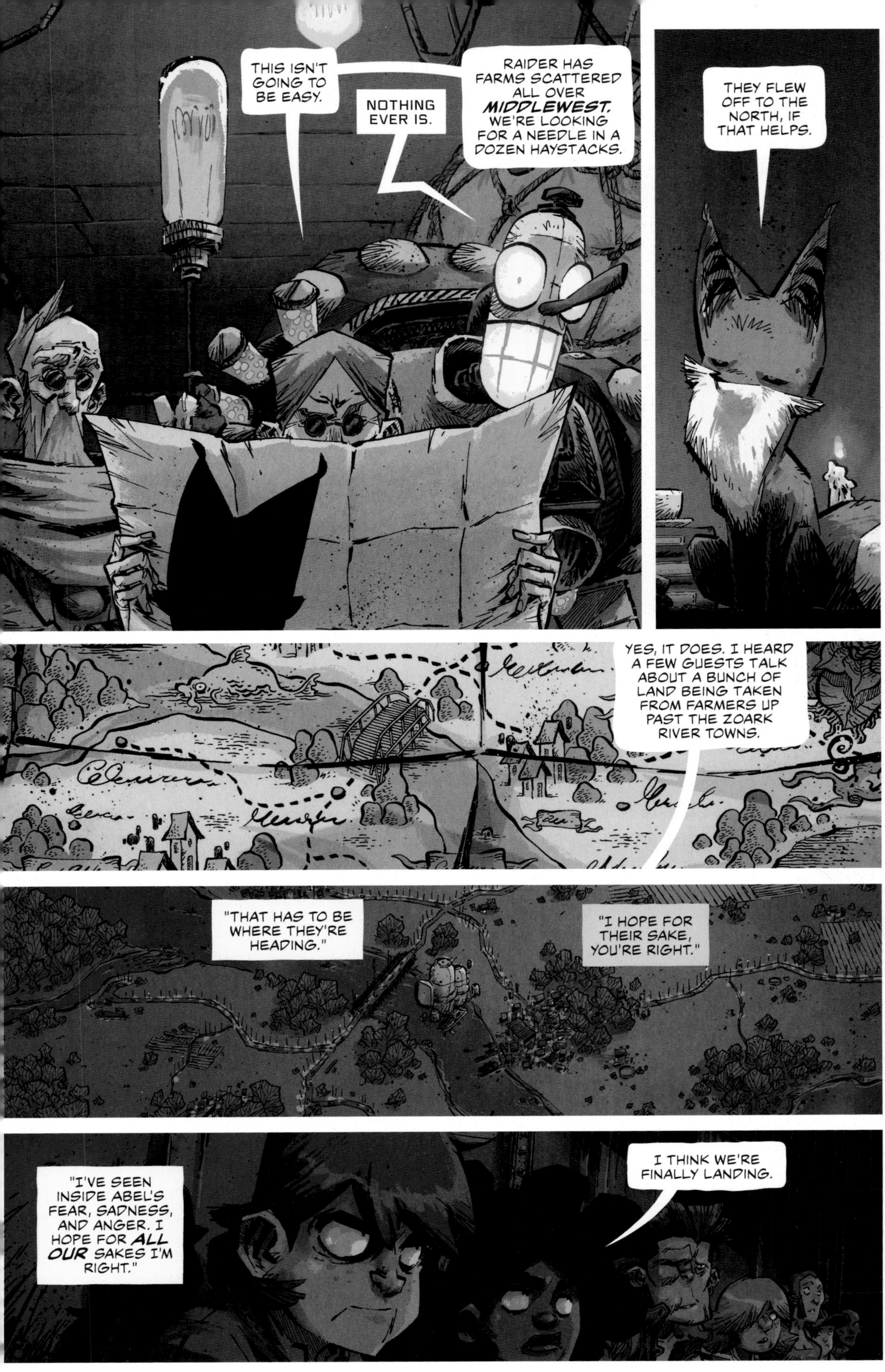
THIS ISN'T GOING TO BE EASY.
NOTHING EVER IS.
RAIDER HAS FARMS SCATTERED ALL OVER MIDDLEWEST. WE'RE LOOKING FOR A NEEDLE IN A DOZEN HAYSTACKS.
THEY FLEW OFF TO THE NORTH, IF THAT HELPS.
YES, IT DOES. I HEARD A FEW GUESTS TALK ABOUT A BUNCH OF LAND BEING TAKEN FROM FARMERS UP PAST THE ZOARK RIVER TOWNS.
"THAT HAS TO BE WHERE THEY'RE HEADING."
"I HOPE FOR THEIR SAKE, YOU'RE RIGHT."
"I'VE SEEN INSIDE ABEL'S FEAR, SADNESS, AND ANGER. I HOPE FOR ALL OUR SAKES I'M RIGHT."
I THINK WE'RE FINALLY LANDING.

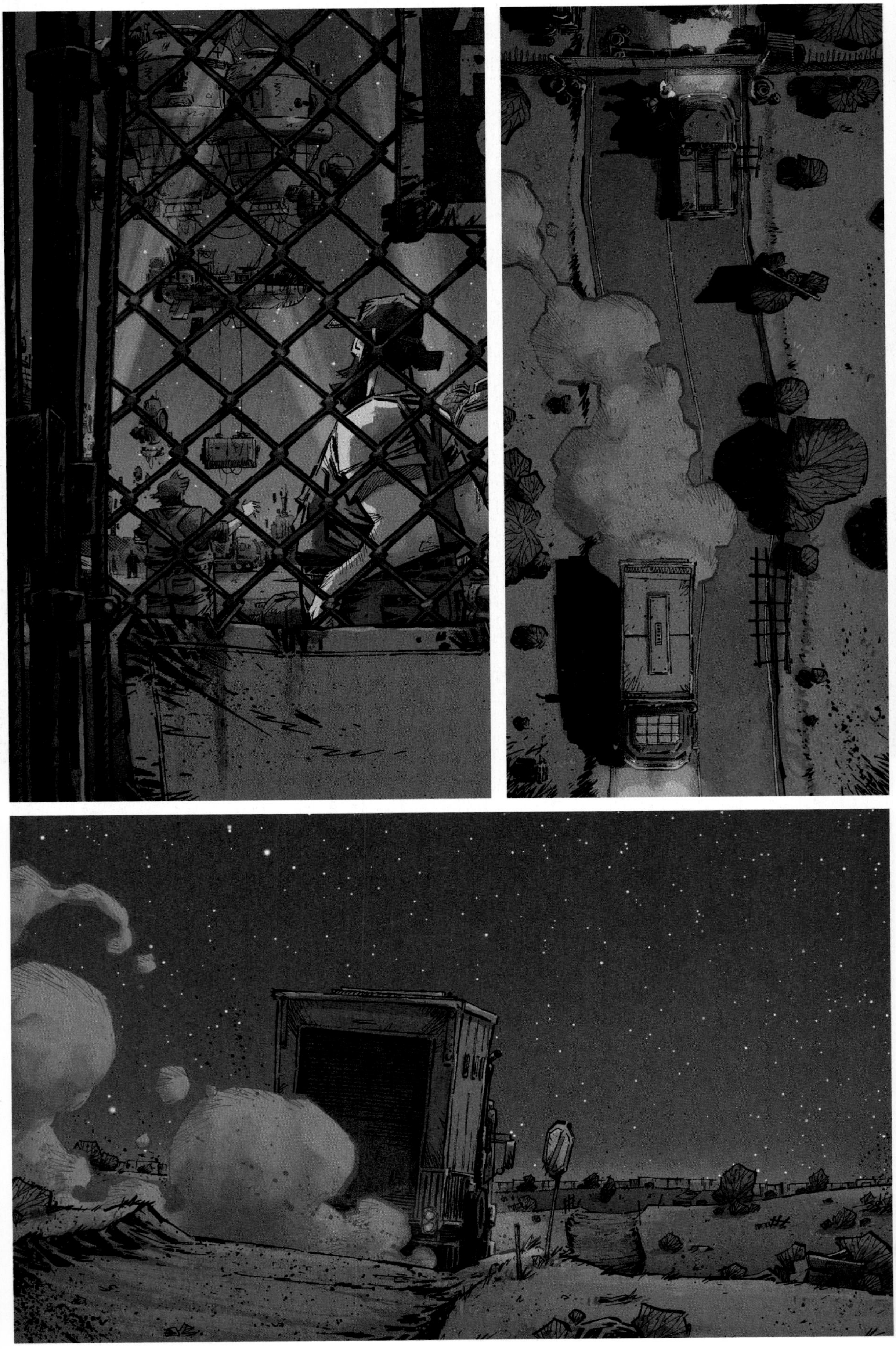

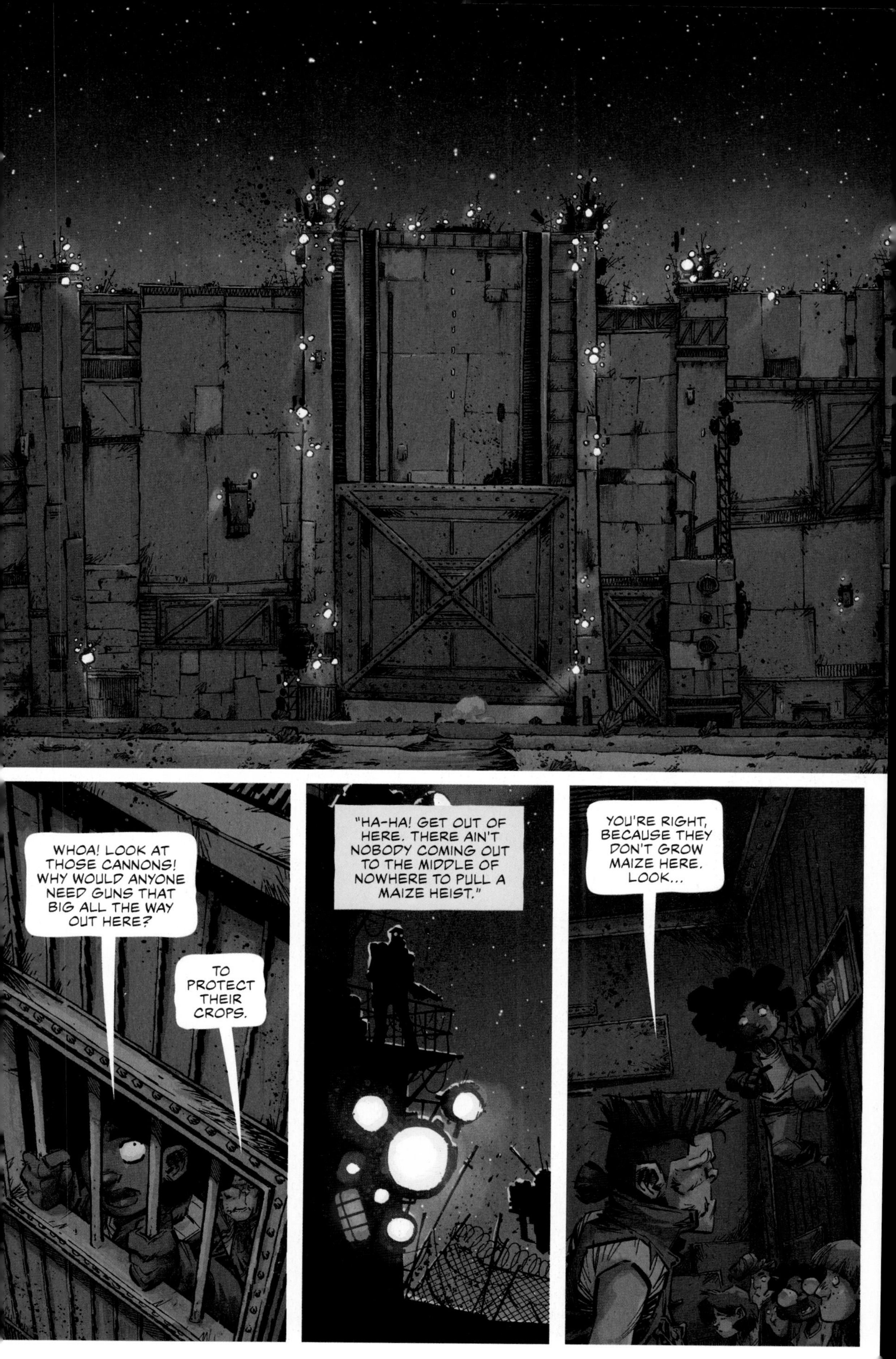
WHOA! LOOK AT THOSE CANNONS! WHY WOULD ANYONE NEED GUNS THAT BIG ALL THE WAY OUT HERE?
TO PROTECT THEIR CROPS.
"HA-HA! GET OUT OF HERE. THERE AIN'T NOBODY COMING OUT TO THE MIDDLE OF NOWHERE TO PULL A MAIZE HEIST."
YOU'RE RIGHT, BECAUSE THEY DON'T GROW MAIZE HERE. LOOK...

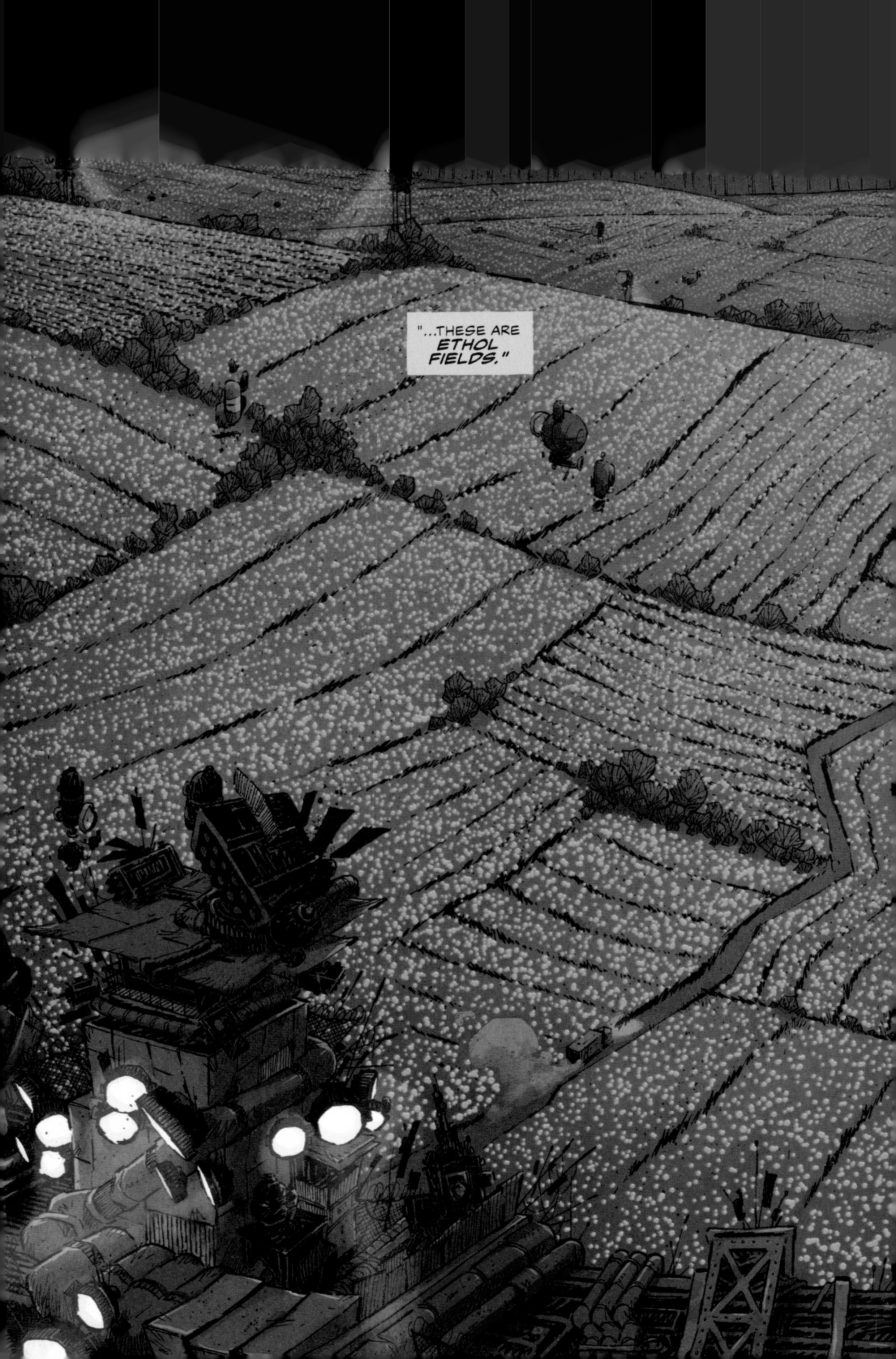
"...THESE ARE ETHOL FIELDS."

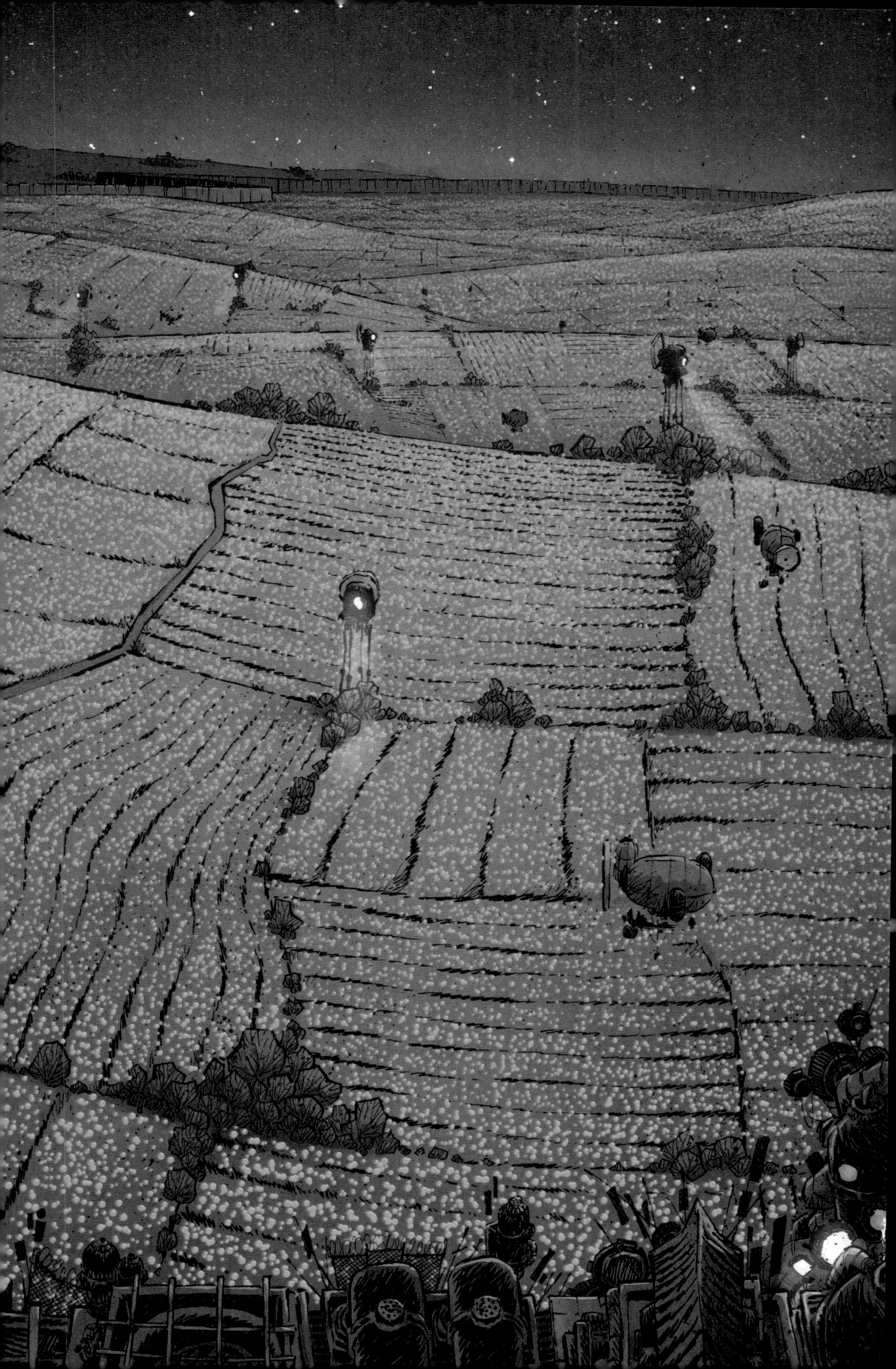

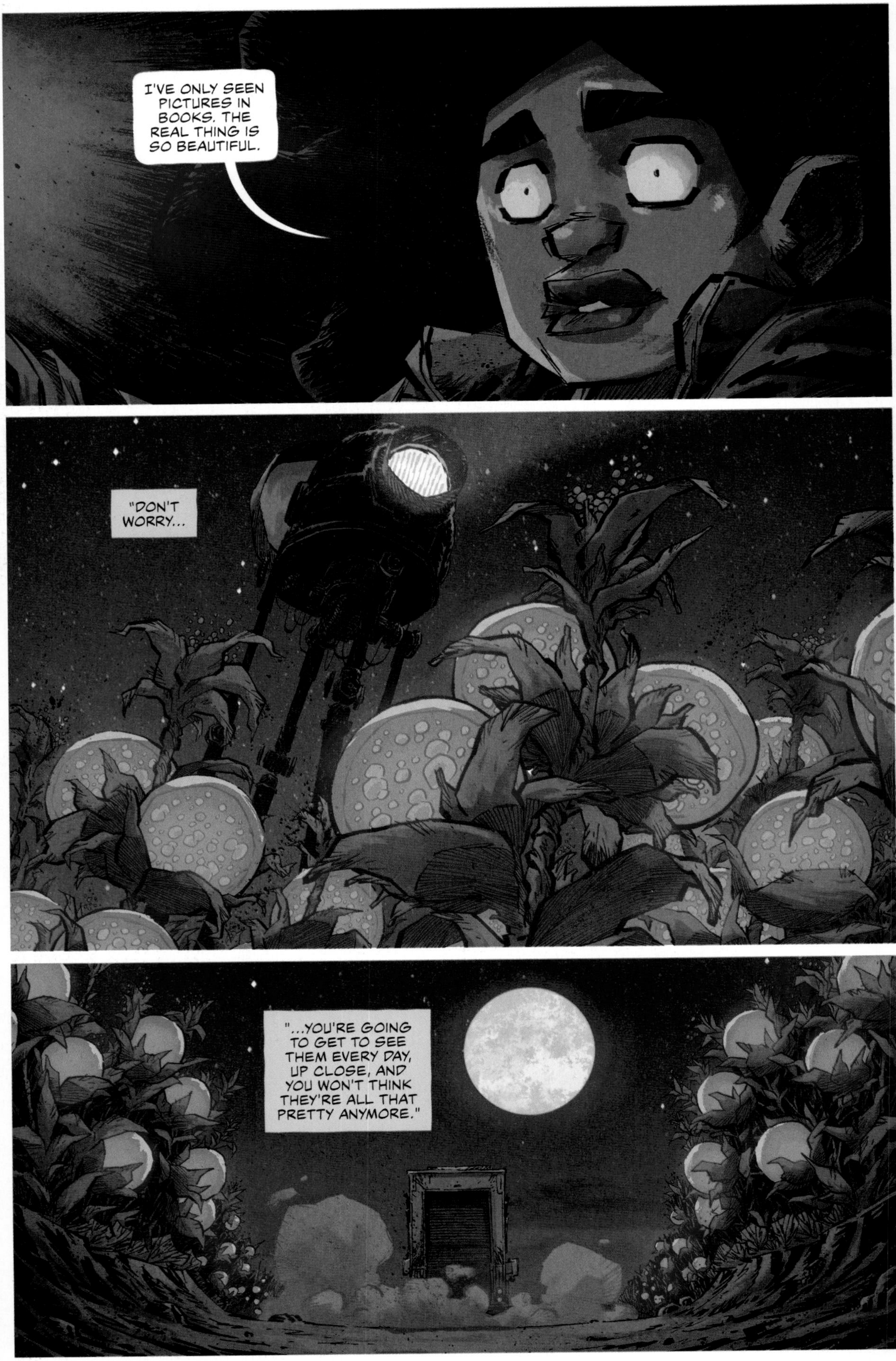
I'VE ONLY SEEN PICTURES IN BOOKS. THE REAL THING IS SO BEAUTIFUL.
"DON'T WORRY...
"...YOU'RE GOING TO GET TO SEE THEM EVERY DAY, UP CLOSE, AND YOU WON'T THINK THEY'RE ALL THAT PRETTY ANYMORE."

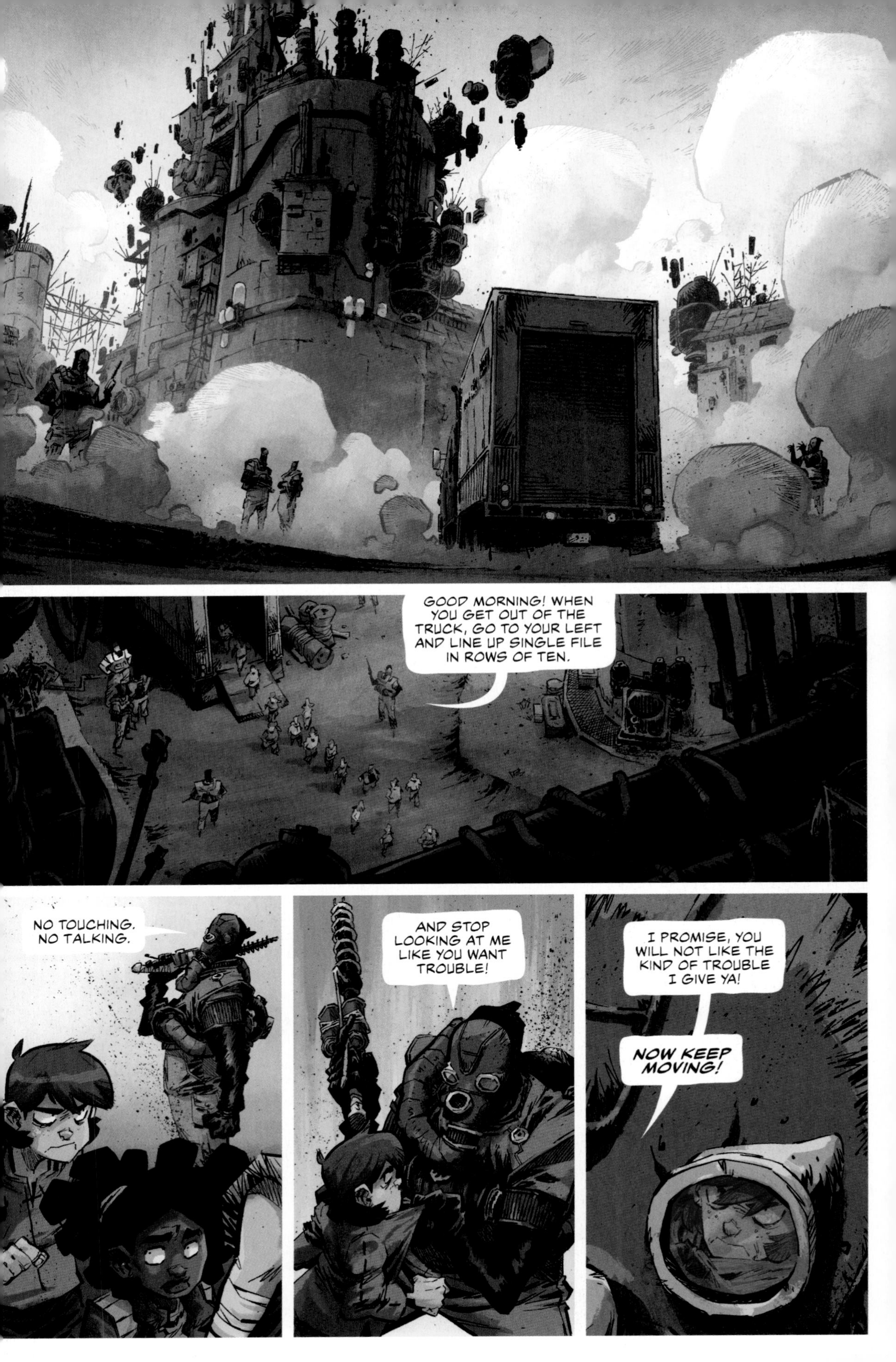
GOOD MORNING! WHEN YOU GET OUT OF THE TRUCK, GO TO YOUR LEFT AND LINE UP SINGLE FILE IN ROWS OF TEN.
NO TOUCHING. NO TALKING.
AND STOP LOOKING AT ME LIKE YOU WANT TROUBLE!
I PROMISE, YOU WILL NOT LIKE THE KIND OF TROUBLE I GIVE YA!
NOW KEEP MOVING!

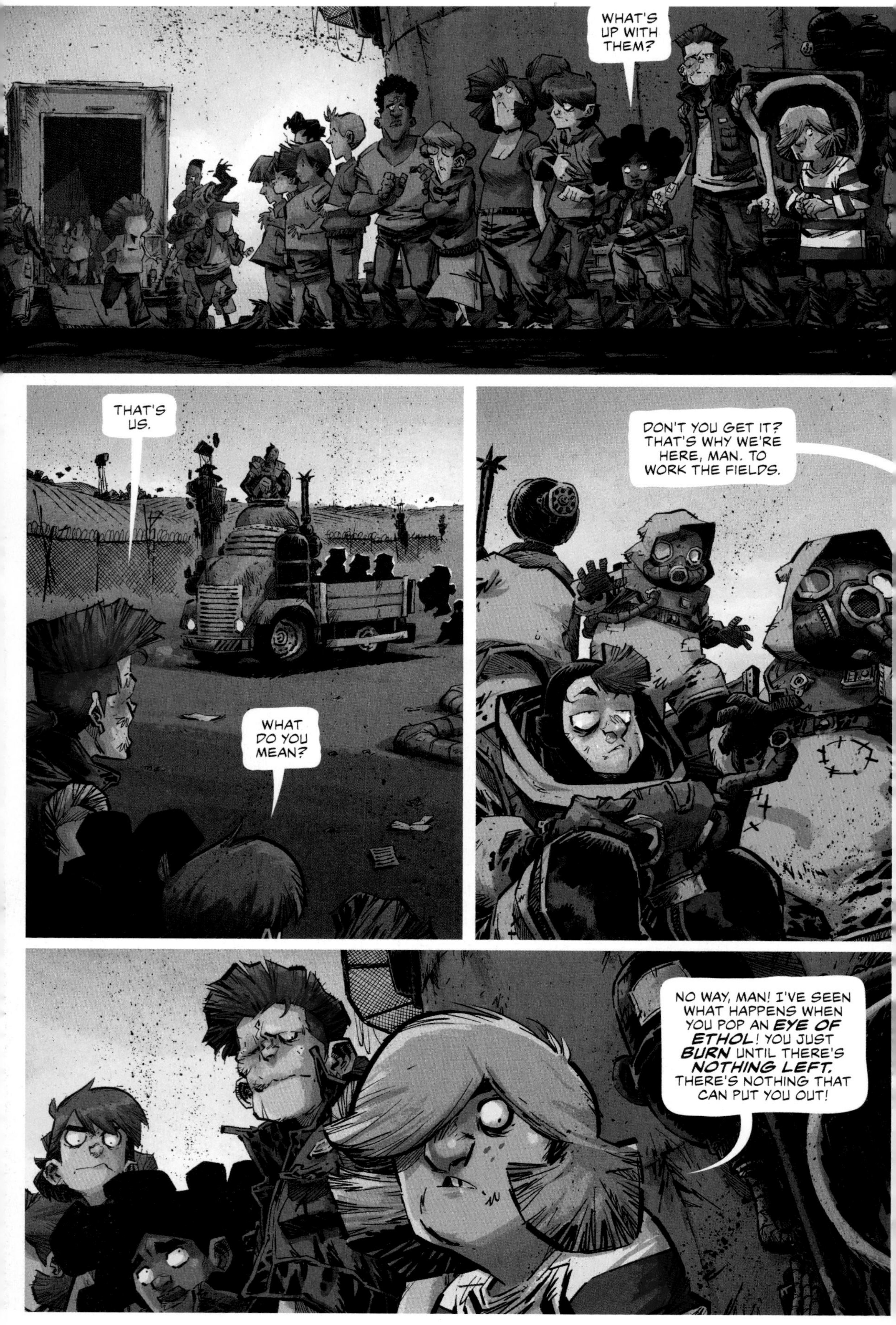
WHAT'S UP WITH THEM?
THAT'S US.
WHAT DO YOU MEAN?
DON'T YOU GET IT? THAT'S WHY WE'RE HERE, MAN. TO WORK THE FIELDS.
NO WAY, MAN! I'VE SEEN WHAT HAPPENS WHEN YOU POP AN EYE OF ETHOL! YOU JUST BURN UNTIL THERE'S NOTHING LEFT. THERE'S NOTHING THAT CAN PUT YOU OUT!

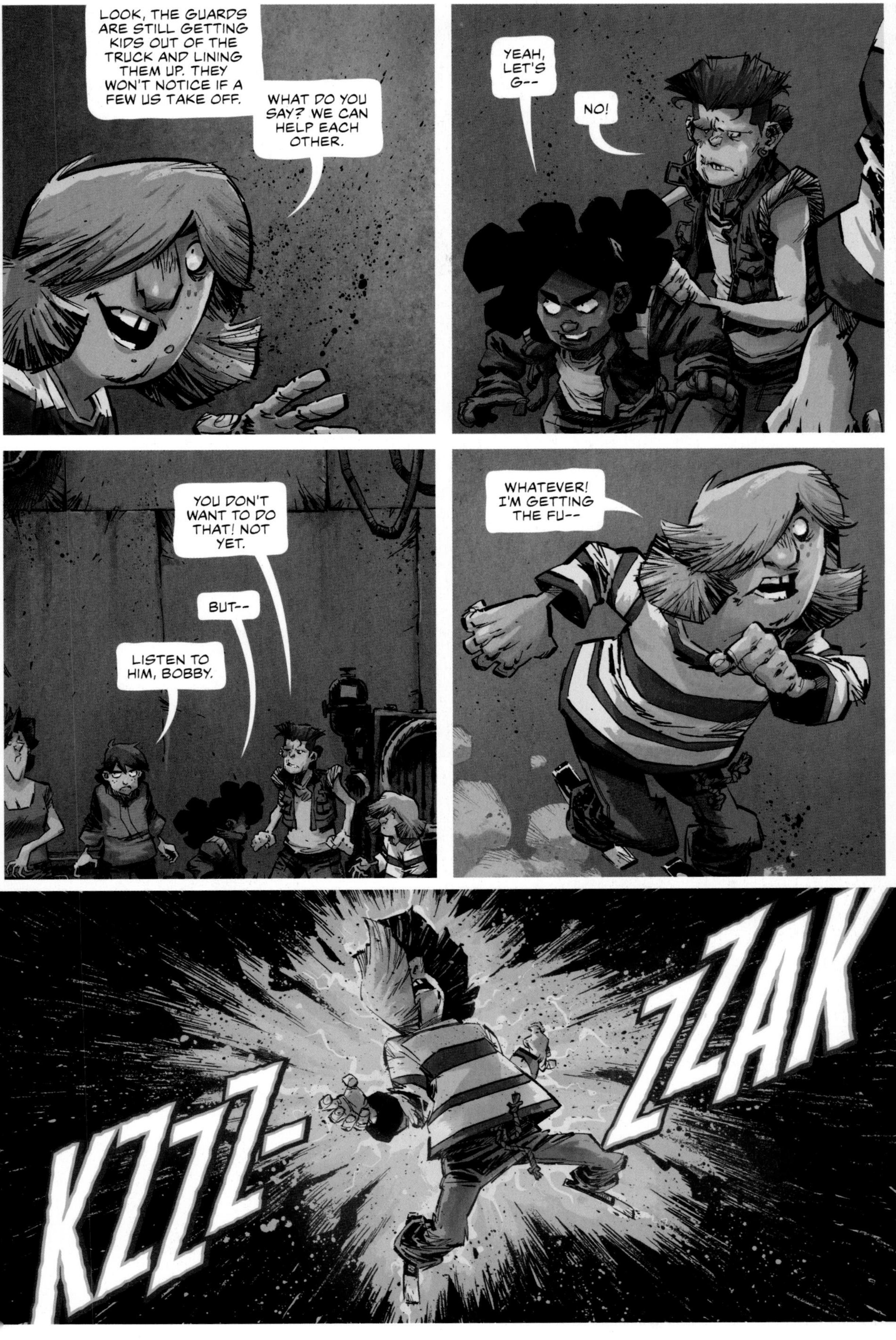

LOOK, THE GUARDS ARE STILL GETTING KIDS OUT OF THE TRUCK AND LINING THEM UP. THEY WON'T NOTICE IF A FEW US TAKE OFF.
WHAT DO YOU SAY? WE CAN HELP EACH OTHER.
YEAH, LET'S G--
NO!
YOU DON'T WANT TO DO THAT! NOT YET.
BUT--
LISTEN TO HIM, BOBBY.
WHATEVER! I'M GETTING THE FU--
KZZZ-
ZZAK

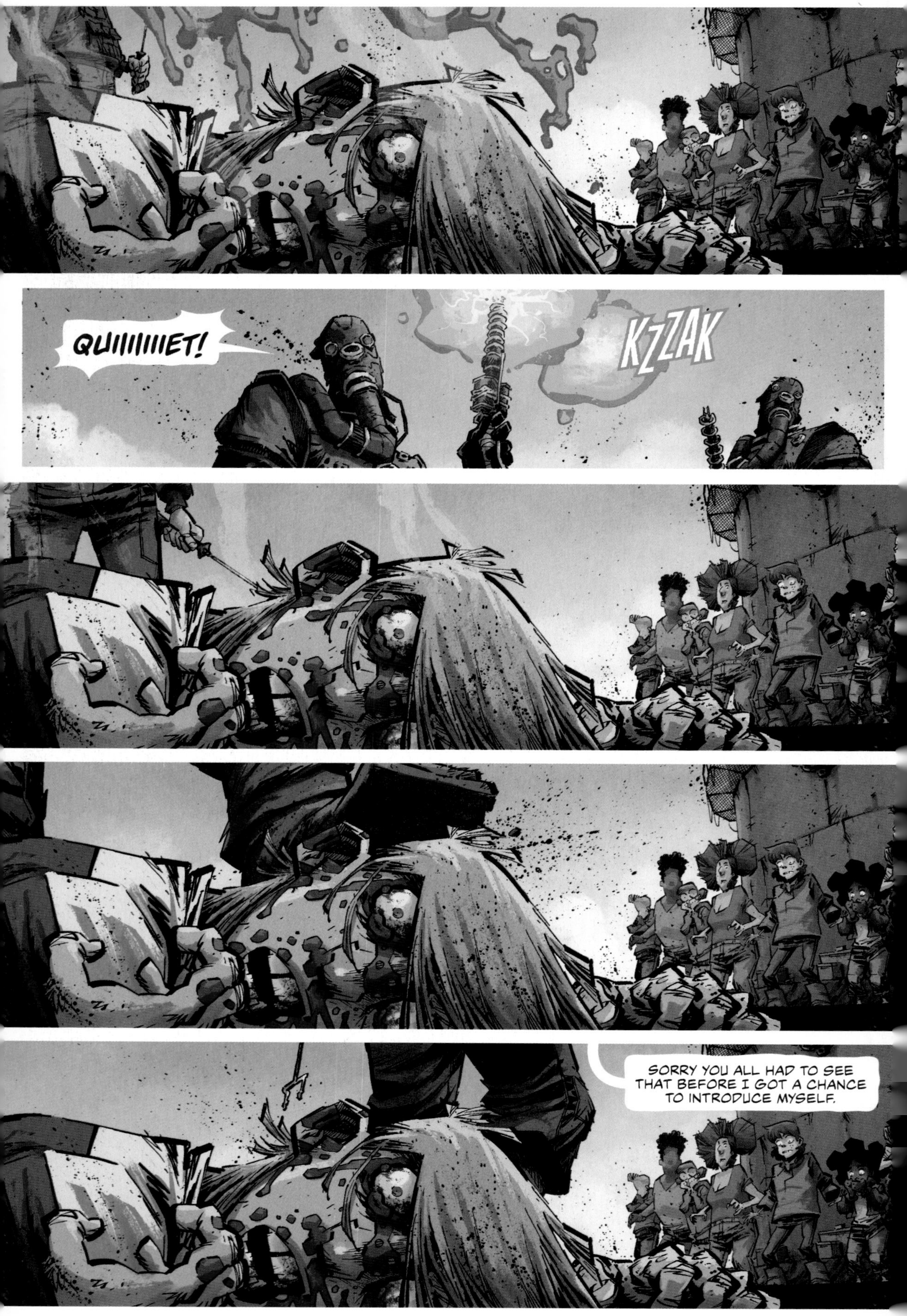
QUIIIIIIIET!
KZZAK
SORRY YOU ALL HAD TO SEE THAT BEFORE I GOT A CHANCE TO INTRODUCE MYSELF.

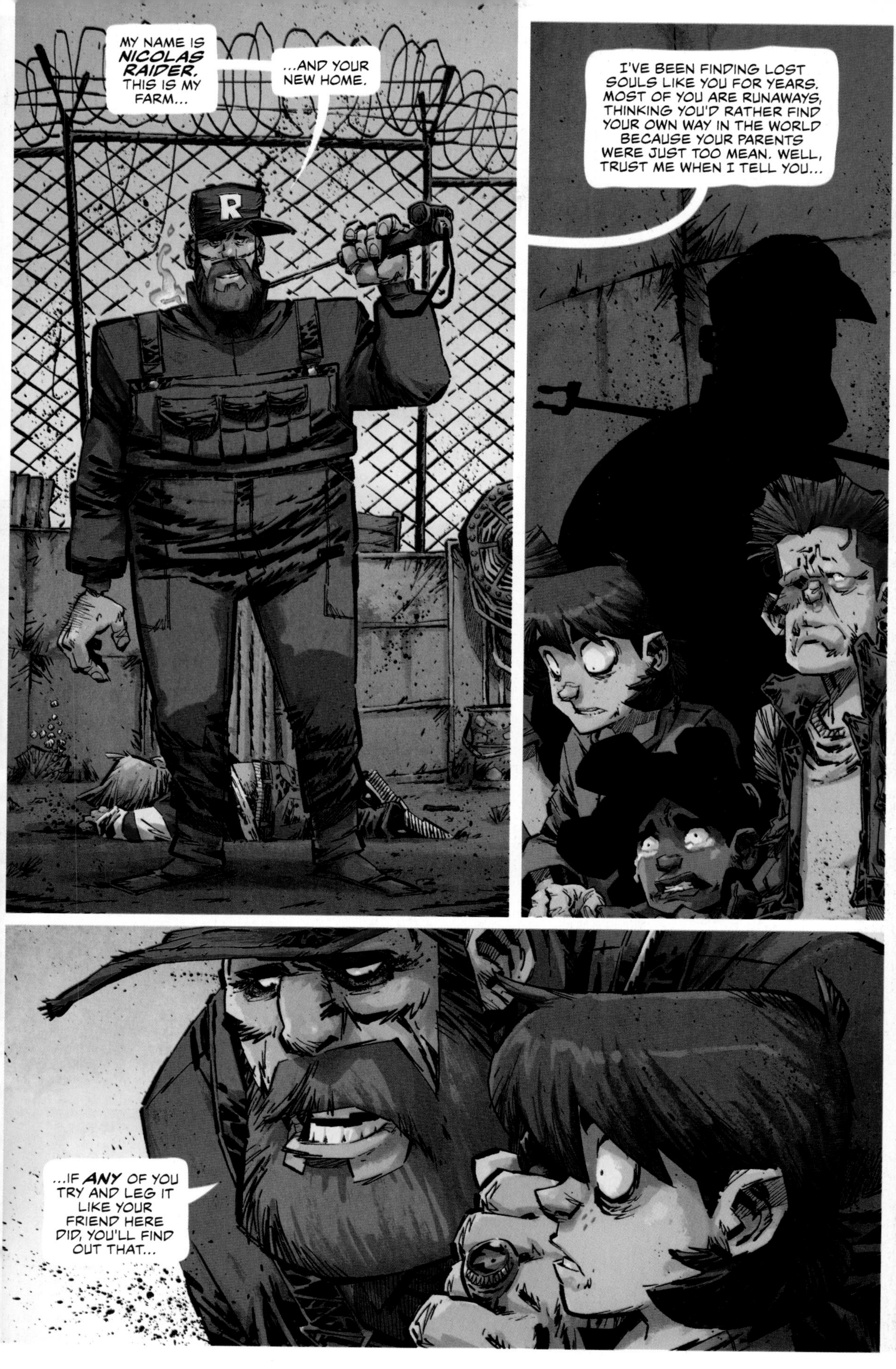

MY NAME IS ***NICOLAS RAIDER.*** THIS IS MY FARM...
...AND YOUR NEW HOME.
I'VE BEEN FINDING LOST SOULS LIKE YOU FOR YEARS. MOST OF YOU ARE RUNAWAYS, THINKING YOU'D RATHER FIND YOUR OWN WAY IN THE WORLD BECAUSE YOUR PARENTS WERE JUST TOO MEAN. WELL, TRUST ME WHEN I TELL YOU...
...IF ***ANY*** OF YOU TRY AND LEG IT LIKE YOUR FRIEND HERE DID, YOU'LL FIND OUT THAT...

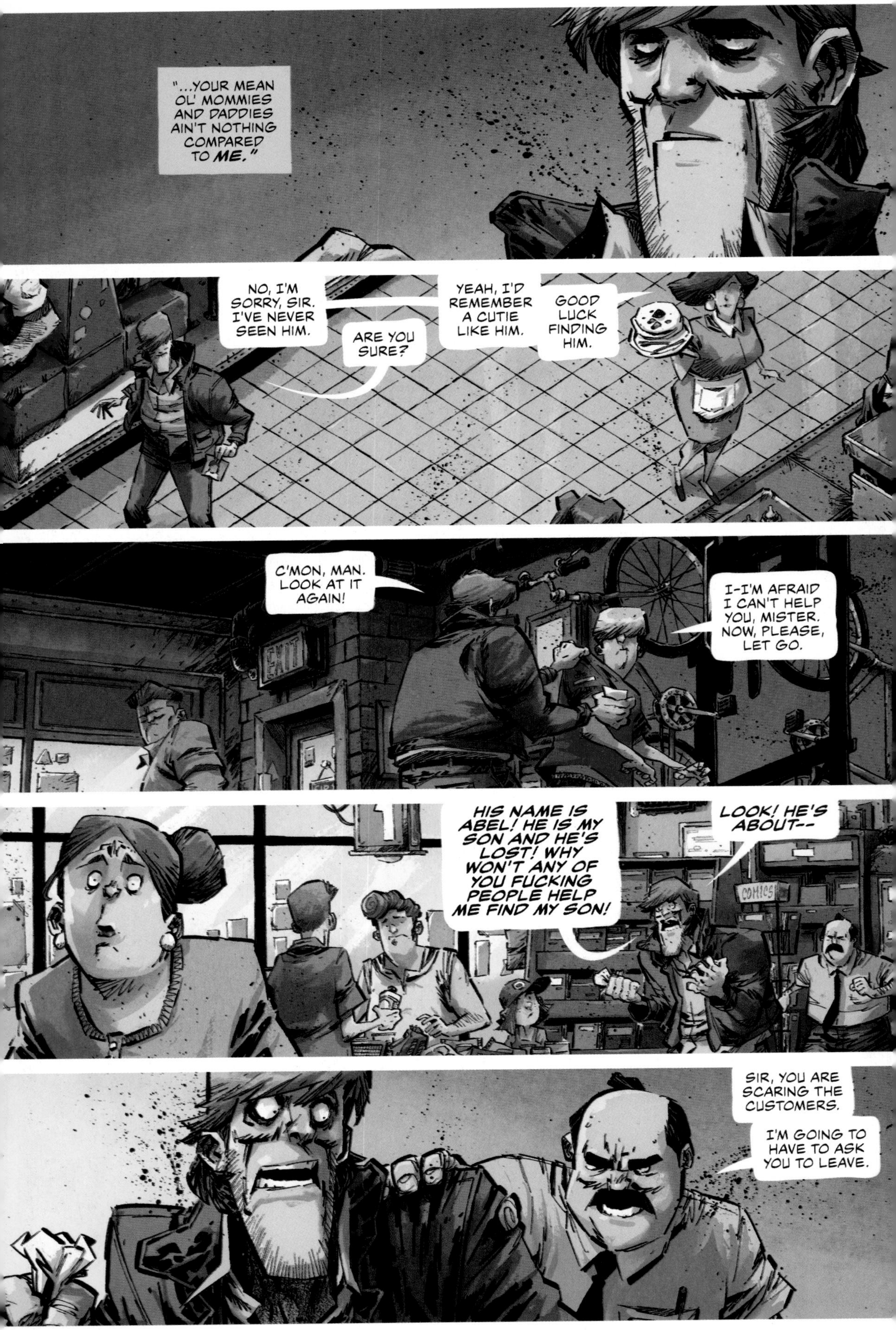
"...YOUR MEAN OL' MOMMIES AND DADDIES AIN'T NOTHING COMPARED TO *ME.*"
NO, I'M SORRY, SIR. I'VE NEVER SEEN HIM.
ARE YOU SURE?
YEAH, I'D REMEMBER A CUTIE LIKE HIM.
GOOD LUCK FINDING HIM.
C'MON, MAN. LOOK AT IT AGAIN!
EXIT
I-I'M AFRAID I CAN'T HELP YOU, MISTER. NOW, PLEASE, LET GO.
HIS NAME IS ABEL! HE IS MY SON AND HE'S LOST! WHY WON'T ANY OF YOU FUCKING PEOPLE HELP ME FIND MY SON!
LOOK! HE'S ABOUT--
COMICS
SIR, YOU ARE SCARING THE CUSTOMERS.
I'M GOING TO HAVE TO ASK YOU TO LEAVE.

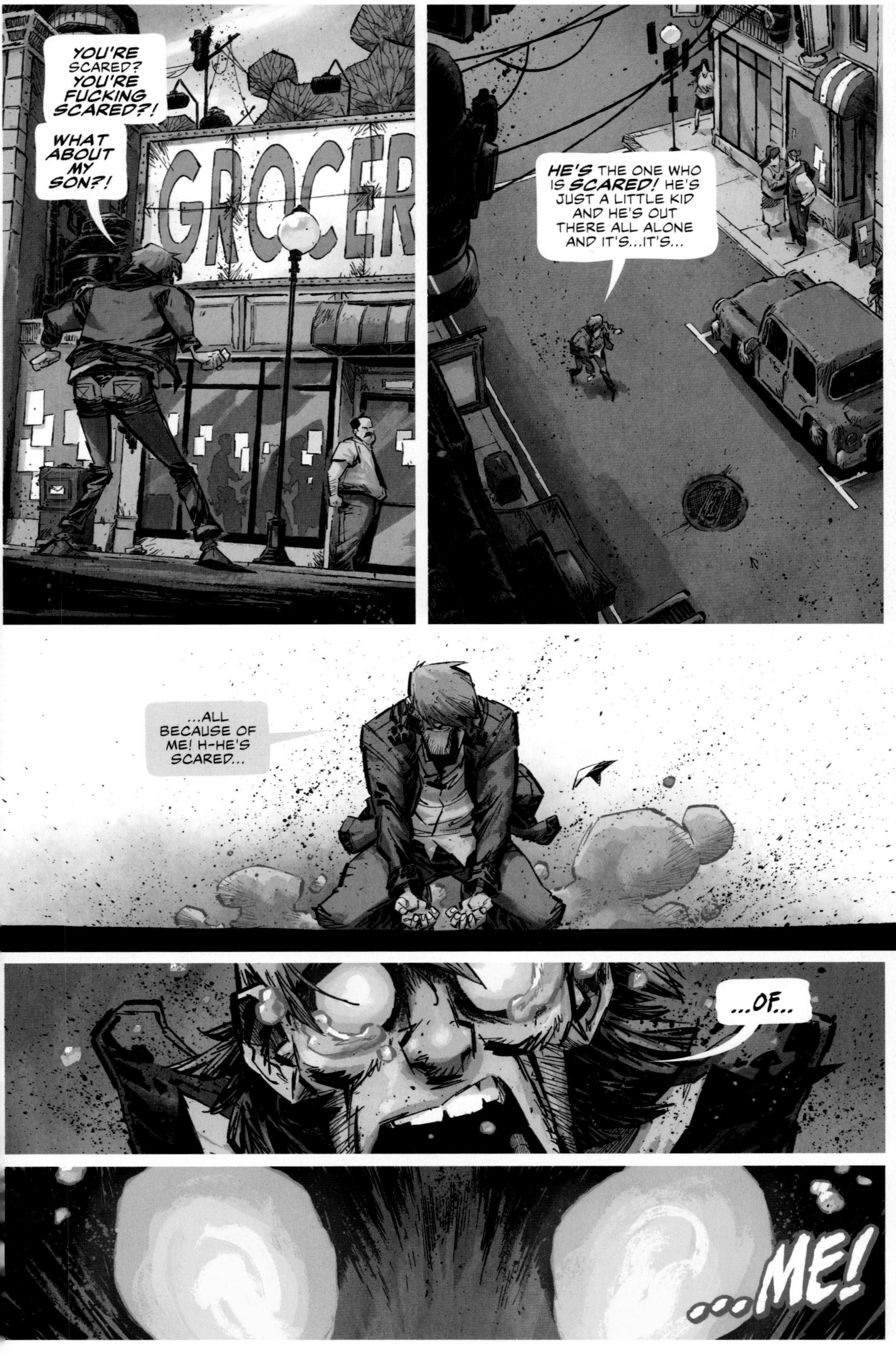
YOU'RE SCARED? YOU'RE FUCKING SCARED?!
WHAT ABOUT MY SON?!
GROCER
HE'S THE ONE WHO IS SCARED! HE'S JUST A LITTLE KID AND HE'S OUT THERE ALL ALONE AND IT'S...IT'S...
...ALL BECAUSE OF ME! H-HE'S SCARED...
...OF...
...ME!

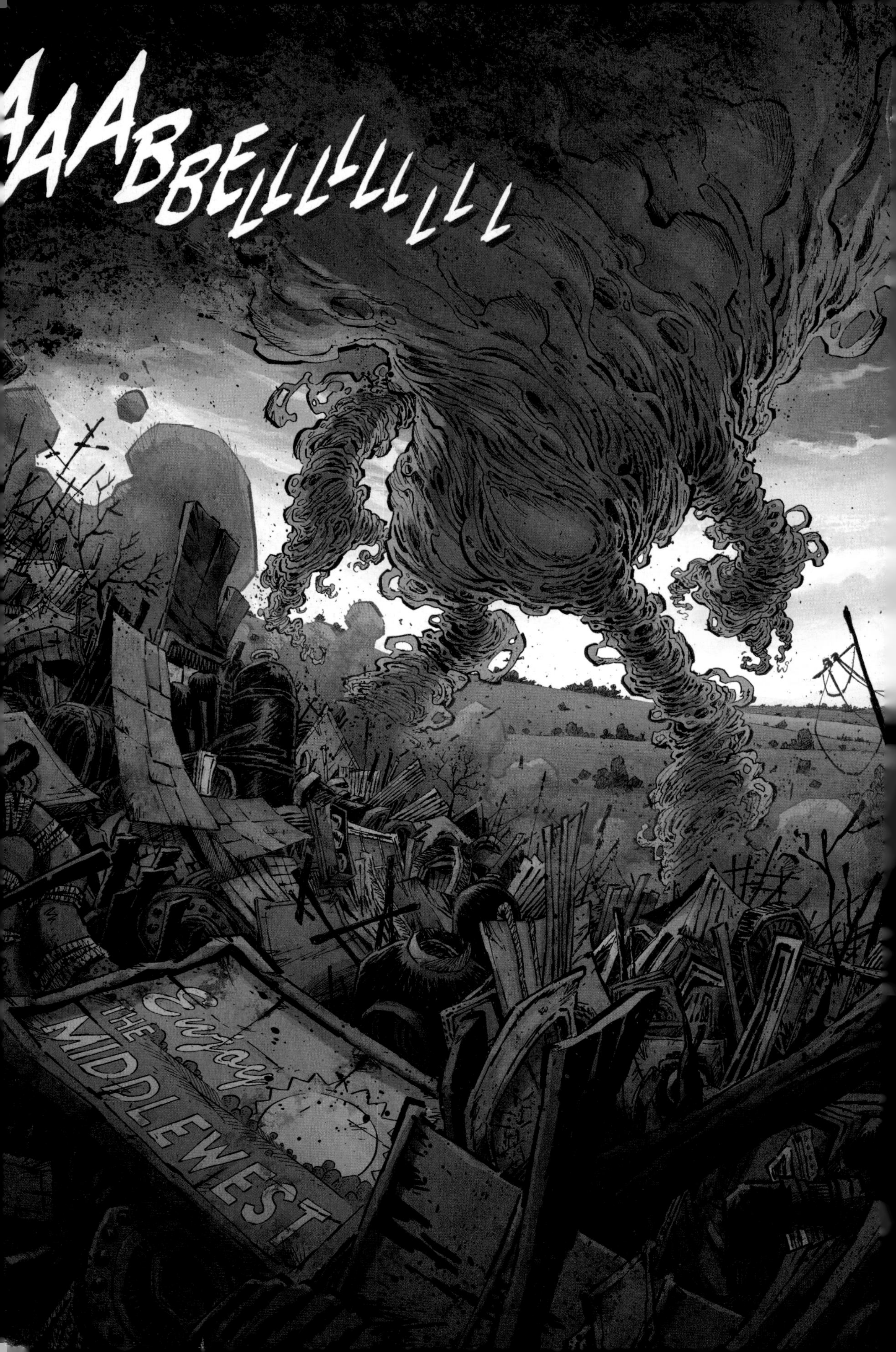
AAABBELLLLLLLLLL
Enjoy THE MIDDLEWEST

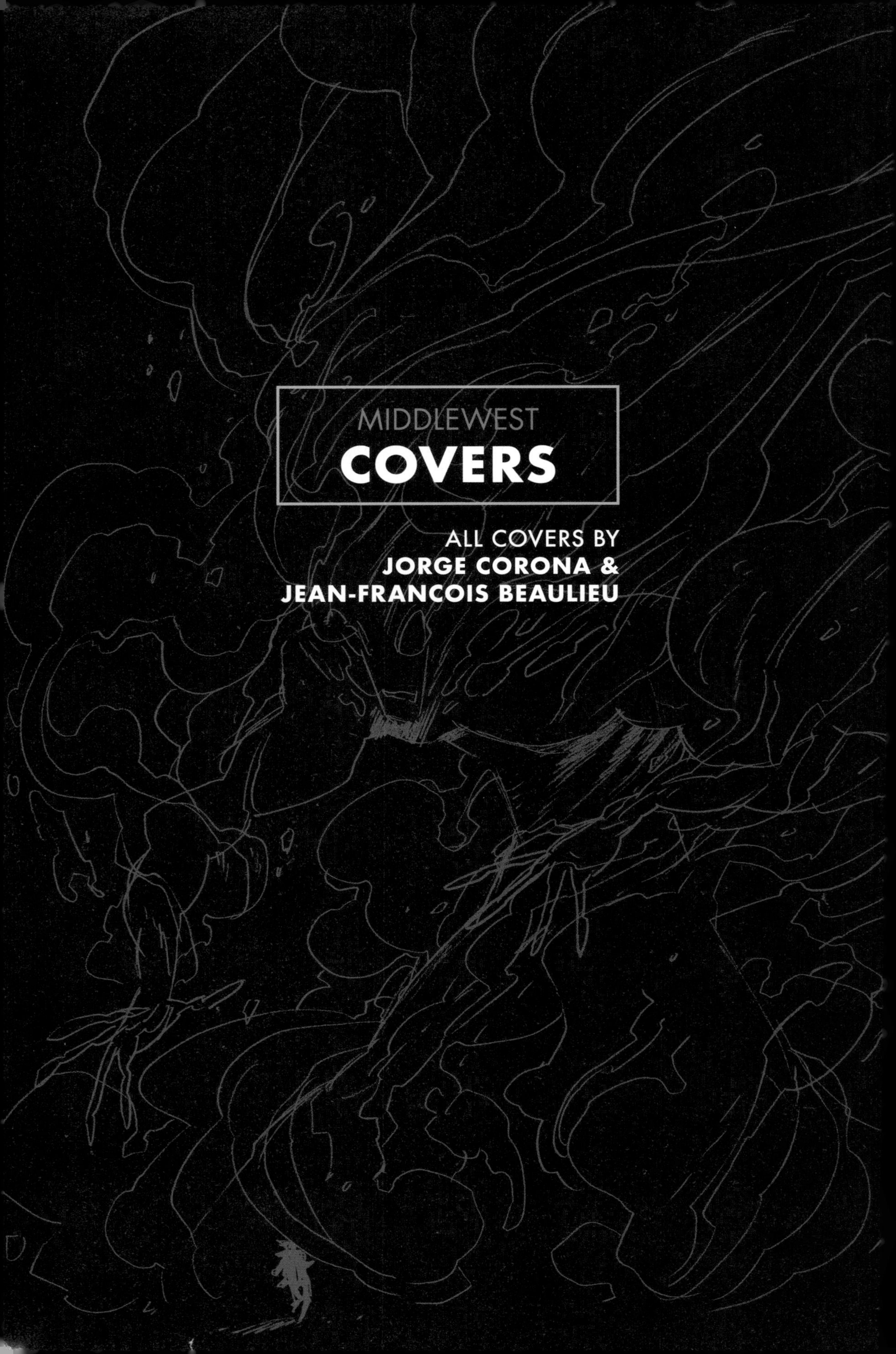

MIDDLEWEST

COVERS

ALL COVERS BY
JORGE CORONA &
JEAN-FRANCOIS BEAULIEU

ISSUE #7

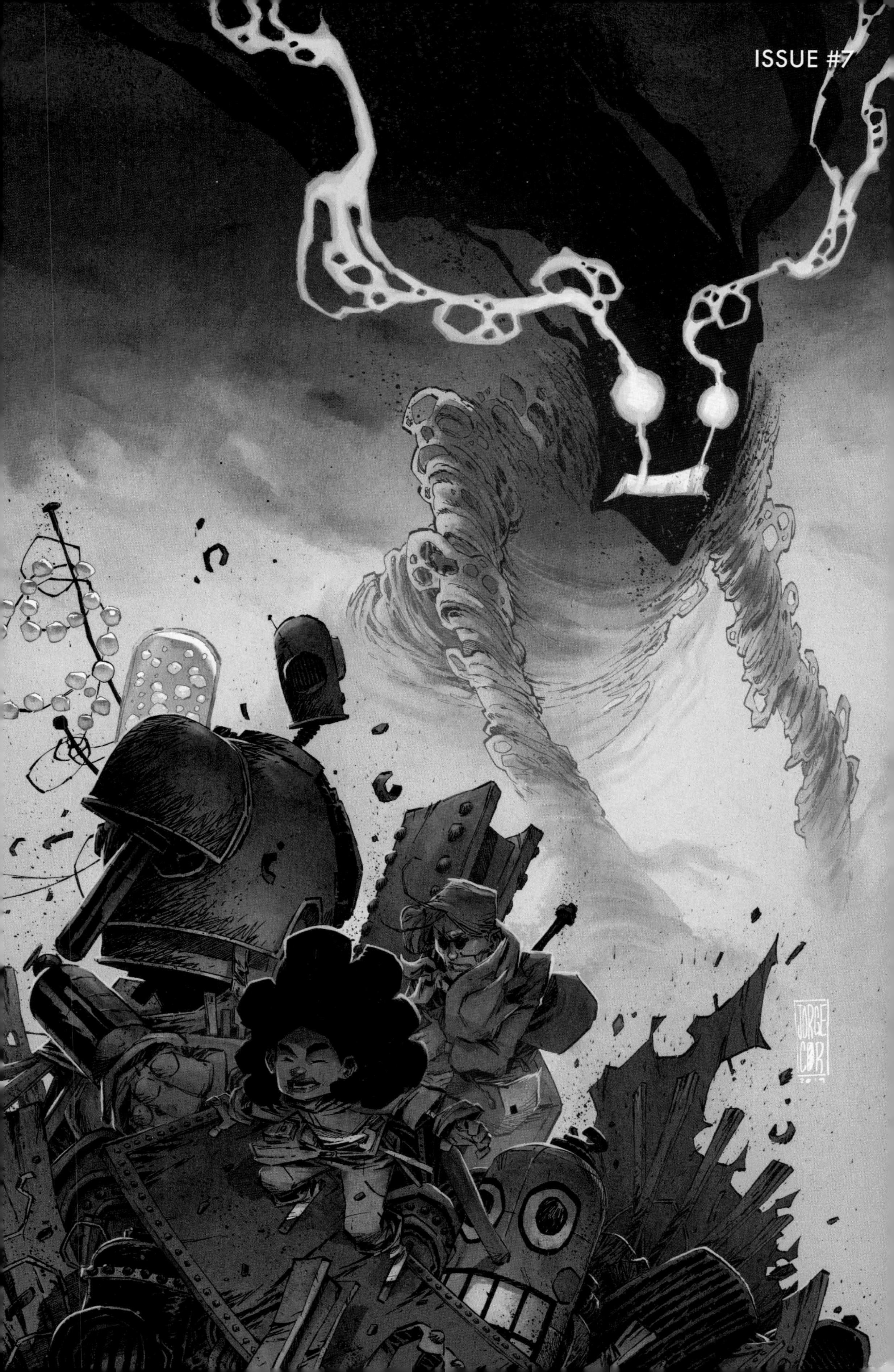
JORGE
COR

ISSUE #8

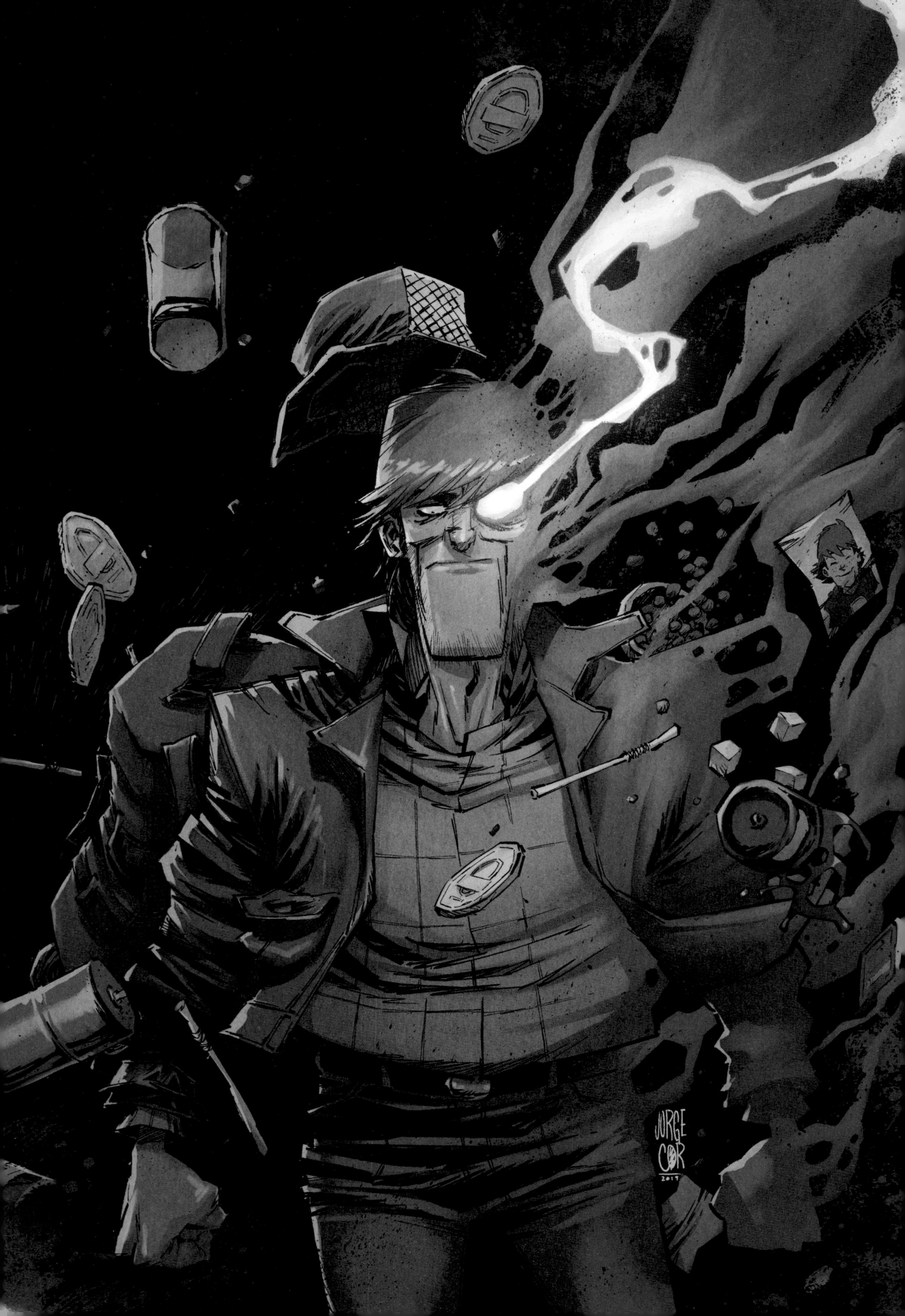
JORGE COR
2017

ISSUE #9

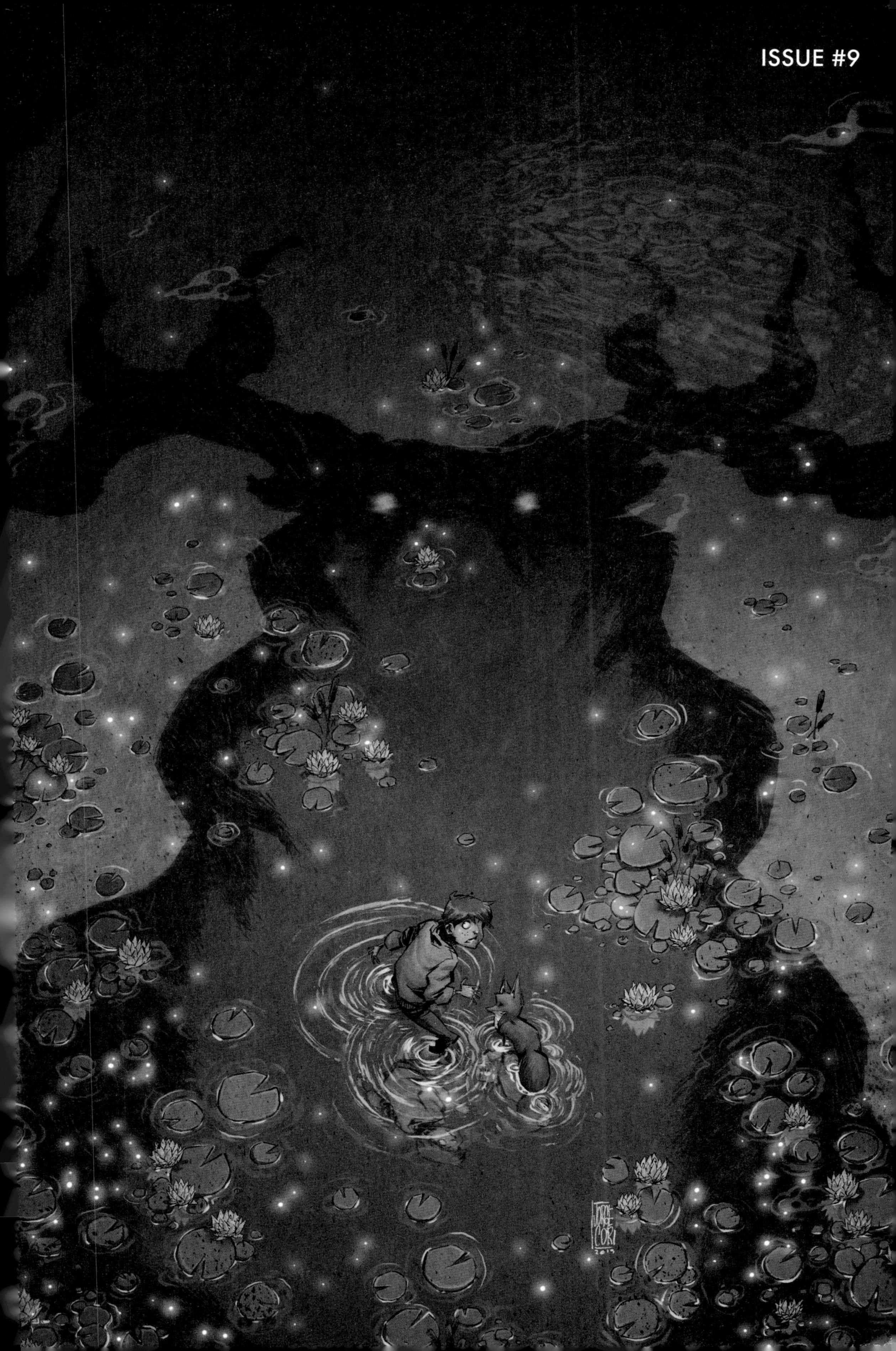

ISSUE #10

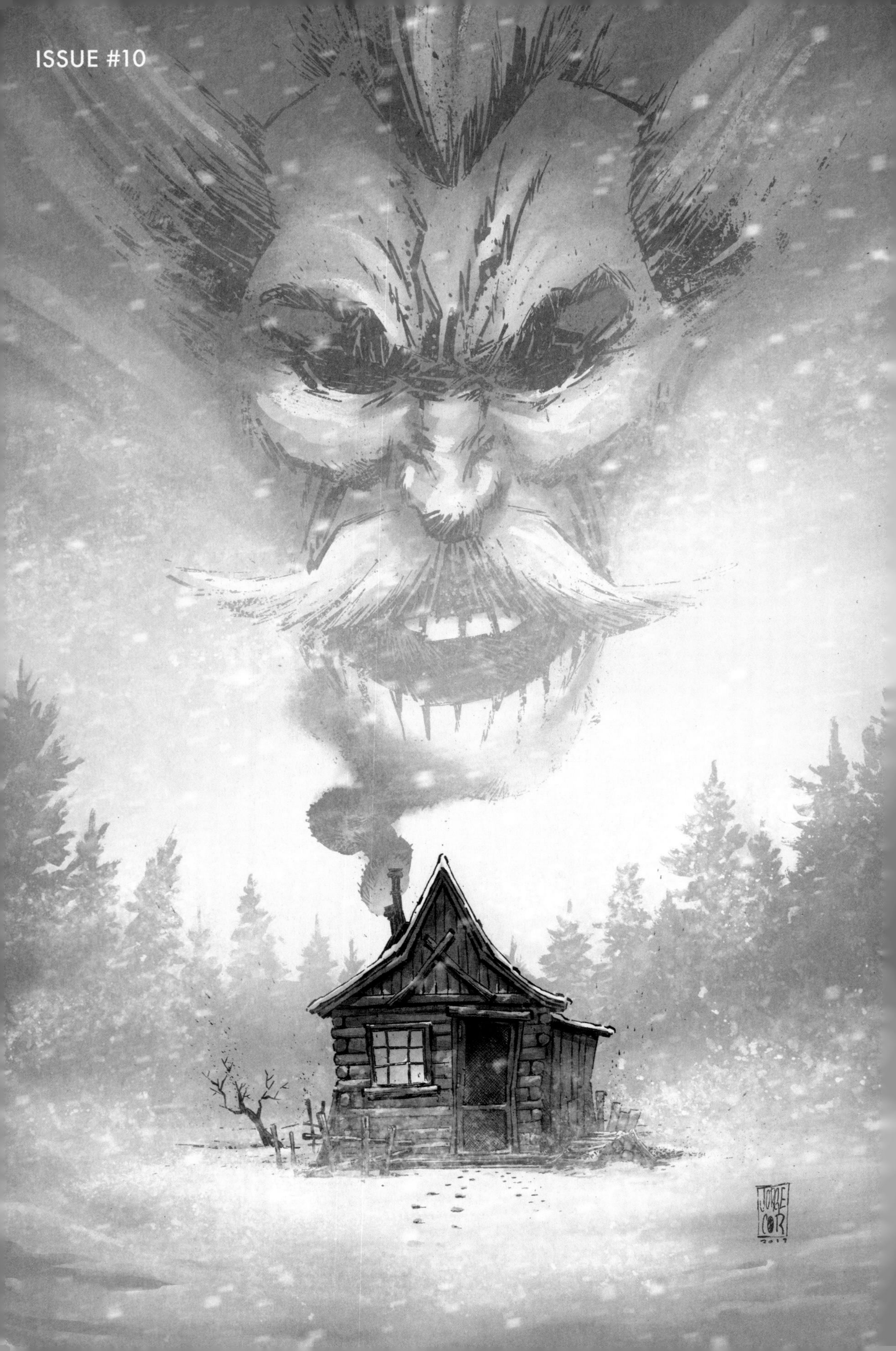

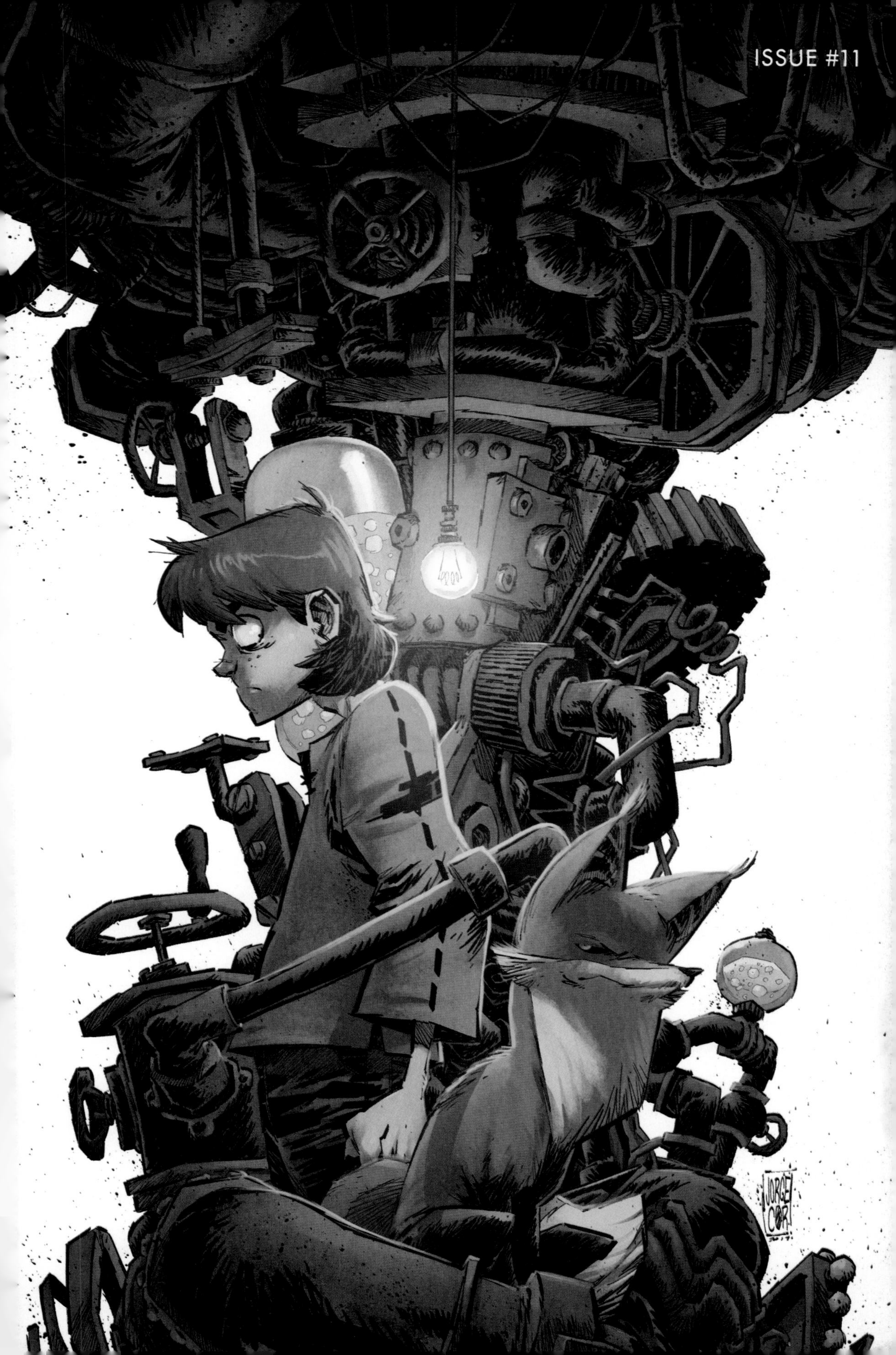
ISSUE #11

ISSUE #12

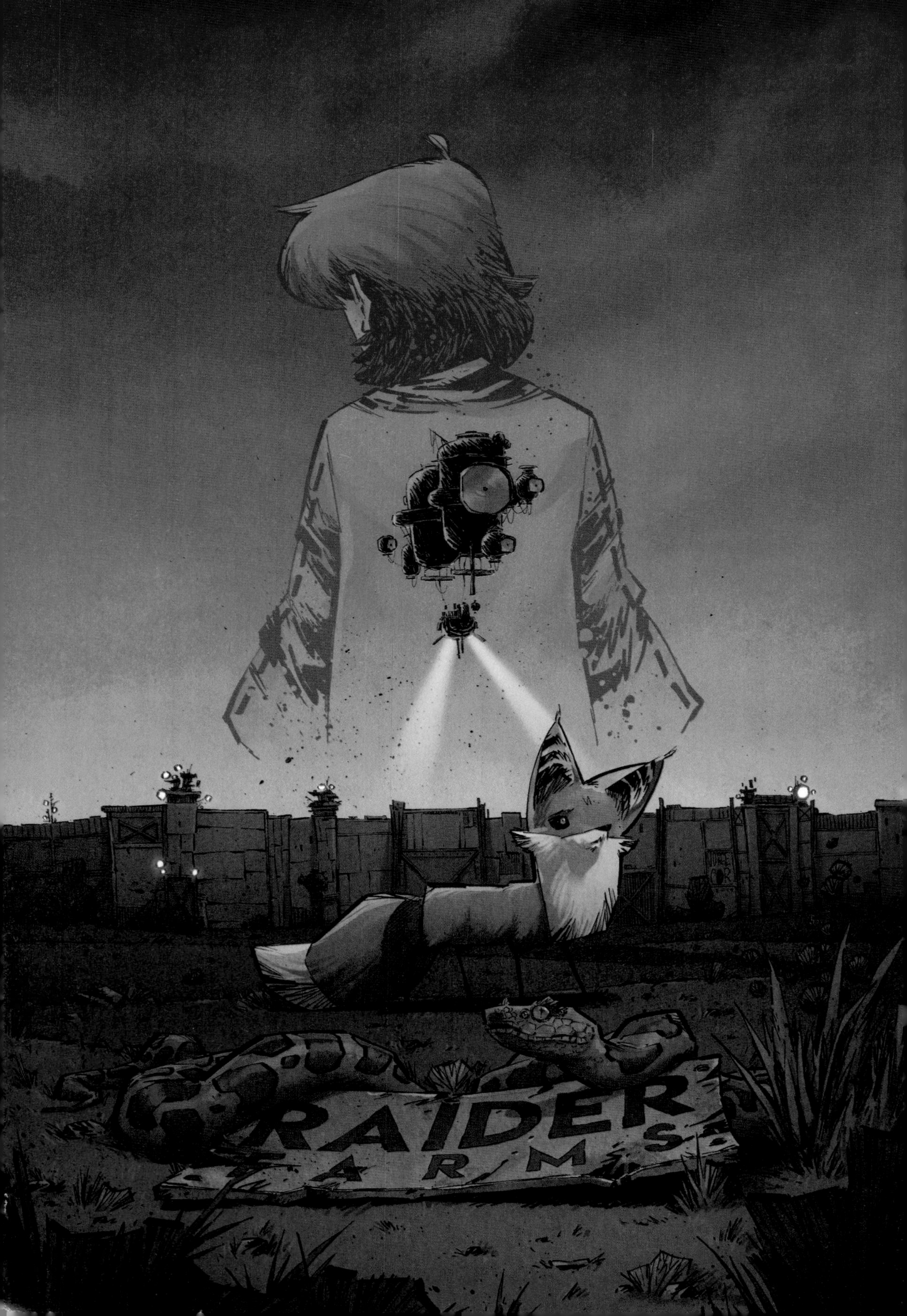
RAIDER
ARMS

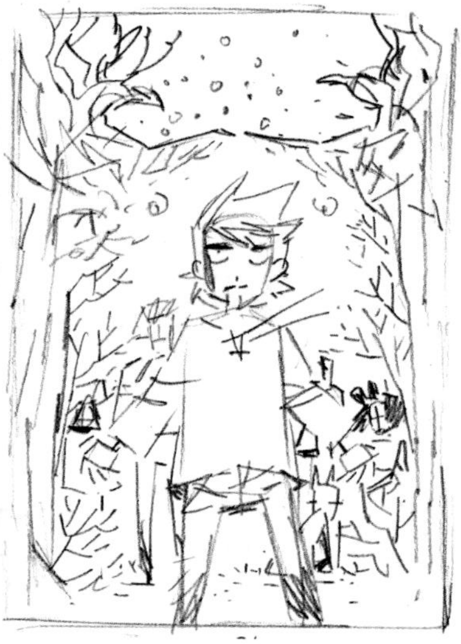
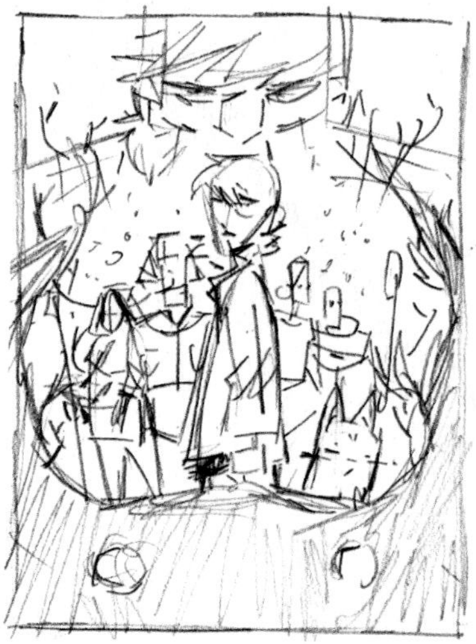
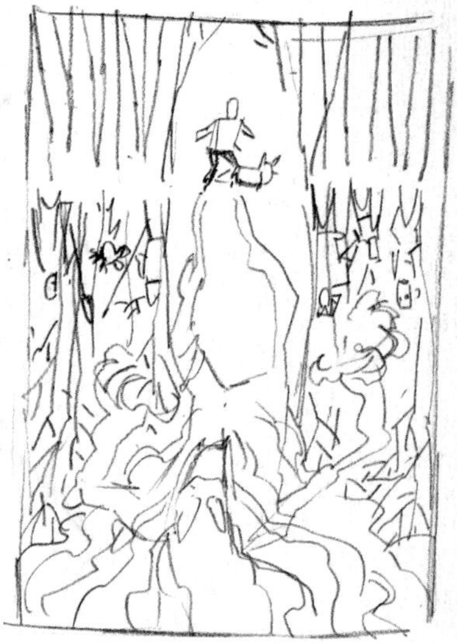
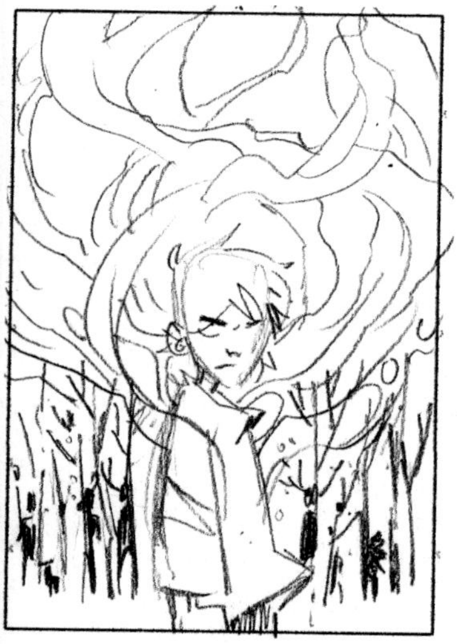
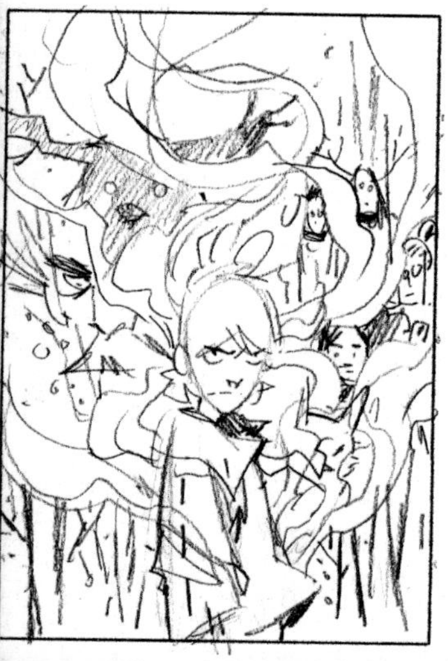
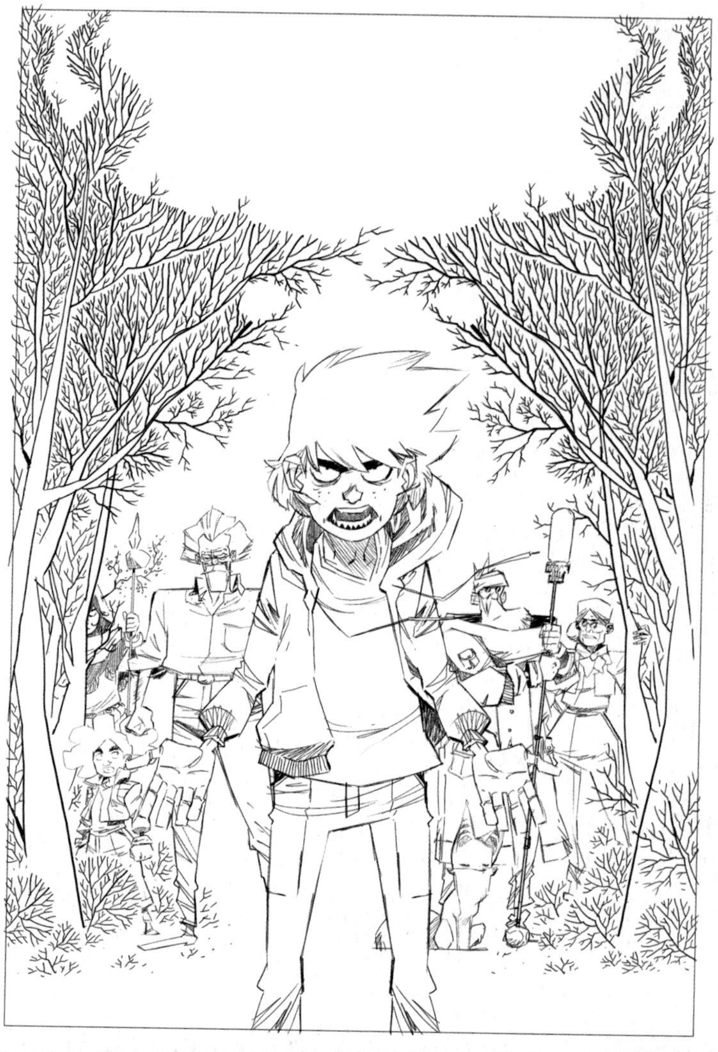

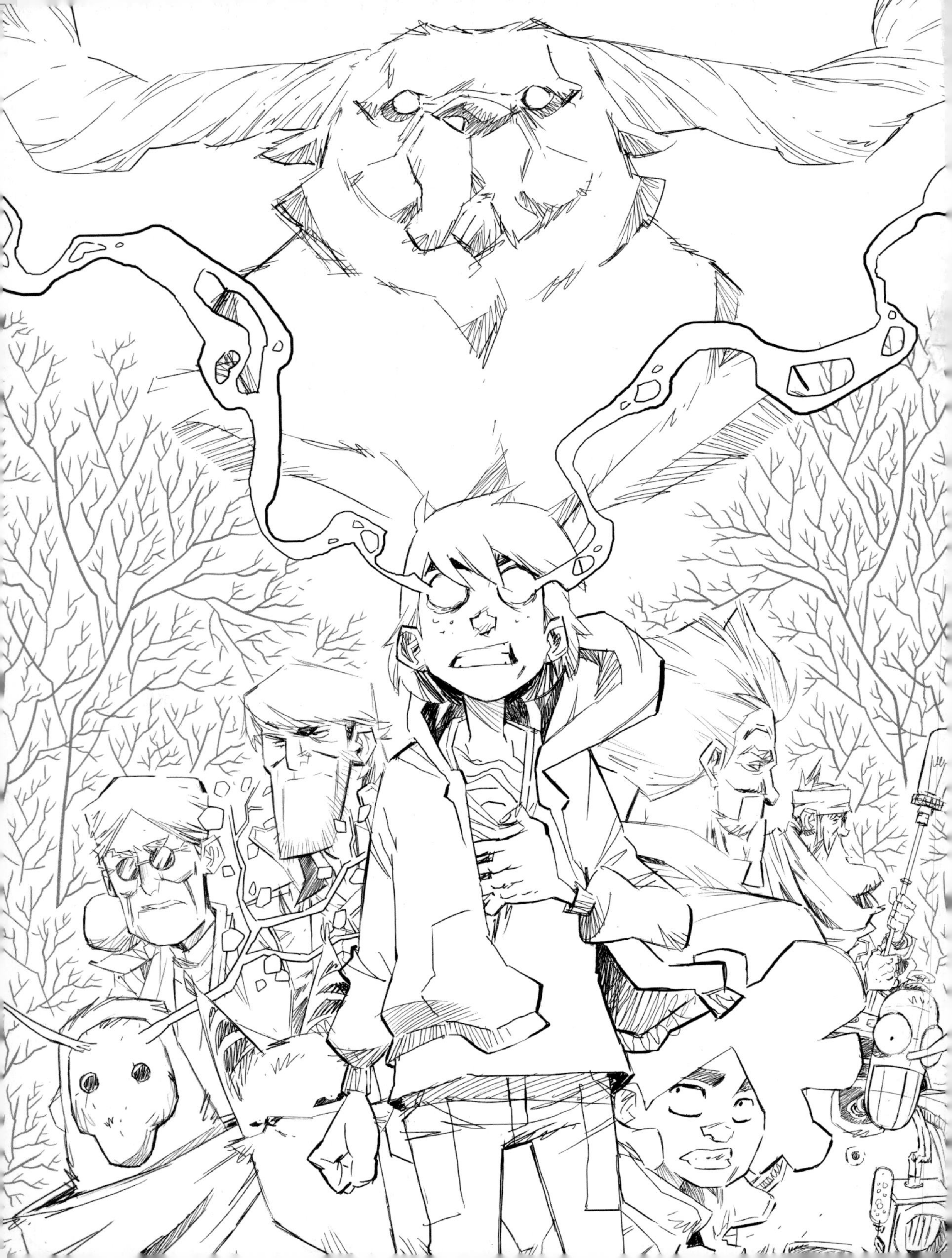